"He was right there!" Cinder moved closer to the curb and scoured the street in each direction. "He was dressed as a ninja. Natasha saw him, too."

"I believe you." Gian joined her, stepping into the street to better see. "He's gone now, whoever he was." Pulling her close, he wrapped her in his cape. "You had yourself a real Halloween spook, didn't you?"

"He was watching me. I know he was."

Rubbing her back, Gian gave the street one more look. Halloween was a night for fun and sweets, a time for pretend-monsters to roam the night. Someone had scared Cinder, and that was enough to make that monster real. "Whoever it was . . ."

"Natasha thought he might have been Karl."

"That doesn't surprise me," Gian said. "Let's close up the dojo and I'll take you home. There's probably some gut-gashing, blood-splattering movie on cable we can watch."

"I thought you wanted to get out of that costume," Cinder reminded him. Within the safety of Gian's cape, her adoration and affection for her superman overrode the creepy feeling the ninja had given her.

"I do. The sooner the better." His hands roamed down her buttocks and, for an instant, he wondered how far he could go with his voluminous cape concealing his actions.

BURN

CRYSTAL HUBBARD

Genesis Press, Inc.

INDIGO LOVE SPECTRUM

An imprint of Genesis Press, Inc.
Publishing Company

Genesis Press, Inc.
P.O. Box 101
Columbus, MS 39703

Copyright © 2010 Crystal Hubbard

ISBN: 13 DIGIT : 978-1-58571-406-3
ISBN: 10 DIGIT : 1-58571-406-2
Manufactured in the United States of America

First Edition

Visit us at www.genesis-press.com
or call at 1-888-Indigo-1-4-0

DEDICATION

This book is dedicated to C.A.K. and G.P. Thank you for your courage, guidance and friendship, and for trusting me with your stories. This book is also dedicated to C.W., who dances with the angels.

PROLOGUE

Zebulon Rice thought himself a lucky man.

He took his time climbing the carpeted stairs of the three-bedroom Gambrel farmhouse he and his grandchildren had been hired to empty. At seventy-years-old, he did everything at his own pace to save the wear and tear on his joints, especially his knees and knuckles, which seemed to have aged slightly faster than the rest of his body. His grandchildren, twenty-year-old Zebulon III, eighteen-year-old Jedediah, and sixteen-year-old Rhoda, were the runners and lifters, the backbone and muscle of Rice & Family Movers. Zebulon, the great-great-grandson of the escaped slave who had founded the family business with the money he'd earned slopping docks in Quincy, was the brains of the operation. His wife, Teresina, was its heart. She booked their appointments, managed the finances, and gave birth to five strapping sons, all college graduates, who had provided the next generation to keep Zebulon & Family running well into the twenty-first century. *Yessir, I'm a lucky man*, Zebulon thought with a swell of pride. *I might not have a big Gambrel farmhouse in Manchester-by-the-Sea, but I know I'm richer than the folks giving up this place.*

Zebulon's craggy brown hand eased along the hand-carved pine banister. His experienced eye had fallen in love with the farmhouse at first sight. The house had to be over a hundred years old and had been constructed of pine, likely from the very trees that had been felled to clear ground for the house and acres of what had once been farmland. A few working farms still existed in the town, but this wasn't one of them. Fortunately, the owners had possessed the good sense to maintain the fields, keeping them so well they looked like an endless expanse of emerald carpet.

The interior of the house had been cared for just as well. The rafters in the high ceilings were original to the structure, as were the banisters and living and dining room floors. He was an amateur at best, but Zebulon had learned a lot about home renovation and restoration in the course of his nearly fifty years in the moving business, and he had to squint and really snoop to notice places where new wood, tile, stone or slate had repaired the old.

At the top of the stairs, he noticed a dark droplet about the size of a quarter on the ivory carpet, and he smiled. No wonder the old bones of the stairs don't creak, he chuckled to himself. The joints had been recently oiled.

Zebulon tugged a bandanna from the back pocket of his work overalls. As he bent over and wiped away the droplet of oil, he hoped that someone would care for him in his old age as well as the departing residents of the farmhouse had cared for it.

He brought the bandanna closer to his face and sniffed it, hoping to identify the type of lubricant used to condition the stairs. *Funny,* he thought, new wrinkles joining the old on his brow. *This don't smell like oil.*

He touched the smear on his handkerchief, rubbed it between his thumb and forefinger. His eyes wide, a sudden burst of adrenalin jolted his heart. He looked back down the stairs. "Zeb, is somebody hurt?"

His grandson, a handsome kid with a bright smile and sparkling black eyes in a face as dark as freshly brewed coffee, appeared just inside the front door. "What's the matter, Granddad?"

"I said, is somebody hurt," Zebulon repeated. "Got some blood up here."

"Naw, we're all good," Zeb told him. "Jed's tying down the last of the furniture in the truck and Rhoda is checking our moving list against the homeowner's inventory. We're good to go, Granddad, just as soon as we get Mrs. Wyatt's check."

"Boy, lower your voice," Zebulon insisted with an impatient slash of his hand. He walked a few steps down the stairs to speak more quietly with Zeb. "You don't ever talk about money until the job is done to the client's satisfaction. What if Mrs. Wyatt had heard you?"

Zeb rolled his eyes. "I think Mrs. Wyatt might be preoccupied."

"Oh, yeah? Why's that?"

"She's been up there in the master bedroom for the past half hour." Zeb snickered. "Jed and I caught a peek of her in the window when we were putting the mattresses in the truck. Saw her splashing red paint on the walls. Guess she's leaving a surprise for her ex-husband." He shook his head. "He sure must have done something awful to piss her off like that. She seemed like such a nice lady."

"Splashing red paint in the—" Zebulon's tongue froze. "Is that officer still outside?"

"He was when I came in," Zeb said and shrugged. "What's he here for? To make sure we don't steal anything?"

But by then Zebulon had swept past him and out the wide front door. One of Manchester-by-the-Sea's finest was sitting in a squad car reading the sports headlines on the back page of the *Boston Herald*.

"This heat getting to you?" the officer asked when Zeb slammed against the driver's door. "You don't look so good."

"I think someone's in the house," Zebulon panted. He snatched off his grimy St. Louis Stars cap and swiped the back of his hand across his sweaty brow. "And I haven't seen Mrs. Wyatt in a while now."

The officer, his balding pate gleaming pink in the summer sun, calmly opened his newspaper. "No one's gone in or out except for you, your workers, and the soon-to-be *Ms.* Wyatt," he replied, stressing the buzz at the end of Ms.

"Thank—" Zebulon began, turning toward the house.

"Oh, her husband might still be there," the officer interrupted indifferently. "He wanted to pick up a few things before the little missus ran off with them. I'm sure you . . ." The officer looked up from his paper to see Zebulon awkwardly rushing back into the house.

"Granddad, what's the matter?" Zeb asked on the old man's heels.

"Shh!" Zebulon hissed, ushering his grandson behind him as they climbed the stairs.

The loose cartilage in Zebulon's knees sounded like popping corn, and he worried that the noise would herald his approach. His lungs burned and seemed to harden in his chest as he fought to quiet his breathing. The thick runner covering the upstairs corridor muffling his footsteps, he passed one empty bedroom, a bathroom, and a second bedroom. The door to the master bedroom at the end of the corridor was closed, but the seam of light beneath it revealed unhurried movement.

"Go get the officer," Zebulon whispered to Zeb. "Now," he mouthed angrily when Zeb took too long to get going.

Zebulon heard nothing until his toes touched the base of the door. Whispers, too soft and garbled for him to understand, but loud enough to make his bladder seize, prompted him to grip the doorknob and slowly, quietly, turn it. Hanging back, Zebulon allowed the weight and momentum of the door to open it further.

Later, when he testified in court, Zebulon would recall the easy, silent movement of the brass door hinges, and he'd again wonder what kind of oil had been used to care for the joints. But in that moment when he'd entered the master bedroom, all coherent thought fled Zebulon's mind.

He first thought Mrs. Wyatt wasn't in the room, that the naked man kneeling behind the bags and boxes Mrs. Wyatt had planned to transport in her SUV was some bold vagrant who had begun squatting in the house before the owners had completely vacated. The streaks and splatters of blood on the windows and ceiling spoke of a far different circumstance, one that drew Zebulon into the room.

It never occurred to Zebulon to be afraid, not after the coppery wet pungent smell of fresh blood assaulted his nose, not even after he spotted a slim, feminine hand filled with blood on the floor. The autonomic response of fear greased his aching joints, clearing the pain from them. It flowed through his ancient muscles, steeling him as he moved closer to peer behind the boxes concealing all but the bloody palm.

The kneeling man's back and shoulder muscles bunched as his blood-streaked right arm flew up, flinging fresh blood onto the ceiling and Zebulon's overalls. His arm slashed down, its movement ending in a nauseating splat.

Zebulon rounded the boxes and could go no farther. He recognized the yellow and black fabric scraps that had been Mrs. Wyatt's pretty shorts and tank top. It took him a longer instant to identify the strands of black silk lying all over the clothes and the floor.

The kneeling man, Mrs. Wyatt naked, unconscious, and pinned between his knees, slowly straightened, and Zebulon felt no ache of arthritis as his hands tightened into fists. "Mr. Wyatt," he started cautiously, "why don't you just put the knife down?"

Sumchai Wyatt slowly turned, twisting at the waist enough for Zebulon to see the blood, some crusted, some still damp, coating him from neck to knees and mixing with the sweat running down his face. His knife hand dripped red, the other remained tangled in his wife's hair. What remained of his wife's hair.

"No one will want her now." He smiled and his teeth were filmy with blood. "No one but me."

"Officer," Zebulon shrieked. "We need help in here!"

Zebulon had met Sumchai Wyatt once, when he had moved the Wyatts into the farmhouse four years ago. He saw nothing of the friendly, openly loving new husband who had carried his wife over the threshold before disappearing into the bedroom to christen it as only happy newlyweds could. The man with the sinister grin of satisfaction before him now was a lethal stranger in the midst of killing his wife.

"Put the blade down, son," Zebulon said. He slowly moved his hands in a gesture of supplication. "You don't want to do this."

Sumchai turned and slashed at his wife, startling a tiny shout out of Zebulon, who was relieved to see that Sumchai had chopped off more of her hair and not her flesh.

Though in the back of his mind Zebulon knew that not even two minutes had passed since he'd sent Zeb for the policeman, he wondered what was taking so long. Mrs. Wyatt's face was unrecognizable; so much blood covered her torso, it was hard to see her wounds. She didn't have much time left, if she hadn't already bled to death.

Zebulon wished that a lamp or a chair remained in the room, anything he could have used as a weapon.

Physically, he was no match for the taller, younger, stronger, insane man, but that didn't stop him from rushing Sumchai when he clutched the knife in both hands and raised it high above his head.

Zebulon's momentum sent the knife flying and carried Sumchai off Mrs. Wyatt. The two men landed at the base of the windows. Slippery as a greased eel with his wife's blood, Sumchai wriggled free of Zebulon's hold and nimbly leapt to his feet. On his hands and knees, Zebulon scrambled for the knife, but Sumchai beat him to it.

Two seconds of indecision made the difference between life and death, Zebulon was sure of it. Knife in hand, Sumchai had spent two seconds, his empty eyes as black as his spiky hair, staring between his wife and Zebulon as if deciding who to gut first. Sumchai had taken one step forward when a shot echoed off the walls of the empty bedroom, dropping him to his knees.

Panting, the red-faced officer stood in the doorway, his gun still trained on Sumchai. Zebulon scarcely heard him speak into the radio clipped to his shoulder, calling for backup and ambulances. He was only marginally aware of Zeb, who took off his T-shirt to cover Mrs. Wyatt. Sumchai fell forward, writhing in pain from the wound in the back of his left thigh.

His hips, knees, hands, and back all at once reminding him of his age, Zebulon sat with a protective hand lightly embracing the top of Mrs. Wyatt's head, his eyes fixed on the frustrated rage frozen on Sumchai's face as he stared, unblinking, at the woman he'd once vowed to cherish.

CHAPTER 1

Swift, fluid, elegant, and powerful, the two men engaged in a battle as captivating as an Alvin Ailey dance. A brisk sweep of a long leg took the taller man down, but in an acrobatic display of agility, he rolled out of his opponent's reach and jumped to his feet. He answered the takedown with a series of quick, blunt blows to his opponent's torso, but he pulled his punches, stopping just short of making actual contact since this was only a sparring match.

The encounter was convincing enough to stop the progress of a woman walking past the plate-glass window fronting the studio.

Catching a glimpse of her dark head shrouded in big sunglasses and a filmy black scarf, the taller combatant froze. Before he could blink, before he could block or dodge an oncoming blow, he found himself moving directly into a hard fist as he tried to get a better look at the woman on the other side of the window.

A stinging lump warmed the point of his right cheekbone as he recovered, felling his opponent quickly with a throw that put him in position to deliver any combination of kill shots to his adversary's head and chest.

The students kneeling in prayer positioned along the edges of the thick vinyl floor mat applauded. He offered a hand to his sparring partner, the wide, loose sleeves of their crisp white *gis* flapping like the wings of seagulls.

"Thanks for the match, Gian," said the man who had just gotten back on his feet. "Almost had you that time."

"Good thing 'almost' doesn't count," Gian said absently, his eyes scouring the street for the mystery woman who had stolen his concentration.

She barely stood taller than the students buffeting her as they exited the dojo, but with her head cloaked in a sheer black scarf and wide black sunglasses, she stood out among the seventh- and eighth-graders in their bare feet and gleaming white *gis*. The little bit of her face that was showing appeared much younger than her wardrobe indicated, though the resolute line of her full mouth reminded Gian of the nuns who had taught him his ABCs.

His students performed hasty bows before exiting the dojo, knowing that failure to show proper respect would earn dozens of knuckle pushups at their next class. The woman in the black scarf, clearly a stranger to the rules and etiquette of a dojo, stepped onto the floor mats with her shoes without first bowing, which stiffened Gian's jaw.

His first thought was that she was a parent to one of his students, but she looked nothing like the mothers who sent their children to him twice a week to learn the discipline and athleticism of martial arts. The desperate housewives of Webster Groves, Missouri, wore their bleached, tinted, and processed hair in bobs or stylized mullets. They didn't cover their heads with funeral cloth, particularly not in June, when the radiant heat of the sun off concrete could cause third-degree sunburns. Exposing their heavy, veiny thighs and flapping upper arms in pastel ensembles of walking shorts and tank tops was typical, which made the woman in black stand out even more in her sensible khaki slacks and long-sleeved white button-down.

"Is there somewhere we can speak in private?"

Her voice was deeper than he expected, and a bit raspy. She was shorter than he, but not by much. If she straightened her spine and relaxed her shoulders, she would gain an additional inch or two, bringing the top of her head even with his chin. Her clothes hung off her slender frame but they suited her body type, and he wondered if she'd had a sudden weight loss. His Italian instincts kicked in—he didn't even know her name, yet he wanted to feed her.

"Mr. Piasanti," the woman prompted, shifting her head, presumably to meet his gaze through her dark glasses.

"Sorry," he said, refocusing his thoughts. "My office. We can talk there."

She followed him, each of her steps annoying the hell out of Gian. Her soft-soled flats caused no physical damage to the mat, but the lack of respect irked him to the core. He led her out of the studio and down a short corridor, past locker rooms for women and men—identified only by Chinese symbols—past two more doors and into the spacious office at its end. He held the door open for her. She turned her left shoulder inward to avoid touching him as she moved past him and entered the windowless office.

"Hey, boss," greeted a dark-haired man whose muscular frame seemed too big for the swivel chair he sat in behind a desk cluttered with stacks of papers, *Asian World of Martial Arts* catalogs, a pair of sparring mitts and red ballpoint pens stamped with SHENG LI. "Sionne can cover my five o'clock, so . . ."

The man seemed to lose his train of thought once his eyes found the woman in black. He stood and rounded the desk, his bare feet silent on the worn red and black Oriental rug. "Karl Lange," he said, offering a big hand criss-crossed with thick veins. "Can I help you with something?"

She cupped her elbows in her hands, her shoulders drawing tighter as Karl's close-set black eyes raked over her. Karl moved closer to her, stroking his thumb over the bare skin of his sternum, which was exposed by his unbelted *gi*.

Perhaps subconsciously, the woman moved closer to Gian. "You're in the attic apartment in the big Victorian on Elm, right? My brother's girlfriend's father owns the company that installed your security system. That's some package you got," Karl said with a low whistle. "Ain't even a housefly gettin' in there without the right security codes."

"If Sionne is covering your five o'clock, maybe you should get going," Gian said. Karl's remarks left the woman shivering, and illustrated one of the things Gian hated about living in a small town—everyone knew someone who knew your business. "If you want to get good parking, you'd better get to the stadium early."

"Good thinking, boss," Karl said. "I'll bring you a souvenir."

As he moved past her to the smaller desk in the corner nearest the door, Karl stroked the woman's arm. She cringed, and Gian quickly ushered her into a chair, carefully circumventing her personal space before taking a seat behind the desk.

"What brings you to Sheng Li this after—"

The woman set a stack of bills on the center of his desk. Her touch had been delicate, but the sudden sight of the pile of cash jolted Gian.

"I'd like to take private lessons," she said plainly.

A low chuckle issued from the desk near the door.

"Get the hell out, Lange," Gian ordered.

"Sure thing, boss." Karl picked up his yellow and black duffel bag. "Enjoy your private lesson."

Gian didn't reply, and he and the woman kept their silence until they heard the front door of the studio open and close.

Gian leaned back in his chair and laced his fingers over his abdomen. "There's a schedule out in the front lobby detailing the times for adult instruction. I offer a variety of classes that would fulfill your personal defense, strength and conditioning, and competitive fighting interests. Classes start as early as seven in the morning and end at six. I'm sure you'll find something that will fit into your schedule. You should take a look—"

She grabbed the cash and was rising from her chair when, faster than she would have believed possible had she not felt it, Gian caught her wrist. Her startled gasp earned her release. She dropped the money back on the desk.

"I'm sorry," Gian hastily said. "I shouldn't have . . . You don't have to run off."

"If you don't offer private lessons, I have no interest in pursuing study here," she said, a slight tremble in her voice. "I need to start right away. Thank you for your time." She swallowed hard. "May I go now?"

"You don't need—"

He had started to tell her that she didn't need his permission to leave, but the longer he looked at her, the more he realized that perhaps she did.

She sat the way she stood, as though she wanted to take up as little room as possible. Her hands trembled despite the warmth of the room, and she constantly, nervously, plucked at the edges of her scarf, making certain that as much of her head and face was covered as possible.

"You don't need to look into other dojos," he said with a long sigh and a glance at the brick of cash. "I can accommodate you."

"When can we start?"

"First we have to establish what type of class you're interested in, and then I have to check the schedule, find out which of my guys can work you in."

"No."

"I'm sorry?"

"I want you."

He'd competed in muy thai and mixed martial arts matches against opponents who could shatter a man's jaw with a single punch, yet three words spoken by this strange little woman in black nearly knocked him out of his chair. And she hadn't even meant them the way he'd heard them.

"All of my teachers are highly qualified." He cleared his throat. "They—"

"I'd like private lessons, at least three times a week, preferably in the evening. I was told that you were the best," she insisted, "and—"

"By whom?"

"—I can pay you more if that isn't enough. According to your website, your personal rate for private lessons is fifty dollars an hour plus a twenty-five dollar fee for use of the private studio. This should see us through to the end of August. Please, count it."

Lifting an eyebrow, he tilted his head toward the cash. "My calendar is full, Miss . . . ?"

"Please," she said slowly.

"Miss Please?" he suggested in a weak attempt to put her at ease.

"Please, teach me to defend myself."

Her breathy plea whittled away his resistance. "Why don't I give you a free trial. Decide what you're getting into before you fork over your nonrefundable tuition."

She swallowed hard. "Okay. When?"

"How 'bout now?"

"Now?"

Standing, he returned her money to her. With a short sweep of his arm, he directed her toward a door behind and to the right of his desk. She tucked the cash into her slouchy black purse.

"Take off your shoes," he said, stopping her before she entered the room. "Place them neatly by the door."

She saw that he was already barefoot when she stooped to place her shoes, purse, scarf, and shades by the door.

He stepped into the room and onto the beige mat covering most of the thirty-by-thirty-foot floor. Without looking at her, he stopped her again before she set foot in the studio. "Bow to the room, to show respect for the art you'll learn here."

His hands at his sides, he bent at the waist in a short bow, demonstrating the proper form. He straightened to see her copying him exactly. "Now you may enter the dojo, and bow to me."

She approached him, her eyes cast down. Meeting him in the center of the mat, she executed another bow. He wanted to explain that the second bow was both greeting and a show of respect to the instructor, but his tongue had been glued in place from the moment she'd entered the private studio.

The dark paneling and carpet in his windowless office made his workplace rather cave-like, but the private studio with its bamboo paneled walls was airy and bright, its only ornamentation two Japanese tiger prints and a stone urn containing a neatly pruned bonsai tree. A domed polarized skylight provided clean illumination and gave the place a cozy openness that the main studio lacked. The private studio was so named because it also doubled as Gian's sanctuary. He allowed none of his staff to train or teach in it, and it had been months since he'd used the space for private lessons.

Without her disguise, the woman standing before him was a lovely addition to the room. She wore no makeup to mask the natural glow of her brown skin. Her close-cropped cap of glossy black hair and her big dark eyes made her appear far younger than he first assumed her to be. Her mouth had the compact beauty of a rosebud, but her lips were full and so very inviting.

"I'm not dressed properly," she said softly, still avoiding his eyes.

"You look fine to me," he assured her. He clapped his hands, startling her but successfully breaking the hypnotic hold her lips had on him. "Our first session will be a simple fitness evaluation. Touch your toes, and try to do it without bending your knees. If you can't do it, don't—"

She turned to the side and her upper half dropped. Her palms were flat on the mat on either side of her feet.

"You're pretty flexible there," Gian said. "You . . ."

Her shirt had come untucked, revealing the skin of her lower back. Two long, fine stripes of pale scar tissue drew Gian's eye. "How'd you get—"

She stood upright so fast, the top of her head missed a collision with Gian's chin by mere inches. Tugging her shirt down, she took a step back.

9

"Hands at your sides," Gian prompted, getting back on track. "Now, extend your left leg and raise it as high as you can."

She followed his direction, holding her left leg perfectly straight and hip high. Gian slowly walked around her. He took his time, deliberately testing her. Rock steady, the only indication of discomfort she gave was a subtle pursing of her lips.

"You've studied dance," he stated.

She nodded.

He passed in front of her, his *gi* brushing her left foot. "Your toe point gave it away. Can you shift your leg to the side without dropping it?"

She did so, her right foot digging into the mat to maintain her balance.

"Now raise your arms as high as you can."

His hands clasped behind him, he watched her assume the position. She bobbled a little, but quickly found her center and steadied herself.

"That's very good," he told her. "Relax now."

She dropped her arms and leg and wiped a sheen of perspiration from her upper lip.

"You're very strong and you've got excellent balance," he said. "Some of my best students studied dance before they came to me. Where were you taught?"

"Flexibility, strength, and balance," she said pointedly, her dark eyes finally meeting his. "What's next?"

"Reflexes and agility. I'm going to throw a series of light punches at you and I want you to dodge them."

She inhaled deeply, steeling herself, while Gian took a fight position. A hesitant nod signified her readiness to begin, and Gian threw out his right fist. She shifted left, neatly avoiding it. After a few slow punches, Gian speeded them up, and he was impressed with her reaction. "Very nice," he said. "You're a natural. You're watching my eyes but following my shoulders. You're anticipating the direction of the punch. Have you had fight training before?"

"In a way," she said, slipping under another punch.

Gian said, "I'm going to throw them in combination now. Let's see what you got."

She kept up with him. High, low, jab, cross—she dodged each of them. He moved her all over the mat, chasing her with punches she skillfully avoided until . . .

"Gian, you still here?"

The loud male voice broke her concentration, and she walked into Gian's right fist. She staggered back before tripping over her feet, and she landed hard on her backside. The familiarity of the brilliant, wet pain in the center of her face confused her for a moment, taking her to a place she had hoped never to see again.

"Grab an ice pack and a towel!" Gian shouted to the man who had appeared in the doorway. Kneeling over his victim, he reached for her. "Are you okay?"

She scrambled out of his reach, stopping only when she butted against the wall behind her. Blood seeped between the fingers she pressed to her nose. "I'm fine. It's nothing."

Squatting, Gian ran his hands over his closely cropped head of dark hair. "Damn it, I'm sorry. I should

11

have been paying better attention." He took her elbow to help her up. She stiffened, tightly closing her eyes as she found her feet.

"I think we'll call it done for today," Gian said. He escorted her into the office and sat her in the chair facing his desk. Gently, he guided her head back. "Don't move," he told her. He grabbed antibacterial wipes from his desk and quickly plucked three of them from the canister. Standing behind her, he peeled her hands from her face and replaced them with the wipes and the ice pack that had been left on his desk, applying gentle but firm pressure to the bridge of her nose. "I should have pulled that last one," he said. "You were doing so well, I guess I got a little carried away."

She moved his hands a bit higher, more effectively staunching the flow of blood. "It was my fault," she said woodenly.

He remembered the scars on her back and wondered how many times she had told herself that. "It's never your fault," he assured her. His voice sounded strange to his own ears. He cleared his throat and forced himself to sound normal. "What I mean is I'm the trained professional. I should have been more careful."

"I know what you mean," she said. "This time, it was my fault. I let myself get distracted and I moved right into the punch. It won't happen again."

Gian smiled. "You're a real tough lady, aren't you?"

She raised her head and sat on the edge of her chair. One last swipe of the wadded wipes, and her nose was clear. "What's next?"

"How 'bout you coming back when you're up to it? In the meantime, I've got some paperwork you'll need to fill out. I need an emergency contact—"

"911."

"—a waiver—"

"I take full responsibility for any injuries I might incur."

"That's what you say now," he responded.

"You have my word," she stated firmly. "I won't sue you if I get hurt." She returned the ice pack to him but crumpled the wipes in her hand. "Is this time tomorrow good for you?"

Her wide eyes were unreadable. The longer she stared at him, the more Gian wanted to study her eyes, to learn their secrets. "Uh," he said, tearing his gaze from hers. "Let me check."

He sat in his chair and spun to look at the calendar posted on the wall. "I have a full day of classes scheduled. It's a busy season with the kiddies out of school. I don't finish up until five-thirty."

"Will you be too tired to teach me?"

"I'll switch some things around. It's not a problem. You'll get my best. So I'll put you down for five-thirty?"

She nodded, her fingers fiddling with the hem of her shirt.

He used one of his promotional pens to write PRIVATE LESSON on the 5 P.M. line of his calendar. "There are a few rules you'll have to adhere to."

Her eyes widened in a flash of fear, then narrowed as a spark of anger reshaped her mouth.

13

"They're all a matter of respect," he explained. "Respect is a very important part of the disciplines I'll be teaching you."

Her face relaxed and she nodded.

"You can wear shorts, sweats, T-shirts—whatever exercise clothes you prefer until you purchase a *gi*." He tossed her a catalog and a business card. "You can order one from this place, or you can go to the shop on the card. It's in Maplewood. I require all of my students to wear white. No pinks or tie-dyed *gis* in my dojo."

He smiled to soften the directive, but she merely nodded her acceptance of his rule before she retrieved her belongings. On her way back to her chair, she took the cash from her purse and returned it to the messy desk.

"Would you like a receipt for this?"

"It isn't necessary."

"Then we'll talk more tomorrow." He rolled himself a few feet to the tall filing cabinet behind his desk. He unlocked it, then opened the bottom drawer to retrieve a cash box. "We'll discuss your goals and the best way to achieve them. I take what I do very seriously and I expect my students to do so as well. If you expect me to go easy on you, or if you think this is going to be a social hour, I'll return your money right . . . now."

He turned around to see that he was talking to empty space. He shot out of his chair, nearly vaulting over the corner of his desk, and got to the main studio in time to see the woman, once again shrouded in black, walking out the front door. Only then did Gian realize that he had failed to get her name.

As was her habit, she glanced over her shoulder before unlocking the door to her attic apartment. The steep, narrow stairwell behind her was deserted, but she quickly opened the door and slipped inside, an old arrow of panic piercing her belly as she closed the door a bit too forcefully. Both automatic locks fastened themselves. She turned the three deadbolts before typing a release code into the security console built into the adjacent wall. She had ten seconds to supply the code before the unit sent a silent call to the police, who would respond in less than three minutes if her last security drill was still accurate. After rearming the unit, she secured the heavy chain and notched the steel police bar in its groove and latch.

Opening the door to the foyer closet, she took off her scarf. She hung the scarf on a hook inside the door, then held onto the door frame to maintain her balance while she kicked off her black flats. With her toe, she scooted them neatly into the gap between her white Nike Cross Trainers and a pair of sensible black pumps.

In her bare feet, she padded into the kitchen. She passed her right hand through her hair, her fingertips reading the raised line of a scar hidden just behind her temple. She'd spent the afternoon preparing her dinner, a banquet of broiled prawns accompanied by broccoli rabe sautéed with bacon, red onion, and a drizzle of balsamic vinegar. Dining alone was no excuse for not dining well, but she got something more than physical nourishment from her efforts.

Cooking fed her mind and soul along with her body. It was her therapy, her companionship. The acts of washing, peeling, chopping, slicing, mincing, and dicing kept her on her feet and her hands busy, sometimes for hours, depending on the complexity of her recipe or menu. It wasn't until after she had consumed her meal, when she looked up from her empty plate to see the vacant chairs around the dining table that loneliness tried to sneak up on her. Washing her cookware and plates by hand, drying them and putting them away helped push the loneliness aside long enough to get her to bedtime, when her attention to herself through bathing and grooming took her to the point where she could climb into bed and turn herself over to sleep.

She had gotten into a routine during her waking hours, one that successfully, if not joyfully, moved her from one day to the next. At the end of her day, she clutched a handful of her bedcovers under her chin and succumbed to the heaviness of her eyelids, wishing that she could manage her sleeping hours just as well.

CHAPTER 2

"So, uh, who was the lady in your private studio last night, Gian?"

Gian looked up from the employee schedule opened atop his desk. His black pen froze above the square in which he'd been writing the name of the instructor who had just pried into his business.

"She's a new student, Chip," Gian said, returning to his schedule.

"She had some really good moves. That is, before I interrupted you. Was she okay?"

"She got over it quick enough," Gian answered.

"What am I missing?" Karl asked. He ceased his pacing behind Chip's chair.

"Gian gave his new student a bloody nose last night," Chip explained.

"It wasn't like that," Gian sighed.

"What'd she do?" Karl chuckled. "Back talk you?"

Gian sat back in his chair and eyed Karl, who grew increasingly uncomfortable under the scrutiny.

Karl's impish grin faltered. "Dude, what . . . ?"

Until yesterday, Gian had thought little of Karl's frat boy mentality. But after spending time with his new student, Gian no longer viewed Karl's coarse remarks as harmless. "I'd like to build up my female client base, and

I won't be able to do that if you don't ease up on the caveman crap," Gian said.

Karl opened his mouth to protest, but Gian cut him off.

"I don't want to hear you referring to women as 'hotties,' 'babes,' 'hoes,' 'shorties,' or any other expression you've picked up from MTV."

"So if a female with a really tight ass and big tits comes in—" Karl started.

Gian cut him off. "Female is an adjective, not a noun."

"Okay, Mr. Dictionary, what should I call people who are not guys?"

"Women," Chip volunteered. "Or girls. Calling them by their names has always worked out good for me."

"Who asked you, Squirt?" Karl grumbled.

At six feet, Chip was only a couple of inches shorter than Karl. A former college football standout, Chip was younger than Karl and outmatched him in speed and agility, if not size. Chip's hiring had brought out Karl's competitiveness, making him a better instructor. The younger man's laid-back nature and confidence made him an easy target for Karl's petty nicknaming, but Gian had no doubt that anytime he wanted to, Chip could easily put an end to Karl's insulting nicknames.

"Chip is as much a part of the management team of Sheng Li as you are, Karl," Gian reminded him. "His contributions are just as valuable as yours."

"So who was that ba—" Karl caught himself, rolled his eyes. "Who was that *woman* who came in late yesterday?"

"I don't know." Gian went back to his schedule to hide his embarrassment. "I didn't get her name. You needed next Saturday off for your cousin's wedding, right Chip? I think I can get Aja to cover your taekwondo class. She owes me a couple hours."

"Go on, change the subject, boss," Karl said. "Your mystery pupil should be here real soon. I'll find out her name, her number, and, when she wakes up next to me in the morning, I'll find out how she likes her eggs."

"Isn't your five o'clock Strength and Conditioning class about to start?" Gian directed at Karl.

"No, Squirt's taking it for me. I'm goin' to the casino tonight with some of my state trooper pals."

"Clear it with me the next time you want to make changes in the schedule," Gian grumbled.

"I meant to." Karl grinned. "I just forgot."

"Maybe I'll forget to sign your paycheck this week," Gian proposed.

Karl snapped his bare heels together and offered a mock salute. "Yessir, boss man, sir. I'm out."

"I apologize, Gian," Chip said once Karl had departed. "Karl told me that he got the okay for the switch from you."

"He's getting a little too big for his britches around here lately," Gian said. "He acts like it's his name on the door."

"You could always fire him," Chip suggested hopefully. "Insubordination is one of the no-nos in our employment contracts."

"So's that shaggy mane of yours, Goldilocks," Gian quipped.

Chip gave his long blond curls a good shake. "I'll get it trimmed this weekend. Wouldn't want to risk pissing off the boss."

Gian leaned to the left to get a better look into the main studio and the lobby beyond it. "Your students are here. You're on, cowboy."

"Later, hoss." With that, Chip exited the office, bowed at the entrance to the main studio, and called his students to take their places.

Gian wished that Chip had closed the office door. The fight cries and sounds of bodies hitting the mat were a distraction he didn't need in the face of the mountain of paperwork before him.

Unfortunately, there was no door to close out his biggest distraction.

The woman in black.

Gian glanced up at the red and gold dragon clock mounted above his bookcase on the opposite wall. His new student wasn't due for another twenty-five minutes. He'd assigned his four and five o'clock taekwondo classes to other instructors, giving him a two-hour break. His intention had been to create files for his new students, check the references for a couple of potential hires, find a new housekeeping service for the dojo, and to speak with Chip and Karl about a tournament in which he wanted Sheng Li to participate.

None of his tasks had successfully drawn his thoughts away from the one thing occupying his mind. The one person, rather.

CRYSTAL HUBBARD

"For cryin' out loud," Gian muttered, rubbing his palms over the scrub covering his dome.

It's not like he hadn't seen a pretty girl before. Webster University, which was only a few blocks from Sheng Li, fed him a steady stream of fetching young coeds. Enrollment always shot up in the winter after the university's seminars on personal safety.

Karl never hesitated to hit on the female students, and although he was forbidden to do so at Sheng Li, he managed to get a number here and there from women who cared more about dating someone with good looks than good behavior. But Gian made it a rule to never get personally involved with his students. It just wasn't wise to teach a potential romantic interest how to maim or kill with one blow.

The woman in black was the first real test of his resolve. Gian sat back in his chair, baffled. The woman's boyishly short black hair made her face that much more noticeable. She had the kind of big brown eyes that reminded him of the somber children living in some of the villages he had been stationed in during his tours of duty in the Marines. Just as those children had worked their way into his heart, so had his new student. Only her presence had also moved into his head, keeping him from properly tending his business.

He tapped the end of his ballpoint pen on the new student enrollment form he planned to give her. Of all the blanks on the form, the one he most wanted filled was the first, the one that came after NAME.

21

"Angela," he said aloud softly, trying to shape his memory of her to the name. *No*, he thought. *Angela's too soft.* "Harriet," he muttered. Chuckling, he deemed the name too old-fashioned for her. "Kyla, Halle, Jada," he recited, wondering if she shared a name with one of the actresses he liked. "Rumpelstiltskin," he sighed, abandoning his little game.

~

She sat in the lobby and watched the five o'clock Strength and Conditioning class. The instructor's wild blond curls and dimpled smile seemed to make it easier for his students to follow his commands, which directed them to do things that looked more like torture than exercise. One of his students, a statuesque African-American woman with a long black ponytail, chatted at her neighbors, mindless of the fact that they pointedly ignored her or answered her with red-faced grimaces.

"Zae!" the instructor called sharply, interrupting his own count of the punches his students executed. "Cut the jibber-jabber!"

"Yes, sensai," Zae responded with a clean thrust of her right fist, her punches still in rhythm with those of her classmates. Seemingly aware of the eyes on her, Zae peeped over her shoulder and found their owner in the lobby. "Hey, sweetie!" she cried over the fight cries of Chip's students. "You made it!"

"Drop and give me twenty Marine squats, Zae," Chip ordered. "I must not be working you hard enough if you've got the energy to socialize this late in my class."

With a roll of her eyes and a saucy flip of her pony-tail, Zae moved to one of the bamboo walls and stood with her back to it. Her hands on her waist, she lowered herself on her left leg, her right extended before her, until her backside nearly rested on her left heel. Biting her lower lip, she raised herself and then switched legs, lowering herself with her right leg. The exercise took incredible strength and balance, and Zae performed the reps without touching the wall. She completed her punishment just as Chip dismissed the class.

"Not bad for an old broad," Chip told her as the other students bowed to him before filing out of the studio.

"You're not my sensai once we hit the parking lot," Zae warned, a wicked twinkle in her black eyes. "I'll show you what an old broad can do, kid."

"I'd hate to be the attacker who ever tried to take you on." Chip chuckled. "He wouldn't know what hit him."

"A hundred and forty pounds of pure African-American wildcat," Zae stated. "A hundred and thirty-nine if I take off my earrings."

Clutching at her lower back with one hand, Zae bowed to Chip and then limped into the lobby.

"So you signed up," Zae said, greeting Sheng Li's newest student with a brief hug. "Good. You'll like it here. Let me show you where the locker room is."

Zae led the way, still limping.

"Are you okay?"

Zae cast a sly glance toward the studio before dropping the limp. "I'm fine. I just wanted Chip to feel bad for giving me the squats, the little punk."

"You weren't supposed to be talking in class."

"Who are you?" Zae asked, pitching her voice higher. "The dojo monitor? Honey, please." She smirked and swung open the locker room door.

"Are the lockers assigned, or—"

"Shh!" Zae hissed sharply, stopping before they rounded a tall stand of black lockers. She crouched slightly, leaning forward to get her left ear as close as possible to the voices coming from the other side.

"I've got spaces open at Witness Protection, Fugitive, and CI," said the first voice, a low soprano with a nasal quality.

"What's 'CI'?" a second, deeper female voice asked.

"Confidential informant," another voice provided.

"What would a confidential informant be doing in Webster Groves?" asked someone else.

"Gian used to be in the Marines," the first voice said quietly. "He was Special Forces. Who knows what kind of people he's connected to. Maybe the new girl was sent here by the government to spy on him."

"Gian was awarded a Purple Heart," someone said. "You make it sound like he's G. Gordon Liddy."

"He could be, we don't know. Same as we don't know anything about his new student."

"I'll put five bucks on Witness Protection. She seems like the type."

"How so?" asked a new voice.

"She comes into the library every week and checks out a dozen books. She reads everything—mysteries, self-help, essays, the classics—but she seems to like romance best. And she *always* returns her books on time."

"So that makes her a criminal in hiding?"

"No. It's just that she seems to make a point not to be noticed. She's seen me every week since she moved here last year, but she never says more than hi and thank you."

"It's her name that gets me," said a new voice. "When she came into the bank to open an account, I was like, 'What kind of name is Cinder White?' It sounds totally made up."

The women laughed, and Zae moved into view from her listening post. But before she could speak, Cinder herself quieted the women. "When I was born, my eyes were so dark that my mother thought they looked like cinders. That's where my name comes from. Is there anything else you'd like to know about me?"

Most of the women guiltily looked anywhere other than at Cinder as they collected their belongings and scattered, but one of them opened her mouth to speak. A scathing look from Zae made her close it.

"I'd better get home," the soprano, a tall, thin woman who resembled a stork in her blindingly white *gi*, said uncomfortably. She curled a sheet of paper in her hand. "Gotta make dinner for the kids."

"Yeah, us, too," another woman said, slinging her gym bag over her shoulder.

"Y'all oughta be ashamed of yourselves, betting on somebody like that," Zae chastised.

The stork halted in her tracks and slowly turned. "I got your text message before class, Zae. I put you down for East Coast escapee, just like you wanted."

"Uh, thanks, Carole." A blush rose in Zae's cheeks, deepening her warm brown complexion. "See you at carpool tomorrow morning."

Alone in the locker room, Cinder crossed her arms over her chest. She glared at Zae.

"We showed them," Zae said proudly, clapping Cinder on the shoulder. "Let's get your stuff put away. You don't want to be late for your first lesson."

"Can I get that for you, Mrs. Gale?" Gian tugged open the front door. With a hand at Adelaide Gale's back, he tried to speed her exit from Sheng Li. "Is your husband here?"

"Oh, Louie went across the street for a cup of coffee while I was in class," the elderly woman said. "He's trying to conserve gas. He didn't want to drive me here, drive home, come to pick me up again, and then drive home again. He's so sensible, my Lou—"

"Well, as long as he's here for you," Gian interrupted. "I'll see you next Tuesday, Mrs. Gale."

Before Gian could close the door behind her, she turned. "I won't be in class next week, Gianni," she started, touching a craggy index finger to her chin.

"We're having a potluck at the church to celebrate Reverend Mason's retirement. I'm going to make banana split cake, the one I brought for Chip's birthday, you remember? Everyone likes it so much that—"

"Mrs. Gale," Gian snapped louder than he meant to, startling her. "I've got a lesson now. I don't mean to be rude, but . . ."

"I understand," she sighed. "I sometimes forget what it feels like to be young and in a hurry."

A pang of guilt stabbed at Gian, but he ignored it. At eighty-nine, Mrs. Dale was his oldest student. She had been one of the first to sign up for his taekwondo class eight years ago, when he'd first opened Sheng Li. Mrs. Gale had progressed no further than a yellow belt, but she always showed up on time and ready to work, which Gian respected. But right now he was so anxious to start his private lesson that he was ready to grab the old lady and toss her like a javelin across the street.

"I'm sorry, Mrs. G.," Gian said, forcing himself to mean it. "I hope you have a good time at your potluck, and I'll tell Chip that you'll be absent next week."

"Thank you, dear," Mrs. Gale smiled. "Have a good lesson."

Gian closed the door and, after a cursory bow to the main studio, he trotted across it, down the corridor, and into his office. He paused a second to straighten his *gi* before he opened the door of the private studio.

He bowed, his eyes never leaving his new student. She had been sitting cross-legged in the center of the mat, but she stood when he approached her. She bowed to him exactly as he'd shown her the day before. She straightened, giving Gian a full view of her in her bright new *gi*.

The stark white cotton contrasted beautifully with the dark richness of her skin. The fit was perfect, and she wore it correctly—the Sheng Li emblem was sewn on the left side, the left side of the jacket overlapped the right, and the drawstrings assuring that the garment would stay closed had been tightly tied. Her belt, the *obi*, was the only problem.

She had followed the other rules of the dojo, which were posted in the locker room, so she wore no jewelry, cosmetics or polish on her fingers or toes. She had come to him unadorned, and so lovely that—

He cleared his throat, stroking his chin to make sure that he wasn't drooling. It was heavy lifting, but he forced himself to remember that she hadn't come to him, not in the way he'd been thinking. She'd come to learn, to work, and it was best he never lose sight of that.

Standing in front of her, Gian saw that she was more apprehensive than she had appeared the day before. The pulse at the base of her throat fluttered, and her rate of breathing seemed too rapid. "Are you okay?"

"Just a little nervous." She wiped her palms on the sides of her *gi*. "I saw part of the five o'clock class. Karate looks a little tougher than I thought it would be."

"Do you know what karate is?"

"Is that a trick question?"

He shook his head. "I just want to know what your idea of karate is."

"It's a style of fighting."

He reached for the loop in her white *obi*. Light and quick as a forest creature, she moved out of reach. "I'm sorry," she said, dropping her eyes for a second. "I didn't mean to do that. I didn't want to do that."

"It's okay, forget about it." But it wasn't okay, not for him. Her reaction tugged at something inside him, something that wanted to close her in his arms and press her to his heart. He took a step toward her and went for the loop again. "Who taught you how to tie your *obi*?"

"Azalea Richardson." She held her arms slightly up and out of the way while Gian unknotted her belt and unwound it from her waist.

Gian's eyebrows shot toward the skylight. "Zae Richardson's fighting skills are excellent, but she isn't exactly a model student. I want you to come to me looking like a warrior prepared to fight, not a present ready to be unwrapped."

"She's the one who recommended you to me."

He stooped a little to wrap the belt around her waist, starting at the front. His cheek was so close to her face, he felt the radiant warmth of her skin on his. "I'll have to figure out some sort of finder's fee for her then. Maybe I'll overlook it the next time she starts doing chorus line kicks when I'm running the class through ax kicks."

She pursed her lips but failed to completely suppress a grin.

Gian's hands worked at her back, folding one end of the belt under the other. He repeated the wrapping in the front, feeding the tails over and under themselves and pulling them tight in a neat, flat knot that left the tails hanging mid thigh. "The *obi* has to be tied correctly for your safety. If an opponent grabs you," he said, demonstrating by tugging her closer by the belt, "it won't get tighter and cut off your circulation. Zae knows how to tie an *obi* the right way, but she loops it anyhow. She says it's 'pretty.' "

"There's no room for pretty in karate?"

Gian almost cupped her face to tip it toward the skylight to better gaze upon the prettiest thing he'd ever seen in karate. "Yes, but we have different words for it. Like power. Dignity. Respect. Dedication. Confidence. Courage. Determination. Loyalty. Survival. Those words define pretty at Sheng Li."

"How do you define karate?"

"Karate comes from the Japanese words 'kara,' which means empty, and 'te,' which means hand. Karate is a form of Japanese self defense where the hands and feet are used to strike—" He shot a fist past her and drew it back so fast, she didn't see it, only felt it move the air. "And block." He executed a rapid series of precise arm movements designed to keep blows from his head and upper torso. In his sleeveless jacket, the muscles of his shoulders and arms bunched and lengthened with power and grace. "At Sheng Li we teach a modified form of karate that combines several styles of martial arts."

He loosely rested his hands on his trim hips. "The Sheng Li technique borrows heavily from Thailand's muy thai, eskrima from the Phillippines, Japanese ninjutsu, Korean taekwondo, Malaysian silat and Russian sambo. We'll take it slow," he assured her in response to her horrified expression. "But by the time we're done, you'll be a lethal weapon. There will be very few situations in which you can't handle yourself."

Her head bobbed slightly, uncertainly.

"Are you ready?"

"Yes, sensai."

He smiled a little. "Very good."

"I heard Zae call her teacher that."

"It's good to know she uses the proper terms of respect, even if she doesn't mean them."

Forty minutes into the lesson, Gian picked her up from the mat for the third time in a row. "You're not focused," he said firmly. "Get your head in this or one of us is going to get hurt." He showed her the fighting stance again, getting her back into proper starting position. "Keep your knees slightly bent, your right foot forward, and evenly distribute your weight. Good solid footing makes it harder for an opponent to knock you over, and you'll get more power behind your blows."

She nodded, giving herself a chance to catch her breath and wipe sweat from her forehead before she copied his movements.

"I know this is a lot to put together all at once, so just watch me while I talk you through the low block again," he said. "Your blocking arm will slice down in front while you bend your front leg and straighten your back leg. Snap your hips," he said, his actions following his words, "to get the most power from the block. You're going to use your opponent's energy against him. Make him tire himself out trying to make contact while you use his momentum to deflect his blows." Gian shook his head, throwing sweat across the mat. "You ready?"

She raised her fists in a fighting stance.

Gian threw a punch. It wasn't hard, but it had enough force to send her back a step when she failed to block it and caught it in her shoulder.

"What's the matter?" Gian relaxed his position.

"I think my timing is off."

"That's not what I meant." He went to a corner cupboard and opened it to retrieve two white hand towels. Mopping his face with one, he tossed the other to his sweaty student.

"I know what you meant." She blotted the back of her neck and the shadowy crevice between her breasts. "Can we try that block again?"

"Not until you tell me what's wrong."

"It's nothing." She tossed her towel to the base of the mirror lining one wall, where it landed next to Gian's. She assumed the fighting stance, her brow creased, her jaw clenched. She held his gaze.

The language of her big brown eyes and her body communicated a message with which Gian was all too familiar. *Wounded warrior*, he thought, naming it. But what he said was, "Then it won't hurt to tell me about nothing."

Her fists clenched tighter, but then she dropped them at her sides and brought her feet together. "They have a pool. About me."

Looking at the floor, Gian gripped his biceps and bounced on the balls of his feet.

Cinder touched his forearm, drawing his attention back to her. "You know about it," she stated simply.

His eyebrows arched toward his hairline. A half smile softened his features.

Cinder placed her hands on her hips. "How much?"

He shrugged. "Ten bucks."

A fine, feminine eyebrow lifted.

Gian stared at his feet. "Ten on New Beginning. Twenty on Fugitive."

"Fugi—!" She choked back the rest of the word, turned, and started for the exit.

"C'mon, don't go." Gian trotted after her. He circled in front of her to bar her getaway. "Nobody meant to hurt you."

"It takes more than speculations to hurt me."

It took Gian a moment to correctly read the slight flare of her nostrils and the heat brightening her eyes. That more than speculations had hurt her was a given. Even so, no one liked being talked about unkindly. "None of us meant to disrespect you. People want to know you. That's all."

"They want to know *about* me," she said, a tremble in her voice. "Not one person in this town has expressed an interest in getting to know me."

"From what I've heard, you haven't made it easy."

She flinched. "Just because people don't have anything better to do than talk about other people—"

"Karl says that your apartment is like a fortress, and—" he cut in.

She gritted her teeth. "I need to feel safe."

"From what?" He stepped closer to her, perhaps unconsciously moving to protect her.

"From my—" She stopped herself. "It's none of your business. It's no one's business but mine why I came here, or who I socialize with. I don't owe you or anyone else any explanations." Once more, she turned to go. "Why don't you ask Zae if you want to know every little thing about me? She's the only friend I have here."

"I don't do that." He caught her arm and reeled her back. "If I want to know something about you, I'll ask you myself." He freed her arm and admonished her. "You came here so I could teach you how to stand up for yourself. Here's lesson one: don't run out on me if I get close to a nerve. Stand or surrender. Those are your choices. When you're in my dojo, running is not an option."

Her voice quivered. "Has it ever occurred to you that sometimes running is the only thing you can do to stay alive? Or to keep from killing someone else?"

"Lady, I spent ten years in Special Ops. I've been in situations you couldn't imagine in your worst night-mares, and not once did it occur to me to run. You're gonna learn that about me."

"Don't you need to learn things about *me*?" she challenged. "You never even asked my name!"

Her accusation might have stung if not for the revelation he was about to share with her. "I don't need to know your name. I know *you*."

Her breathing deepened, her skin turning to goose flesh. His earnest declaration started her heart pumping in ways exercise couldn't. If any other man had said that to her, chances were good that she would have been packed and on her way out of Webster Groves within hours. But Gian's certainty gave her a sense of relief and comfort she hadn't experienced in a very long time.

"It's Cinder," she told him. "Cinder White."

He thrust forward a hand. "The pleasure's all mine."

Slipping her hand into his intensified the goose bumps rising along her limbs. His big hand swallowed hers, thrilling it with its warmth and roughness. He gave her hand a quick pump before briefly coddling it in both of his. Cinder believed that you could learn a lot about a person from a handshake, and Gian's told her that he was someone she could trust. Eventually.

"Who are you?" He still held her hand.

"I didn't run away. I relocated. It's not the same thing."

He tried a different question. "Why did you come to Webster Groves?"

"I wanted to live someplace quiet and clean. I . . ." She took a deep breath. "And my best friend lives here."

"Zae Richardson?"

She nodded.

"Zae's a pain in my whole ass when it comes to class, but she's a real good friend to have."

Curiosity brought her eyebrows a bit closer together, but before she could ask the question perched on her tongue, a knock on the bamboo door frame interrupted her.

"Excuse me," Chip said, leaning into the studio. "It's six-thirty, Gian. Pritchard Hok's people just called. Says he's running late but that he'll be here in about thirty minutes."

"Which means he'll be here in twenty," Gian sighed. "He's Japanese, and punctuality is very important to him." He turned to Cinder. "I need to finish some paper-work, shower, and get pretty for a meeting, but I also need you to fill out some forms."

"Okay," she agreed.

"Chip, there's a receipt and a stack of enrollment forms on my desk," Gian said. "Would you give them to Miss White on her way out and lock up for me?"

"Sure thing," Chip responded before disappearing into the office.

"Lesson one is in the bag," Gian smiled as he bowed to Cinder. "You did good."

"Thank you, sensai," Cinder replied, returning his bow. They left the studio, bowing to the mat as they did so.

"Five-thirty Monday?" Gian directed to Cinder before taking a seat at his desk.

"I'll be here."

When she turned, Chip met her with a stack of papers. "Here's your receipt and your enrollment forms, Miss . . . ?"

Cinder glanced back at Gian. "White. Cinder White."

"Pretty name." Chip's dimples teased in and out of his smile. "It's sure better than Chip."

"Chip isn't a nickname?" Cinder chuckled.

Gian's head snapped up from the document he had been reading. Cinder's hesitant laugh had drawn his attention, but her smile kept it. The smile vanished almost as quickly as it had appeared, but its afterimage burned in Gian's mind. He sat back heavily in his chair, totally confused.

Cinder was beautiful, unquestionably. Her somber brown eyes looked black everywhere other than in the bright light of the private studio. The warmth of her dark skin contrasted beautifully with her chilly demeanor. Her full lips constantly drew his eye, whether pursed in concentration or shaping her words, but when she pulled them into that brief smile, Gian had suddenly wanted to fly across the room and grab her by the shoulders. Not because she had smiled, but because the smile had been spent on Chip.

Typically not prone to jealousy, Gian didn't know what to do about the scene unfolding before him.

"My daddy's name is Charles Avery Kish Jr.," Chip started, "so when I was born, my parents named me Charles Avery, too. Only I wasn't number two, I was the third, so they called me Trip, for triple. My big sister, who was three at the time, couldn't say Trip. She called me Chip, and it stuck. I've been Chip ever since."

"That's an interesting story," Cinder said politely. She caught Gian looking at her. "I'll drop these forms off tomorrow morning," she told him. "Goodnight." She gave Chip another brief smile and headed for the locker room.

"Miss White, I'm done for the day," Chip said, following. "Do you need a ride home?"

Gian bolted upright in his chair.

"No, I'm within walking distance," she said.

"It's a nice night," Chip said. "Let me change out of these pajamas and I'll walk with you. That is, if you wouldn't mind the company."

Gian watched, every bit as vested in her answer as Chip seemed to be.

Cinder's right hand worried over her left a few times before she cleared her throat. "I, uh . . ." She cut a glance at Gian.

He forced his eyes back to the Pritchard Hok Industries documents on his desk, but not before he noticed the way her blush deepened her complexion to a shade of beauty that put him in the mind of slow, deep kisses and sweaty bodies grasping in the dark.

"You know what, maybe next time," Chip said amiably—to Gian's relief—just as Cinder replied, "Give me five minutes?"

Chip's dimples deepened.

Gian's face fell.

"See you out front, then," Chip said, and then trotted off to the men's locker room.

At the door, Cinder looked over her shoulder at Gian. "Have a good weekend, sensai."

Even though his document was upside down, Gian continued to study it. He grunted his acknowledgement of her parting words, looking up only after he heard the soft slap of her bare feet departing toward the locker rooms.

CHAPTER 3

"Zae speaks so highly of you and Mr. Piasanti," Cinder said quietly. "She mentioned that you were in the Marines."

"Yeah, Gian and I served in Yemen, the Gulf, Mogadishu. He was my commanding officer." He shoved his hands deep into the pockets of his baggy cargo shorts. "Saved my life a couple of times."

Cinder slowed her pace and glanced at Chip. "Really?"

"Oh, hell yeah. I wouldn't be talking to you right now if Gian hadn't carried my ass through two miles of rebel fire in Mogadishu."

They stopped at the corner of Lockwood and Gore to wait for a car to pass before crossing the street. "How long were you in the service together?"

"Five years." Chip slipped Cinder's gym bag from her shoulder and slung it over his own, and he continued his story before she could protest. "I'd been in the service for two years before I was reassigned to Gian's Force Recon company. Gian had worked his way up to Special Ops by the time he was twenty-five. He enlisted right after high school."

"What are 'ops'?"

"Operations. Our missions were highly classified."

"And highly dangerous?"

"And how." Chip chuckled somberly.

Chip took Cinder's hand and started across Lockwood, waving a hand in gratitude when a considerate driver allowed them to cross. As soon as they hit the opposite curb, Cinder slipped her hand from his. "Is Gian from Missouri?"

"Yeah, he grew up in South St. Louis, on The Hill."

"Which hill?"

"*The* Hill," Chip said. "A lot of Italian immigrants settled between South Kingshighway and Hampton Avenue. It used to be called Dego Hill, now it's just The Hill, thank goodness. Gian's people have lived there since the Piasantis came to the States from Italy. Gian's mom makes the best meatballs, I swear, they—"

"Chip," Cinder started softly, "if you don't want to tell me about the time you and Gian spent in the service, you don't have to."

"No, no, it's fine. I don't mind talking about it. I'm glad to talk about it with you." A flash of his blue eyes and friendly dimples assured Cinder that he was telling the truth. "Our mission in Mogadishu was our last. Gian decided not to re-up when he left Special Ops, and I was discharged to go home to—"

"Why didn't Gian want to re-up?"

He shrugged. "I don't know. He never said. The USMC wasn't too eager to let a good commander like Gian go, so they offered him a position with their training school in the Ozarks. He helped beat grunts into shape for a few years, then decided to open a school of his own to teach the fighting techniques he'd learned over the years. That's how Sheng Li was born."

"Why did he pick Webster Groves?" Cinder stepped aside to allow a group of noisy, pierced, and tattooed teenagers dressed in black and purple to pass between her and Chip on the narrow sidewalk. "Does he have family here, or a girlfriend?"

"I don't know why he settled in Webster Groves," Chip said. "He's the reason I came here, though."

They were passing the Webster Groves town hall when a woman in a sharp business ensemble stopped opening her car door to stare at Chip. Cinder glanced back after they had passed her to see that the woman's line of sight arrowed directly at the seat of Chip's shorts.

Chip continued to talk about his experiences in the service, but Cinder watched him more than listened to him. An orange Tennessee Volunteers T-shirt hung off his broad shoulders, the worn fabric nicely showing off the carved muscles of his upper arms and back. Cinder's gaze, and that of a couple of female pedestrians, followed the movement of Chip's hand when he mindlessly raised his T-shirt to scratch his belly, casually exposing the stacked muscles of his runway-ready abs and the trail of golden hair adorning them.

Cinder examined him from head to toe as one would take in the details of a museum exhibit. From his big feet in their plastic and foam flip flops to the chaos of thick curls atop his head, Chip was a beautiful man. He was a nice one too, who was walking her home, carrying her gym bag, and who'd held her hand to cross the street.

"I was in Nashville recuperating," Chip was saying by the time Cinder transferred her attention from his looks to his words.

"Recuperating from what?" she asked.

"Somebody always comes out on the bad end in a fight. In our last one, it was us."

"What happened?"

"Our last mission was . . . challenging." He sighed. "I got shot in the leg and nearly bled out in the field, and by field I mean a grass hut village surrounded by wasteland and enemy troops for ten miles in every direction."

She looked at him. He stared at his feet as they walked, his mind clearly in a time and place that etched fine lines around his youthful eyes.

"We lost four men before we could get a signal strong enough to radio for an extraction," he went on. "The hardest part was getting to the extraction point two miles away."

"Gian carried you?"

He raised his head and stared forward. "The whole two miles. He didn't break stride or stumble once. He led his men through gunfire and mortar rounds, and he did it with my dead weight over his shoulder. Most people can't even imagine what that must have been like."

I can, Cinder thought.

"I was sent home to recuperate," Chip said. "Three surgeries and a year of physical therapy corrected the muscular, skeletal, and nerve damage in my leg. When Gian asked me to come to Webster Groves and work for him, he wouldn't take no for an answer, even when we didn't know if I'd ever walk again." He slapped his upper thigh. "I've got enough titanium in here to build a battle-ship, but it works almost as good as new, thanks to Sheng Li and Sue Pan."

"Is Sue Pan another form of martial arts?"

Chip laughed softly. "No, she's the physical therapist who helps me out here."

They walked in silence, passing well-lit houses where families sat for dinner, or teenagers laughed and chatted on wide, wraparound porches. Cinder offered a polite smile to an older couple walking a pug that strained against its leash.

A young woman in neon running shoes jogged toward them. She eyed Chip so closely that she nearly collided with Cinder. When the woman passed, Cinder peeped over her shoulder to see the petite brunette runner staring back at Chip, her sweating face split in a leering grin. Cinder studied Chip, forcing herself to view him anew, to see him as the overheated jogger had.

He was the very picture of summer sexiness, and Cinder realized that she should have been enjoying his company. She was. Yet in taking inventory of Chip's good qualities and good looks, she couldn't stop comparing him to Gian.

A few inches taller than Chip, Gian was long, lean, and elegant compared to Chip's compact, gym-built physique. Chip was as quick to smile as Gian was to scowl; he was sunny and open to Gian's authoritative, business-like demeanor.

She sensed a tender vulnerability within Chip's apparent strength that left her affection for him more familial than carnal. She sensed no such vulnerability in Gian, who was as solid and stoic as a Marvel superhero. From what she'd seen so far, Gian was everything Zae had promised: patient but firm, knowledgeable, handsome.

Chip had a mouth built for kissing, but it only made Cinder want to know what it would feel like to press her lips to Gian's head and cradle it to her bosom. Not many men could carry off a near-buzz cut. Gian's square jaw balanced his broad forehead. His eyebrows were manly, not too heavy and not too thin—the perfect awnings for his deep-set hazel eyes. Gian's face never showed his emotions, but his eyes betrayed him every time Cinder looked into them.

He was curious about her, but unlike most people she'd met in Webster Groves, he asked questions outright. When he accidentally bloodied her nose, his face had remained totally calm, but his eyes had telegraphed his concern for her. Gian was so different in appearance and temperament from Chip, yet every bit as beautiful inside and out.

Cinder shook her head to clear it of that last. She hadn't enrolled at Gian's school because of his looks or personality. She wanted only to learn what he knew—how to kill a man a hundred different ways with no weapons other than her hands and feet.

"This is you," Chip said, stopping.

"I'm sorry?"

"This is your house, isn't it?"

She answered with a reserved smile.

"Got some things on your mind?" Chip shoved his hands into his pockets and rocked on his heels.

"I didn't think it showed," she replied. "Thank you for the walk home."

She climbed three short concrete steps leading to the long flagged path in front of the three-story Victorian. Chip vaulted the stairs to get ahead of Cinder.

"I think I already know the answer to the question I'm about to ask you, but I have to ask anyway," he started. "Would you have lunch with me sometime? I'd really like to get to know you better."

With the fiery pink and orange sunset and the warm breeze filtering through his goldenrod curls, Chip looked like a figure from a Renoir painting. It had been so long since she'd gotten a date invitation, and Chip was someone she might eventually like as more than a friend. The last thing she wanted to do was give him reason to expect more than she could give, so she phrased her answer very specifically.

"That would be nice," she said. "Maybe we could invite Zae along with us. She really likes you and she rarely goes out because of her teaching schedule."

Aiming a dejected smile at his feet, Chip sighed. "I was thinking just the two of us could go out."

"I'm flattered, but I wouldn't be very good company." She took her bag from him and dug out her house keys. They climbed the three wide wooden stairs to the asymmetrical porch of the maroon and black house.

Chip followed her. "You were great company tonight."

She dared not tell him that their walk was the first social interaction she'd had with someone other than Zae in the fifteen months since she had moved to Webster Groves. That Chip thought her great company was a much-appreciated compliment.

"C'mon, it's just lunch," Chip said, his voice playfully seductive. "If you hate me afterward, we can pretend it never happened."

Her back to the door, Cinder fiddled with her keys. "I find it hard to believe that anyone could hate you."

"So is that a yes to lunch?"

"I can't, Chip. It wouldn't be fair to you."

His smile never wavered. "I had a feeling, but I had to try."

"Why were you so sure that I'd say no?"

He backed toward the stairs. "Because just about every question you asked me tonight was about Gian Piasanti."

Gian tugged at his tie, which seemed to be slowly strangling him. He sat opposite Pritchard Hok and his partner, a long-legged brunette with grasshopper green eyes. The mellow notes of a viola accompanied the pleasant murmur of conversations about the dining room. Isis was one of Gian's favorite restaurants because of its eclectic cuisine and décor, which was just chic enough to pass for upscale when he entertained people like Hok. But for the first time ever, he had no taste for the chef's special menu, no ear for the live viola, and no eye for Hok's stunning partner.

Kuriko Lavenich was the reason Gian was in talks with Pritchard Hok, founder and CEO of an eponymous health, fitness, and sports conglomerate based in Korea. One of Gian's former students had demonstrated the Sheng Li technique at a fitness expo in Hong Kong and had impressed Kuriko, who had flown all the way to Missouri to meet "the man behind the mastery."

A second meeting in New York City a month later had further convinced Kuriko to seek a deal between Sheng Li and Pritchard Hok Industries. Although he could never be sure if it had been his acumen in the boardroom or in the bedroom that had inspired Kuriko to sell the Sheng Li technique to Hok, Gian was glad to be given a chance to join a company that could make Sheng Li a worldwide brand. If the movement of Kuriko's toe along his inseam was any indication, all they had left to do was put the deal to bed.

"It took a great deal of convincing to get the sponsors to agree to hold the International Martial Arts tournament in St. Louis," Pritchard said, running his fingers through his long, silver hair. "This will be the first time we've ventured into foreign territory."

His measured tone and boarding-school-bred English accent belied the gravity of his words. Gian understood corporate speak, and he translated "convincing" to mean money, "foreign territory" to mean anyplace other than New York, Boston, Miami or Los Angeles.

"With Kansas City and Chicago so close by, St. Louis is an ideal location for the tournament," Gian said. "Students and fans of the martial arts will turn out to see fighters they've only seen on ESPN. I'm sure you've already noticed how much more economical it is to host the event here, with hotels, transportation, and tournament venues costing a fraction of what they do on either coast. You'll more than recoup your investment, Mr. Hok."

"The money isn't the issue most concerning me, Mr. Piasanti." Pritchard grinned. "This tournament will be an audition for you and your Sheng Li fighting techniques. It will be your introduction to the international fight community. Your competitors and potential franchisees must be impressed with a dynamic presentation. If you fail . . ." He raised a speculative eyebrow and swirled the last of the red wine in his goblet.

"I won't fail," Gian stated, his jaw hardening. "My students won't fail."

Pritchard smiled. Kuriko's toes burrowed deeper into Gian's crotch.

"That's the fighting spirit, Mr. Piasanti." Pritchard raised a hand and summoned their waiter with two hooked fingers. "I shall leave you and Kuriko to enjoy dessert, and perhaps, catch up?" Their server scurried to their table and cheerfully accepted Hok's black credit card.

"Thank you, Hok," Kuriko said, her Russian accent turning "thank you, Hok" into "zank you, Howk."

"Stay," Gian said, perhaps a bit too quickly. "The green tea ice cream is pretty good here."

Kuriko narrowed her eyes at Pritchard, and her shoulders rose with the deep breath she took through her nose. If her body language hadn't been specific enough, Kuriko's next words made her preferences clear. "I am sure that you have better things to do this evening than sit in on old home week between me and Gian," she said. "I'll see you at the airport in the morning, Hok. Goodnight."

Pritchard muttered his farewells and left, Kuriko's eyes tracking him until his driver was closing him in his Town Car. When Kuriko returned her gaze to Gian, he nearly shrank from the heat blazing from her eyes. The last time he had seen that fire, he had ended up dehydrated and exhausted after two days and two nights in Kuriko's suite at the Mandarin Oriental Hotel. With Manhattan's skyline sprawling in the background, he and the limber marketing executive émigré had wiped the walls with each other.

Gian had looked forward to her return for this meeting, and not just because of the business opportunity it heralded. Kuriko's intelligence matched her unusual beauty, the result of her Japanese and Ethiopian-Russian ancestry. Gian watched her comb her fingers through her straight black hair, and he had a vague memory of that hair tickling over his torso. As she spoke, he watched her ruby lips form her words. When she asked their waiter for sugar cane juice to sweeten her coffee, her lips wrapped around the word "juice" and reminded Gian of her lips wrapped around the heaviness between his legs, which now rested snugly beneath Kuriko's bare toes.

"Pritchard is obviously quite serious about partnering with you and making Sheng Li an international brand, but he'll proceed no further until he sees the reception you get at the International Martial Arts Championships." Kuriko leaned over the table, her long hair nearly sweeping into her coffee. "He'll be watching your exhibition matches most closely."

Gian sat back in his chair, shifting to clear his crotch of Kuriko's foot. "Why's that?"

"There are rules to the championship matches. The combatants are highly trained athletes skilled at competition fighting. The audience is familiar with them, for the most part, and knows what to expect, a winner and a loser. There are no rules for the exhibitions and the fighters are either unknown or old ponies trotted out for a last kick. The first round match-ups are random, so you never know who will be matched with whom. That's what makes them far more exciting to the audience. Exhibitions win far more new students than championship matches, and we want the viewing public to hunger for you and Sheng Li after the tournament." Her long, slim fingers went to her neckline, lightly playing with it so that Gian was forced to notice the deep plunge of her cleavage. "You make it very easy to hunger for you, Gian."

The left side of his mouth hooked into a subtle grin when Kuriko's toes grasped at the place his crotch had been. He gave them a light squeeze before moving her foot, guiding it back to the floor.

Kuriko pushed her coffee aside and rested her arms on the table. She sat up straight, instantly changing her posture from bedroom to boardroom. "You don't seem yourself, Gian," she said briskly. "If you don't think you'll be prepared for the tournament, it would be best if you told Hok now. Better to delay the launch of Sheng Li than force it before you're completely ready."

"I'm on track with my preparations for the tournament. Don't you worry. This thing will happen."

"Then why won't you come back to my hotel with me?"

At the nearest table, an older lady with a glossy blue rinse hid an amused smirk behind a fork wrapped in glassy rice noodles. Her dining companion's eyebrows rose; his wide eyes darted between Gian and Kuriko. Shaking his head, he chuckled, and Gian knew exactly what he was thinking: *You're crazy for not going to the ends of the Earth with this woman.*

"I didn't know that I'd been invited." Gian sighed.

"You have a standing invitation."

Or appointment, Gian thought. He ran his hand over his head. Kuriko had made it very clear that she desired nothing more than "a bit of fun" from him or any other man. Pritchard Hok Industries took her all over the world, and Gian had no delusions that he was her only fun.

But even as he recalled the many varieties of fun they had enjoyed in New York City, he had no desire to revisit them. Funnily enough, he had no desire for her at all. She had touched him intimately in a semi-public place, yet his flesh hadn't stirred. He hadn't been with a woman in months, not since his last visit to Manhattan for his initial meeting with Pritchard Hok. He had looked forward to this meeting all day for its own sake—not because he had a sure thing in Kuriko.

Kuriko had sat before him all through dinner, teasing him with her eyes as much as her toes, yet her obvious interest had failed to dislodge the reason for his inability to devote his full interest to her. He couldn't stop thinking of Cinder and what her toes might be doing to Chip.

The day after his meeting with Pritchard Hok, Gian stood in his kitchen waiting for his teaching staff to fill their plates and seat themselves in his media room. Karl jumped ahead of Sionne to pick over the spread Gian had laid out, heaping his plate with chicken wings, baked ziti, pasta salad, and spare ribs.

"Need any help with that?" Gian watched Karl top his mountainous plate of food with three steaming garlic knots.

"I'm good." Karl plopped a dollop of bleu cheese dressing onto his buffalo wings, slopping a glop onto the floor. Tucking two bottles of Schlafly ale under his arm, he carefully stepped over the mess and left the kitchen. "I got dibs on the La-Z-Boy!"

Gian took a napkin from the package on the counter and stooped to wipe up the dressing. The bamboo flooring was durable, but the last thing he needed was one of his instructors slipping and breaking an ankle in the midst of training for the most important tournament in Sheng Li's short history.

"This is some spread, chief," Sionne said, passing Gian a second napkin. "You cook, you clean. You're gonna make a great little wife someday."

"Up yours, junior," Gian grumbled.

At almost three hundred pounds and six and a half feet tall, Sionne Falaniko was Gian's biggest fighter. His background in mixed martial arts made the Samoan a fierce competitor, but Sheng Li had refined his skills and shaped his talent, helping him to six national fighting titles.

His native tattoos and size gave him an imposing appearance, but a minute in Sionne's company was all it took to realize that inside the well-muscled fighting machine raged the heart of a kitten. One of Gian's best instructors, Sionne's specialty was teaching the basics of martial arts to children aged five to eight.

"Are you gonna need your La-Z-Boy, chief?" Sionne asked. He clutched two plates in his hand, each resembling a model of Mt. Everest sculpted from pasta and red sauce. "If you want Karl moved, I can move him."

"No, Karl can keep it. Are you gonna need an ambulance after you eat all that?"

"This?" Sionne raised the plates. "This is just the first course."

Thankful that Sionne had taken up martial arts and not competitive eating, Gian followed him into the media room, carrying bottled water for each of them.

Chip entered behind Gian, taking a seat on one of the two oversized sofas on opposite sides of the yellow pine cocktail table Karl was using as a footrest. Gian walked between the La-Z-Boy and the table, knocking Karl's feet onto the floor. Half of Karl's food jostled onto his lap.

"What the hell, man," Karl cried, half-chewed chicken spraying from his mouth.

"You're in a recliner," Gian responded coolly. "You want to put your feet up, use the footrest built into the chair."

"Damn it, Gian," Karl swore. "I just bought these jeans."

"It shouldn't be too hard to find another pair," offered Cory Blair, a weekend instructor who attended Washington University. "There's a Tuffskins outlet in St. Charles."

"That's real funny, Urkel," Karl sneered over the laughter of his co-workers. "Shut up before I kick your ass back to school."

"That's enough, guys," Gian announced, quieting them. "Let's get this meeting underway."

He opened the armoire occupying the wall adjacent to the two sofas, revealing a forty-seven-inch flat screen television. At Gian's bidding, Chip and Cory lowered the room-darkening shades covering the windows behind the sofa they shared.

"If I'd known there was going to be a movie, I'd have brought the cupcake I took to the Tropicana last night," Karl said. "Gian, this is the best makeout pad I've ever seen! Dude, I bet they drop their panties the instant they see this place. Hell, if I'd have known you were living this large, I'd have invited myself over a long time ago. No wonder you pay us pennies. All Sheng Li's dough goes into your mortgage."

"All Sheng Li's dough goes back into Sheng Li," Gian said stiffly. "This was one of my brother's model homes. I got it for next to nothing."

"Eat that up," Cory muttered.

"This is one of Pio's green homes?" Chip asked.

"Yes. But I didn't invite you bums here to talk about my house," Gian said. "I want to discuss the International Martial Arts tourney with you."

"Man, that's five months away," Karl complained.

"And some of us need every second of that time to train." Gian pressed a key on the remote clutched in his hand. The television blipped on and he hit another button, this one powering the DVD player.

"Ever done it in a recliner, Gian?" Karl asked, fooling around with the chair's back and footrest settings.

"If that's an invitation," Gian started, "I'm flattered but not interested."

Chip and Cory laughed, which made Karl launch himself out of the chair. Sionne, incredibly agile and fast for his size, popped off his ottoman and blocked Karl's path to the sofa.

"Guys, c'mon," Gian sighed. "The faster we get through this meeting, the sooner you can get out of here."

Glowering at Chip and Cory, Karl resumed his seat. "So how 'bout it, Gian," he persisted. "You ever done it in this chair?"

"The day I discuss my sex life with you, will be the day—"

"What sex life?" Karl mumbled. "I thought you were married to Sheng Li."

"At least I'm not married to my right hand," Gian replied.

"Oh, snap," Cory shouted, drawing his knees to his chest in exaggerated paroxysms of laughter.

"Who was that girl I saw you with at the Tropicana last night, Cory?" Karl sneered. "Her ass looked like two bowling balls wrapped in basketball skin."

"At least my girl had an ass," Cory coolly responded. "Yours had a billboard booty."

"It's 'cause I keep her on her back," Karl said.

"You're such a pig, man," Chip muttered.

"Better a pig than a Boy Scout," Karl scoffed. He grabbed the bulge between his legs. "I got females begging me to feed their kitties. All you got outta your girl last night was a walk." He clasped his hands under his chin and batted his eyelashes. "Oh, how sweet," he started in a teasing falsetto. "Opie took Frieda for a walk down Limp Lover's Lane."

Sionne belched. "Who's Frieda?"

"For cryin' out loud, I could smell that," Gian winced. "Did you have hotdogs before you came here?"

"Who's Frieda?" Cory asked.

"Cinder White," Karl said. "Gian's private lesson. Or maybe she's into Chip's privates now."

Gian's jaw hardened.

"Why do you call her Frieda?" Chip asked.

"Frieda is a black girl's name," Karl smirked.

"Actually, it's German in origin," Cory said. "It means 'lady.' My sister and her husband are having twins. All they do is talk baby names."

"If they're girls, she could name them Frieda and Hazel," Karl said. "Or Leroy and Tyrone, if they're boys."

"Why don't you shut up, you ignorant prick," Cory snapped.

Karl kicked the footrest back into place and sat taller in the recliner. "Why don't you make me?"

"You know I can," Cory warned.

"Let's dance, Lionel."

Both instructors stood and started to square off, but Gian quickly stepped between them, Chip taking Cory's arm in a brotherly grip.

"Settle down, guys," Gian said, his tone reminding them that he could take the both of them if he had to. Fast, slim, and strong, Cory was the youngest reigning Junior Regional Martial Arts champion ever, and the first African-American to win the honor. Karl rarely competed, but his mean streak and the solid muscle packed on his large frame might have been enough to give him the edge in a fight with Cory. It was a match-up Gian would have enjoyed watching on the mat, not in his house.

Karl and Cory returned to their seats, although they continued to give each other the stink eye.

"Save this for the tournament," Gian told them as he paced the room. "The footage you're about to see will show you what you'll be up against. You're gonna need everything you've got to win. And winning this tournament is about more than prize money or trophies. This is where the best of the best meet to prove who most deserves that title. You take everything you have to the mat, and you spend it, every bit of it. When you walk into that arena and face off with your opponent, you'll do it for honor." He glanced at Chip, then Cory. "You'll do it for respect." He threw a glance at Karl.

Gian stepped around the cocktail table to pull Sionne's plate from him before he could dive into a third helping of pasta. "You'll do it to show your peers that you're a champion on and off the mat."

Gian returned to the armoire and pushed PLAY on the remote. "You four are Sheng Li's best chance for a team title and to medal in the individual fight classes. I'd like each of you to nominate a student or two who you think would make a good showing in the exhibition matches. Competitors will be matched up according to skill level alone, not weight, so keep that in mind." He turned to Chip. "I've already got Zae Richardson on my list, so I'd like you to choose two of your other students."

"Which belt class are you putting Zae in?" Chip asked.

"Any one she wants."

They chuckled, each of them having survived in-house run-ins with Zae.

"Put her in the black belt class." Cory grinned. "I'd love to see her tear up that bulldog from the Philippines." He pointed to the television. "Did you see his take-down?"

They quieted to watch the fight footage, Gian's animated play-by-play providing insight to the styles and habits of the men they would likely face in the tournament. Once the DVD was over, Gian dismissed them with copies to study on their own time.

Chip volunteered to stay and help Gian clean up the kitchen. "My mother's baked ziti normally feeds twelve," Gian said, scooping the half-cup leftover portion into a small plastic storage container. "Or one Sionne."

"Karl made off with the last of the ribs," Chip said. "Gian, he's totally outta control."

Gian plunged the empty casserole dish into a sink full of hot, soapy water. "Maybe he wanted something to chow on while he watches the Cards tonight."

"I'm not talking about him stealing your leftovers."

Gian glanced up from the dish he was washing and sighed. "Yeah, I know. He's gotten worse ever since he lost his job at the auto plant."

Chip leaned against the counter nearest Gian. "That's not your problem. But sooner or later, he's going to become yours. He's always been obnoxious, and now he's downright mean."

His white shirtsleeves rolled up to his elbows, Gian stared forward as he washed the ziti dish. Through the wide, bare window before him, he watched a hawk soar above the treetops. The hawk either lived in or planned to prey on something scurrying through the organized wilderness of the Shady Creek Nature Conservatory abutting Gian's big backyard.

"I can't fire him," Gian finally said. "Sheng Li is all he's got left."

"So why's he trying to throw it away?"

"He's in a bad place right now. You and I know what that's like. It'll pass."

Staring at his flip flops, Chip grabbed his left elbow with his right hand. "Are you sure?"

"No."

"He's got a real burr in his saddle about Cinder."

"You noticed?" Gian asked wryly.

"He's not the only one preoccupied with her."

"Cory asked about her yesterday." Gian laughed. "Not that he'd know what to do with her if she was into twenty-year-old college juniors."

"I don't know," Chip said. "Cory's got his goofy moments, but I don't see anything wrong with a younger man seeing an older woman."

Gian nearly dropped the freshly rinsed casserole pan. "You wouldn't mind seeing Cory with Cinder White? Our little Cory?"

"Not if that's who she wanted to be with. But he's not who she's into."

Gian pulled the stopper from the drain and the stainless steel sink emptied with a soft sucking sound. He dried his hands on a white, waffle-weave kitchen towel. "I'd love to hear all about your love connection with Cinder, but I got laundry to do and some yard work that needs—"

"It's not me, Gian," Chip cut in. "I think it's you."

Gian's interest in the conversation renewed instantly. "Did she say something? How do you know?"

With a tiny grin, Chip shook his head. "The ol' Kish charm didn't move her one bit last night. She only wanted to know about you. I don't think she even realized it until I pointed it out."

Gian's chest seemed to inflate and his step was lighter as he went to the refrigerator. Karl's fingerprints in barbeque sauce were on the door handle, but Gian didn't seem to care. He simply wiped them away with paper towels. "There's something about her. It's like with Lucia." Forgetting about his laundry and yard work, he took a couple of beers from the refrigerator and handed one to Chip. "They're so different, but they're so much alike."

"You think so?" Chip followed Gian back into the media room.

Gian sank into a loveseat while Chip took the recliner. "I want to be wrong," Gian said softly. "I hope to God I'm wrong."

CHAPTER 4

"Is there something wrong with you?"

Zae had stopped in the middle of the baking aisle in Freddy's Market to bark her question. Mindless of stares from housewives dropping flour or sugar into their carts, Cinder drew to a halt, her response to Zae's question succinct. "No."

"Chip Kish asked you out, and you're only telling me now, two months later?" Zae started piling two-pound bags of confectioner's sugar into her cart.

"What are you going to do with twelve pounds of powdered sugar?" Cinder asked.

"Make twelve pounds of frosting. Why did you turn down Chip? What did he do wrong?"

"Nothing." Cinder moved closer to Zae, almost toppling a floor display of discontinued brownie mixes in the narrow aisle. "I haven't felt anything for anyone in such a long time, I'm not sure I'm capable of it anymore."

"You need to see a doctor," Zae deadpanned. "Chip Kish is sick."

"Sick with what? He looked fine when I saw him at Sheng Li last night."

"Sick means good," Zae explained. She chose two packages of shortening sticks and set them on top of her confectioner's sugar. "It means fine. Handsome."

"You've been reading Dawn's e-mails again, haven't you?"

"Yes, once Eve translated them into English for me."

They left the baking aisle for the Deli & Meat counter at the back of the store. "Why don't you go after him yourself if you think he's so sick?"

Zae bent over to peer more closely into the glass case housing the prepared salads and heat-and-eat entrees. "It doesn't sound right when you say it."

"Why don't you ask him out?"

Zae stood and, with one hand planted on her hip, said, "Woman, heal thyself. Once you pull a Lazarus on your own love life, then you can try to rebuild mine."

Cinder held Zae's gaze. Cinder's experience maintaining a blank expression served her well, but she had never been able to cloak her feelings from Zae.

"I'm sorry." Zae ran a consoling hand along Cinder's bare upper arm. "I shouldn't be so defensive. Or so resistant to . . ." She took a deep breath to force out her next words. "Starting over."

"You don't have to apologize," Cinder assured her. "You're right, about all of it. There is something wrong with me, and I've known it for a while now. I just don't feel right. I don't feel at all."

"It takes time to fully recover from what you've been through. It hasn't been two years."

"I don't mean that way." Cinder lowered her voice. "I haven't had *that* urge, in so long. I can't remember the last time I felt . . ." She widened her eyes and tipped her head to one side, hoping Zae would know what she meant.

"Horny," Zae blurted.

The apron-clad butchers behind the counter looked up from their cutting and wrapping.

"Mind your meat, man," Zae directed them before turning back to Cinder. "You have to do something about that. You can't let what happened back East permanently change your life."

"But it did."

"You're in charge, kiddo. You can determine how it's changed you. Whether it's for the good or the pitiful. You've already made positive strides toward putting the *you* back in you. You moved to Webster Groves, you're learning at Sheng Li. You won't ever be the woman you were before everything went down back East. You'll be better."

"If I can rebuild my life," Cinder started pointedly, "then so can you."

"I set myself up for that, didn't I?"

"Good advice works both ways." Cinder smiled. "It's been eight years since Colin died, Zae. You're still young . . . relatively."

"Girl," Zae said, warning in her tone.

Cinder laughed.

"It's good to see you smile again," Zae said, her own brightening.

"I'll say."

Cinder turned, Zae looking over her shoulder, to see who had spoken.

"Good afternoon, ladies," Gian said. His eyes on Cinder, he added, "I'm with Zae on this. It really is good to see you smile."

In two months of training her, she hadn't cracked so much as a grin. Now her smile, lovely as it was, seemed permanent as the heat of a blush gave her face new radiance. This was the first time in weeks that he'd seen her in something other than a *gi*, and he spent a moment studying her.

The voluminous jacket and pants of her *gi* hid the elegantly sleek muscles of her arms and the fuller, more defined muscles of her legs, all of which were on display in her pale sleeveless top, denim cut-offs, and high espadrilles. He'd noticed the subtle changes in her face that had come with her hard work at Sheng Li and a healthy weight gain. No longer gaunt, her cheeks were sensuously plump. Her eyes appeared vibrant and relaxed rather than sunken and wary.

The sadness she carried with her remained, but it only added to her mystery, her beauty. Chip's revelation, that he thought Cinder had an interest in him, had fertilized the seed that had been planted the first time he had seen her. Standing in front of the meat counter at Freddie's Market, Gian's feelings for Cinder began to bloom.

"What can I get for you, Mrs. Richardson?" the butcher asked, a wide smile beneath his thick white mustache. "I've got slab bacon on sale."

"I'll take three pounds," Zae said.

Cinder nudged her.

"Make that five," Zae amended.

"Someone's having a big breakfast in the morning," the butcher exclaimed, tearing off a sizeable piece of white paper from the roll behind the counter.

"It's this one here." Zae bumped Cinder with her hip. "She could live off bacon."

The butcher winked at Cinder. "Is that so?"

Gian hung his shopping basket over his right arm so he could stand closer to Cinder to hear her answer.

"Bacon is proof of God's existence." Cinder's placid tone contradicted the passion of her words. "If there was bacon juice, I'd drink it. If there was bacon perfume, I'd wear it. I wish there was such a thing as bacon ice cream. If—"

"See what I mean," Zae interrupted.

"What other foods do you like?" Gian asked Cinder.

"Donuts," she and Zae answered together. "LaMar's vanilla long johns are my favorite," Cinder told him.

"Mine, too," Gian said.

Zae stepped around Cinder to face Gian. "She once put three strips of bacon on top of a LaMar's long john and ate it like an entree."

"I'll have to add that to my recipe collection." Gian chuckled.

"Me, too," the butcher said and laughed.

Zae took her massive package of bacon from the top of the counter and asked for bone-in chicken breasts and lamb chops. Cinder peered into Gian's basket. Then she looked at his face. "This is what you live on?"

"Sure." He shrugged one shoulder.

Cinder inventoried his selections. "HoHos, Cool Whip, Velveeta—"

"Velveeta is great for nachos," Gian said defensively.

"It's great for sealing cracks in your bathroom tile, too," Zae muttered.

"How do you stay in such great shape eating stuff like this?" Cinder wondered.

Gian patted his abdomen. "You think I'm in great shape?"

Her blush deepened, but she maintained eye contact with him. "Yes. I do."

It was Gian's turn to blush, and he dropped his chin in a weak attempt to hide it.

"Gian?"

The high-pitched, nasal squawk came from a tall, skinny woman in white low-rider shorts and a plaid halter. She exited the dairy section and headed straight for Gian. "Well, hey, what brings your hot buns into this neck of the woods?" The woman grasped the handle of her shopping basket in both hands, and she stood in such a way as to use her basket to create a gap between Cinder and Gian.

"Hi, Tracy." Embarrassment flared in Gian's cheeks. He cast an uncomfortable glance at Cinder and Zae, who whispered in Cinder's ear. "I'm conducting a karate class at Clark this afternoon."

Tracy's heavily lined and shadowed eyes widened in exaggerated surprise. "If I'd known you were teaching an Afternoon Enrichment class at the elementary school, I'd have signed my brood up." She held up a finger and craned her long neck to peek down the dairy aisle. "Garrett! Chesney! Emory!" she shrieked. "Mommy is getting extremely impatient with you! Climb down and come here, right now!"

"Where's Granddad with his belt," Zae muttered.

Cinder laughed out loud at Zae's reference to the way Granddad from *The Boondocks* would have handled unruly children in a grocery store.

Gian snickered, certain he could have held a straight face if Cinder's laugh hadn't been so contagious.

Three children with shoulder-length blond hair barreled out of the dairy aisle and zoomed past the meat department. Tracy stepped in their direction to watch them race into the produce section. Cinder took that moment to lean toward Gian. "Are those girls or boys?"

"Probably," Gian answered.

Tracy turned back to Gian, her sun-damaged face drawn in severe lines meant to resemble an expression of motherly pride. "Aren't they adorable? So full of life and imagination. There are times I look at them and ask myself, what more could I possibly need?"

"A tranquilizer gun," Zae suggested.

"Who are your friends, Gian?" Tracy's tone chilly, she finally acknowledged Cinder and Zae with a glassy smile.

"Zae Richardson, Cinder White, this is Tracy Leach-Roche," Gian said.

"I'm just Leach now," Tracy corrected him. "I dropped my ex-husband's surname."

"Zae and Cinder are two of my best students at Sheng Li," Gian went on. "Zae got her second black belt last winter and Cinder is my prize pupil."

The beauty of Cinder's innocent surprise caught Gian off guard. His heart surged, a breath caught in his chest, and in the short second it took him to regain control of himself, he was certain the three women could read his burgeoning feelings for Cinder as if his heart and head were transparent.

Tracy, a wrinkle like a hatchet mark appearing between her overly tweezed eyebrows, very precisely said, "Prize pupil?"

Gian kept his eyes on Cinder. "You'd never know that she hadn't had any prior training when she came to me. She's amazing."

Cinder smiled, this one unfolding slowly, this one meant for Gian only. His appreciation for the gift was such that had they been anyplace else other than the meat counter of Freddie's Market, he would have cupped her face and drawn her in for a kiss that would have shown her exactly how much he loved that smile.

"I'll just bet she is," Tracy muttered tersely through an icy grin that shattered with the sound of a loud metallic crash from the produce section. "I'd better see what my darlings are up to. Good running into you, Gian." She gave Cinder and Zae a dismissive glance, saying, "Cindy, May."

At the end of the produce section, Tracy ran into a group of women she knew. Another crash, followed by the voice of an angry Freddy's employee, sounded while Tracy huddled with her friends, each of them doing a poor job of sneaking glances at Zae, Cinder, and Gian.

"You might want to get out of here before the hyenas finish strategizing, Gian," Zae warned. "They look like they haven't had meat in a long time."

While Zae and Cinder collected their neat white bundles from the butcher, Gian vanished into the cereal aisle and raced for the two check-out stands.

Zae leaned in close to Cinder. "You better go after him," she directed. "Tracy Leach-Roche don't play. She's been trying to fix Gian up with her motley crew of fellow divorcees ever since he shot her down at last year's Christmas parade. She seems to think that getting him with one of her friends is the next best thing to having him herself."

"You know Tracy?" Cinder asked.

"I know *of* her. Her oldest goes to school with my twins."

Cinder and Zae steered their shopping carts into the cereal aisle. Without looking at what she was doing, Zae grabbed two boxes of shredded wheat from the shelf and put them in her cart as she spoke. "You saw the way they broke as soon as Gian left us. They're on the hunt," Zae whispered through gritted teeth. "Go get your man, girl!"

"He's not my man," Cinder said.

"Do you want him to be?" Zae speeded up, narrowly missing a shopper parked in the center of the aisle. "Then you better get up here!"

Cinder's heart drummed so hard, the beating reverberated in her ears. There had been a time when asking a man out had been as easy for her as blinking or breathing, but a lot had changed in the intervening years. She had changed. How much, she didn't know. But when she exited the cereal aisle and saw Tracy overlooking three of her friends surrounding Gian, Cinder decided that there was one part of her long-lost self she could recover.

She didn't need the extra little push from Zae to shove her cart through the gaggle of grinning ex-wives at register two. Cinder threw her shoulders back in a move that would have made the most of the long hair she'd once had. Without as much as an "excuse me" or a nod of acknowledgement, she shouldered her way to Gian.

"Would you care to have dinner with me?"

She congratulated herself on how normal her voice sounded despite the nerves that made her stomach dance and her palms moist.

One of Tracy's friends, a petite woman with banana-blonde waves and chocolate roots, pressed her right hand to her throat. "Pardon me, but we were having a conver—"

"Yes," Gian answered, cutting the blonde off. "I'd really like that."

Gian watched relief and joy shape Cinder's face once more into something so beautiful, everything and everyone else fell away. The offended nattering of Tracy's posse, the protests of Tracy's children as she denied them candy, even Zae's attempt to tug Cinder into the checkout line went unnoticed until Cinder had backed away with her cart to place her groceries on the conveyor belt.

"See," Zae said, sneaking peaks at Tracy's disgruntled pals. "That wasn't so hard, was it?"

"No," Cinder smiled proudly. "It was easier than I thought it would be."

She had been anxious and scared asking him out, then exhilarated when he'd said yes. She reveled in her emotions, reacquainting herself with feelings she hadn't experienced in a long time.

With fewer items, Gian was checked out before Cinder. On his way to the exit, he paused near the bagging platform at the end of her check-out stand. "See you at Sheng Li tomorrow?"

Cinder nodded, smiling in agreement.

"We can make plans for dinner then," he added.

Cinder's throat went dry. "Sure," she warbled.

She watched him leave the store and go to his car. Asking him out had been easy. Going on the actual date—that would be the hard part.

~~~~~

"You have beautiful veins," the phlebotomist said, patting the crook of Cinder's elbow with two stiffened fingers. "I've got the Alaska pipeline here."

The stretchy blue tourniquet tied just above Cinder's elbow popped her veins out so prominently that the American Red Cross worker had no trouble finding a good one to stick. "They say that every time I give blood," Cinder told her.

"Good veins, good blood, good attitude," the woman said. "You're the kind of donor we love to see." She unwrapped a needle. "You're going to feel a little stick now . . ."

Cinder looked away. Needles didn't bother her as long as she didn't watch them pierce her skin. Her technician's skill was excellent. Cinder barely felt a thing. "That's the best stick I've ever had," she said. "Could I get your business card so I can call you anytime I need a blood draw in the future?"

"I like to use butterfly needles," the technician said. "They're more comfortable." She looked up from the pouch collecting Cinder's blood. "Sounds like you've had a lot of experience with blood draws."

Cinder nodded but didn't elaborate. She looked around the Hixson Junior High gymnasium. "It looks like a MASH unit," she remarked. "Like in that old television show."

The technician agreed with a laugh, but Cinder was distracted by a donor two stations away. Gian reclined on a maroon padded chair, his left arm being drained. The network of veins in his exposed forearm reminded Cinder of vines along the trunk of a cypress tree. Gian spoke amiably with his phlebotomist, who seemed thoroughly charmed by the conversation, until his gaze happened to land on Cinder.

His mouth stopped moving, he didn't blink. His right hand rose in a casual wave, which Cinder returned. It had been less than twenty-four hours since they had run into each other at Freddy's Market, but the unknowing observer might have thought it had been years if judging by the intensity of their connection.

"There you go," Cinder's technician said after removing the needle. She peeled open a bandage and adhered it over the draw site. "I'm going to walk you over to the canteen, where I want you to lie down for about twenty minutes so we can make sure that you have no problems with dizziness, weakness, or nausea. One of the volunteers will bring you some juice and cookies."

Cinder was escorted to an empty gurney. A volunteer adjusted the bed's incline to make Cinder more comfortable. Gian finished his donation a moment later, and was ushered into the canteen by his phlebotomist. Cinder was secretly thrilled when he chose the gurney beside hers rather than the distant one his phlebotomist had selected.

"Hi," he greeted her, climbing onto the gurney. He rolled down the sleeve of his white button-down, covering his draw site. "Are you stalking me?"

Cinder's smile vanished.

"I was just kidding." He chuckled. "We keep running into each other."

"Sorry," Cinder said softly with a self-conscious smile. "I knew that."

"Guess what I had for breakfast this morning," he said to keep her talking.

"Coco Puffs."

"Nope. Try again."

"You look like you might be the Fruit Loops type."

"Yeah, when I was seven."

An elderly woman in pearls pushed a cart laden with paper cups of juice and a big circular tray of cookies. "Can I get you something?" she asked brightly.

"Sure, what are you selling?" Gian asked.

The woman's smile widened and she gave Gian's foot a playful swat. "Orange, cranberry, grape, and grapefruit juice, and chocolate chip, oatmeal, and sugar cookies."

"I'd like—" Cinder started.

Gian cut her off with, "This is my treat." He turned to the refreshment keeper. "The lady will have . . ." He studied Cinder. He had no idea what she'd like, and he wanted to make the best guess. "A grapefruit juice and two chocolate chip cookies."

"I don't like chocolate," Cinder said.

"Seriously?"

"Can't stand the stuff."

"Oatmeal and sugar, one each?"

"Perfect, thank you," she said.

Cookies and juice in hand, Gian and Cinder waited for the refreshment lady to move on before they resumed their conversation. But the woman simply stood between the feet of their gurneys, watching them.

"I want to see you drink some of that juice before I go," she explained. "We don't want you passing out when you get up to leave."

Gian raised his flowered paper cup in a toast and threw back his grapefruit juice in two big gulps. Cinder daintily sipped hers.

"Very good." The volunteer took their empty cups and replaced them with full ones. "Thank you for donating today." She returned to her cart to get two little round stickers. She pressed one to Gian's breast pocket, the other to the short sleeve of Cinder's airy blouse. "Such nice kids," she said affectionately, pushing her cart to the next pair of gurneys.

"I can't remember the last time anyone called me kid," Gian chuckled lightly.

"How old are you?"

75

"Thirty-nine. Forty, in December."

"Cream of Wheat."

"What?" Gian laughed.

"That's what you had for breakfast."

"I said thirty-nine, not sixty-nine. Guess again."

"I give up."

"That's not what I teach you at Sheng Li."

"Stand or surrender." Her eyes sparkled merrily. "I surrender."

"I had a vanilla long john with bacon strips on top."

She laughed, almost spilling ruby red grapefruit juice on her lap.

"So why don't you like chocolate?"

The light in her eyes dimmed. "I used to. I just . . . does it matter why?"

"You're the only woman I've ever known who doesn't like chocolate." He decided to let her off the hook, for now, to fully restore her good mood. "I'm glad I found out about your aversion to chocolate now instead of later. I was planning to take you to Bissinger's after we go out for dinner. They've got the best chocolates in town."

"I invited *you*," Cinder reminded him. "I'll choose the place. And I'm paying."

"What do you do?"

"Do for what?"

"For a job. For a living." He shifted, lying on his side to fully face her.

Cinder wallowed in the depths of his eyes. The high windows allowed enough bright, clean light to illuminate the flecks of gold and grey muddying the inky blue-green of his gaze. His hair had grown a lot since she first met him. Just short of being too long for military service, it was the perfect length to run her fingers through. He tried to guess her occupation, but Cinder heard few of his words, not when watching his lips shape them held her full attention.

A late summer tan darkened his complexion, doing nothing to conceal the shadow of his beard and mustache. His face, so overwhelmingly masculine, was a thing of beauty that made it hard for Cinder to look away or think about anything other than touching him.

Even his nose was attractive, and Cinder typically gave noses little regard. Gian's was straight, in excellent proportion to his face, slightly wide at its base, with perfect nostrils. He had a very shallow cleft at the tip of his nose, and Cinder wondered what it would feel like against the tip of her tongue.

"Hey," Gian said. "You still there?"

She gave herself a mental shake. "I'm sorry. My mind wandered."

"Where to?"

"Not far."

One side of his mouth rose in an amused grin. "I'm glad you're back. So what do you do when you're not throwing me around Sheng Li?"

She traced the pattern of the sugar granules on top of her cookie. "You give me too much credit."

"Not at all. You've developed so much faster than I thought you would. I wish all my students were so dedicated."

"All your classes are full," Cinder said. "The women in Zae's class get there twenty minutes early, just so they can get good spots on the mat."

"Sure, if the good spots are the ones closest to Chip. My female students love him, even the little ones in our grasshopper class."

"Why did you leave the Marines?"

"Why did you leave the East coast?"

The smile left Gian's eyes. Cinder's hand involuntarily closed around her cookie, breaking it into pieces.

"I—" they began at once.

"It's complicated," they said in sync.

They laughed, which broke the momentary tension. "Maybe we should stick to the light stuff and save the heavy duty goods for our second date," Gian suggested.

"Planning ahead?"

"Absolutely."

"When would you like to have dinner?"

"Tonight." He held out his hand for her cookie pieces.

She gave them to him. "We have a lesson tonight."

"We just gave blood." He ate the remains of her cookie in one bite and brushed the crumbs from his shirt. "We should take it easy for the rest of the day. We can make the class up tomorrow, if you can get off work."

"I'm a graphic designer. Self-employed. I work from home. I come and go as I please."

"A graphic designer, huh? I figured you for the creative type."

"I don't know how creative I am, but I do okay."

"Thank you," he said earnestly.

"For what?"

"For trusting me."

She squinted in curiosity. "I don't—"

"You just told me what you do for a living."

She replayed the last part of their conversation in her head. "I didn't mean to."

"I know. But I'm glad you did."

"What made you decide to start your own karate studio?"

"I wanted my own business, so I thought I'd do something that I know. Martial arts."

Cinder swung her legs over the side of her gurney. Propping her left elbow on the inclined back, she braced her left hand against her head and crossed her legs. "Did you learn all those fighting techniques in the Marines?"

"You read the promotional material in my lobby?

"No," she admitted. "Chip told me that you two were in the service together. How old is Sheng Li?"

"Eight years."

"Zae told me that you've won a couple of business awards from city hall, and that *Riverfront Times* voted Sheng Li Best Workout for the past three years in a row."

"I couldn't have done it without Zae and Colin." He lay back on the gurney, his fingers laced behind his head, cradling it. "Colin approved the loan that helped me get the studio off the ground. He and Zae were the first ones at the grand opening." He grinned. "They and their kids were the *only* ones at the grand opening." Gian rolled onto his side again to face Cinder, who listened attentively.

"The place was a ghost town until Zae got involved," he said. "She strategized, rallied her troops, and swept Webster Groves, Maplewood, Kirkwood, Glendale, Oakland, Richmond Heights, Clayton—she hit every town between here and the riverfront. I'd never seen anything like it. If she'd joined the Marines, the war in Iraq would have been over in two months."

"She's a great general." Cinder smiled. "She'll fight to the death and she'll never leave a man behind."

"She called in favors and gave me her connections. I got spots on local morning news shows, premium booths at health and fitness expos. She put me in touch with an insurance agent who gave me great deals. She hooked me up with the athletic department at her university so I could hire assistants who worked for college credit instead of money. That's how I found Cory. She got seniors involved with Sheng Li by encouraging me to create a low-impact exercise program for the elderly. One of her most brilliant ideas was for me to get involved with the after-school enrichment programs in the Webster Groves' elementary schools. Each of my instructors goes to a school, and he teaches—"

"Why don't you have female instructors?"

"What?"

"Why don't you have any female instructors?"

"I have one, Aja. She's a part-timer who teaches the Dangerous Housewives self-defense and strength conditioning class on Monday, Wednesday, and Friday mornings, so you haven't run into her yet. Aja is the only woman who's ever applied to work for me," he said.

"Why is that?"

"I don't know." He was genuinely bewildered. "I'm an equal-opportunity employer."

"Have you tried recruiting female instructors?"

"Are you conducting an investigation of my hiring practices?"

"No." She giggled.

"Then can I finish my story?"

"Please do."

"The after-school programs opened the floodgates," he said. "Overnight I went from twenty percent enrollment to one hundred percent. I had to turn students away. When Zae suggested I develop a self-defense class for housewives, I didn't think anyone would be interested. But I ended up having to schedule two more sessions to keep up with the demand."

"Zae is the best friend I've ever had," Cinder said. "She's a blessing."

"When Colin died, I tried to be the kind of friend to her that she had been to me," Gian said. "She and the kids kind of closed ranks. Sheng Li was the last loan Colin approved before he got sick. When he died, I think Zae invested in Sheng Li's success because it was something Colin wanted to see do well. Either that, or she just wanted free classes for the rest of her life."

"Is that how you repaid her?"

"She wouldn't take money, and I had to offer her something." He laughed. "About a year after Colin passed away, I tried to fix her up with a couple of different guys I knew in the service. She scared off one of them, and she challenged the other to an arm wrestling match. He lost, so she wouldn't go out with him. This guy was a serious jarhead. I think he bench pressed two-ten, and she beat him."

"That's one of her favorite tricks." Cinder laughed. "She's got long forearms, and she's freakishly strong. It's physics. Chances are good she can beat most guys."

"You've known her a long time?"

"She was taking a few classes at Boston University when I was there," Cinder said. "We had modern communication together. I didn't know she was ten years older than me until I met her kids. The twins were almost eight then, and C.J. was three. Colin was working at Fleet Bank. When Fleet was bought out, Colin took a job with Heartland Bank in St. Louis, and they moved to Missouri. Zae and I kept in touch. I saw the Richardsons every time they went back to Massachusetts to visit Colin's family."

"I remember a trip Zae made alone about a year and a half ago," Gian said. "She told me she was going to . . ." He thought a moment. "I think she said Lancaster-on-the-Sea, something like that?"

Cinder dropped her eyes. "Manchester-by-the-Sea," she whispered.

"Then about six months later, you moved here. Zae didn't say a thing about you, other than that she had a friend staying at her house."

Cinder twisted the tiny gold post earring in her left earlobe. Her gaze never left Gian. "We should go."

"Why?" Sure that he'd pressed her one time too many, Gian wanted to kick himself. "If I've said something inappropriate, or—"

"I think they want us to leave," she said simply.

Gian finally noticed that the sun had left their side of the building, and the overhead fluorescents had been turned on. Every gurney in the canteen was empty, but for his and Cinder's, and the volunteers were bagging up leftover cookies and taking out the trash. The American Red Cross workers and their refrigerated cases of blood were gone.

"We closed the joint," Cinder said. "Are you hungry?"

"God, yes." He patted his belly and hopped off the gurney. "May I?" He offered his hand to Cinder to help her down.

In the course of their private lessons, his hands had been all over her. But slipping her hand in his in response to his gesture of gentlemanly courtesy opened a new possibility for intimacy, one Gian hoped Cinder wanted to explore as much as he did.

~~~

"We were in line at Michael's Arts & Crafts in Saugus," Cinder said through her giggles, "and there was this guy in front of us. He was young, probably about twenty-five or so. Blond hair, blue eyes, kinda muscular. The frat boy type, but a little older." She used her chopsticks to swirl a piece of spider maki roll in a tiny white dish where Gian had mixed a pinch of wasabi into a small quantity of soy sauce. "He's buying this big ol' poster-sized frame. Zae looks at it and says, 'You have a lovely family.' The guy eyeballs her like she's got horns, and he says, 'This isn't my family. This picture comes with the frame.' " Cinder laughed and tucked her sushi into her mouth. Shoving it into her cheek, she continued her story. "Zae waits a second or two, then points to the woman in the frame and goes, 'Your wife is beautiful.' "

Gian covered his mouth with his loosely curled fist to avoid spraying Cinder with partially chewed seaweed salad.

"The poor kid says, 'Lady, this isn't my wife.' He taps the photo and goes, 'These aren't my kids. This guy isn't me. He doesn't even look like me. I've got blond hair, this guy's dark-haired.' " Cinder finished chewing her sushi and took a sip of warm sake. "Zae stands there, nodding in total understanding, and the guy turns around and sets his frame on the counter to pay for it. Zae taps him on the shoulder, points to the photo again, and says, 'What's your dog's name?' I thought I was going to pee my pants, I was trying so hard not to crack up!"

"Zae's antics are so funny when they're aimed at someone else. That poor guy . . ."

"He loved it," Cinder said. "When we left the store, he was waiting in the parking lot to ask Zae for her phone number. She didn't break stride when she told him she was married and had three kids."

"Ruthless." Gian shook his head. "Colin probably never had a dull moment with her."

Cinder's mirth faded. "She loved him so much. She still loves him. It's easy to be alone, but loneliness can eat you up. I've tried to tell her that she needs to move on, and she knows that, but . . ." She sighed.

"The heart can't exactly be reasoned with," Gian finished. "None of Zae can be reasoned with, once she makes up her mind about something."

"You seem to know her as well as I do. She's lucky to have you."

"I'm lucky to have her, too," Gian said. "She saved my life."

"Mine, too."

Weeknights were slow for Sansai. Cinder and Gian sat alone in their candlelit corner of the Japanese restaurant. The muted gold and amber color palette complemented Cinder, the décor emphasizing the dark coffee of her eyes and putting a glow in her warm complexion. She wore a light, off-white cardigan, a matching linen blouse and white capri pants, an ideal ensemble for a late summer night in Missouri.

Gian set down his chopsticks and took her hand, clasping it near the votives flickering in the center of their table. "Could I ask you what you mean by that?"

Her free hand went to her hair. Out of nervous habit more than necessity, she smoothed her short locks behind her ear. "I was married. His name is Sumchai Wyatt."

Gian leaned farther over the table to better hear her. "Interesting name." He slightly tightened his hand around hers to still the tremble in it.

"His mother is from Thailand," Cinder explained. "His parents met when his father was a U.S. Army engineer with the 44th Engineer Group in Korat during the wars in Vietnam and Laos."

"The Korat," Gian repeated. "That's central Thailand. It's brutal terrain, even now, after decades of development."

"Sumchai idolized his father, but he never thought he could live up to him. His mother's English was never very good, and Sumchai was her translator until he left home. She kept him isolated from other kids, supposedly because she thought American children were too spoiled and inferior in intellect. She ruled with an iron hand, which she used upside Sumchai's head whenever she thought he wasn't living up to her expectations. He tried to join the Army, but he didn't pass the psychological evaluation." She smiled sadly. "I wish I'd known that before we got married."

Gian held his tongue. There were so many questions he wanted to ask, but he knew it was best to follow her lead.

"He swept me off my feet." She smiled, her unshed tears sparkling in the candlelight. "I'd just finished my master's degree in graphic design at Boston University. Sumchai was still working on his master's in education. We'd gone back to our old high school to participate in a career day for the students, and we saw each other. From that day on, we were always together." She wiped her eyes, cleared her throat and continued. "He said all the right things. He did all the right things. He made me feel like I was the most important person in the world. I was so caught up in the illusion he created, I didn't notice that the closer I got to him, the further I got from my friends and family."

"How long were you together?"

"We were married for three years." Her hand seemed to convulse, closing hard around Gian's fingers. "But according to him, we'll always be together . . ."

CHAPTER 5

Like a pair of dead snakes, two black seamed stockings lay coiled on the ivory tile of the master bathroom floor. A ragged thumbnail had ruined one and Cinder had snagged the other on the door of the under sink cabinet on her first attempt to leave the bathroom. She sat on the edge of the deep bathtub and slowly, carefully, rolled a new stocking onto her right leg.

Once done, she stood and slipped her feet into the scandalously high black patent-leather heels she had purchased that afternoon at Shock & Ahh!, an adult toy and fashion store in Cambridge. She'd gone in for the stockings, but the mohawk-wearing grandmother who owned the shop had convinced her that the stilts, seamed stockings, a sheer black mini slip dress and a matching satin G-string comprised a tastefully sexy ensemble no man could resist.

She studied her reflection in the triple-paned mirror mounted above the his-and-hers sinks. This Bizarro Cinder was the complete opposite of the advertising graphics manager whose typical wardrobe consisted of pleated slacks and modest, long-sleeved blouses.

Her freshly styled sable hair fell past her shoulders in soft, full waves that gave her a sexy, kittenish appearance. She had heavily lined her eyes and made them up in smoky plums and earth tones that accentuated their color and shape. The silky dress covered her while completely exposing her. The G-string was so negligible, she wouldn't have known it was back there if she hadn't seen the front of the underwear, which was only slightly larger than a Doritos chip.

The ruined stockings went into the waste bin between the sinks and the toilet, and then Cinder hurried into the bedroom. She fussed over her arrangements: fresh rose petals sprinkled on the new white satin duvet; sparkling grape juice—Welch's, always Welch's—that Sumchai preferred to actual champagne, stood in a silver ice bucket dotted with condensation; hazelnut chocolate truffles Sumchai ordered from a little shop in Paris; and the finishing touch, dabs of Bulgari Blu Notte, the one scent Sumchai allowed her to wear, behind each ear and knee. Observing another one of her husband's preferences, she had drawn the sheers and drapes over the tall, wide windows even though doing so closed out the beauty of the sun setting over Singing Beach.

Downstairs in their freshly remodeled kitchen, Sumchai's favorites sat in the warming oven—rice cooked with lemongrass and wood ear alongside chicken stir fried with straw mushrooms, egg, tomato, bean sprouts, onion, and sprinkled with diced cucumber and chopped peanuts. For dessert, she'd driven all the way into Brookline for sweet bean paste buns from Japonais, the bakery he'd taken her to on their first date.

Her heart lurched with excitement when she heard her husband's key in the backdoor. Giddy, she positioned herself at the head of the bed, careful not to disturb the petals any more than necessary.

"Cin!" His voice echoed in the mud room.

"I'm up here!"

His footsteps on the stairs harmonized with the eager beat of her heart, which leaped the moment her husband filled the doorway.

Sumchai Wyatt was a beautiful man who had inherited his mother's black eyes and his Irish father's prominent square jaw. He also had his father's imposing height and lean, muscular build. Even though he had never been a soldier as he had wanted, the hours he'd spent at the gym had given him a soldier's physique. His straight black hair was the same color as his slightly angled eyes, and he had his mother's olive complexion. His temperament was all his own.

"What did you do?" Sumchai's deep voice dropped an octave in suspicion as he stared at her.

"Nothing." Cinder laughed. "I wanted to surprise you."

"I'm surprised," he said, slowly approaching her.

It was hard to tell if he was pleased or . . . not. His expression remained blank, his eyes unreadable. Cinder reclined on the pillows, one arm draped over her head, the other across her torso. "Come over here and tell me about your day," she invited.

He approached the big sleigh bed but bypassed it to go to the dresser. "My day was great," he remarked, his tone belying his words. "It started off with my interview at Winchester Prep. That turned out to be a total waste because the salary the principal was offering was a third lower than what the employment agency told me it was. Then I had to rush south to Randolph for a meeting with the board of administrators at Williams-Coe." He took off his watch and tossed it onto the silver jewelry tray on his side of the dresser. Unbuttoning the cuffs of his striped business shirt, he said, "They had their minds made up about me before I sat down. Another waste of time."

He hadn't come to her, so Cinder went to him. "They wouldn't have had you in for an interview if they had already made up their minds about you." She slid her arms around him and pressed her cheek to his broad back.

In a quick, smooth move, Sumchai turned, took her by her shoulders, and shoved her onto the bed. "They called my old school for a reference and spoke to the principal," he sneered. "He wasn't listed as my reference! Why didn't they just talk to the vice-principal? She was the one named on my resumé!"

"Chai, it's just one school," she tried to reassure him. She went to him again and hugged him from behind. "Did you really want to commute all the way into Randolph every day? It's so far away from Manchester-by-the-Sea."

He continued as if she hadn't spoken. "I got a flat on the way home, so I had to change it while pricks are whizzing by me at eighty miles an hour on I-95. I ruined these pants."

Cinder noticed the streak of road grime on the left leg of his khaki slacks. "I'll take those to the dry cleaners tomorrow. Don't worry about them." Peeking around him, she started unfastening his belt. When she went for his zipper, he took her wrists and threw off her hands. He stared at her reflection in the mirror mounted at the back of the dresser. "And the cherry on the top of this crappy day is that I come home to find my wife dressed like a slut."

Stung, Cinder backed away. "It's been a long time since we made love," she started. "I wanted to try—"

"Whose fault is that?" he muttered, yanking at his tie. "Yours."

Sumchai turned. In her "slut" heels, she was eye to eye with him. Her hands on the hips of her "slut" dress, she elaborated. "I know you've been under a lot of pressure since you got fired, and I've been understanding. I've supported you. But you've been bringing your stress into this bedroom, and I don't like it. Every time we have sex, you're cold and distant. The last time, you were so rough and—"

"I got the job done, if I recall correctly," he said slowly, quietly.

"Actually, you didn't." Cinder deliberately ignored his lethal calm and the flat shine in his dark eyes, the early warning signs that a storm was dangerously close. "I was responsible for my own. You just happened to be there."

"I see." His hands clenched into fists.

"No, you don't." She took his stiffened jaw in her hands, hoping to diffuse his mounting anger. "I miss the way we were before we got married. Do you remember the time you took me to Stowe, and you cried after we made love in front of the fire? I want that back. I want you to relax and let me show you how—"

He roughly shoved her, his movement so sudden that Cinder had no time to prepare herself for the spill. She stumbled off her shoes and landed in an ungainly heap at the side of the bed. Sumchai yanked her back to her feet by her right arm. "What? You think I need a lesson in fu—"

"Chai, stop it, that's not what I meant," she cried. She tried to wrench her arm from his grasp, but he was too strong.

"You want to seduce me, slut?" he spat, his spittle speckling her face. "You think I need to be taught how to screw my wife?" He let her go and she fell to the bed. "I come home after a crappy day and all I get is more criticism and disapproval?"

He paced the side and foot of the bed, ranting. "I didn't deserve to get fired," he muttered.

Cinder squinted her eyes tight. Every argument, every disagreement always returned to Sumchai's greatest disappointment. His greatest failing.

"The only reason I hit that kid is because he deserved it," Sumchai ranted. "He disrespected me, but no one cares about that, not even you!" He slammed his fists on the top edge of the footboard, scaring Cinder into crawling down the bed to get to him, to see if he was injured. Sumchai snatched his hands out of her reach, continuing his tirade. "You don't think I know that you've had to support me? That I don't know that makes me less of a man?"

"No, it doesn't, and you know it," she said. "Everything happens for a reason, Chai. If you hadn't lost your job, I would never have worked up the courage to ask for a promotion. I'm proud of myself for being able to support us. You should be, too, because now you can take the time to find a position that will make you happy. You don't have to take the first thing you're offered just so we can make the mortgage."

He stood at the foot of the bed, breathing heavily, rage still hardening his features. "In Thailand, women never forget that they exist to serve their husbands and sons," he said darkly. "I should have married a woman like my mother."

Cinder gave up trying to reason with him. "Your mother threw a dinner party for me when I got promoted. I wish you'd been as happy for me as your family was. And as for sons, I'm not the one responsible for us not having one. I'd love to have a little boy with your eyes, and—"

Sumchai didn't move, but no sooner than her words left her mouth, Cinder saw something snap in his eyes. "You carry the Y," she hastily told him, all the while knowing that she had crossed into dangerous territory. "That's all I meant. I wasn't referring to your ability to—"

He scrambled over the foot of the bed and pressed her to the mattress with such force, one of her shoes flew off. Straddling her, he ripped off her filmy dress. Ignoring her screams of pain and protest, he caught her arms, wrapped them from wrist to elbow with the torn garment and secured them to the headboard. She tried to buck him off, but his weight and determination rendered her efforts useless. With one hand he forced her legs apart, the other unbuttoned and unzipped his pants.

His hands rough, invading, damaging, he barely moved her G-string aside before he shoved into her with such force that her head banged into the teak headboard. Deaf to her pleas to stop, he pounded into her, arching upward to avoid looking at her tear-streaked face. He prefaced his climax by taking handfuls of her hair, pulling it so hard the skin of her face went taut. Her agonized cries matched his grunts of release. When he finished, he rolled off her, lying beside her to catch his breath. "I think I might like having a personal slut," he panted.

Too angry and still too stunned to think of anything bad enough to say in response, Cinder stared at the ceiling fixture. The lead eagle medallion supporting its frosted glass globe was original to the farmhouse, but they had purchased the globe shortly after moving in. They had spent a Saturday comparison shopping at home goods, antique and lighting stores, searching for the perfect globe. Such a small task, yet it had been so much fun driving around with her new husband on a rain-glossed day.

But as she lay there, bound and sore, she recalled a few details about the way he had treated her that day. The comments he'd made in front of sales assistants, making fun of her choices and suggestions—they had seemed amusing and harmless then, in the wake of their new union. With pain and humiliation lending clarity to retrospection, she saw his behavior for what it had been. Abuse.

She thought back to the last time he had left marks on her, at an anniversary party for Zae and Colin. She had danced with Colin's younger brother to one too many Earth, Wind & Fire songs and Sumchai had escorted her from the dance floor, holding her upper arm so tight his fingernails had broken her skin. He'd apologized and she'd forgiven him. But she hadn't forgotten.

Every insult, every smack, slap, pinch, kick, and push came back to her, snowballing into something so big and ugly, Cinder could no longer ignore it, not in light of what he had just done.

Sumchai left the bed and stripped off his clothes as he strolled into the bathroom. Cinder's hurt and humiliation morphed into fear that didn't lessen until she heard the quiet whoosh of the shower. She wrenched her arms, struggling to free herself from her bonds even if it meant snapping one of the slats in the headboard.

She slid her forearms together, working them back and forth an inch at a time. Although she tore her skin in the process, she managed to release one arm. The other came out much easier. Freed, she scooted off the bed. She picked up the striped button-down Sumchai had discarded on the floor and put it on as she slipped out of the bedroom and hurried down the carpeted stairs.

She had retrieved her car keys and purse from the kitchen and was approaching the front door when, faintly, she heard the shower stop. She opened the heavy front door and left it standing open, so he wouldn't hear its tell-tale latch upon its closing.

"You'd better be down there getting dinner on the table!" His command chased her to the driveway, where she got into her sensible Audi and started it. Sumchai's big pickup blocked her in the long driveway. She tested her car's maneuverability by backing over the low stone border she had spent three afternoons putting in, onto the lawn, and down to the two-lane street.

Her tires spun for a moment, long enough for her to see her husband's silhouette against the bright light bleeding from her front door, before she zoomed away, her headlights blazing a path in the night.

~~~~~

"Did you go back to him?"

Gian still held her hand and Cinder was grateful for it. It was the only thing that had steeled her enough to tell him her reason for leaving her husband.

"I wanted to," she admitted. "I tried to. The night I left, I showed up at my parents' house with nothing but the shirt off Chai's back and my car keys. My dad wanted to kill him, especially when Chai got to the house a half-hour after I did."

"That guy had a lot of nerve," Gian said. "I hope you called the police."

She nodded, her eyes fixed on the votive. The bright flame seemed to skim the liquid surface of the melted wax. "He spent two nights in the Middlesex County jail because I wouldn't post his bail. He couldn't get arraigned until Monday morning."

"I'll bet that pissed him off."

"I didn't do it to piss him off. I needed some time to get my clothes and things out of the house."

"Most women wouldn't have found it so easy to just leave like that." Gian summoned the waiter.

"It wasn't easy," she stated firmly. "I still loved him, at that point. I couldn't just turn that off, no matter what he'd done to me. But I sure as hell wasn't going to stay there and let him do it again. I was in love, not insane."

"Point taken," he conceded.

A smiling waiter appeared and took Gian's order for coffee. Once the waiter hurried back to the kitchen, Cinder continued. "He called or drove by the house every night for two weeks, until I threatened to get an order of protection. He left me alone after that. One day, about a month later, I called him."

Gian opened his mouth but Cinder spoke over him. "I wanted to help him. I thought medication or therapy, something, would help him control his temper and manage his impulses and paranoia."

"What was he paranoid about?" Gian asked.

"He was convinced that I would leave him."

"He forced you to."

She smiled somberly. "I tried not to. I really did."

"I can see that you did."

"We started seeing each other. We'd meet for lunch and he'd tell me about his job search. The lunch dates went well, so we started having real dates. He was so nice, the way he'd been when we were first dating. He promised to see a therapist and told me that he would be willing to go to marriage counseling. It took him three months to blow it."

"How so? Did he hurt you again?"

"He came to pick me up for dinner and a movie one Saturday, and my cousin David was visiting. He was twenty-six years old, and he'd just gotten his degree from the Massachusetts School of Law. He'd come to my parents' to pick up a graduation present. It was a sterling silver Cross pen with his name engraved on it."

The waiter returned with a busboy, who collected their plates and empty sake cups to make way for coffee and a small tray of delicate almond cookies.

"David was leaving when Chai pulled into the driveway," Cinder continued once she and Gian were again alone. "I was on the front porch giving him a hug. Chai got out of his car, charged across the lawn, jumped onto the porch, and threw David against the side of the house. He broke David's nose before my dad and I could pull him off."

"What the hell was wrong with your ex?"

"Chai thought David was a date." Tears spilled over her lower lashes when she blinked, and they sparkled in the candlelight until she wiped them away. "David came to our wedding. Chai had met him before, he knew David was family! That was it, for me. He hadn't changed. There were things wrong with him that I would never be able to fix. Everything he'd said about getting help was a lie. I couldn't go back to him and the toxic life we'd built. I'd been living with my parents for a year, and it was time for me to rebuild my life. I filed for divorce a few days later."

"How did your ex handle it?"

"Not well," Cinder said tremulously. "He wouldn't sign the papers."

"There are ways to divorce someone, whether they want to be divorced or not," Gian insisted, sitting back in his chair.

"Those ways took time," Cinder said.

"So when did you get your divorce?"

"Shortly after I last saw him."

"You're being cryptic." A tinge of impatience tainted his words. "When did you last see him?"

She swallowed hard and still struggled to get her next words out. "We agreed to sell our farmhouse in Manchester-by-the-Sea. The day I was emptying it, he violated the order of protection I'd taken out on him."

"Tell me what happened." He scooted his chair in closer and took both her hands. "I—"

"Sir, ma'am," interrupted their waiter. "We closed a half hour ago. May I bring you your check?"

"Of course, thank you," Gian said.

"We're making a habit of overstaying our welcome." Cinder took her purse from under her chair and withdrew her wallet.

"Uh-uh," Gian said. "I'll get this."

"I invited you to dinner, sensai," Cinder argued. "That means I cover the check."

"I don't feel right, letting a woman pay for me."

"That sounds like something caveman Karl would say."

The waiter returned with their bill tucked in a small leather folder. Cinder plucked it from his hand before he stopped at the table.

"That was impressive," Gian said. "Your reflexes are really good. I think you're ready for group classes."

"I don't want to be in a group."

"You need to spar with other people besides me," he told her. "You have to learn to adapt your fighting style to your opponent's, and you're too familiar with my moves now. I don't think I'm challenging you enough."

"I'm paid up through the end of the month for private lessons."

"Sionne is teaching a class tomorrow at five," Gian said. "There are only seven students. Just try the class, on the house. If you hate it, no harm, no foul. But if you find you're getting something out of it, we can apply your tuition credit to the cost of a group lesson."

"I'd rather not—"

"Here you go," Gian said, butting Cinder's credit card aside to hand three twenties to the waiter, who had returned for the check. "No change."

"Thank you, sir, and good evening." The pleased waiter escorted Gian and Cinder to the exit and held the door open for them.

"Oh!" Cinder squeaked. The waiter closed the door so fast behind her, it struck her backside.

"Maybe we should go out earlier next time," Gian suggested. He took her hand and they strolled across the parking lot to their cars.

"I'd like to go to the zoo," Cinder said. "I've read that the St. Louis Zoo is one of the best in the country. I went to the Franklin Park Zoo in Boston once, and I hated it. The animals looked so sad, like they knew they were serving life sentences."

Gian laughed, the booming sound carrying through the near-deserted parking lot.

"That wasn't nearly that funny," Cinder chuckled.

"No, it wasn't," Gian agreed, stopping between his SUV and Cinder's Audi. "But you said it, so I liked it."

Toe-to-toe in the awkward silence following Gian's remark, Cinder was unsure if she should hug him, shake his hand or . . .

"May I kiss you?"

His eyes moved over her face. More plea than request, his words were as quiet and pleasant as the night itself. Moonlight streaked his hair with silver and darkened his eyes. His white shirt, preternaturally bright in the cold wash of the overhead lights, led her to think of him as a guardian angel, some divine appointee to protect her though she had never asked for it. His rolled-up sleeves exposed thick, well muscled forearms, and Cinder fully realized that, were he the type, he could have had his kiss whether she wanted to grant it or not.

"Thank you," she said, the hammering of her heart muting her words. "For asking."

"What's your answer?"

"Yes."

Awkwardness vanished. Gian bowed his head, Cinder raised hers. Their lips met delicately, growing more eager once fully acquainted. Powerfully gentle, the heat of Gian's kiss flowed through her. Dormant sensations flourished under the nourishment of his kiss.

Gian's hands clenched in his pockets. His abdomen tightened from the effort it took to restrain himself from spreading her over the hood of her car and kissing every part of her. The touch of his tongue to hers, chaste at first, triggered rapid-fire reactions throughout his body. His most responsive tissues instantly hardened. His heart raced, his breath quickened, every part of him reaching for Cinder.

Her arms went around him, hesitantly at first, but with more confidence when her fingers splayed over the muscles of his lower back. She drew his torso to hers— the move he had hoped and waited for because it invited him to return her embrace. His arms circled her waist and shoulders and he held her even closer, moaning into their kiss.

When they separated to breathe, Cinder laughed.

The merry sound made him laugh, too. "What's so funny?"

"I don't know." Her eyes delved into his.

"You were laughing for no reason?"

"I'm happy." That was it, unadorned. She was so happy, it flooded from her in the form of laughter.

"Why do you sound so surprised about that?" He nuzzled the top of her head with his cheek and chin.

"I didn't expect this to happen." She pressed her cheek to his chest and deeply inhaled his scent. She had come alive in his company. With each passing week since her first lesson with him, she had emerged more and more from her cocoon of solitude. Sure, she had been nervous and scared to ask Gian out, but looking back on it, she had enjoyed even those feelings. It had been too long since she had felt anything other than apprehension and uncertainty. She embraced those feelings because they brought happiness, yearning, contentment, and desire with them.

Gian was not what she expected of a former Marine. He was a leader without being oppressive or domineering, and he readily earned respect because he was willing to give it. He made it so easy for Cinder to view him as a warrior as easily as . . . a lover.

"Are you glad it did?"

She nodded.

"Yeah?"

"Yes." She laughed.

"Good."

He scraped the edge of his neatly trimmed index fingernail between his incisors, lifting away a glistening orange dot. "Maybe we shouldn't have done sushi. I think this belongs to you."

Laughing, Cinder said, "You had the California maki with the flying fish roe, not me. That's all yours."

"Want some?" He offered it to her on his fingertip.

"No, but thanks." She giggled, catching his wrist.

"What's mine is yours," Gian taunted in a schoolyard sing-song.

"Really, I'm good." Smiling, Cinder sidled away from him until she was free of their cars.

Gian chased her. Laughing and squealing, Cinder ran, neatly stepping out of his reach and blocking his attempts to catch her.

"Nice," Gian told her. "See what I mean? You know me so well now that you anticipate my moves. I can't get a hand on you until you let me. You're ready for new opponents."

She sobered a little. "I don't think I am."

"You read my body very well. Can you tell what move I want to make next?"

"You want to kiss me again."

"I rest my case."

He reeled her in for a second kiss. Had they been using their mouths for speaking, they would have agreed that it was twice as nice as the first.

~~~

Gian lay in bed, his head resting on his right forearm. Staring at the ceiling, he sighed. He had kissed Cinder goodnight over an hour ago, and he was still too high to sleep. Memories of the sweetness of her mouth and the softness of her lips acted on him as would a drug, loosening his joints and relaxing his muscles. He couldn't remember the last time he'd so enjoyed the company of a woman and ended the night on a kiss that left him more thoroughly satisfied than a weekend with the limber and imaginative Kuriko.

Beneath a thin cotton sheet, Gian's body reacted to his thoughts of Cinder. "At ease, boy," he muttered. The one-eyed soldier between his legs paid no attention to his orders tonight, not as long as Cinder White was on his mind. She had given him a lot, but there was so much more he wanted to know about her.

What had been her favorite game as a child? Who was her favorite teacher? Did she have siblings? What of her parents? What was her favorite candy? What was her favorite color? Did she prefer pearls to diamonds? The Red Sox to the Cardinals? Did she like The Three Stooges, and if so, which was her favorite?

Those questions spiraled into more intimate ones. He wondered if she slept in the nude, in a sexy nightie or an old T-shirt. What sounds did she make at the height of passion? Did she gasp and grunt, hold in her noises, or did she cry out in abandon, speaking the language known only by those who really knew how to revel in the giving and acceptance of pleasure?

The most important question, though, the one keeping him up, was far more simple: Was Cinder awake and thinking of him?

He rolled out of bed, intending to get a drink of water. Scratching himself through the thin cotton knit of his grey sports briefs, he shuffled toward the kitchen. A soft, mechanical hum from his office sidetracked him.

He backtracked and entered the dark room, drawn by the unflattering, over-bright light of his monitor. The padded seat of his swivel office chair creaked under his weight, and its wheels cried out when he scooted the chair up to his desk. A wiggle of his mouse brought up his home page, and without a moment of hesitation, he typed Cinder White in the search box.

He got three results, all for an athletic shoe called the Cinder, which came in white.

He tried her ex-husband's name, spelling it three different ways before his search yielded the first ten of thirty-six thousand hits on Sumchai Wyatt. Gian had to read the headline of the first one twice before he could bring himself to double-click on it, opening the page.

North Shore teacher found guilty of
first-degree assault in spousal abuse case

Cady Winters-Bailey
Special to the Herald-Star

A Middlesex Superior Court jury yesterday convicted Manchester-by-the-Sea high school teacher Sumchai Wyatt of first degree assault, the most serious of 18 felony counts against him following the June 9, 2007 attack on his wife, Cinder B. Wyatt. The jury delivered mixed verdicts on the remaining 17 counts.

After two days of deliberations, the jury of eight men and four women found Wyatt guilty of eight charges, including torture, spousal abuse and child endangerment. Wyatt was found not guilty of seven counts, among them false imprisonment, making death threats and second degree assault. The jury remained deadlocked on three charges of assault, making death threats and assault with a deadly weapon.

Jurors heard from 56 witnesses and reviewed 310 exhibits during the two-month trial, including the police photos below reprinted with the permission of Dee Bolds, an administrator with Project Protection, a North Shore advocacy group for victims of spousal abuse . . .

Gian stared at the disclaimer above the photo—WARNING: THE FOLLOWING IMAGES MAY BE DISTURBING TO SOME READERS—for a long time before he took a deep breath and looked at the photographs accompanying the article.

Twelve years of active duty as a Marine in several war zones hadn't prepared him for what he was seeing. The first photo depicted a young woman on a hospital gurney. Her bloody, swollen face made it impossible for him to identify her. He had to trust the caption, which read: Cinder B. Wyatt upon admission to North Shore Medical Center.

Cinder was naked, but there was so much blood on her body, the newspaper probably didn't need to cover her breasts and crotch with black bars. The photo was more than two years old and Gian had seen Cinder only whole and healthy, but his heart still pounded hard, his stomach still knotted as if her pain and suffering were fresh.

A second photo showed Cinder in a hospital bed. A large bandage covered half her forehead above her left eye, which was black and swollen to the size of a baseball. A circular close-up set in the photo revealed the stitches that had been used to reattach the lobe of her right ear.

She wore a uniform of casts and bandages, her left shoulder, feet, right knee, and right arm the only exposed parts of her. Oxygen fed into her nose, and an intubation tube jutted from her puffy and torn lips.

Gian touched his monitor as if he could feel the uneven scrub of her hair, which had been crudely chopped off.

He read on, determined to learn as much as he could about what she had endured.

. . . Said Bolds: "I'm sure there are people who wouldn't want these photos publicized, but I think it's important for people to see precisely what abusers do to their spouses. A battered woman might look at those photos and see herself the next time her spouse decides to go upside her head, and she'll get out before that happens."

Fourteen months prior to the attack on his wife, Wyatt, 35, had been released from his position as history teacher and soccer coach at West Reading High School after a physical altercation with a student.

While not underplaying the severity of Wyatt's crime, his attorney attempted a creative defense, blaming Wyatt's actions, in part, on extreme emotional duress and cultural conditioning.

"My client is a proud man of Thai descent," defense attorney Vincent Gorman said. "He comes from a culture where women are meant to care for the home and children and men are meant to support the family. Losing his job and his role as breadwinner led to a severe psycho-emotional breakdown for Mr. Wyatt, who has no memory of the crime. The jurors didn't take that into consideration during the trial, but I hope it makes a difference in sentencing."

Wyatt has been held in custody without bail since his June 11 arrest despite attempts by his counsel to get him released on bail.

Said former Commonwealth prosecutor Evelyn Cranston, who has commentated on the case for TruNewsTV, "Wyatt's defense screwed the pooch for him when they allowed him to testify that the 'psycho-emotional stress' of being financially supported by his wife led to his attempt to beat her to death.

"What judge in his or her right mind is going to name bail for a defendant who testifies to having no memory of his crime? If it's true, and this is an 'If' the size of Texas, what's to stop him from going out and beating the (expletive) out of someone else? Wyatt is where he belongs and I hope his sentence keeps him there for the rest of his life."

Gian scrolled down, skimming over the rest of the lengthy article. He stopped at a third photo. According to its caption, the image was a captured still from an interview televised by TruNewsTv shortly after Sumchai Wyatt's sentencing hearing. In it, Cinder was more recognizable, yet still unfamiliar. Her hair was short, but it was nicely styled in an adorable pixie cut. Her physical wounds appeared to be healed, but her thin frame, gaunt face, and flat eyes indicated that her emotional injuries were still fresh.

Gian clicked on the link beneath the image, which took him to TruNewsTV.com's video archives. He clicked on the white arrow centered in the middle of the video box, and it began to play.

"Twenty-eight-year-old Cinder Bloch had a very happy upbringing in Milton, Massachusetts," started TruNewsTV reporter Andrew Dalton, who Gian recognized from the expose shows Drake regularly did for the network. "Her parents, a Northeastern University English professor and a third-grade teacher, built a home for their daughter, full of warmth, love, and humor, as evidenced by young Cinder's name."

Dalton, who was reporting from Manchester-by-the-Sea in Massachusetts, turned and half raised an arm toward the huge farmhouse in the background. "But as their daughter's marriage to Sumchai Wyatt progressed, the Blochs came to realize that Cinder's home was nothing like the one they had made for her."

Gian settled into the chair, glancing at the running time of the tape. At twenty-two minutes, an entire segment of the news show was devoted to Cinder. The camera cut away from the charming farmhouse to a picture of a woman. The photograph captured the sparkle in her eyes, which were so dark, they reflected the photographer's image. Her wide, bright smile forced a lazy grin from Gian, who again reached for the screen to touch the long fall of black hair framing the woman's face.

Cinder. Younger, happier.

Cinder, before it all went bad.

"Cinder Bloch, 28, met Sumchai 'Chai' Wyatt during a Career Day event at their high school alma mater, Wakefield's Eichorn High School. Nicknamed "IQ" High by local residents, Eichorn's student body consists of some of the brightest students in the United States. Chai, a math prodigy, was a senior at Eichorn when Cinder was a freshman. Yet the two wouldn't meet until that fateful career day ten years after Cinder's graduation . . ."

Gian spun his chair to face his tall windows instead of his monitor. A cool breeze carrying a hint of the approaching fall stirred the sheers drawn over the window. The sheers muted the glow of the full pearl moon, which seemed to stare back at Gian. He saw none of its beauty, not with the new images of Cinder tattooed onto his retinas. His stomach roiled and burned, and for a moment, he thought whatever was left of his dinner would come up. He was no stranger to senseless and brutal violence—he'd been a soldier. What Cinder had suffered was worse than anything he'd witnessed in war simply because she had been victimized by someone she had trusted, who had claimed to love her.

Gian had never met Sumchai Wyatt and hoped he never would. He knew he'd have no problem killing him on sight.

CHAPTER 6

Chip walked among the couples squared off for sparring, checking their stances and fighting positions. "I want you to strike your opponent with an open fist, and—"

Zae giggled.

"What's so funny, Mrs. Richardson?" Chip asked amiably.

"That's an oxymoron," she grinned. "By definition, a fist is a closed hand. If the hand is open, it's not a fist."

In a fast, fluid motion, Chip demonstrated the open fist strike on Zae, catching her upper right shoulder and sending her bum-first to the floor. "Oxymoron or not, it's still effective, isn't it? Now I want you all to try that move."

From the lobby, Cinder watched Zae pick herself up, rubbing her offended backside. Chip's class was nearly over, which meant that she would soon have to take a place of her own on the big mat for her first group class.

Sionne had always seemed kind and patient, and Zae had no complaints about him, so Cinder had decided to man up and take the class, even though she had no confidence at all that she was at the level Gian thought she was.

Cinder wanted to get in and out of the locker room before Zae's class ended. She started there, making a quick stop in Gian's office. A dark head was bowed over Gian's desk, and she started to greet him.

But he wasn't Gian.

He looked up and Cinder stammered a hello to Karl.

"Hey, don't run off so fast," Karl called after her once she'd backed clear of the doorframe.

Cinder kept walking, pretending she hadn't heard him. Karl's long legs caught up with her, circling her to obstruct her path to the locker room. Cinder wondered if he'd vaulted over the desk to get to her so quickly.

"Hey, Cinder, I've been meaning to ask you something," Karl continued, "ever since you started coming here." He swiped a forefinger under his nose and moved closer to her, nearly backing her up against a vending machine. "I, uh, am usually pretty good at this sort of thing, but you make me really nervous."

The feeling is mutual, Cinder thought, little appeased by his lopsided grin.

"I was hoping you were free tomorrow night," he said quietly. "We could have dinner and catch a concert in Forest Park, or—"

"Karl, I'm so flattered," she started. "I—"

"So what time should I pick you up?" He stroked a fingertip along the lapel band of her *gi*.

"I have to say no," she finished.

He stood to his full height, drawing away from her.

"I already have plans for tomorrow night," she explained.

"Well, what about the night after that? Or maybe Saturday?" He smiled, and for once, it didn't leave Cinder with the feeling that he wanted to peel the skin from her face with his teeth. "Once you get to know me, you'll see that I'm really a nice guy."

"I'm seeing someone."

"Oh, yeah? Who?"

"I don't think that's any of your business, Karl." She sidestepped away from him.

He grabbed her by the arm. "Is it Gian?"

She shrugged free of his grasp. "I'm sorry if I've upset you, but—"

"You're *sorry*?" Karl's friendly, open expression instantly hardened.

Cinder clutched the strap of her gym bag, hunching her shoulders.

"Don't be so stuck on yourself," he scoffed. "I don't need your pity. I can go out right now and find ten gals prettier and skinnier than you to spend my time with. Peace out, homegirl. Isn't that what you people say?"

Cinder hurried to the locker room to put away her bag. Even though she had done nothing wrong, she couldn't help feeling that she had yet to be punished for refusing Karl.

Cinder took deep breaths to steady her heart rate. None of the veteran students had looked pleased when Karl entered the studio and informed them that he would be teaching Sionne's class. One of two new students in the class of seven, she was Karl's first target.

"We meet again." He spoke low in Cinder's ear. "And so soon." He threw out a fist, the force of it shoving air currents around Cinder's head. She blinked, but made no other outward sign of fear or shock.

"I've never seen anyone pass Karl's flinch test before," one of the male students, eyeing Karl, softly whispered.

Karl hurried to him and placed his fingertips against the student's head. He pushed, cracking his knuckles against the man's skull. Karl followed it with a quick punch. He didn't make contact, but the student flinched just the same.

"Twenty for flinching," Karl said, ordering the guy to the mat for twenty push-ups to be executed on his knuckles.

Karl returned to Cinder, circling her. "You're going to pair off and show me what Sionne's been teaching you, and then I'll spend the rest of the hour teaching you how to do it all the right way."

He paired them up, leaving Cinder standing alone. "I guess it's you and me after all, baby girl."

She bit her lip.

Karl, his hands at his waist, bent to speak directly into her left ear. "What's the matter? You don't like being called baby girl?"

"They're just words, sensai," she said. "Words can't hurt me."

Karl's big body overshadowed her, his thick, overly muscled arms making him appear even wider. He threw a strike, stopping his fist mere centimeters from Cinder's cheek. Every other student flinched, but Cinder remained frozen.

"You really think you're tough, don't you?" The friendliness of his inquiry failed to blunt the menace in his challenge. "Assume the fighting position."

Four groups of two squared off, and at Karl's signal, they began throwing and blocking slow strikes and kicks. So intent on his fight with Cinder, Karl paid no attention to the other students, one of whom carelessly walked into a blow to the eye.

Cinder ducked and blocked, neutralizing Karl's strikes and kicks. She had never watched him teach as she had Sionne and Chip, so she had no knowledge of his fighting style or habits. He stalked her over the mat, and she realized it didn't matter. Karl wasn't teaching. He was pursuing a personal grudge.

"Sensai, you said we're only sparring," one of the male students remarked.

Cinder barely noticed that the rest of the class had become the audience for her and Karl. The more skillfully she avoided contact from him, the more complicated his moves became. He implemented skills far outside her realm of experience, and even though Gian had taught her well, she knew that her reflexes and blocking techniques wouldn't serve her much longer.

Karl executed a drop spin, his long leg sweeping her feet from under her. She felt as if she'd been struck by a tree trunk as she rolled out of reach of his subsequent ax kick, his foot coming down on the mat hard enough for the impact to move painfully through her upper body. With a frustrated growl, Karl lunged at her, grabbing her by the waist and throwing her across the mat. Two of her classmates intervened.

"Sensai, I think that's enough," the male student said. Karl responded with a short chop to his windpipe. The fellow dropped to his knees, gasping for air, his hands clasped at his throat.

"Karl!"

Gian's voice boomed throughout the studio, freezing Karl in place as he leaned over Cinder and the woman protectively kneeling beside her.

"My office," Gian demanded. "Now."

Panting, Karl spent an extra second glaring at Cinder before he turned and stomped out of the studio, flinging sweat from his face.

No sooner than Karl exited the studio, Zae entered, Chip close behind her. Cinder picked herself up from the floor and thanked the woman who'd come to her aid.

"Karl has lost his damn mind," Zae proclaimed. "What did you do to make him so mad?"

"He asked me out before class," Cinder quietly explained. She went to the man who had tried to stop Karl. Chip was checking out his throat.

"And you turned him down," Zae said.

"You're going to have a nice bruise, but I can't tell much more than that," Chip told Karl's victim. "Let me take you to Urgent Care, just to make sure nothing is broken."

Chip dismissed the class. Shouting from the corridor drew everyone from the studio. Gian and Karl had made it to the office, but the noise of their confrontation didn't stay confined to it.

"That girl came through hell to get where she is now, and I won't have you turning Sheng Li into a place she can't call home!" Gian shouted. "Grow up, you dumb self-centered bastard!"

"You're not the biggest cock on the walk, Gian! Criticize my teaching all you want, but I'm the best you've got here!"

"You're fired, Karl." Gian lowered his voice, so the gang in the corridor shuffled closer to the office to get a better listen. "I've had too many complaints about you from students, the staff, even the cleaning service. I can't keep you on."

Zae punched the air in a silent sign of triumph.

"It's her." The darkness in Karl's voice raised the fine hairs at Cinder's nape. "If you got your head out of that woman's ass for one second, you'd see that—"

"If you so much as look at her funny ever again, it's gonna end badly for you, son."

Gian's cold warning gave Cinder an unexpected thrill.

"Oh, I'm your son now, Gian?" Karl challenged. "Is that it?"

"Yeah, that's it."

Brusque, heavy movement in the office sent Chip running in there, his entourage of Zae, Cinder and two students behind him. Chip tried to position himself between Gian and Karl while everyone else crowded the doorway.

"What are you gonna teach me, pops?" Karl demanded, angling around Chip to strike at Gian. "You gonna teach me this?"

Karl's right fist shot past Chip, aimed right at Gian's face. Gian caught Karl's wrist and gave it an expert twist, bringing him to his knees with a pained cry. He leaned over Karl to speak into his face. "Go near Cinder, her house, her car, anything, and I will end you. Do you understand me?"

Karl muttered a stream of curse words under his breath, earning a savage little twist to his hand.

"All right!" he screamed. "Fine!"

"Get your crap and get the hell outta my dojo," Gian ordered.

Karl stood and went to his desk. Angrily, he threw his belongings into his duffel bag and stormed out of the office, sharply catching Zae in the shoulder with his bag on his way to the lobby.

"You big—"

"Just let him go," Cinder said, stopping Zae from pursuing Karl.

Chip left the office with Gian close behind him. Gian seemed surprised to see a bunch of people in the corridor. He briefly cupped Cinder's cheek and said, "Would you wait for me in there?" He nodded toward the private studio. Without waiting for her answer, he fell into step beside Chip.

"I just want to make sure he leaves," Gian said.

"Without breaking a window or kicking a hole in the wall on the way out," Chip added.

Cinder sat alone in the private studio long after Chip had escorted Zae into the women's locker room to ice her shoulder. The longer she sat, the more confused and angry she became. When Gian finally entered the room, she stood and greeted him with a hard push and an even harder demand. "Who do you think you are?"

"Cinder, what—"

"I told you I didn't want to be in a group class, I told you I wasn't ready, but you insisted! And then you weren't even here at five-thirty!"

Gian's solid figure didn't budge under her first push, so Cinder planted her feet and gave him another hearty shove. She smiled inwardly at the way he had to take a step back to maintain his footing.

"If you had been here for our class, I wouldn't have run into Karl," she continued. "I pay you for *private* lessons specifically so I don't have to deal with humiliation!"

"You held your own against Karl," Gian said proudly. "He humiliated himself, not you. You don't have a damn thing to be embarrassed about. You're one of the most courageous women I've ever met."

Right then, staring into his eyes, she knew he wasn't talking about what had happened in the group class. "Who told you?" She wanted to push him again. "Was it Zae?"

"Told me what?" Gian braced his hands in front of himself to ward off another attack.

"Is that what you do when I'm not around? Talk about me like I'm some kind of victim who needs to be protected?"

It took Gian another couple of seconds staring into her feral brown eyes before he figured out what she was referring to. "I Googled you."

"What?"

"Last night. I couldn't sleep, and you said some things that got my curiosity going. So I Googled you. But I couldn't find anything, so I Googled your ex."

She swallowed hard. "Then you know all about what happened back East."

The disappointment and finality in her voice weighed on Gian's heart, bringing back the hurt and helplessness he'd felt the night before. "At first I couldn't sleep because I couldn't stop thinking about the time I'd spent with you," he confessed. "Then it was because I couldn't stop thinking about what your ex-husband did to you."

"That makes two of us then," Cinder snapped. Her lower lip quivered, but she held her tears. "I wanted to tell you. I would have."

"I know."

"I don't need to be rescued." Her tone defied him to contradict her.

"I know," he agreed. "But that won't stop me from trying to be your hero."

"I said too much," she chuckled sadly. "When I got home last night, I knew it. I told you just enough to give you a pry bar to open all the doors I've tried to keep closed."

"Cinder, I've never known anyone so . . . so . . ."

"Stupid?" She attempted to finish his sentence for him. "Gullible? Blind?"

"Strong." He caressed her shoulders, working his hands up to cup her face.

Cinder's anguish vanished. She covered his hand with hers, turning her face to press her lips to his palm.

"It would have been different if Sionne had been teaching the class," she conceded.

"Well, according to Chip, Karl told Sionne that he'd cleared the switch with me. Karl wanted Sionne to take his class tomorrow night. Apparently, he was planning a big date."

Cinder's lips parted. "Karl asked me to dinner for tomorrow night."

"I hope you said no," Gian remarked.

"I did. That's when he got mean."

"I'm sorry I wasn't here for you."

"I can take care of myself. I might not need you to rescue me, but I do need you to keep teaching me."

"That would be my absolute pleasure."

"Then let's go."

"Okay. How 'bout dinner?"

She smiled. "I don't mean leave. Let's go right now." She bowed to him, and then struck a fighting stance. "Right here."

"I figured you had enough fighting for one night."

"It's not fighting when it's with you, it's learning. Karl did things that I've never seen before. I don't want to be surprised like that again. So start teaching me, sensai. I'm yours."

Gian spent a long moment just staring at her. In the quiet studio, with the sunset filtering through the sky-

light to brush Cinder in pale oranges and purples, Gian
wanted to remember her as she was in this instant—the
moment he knew he was in love with her.

Cinder paced before her living room, windows
wishing she had been more specific. When she invited
Gian to her apartment, he had asked what time he should
arrive. "After six," she had said.

After six turned out to be an enormous place filled
with imagined door buzzers, minutes that lengthened
into years, and hallucinations of Gian's car every time she
poked her head between her curtains.

A fresh loaf of herbed sourdough bread warmed in
her oven; an antipasto tray, wine, beer, soda, juice, and
bottled water chilled in her refrigerator. She had changed
clothes three times, first wearing a pair of knit shorts, a
matching tank top and espadrilles, then switching to
white capri pants with a pink baby doll T-shirt and
strappy sandals. She settled on comfort over cute, and
put on a simple black dress, a sleeveless cotton garment
with a straight bodice and a flared skirt. She looked a
little like a chic nun. As much as she hated to admit it,
the look suited her.

Barefoot, she wore a path in the flooring at the
window as she walked back and forth, nibbling the nail
of her right thumb. She wasn't nervous, exactly. It took
ten more passes in front of the window and four more
peeks out the window before she could name her feelings.

Eagerness. Excitement. Beneath those, a layer of her favorite emotion—anticipation. Gian was the first man she had dated in almost eight years, and he stirred up all the best things she remembered about dating. Getting to know Gian was as easy as breathing and the most fun she'd had in a very long time. Unless she was mistaken, Gian was enjoying getting to know her, too.

Her buzzer sounded, and she rushed to the console mounted beside her front door. Pressing the talk button, she spoke into the speaker. "Gian?"

His voice sounded through the speaker. "Buzz me up before my ice cream melts."

"What kind of ice cream?" Cinder asked, smiling.

"The sooner you buzz me in, the sooner you'll find out."

Cinder leaned on the buzzer, and faintly, from three floors down, she heard the distinct click of the front door unlocking. Gian's footsteps on the stairs grew louder as he got closer. So eager to see him, Cinder didn't look through her peephole before she threw open the door.

"Hey," Gian said, the word stretching into a contented sigh.

Every time he saw her felt like the first time. He wondered if he'd ever get used to her beauty, if there ever would come a time when the first glimpse of her smile or her eyes wouldn't start his heart beating faster, or send the too-familiar ache of need flooding into his belly.

She wore no makeup, no jewelry, not even shoes. Her sleeveless black dress with its straight neckline and bell-shaped skirt couldn't have been more prim, yet she had never looked sexier. He handed her the condensation-dampened bag containing the ice cream so he could grab the waistband of his jeans, adjusting them to hide the growing evidence of his attraction to her.

"The Dream Cream Shoppe?" Cinder read the print on the bag, ushering Gian in.

"It's in Kirkwood." Gian watched her spend a good minute locking the deadbolts and fastening the chains on her door.

"It sounds pornographic." Cinder chuckled. She went to the kitchen to put the ice cream in the freezer, Gian following her.

"It's called Dream Cream because they'll put any flavoring you want in ice cream," Gian explained. "So what's for dinner?"

Cinder closed the door to her freezer compartment. "It's so hot, I thought I'd do something light. Zae recommended an antipasto tray, so—"

"I love antipasti," he said. "Ever been to Favazza's on The Hill?"

Cinder quickly turned to grab two wine glasses from an overhead cupboard. "I've been there once or twice." *Just this afternoon*, she added to herself. Zae had told her that Favazza's was one of Gian's favorites, and she'd gone there for her ingredients, doubling back within sight of her apartment when she realized that she'd forgotten freshly shaved parmesan cheese.

"Would you like wine?" Cinder asked. "I've got—"

"Anything is fine."

Taking a muscato d'oro by its neck, Cinder drew it from the fridge and set it on the counter.

"Do you have an opener?" Gian asked.

"Sure."

Cinder reached for the magnetic strip mounted along the wall behind the counter. She took a red-handled corkscrew from it and held it in her hand, staring at it for a moment before handing it off to Gian.

"You okay?"

She nodded. "My ex-husband never . . ." She touched a hand to her face, her throat, tamping the anxiety that always threatened when random thoughts of her past invaded her present. "He would never have volunteered to help. He thought it was my duty to wait on him. I thought so, too. I mean, I didn't mind doing things for him. I didn't realize until after everything happened that I did so much for him because I was afraid of disappointing him. Literally afraid."

"My parents taught me that a husband should worship his wife," Gian told her. "That a family's true wealth is its happiness, and if mama ain't happy—"

"Ain't nobody happy," Cinder finished with him. She smiled, her anxiety dissipating before it could plant roots.

Gian filled their glasses and carried them into the living room while Cinder brought the antipasto tray, saucers, and cutlery.

"This smells so good." Gian took a seat on the shorter section of Cinder's L-shaped leather sectional.

Cinder placed the tray on her coffee table, edging it close to Gian. Tucking her legs beneath her, she reclined on the long section of her sofa, her wine glass in hand. "Please, help yourself," she offered.

Gian's gaze moved from Cinder to the tray and back again, the sight of both making his mouth water. She had outdone herself with the antipasti, presenting many of his favorites—mortadella, prosciutto, roasted red peppers, black and green olives, sweet onion slices, crostini, and a finishing touch of wide, freshly shaved parmesan reggiano ribbons.

Gian spent a minute preparing the perfect bite, a crostini layered with all the flavors and textures before him. He offered it to Cinder, his hand cupped under her chin to catch crumbs.

She felt a little silly being fed, but the gesture gave her pleasant goose bumps nonetheless.

"Good, isn't it?" Gian asked proudly.

Her mouth full, Cinder grinned, nodding. Once she'd swallowed, she said, "It's so different from the antipasti I had in Boston, in the North End. I asked the counter guy at Favazza's to recommend items, and he chose so many different meats."

"Us landlocked Italians have a slightly different palate than those seaside guineas," Gian said. "We like our meat down here same as those Boston Eye-talians like their seafood." He chomped into his own crostini, which was loaded high with meat, cheese, and vegetables. Speaking around it, he said, "The wine is nice. It really complements the food."

"I was worried that you wouldn't care for it," Cinder admitted. "It's kind of a girlie wine."

"I didn't know wine had genders."

"This muscato is light and sweet, and it's got a little bubble to it," Cinder explained. "Its notes of vanilla, honeysuckle, and peach remind me of perfume, something feminine. It's the opposite of a shiraz, for example. A spicy, masculine red like that is something I'd serve with barbeque or Mexican food."

"The sweetness of the muscato is what makes it work with the saltiness of the antipasti. How did you come to know so much about wine?"

"My ex used to collect it."

Gian slowly wiped his hands on a cloth napkin. "What happened to him after the trial?"

Cinder swallowed a big gulp of wine, steeling herself. "He was sentenced to three years in prison."

"Three years?" Gian nearly shouted. "For attempted murder?"

"He was charged with assault, not murder. The jury bought his psycho-emotional breakdown story and gave him a lighter sentence. The prosecutor didn't want to take the risk that another jury at appeal would let him off altogether. The defense argued that Sumchai posed no danger to anyone but me."

Gian quickly calculated the math. "So he'll be out in about eighteen months?"

"Half that, if he gets credit for good behavior and parole."

Gian, hands on knees and elbows wide apart, studied Cinder's apartment. He'd noticed all of the locks and chains on her front door and the wall-mounted console for her security system, and now he noticed armed motion sensors blinking in the corners of her living room windows.

Her bone-colored walls and hardwood floors were bare, the sparse furniture elegant in its plainness. She had nothing of extreme value that he could readily see, and his only logical conclusion was that the high security was in place to protect one thing: her life. "You think he'll come after you."

"I know he will." Her dark eyes fixed on Gian, telegraphing her certainty.

He leaned back into the sofa and stared forward. The hot, humid dusks of summer had given way to the arrival of early fall, and a cool, dry breeze moved Cinder's sheer curtains in a mesmerizing dance. Everything about Cinder, from her social habits to her apartment, seemed temporary. In her year in Webster Groves, she'd made no new friends, left no mark of her presence anywhere other than at Sheng Li. She was preparing, and waiting, he saw that now.

"Are you planning to leave, if he comes here?"

"If I run from him again, I'll have to keep running. But if I stay, if I face him, I might not live through it."

"You're not alone." Gian moved to her part of the sectional, sitting close enough to enclose her hand in both of his. "You don't have to do any of this alone."

Pulling her hand gently from his grasp, she disagreed. "Yes, I do. I won't have anyone else getting hurt because of Sumchai Wyatt."

"You changed your last name," he said, varying his approach. "Why White?"

"When I was recovering from the attack, one of the counselors at Project Protection told me that the best way to remember a new last name was to choose one similar to the old one. If I ever accidentally said 'Wyatt,' it would be easy to cover it with 'White.' I couldn't use my maiden name because—"

"Your parents had a sense of humor," Gian interrupted.

"Yes," Cinder chuckled. "I can't tell you what it was like growing up with a name like Cinder Bloch."

"You and my brother could trade war stories."

"Why's that?"

"Pio Piasanti?"

After a beat of silence, laughter burst from Cinder. She threw back her head, laughing so hard that she couldn't breathe. "I'm sorry," she managed, wiping tears from the outer corners of her eyes. "It's just that I can totally imagine the names and jokes kids must have made about your brother's name."

"Have you seen your parents since you moved here?"

"No." Her laughter tapered off. "But I talk to them once a week. They want to come visit, but they're close to my former in-laws. They mean well, but I don't want them to accidentally say something to the Wyatts that they might repeat."

"Your parents don't know where you are?"

She shook her head. "It's better this way. For now."

"You amaze me."

Not knowing what to say in response to his heartfelt statement, Cinder said nothing. But Gian persisted.

"I won't lie and say that I know what it's been like for you, but we have more in common than you think. The way I see it, you're just as much a veteran of war as I am. The only difference is that you're stronger than I am. I had the U.S. military behind me when I went into battle. You had to do it alone."

Just that fast, Cinder went from laughter to the verge of tears. So many people had told her in so many ways that she was brave, a survivor, but none so eloquently as Gian. She hadn't cared for any other opinion as she cared for Gian's. He was the first man she had grown close to since her divorce and the first she'd come to trust.

Mostly.

But she wanted to trust him completely.

"I want to see you naked."

He had been drinking his wine, and her confession so surprised him that he sucked a little of the vino up his nose. Cinder dropped her feet to the floor to take a fresh napkin from the coffee table. She gave it to him, pressing back a tiny smile as he sputtered and blew his nose.

"I didn't mean to shock you," Cinder said.

"That wasn't something I expected you to come out and say like that."

"Could I see you?"

He gave his head a little shake of confusion.

"I'd like to look at you."

She elaborated no further, but he saw something in her eyes that gave him a clear understanding of what she was asking of him. Vulnerability and fear mingled with hope and longing in her expression, and Gian knew then that he would do anything she asked if it removed any lingering doubts she had about him. He held her gaze as he unbuttoned his shirt and unfastened his belt, then stood to undo his button fly. With a self-effacing grin, he let his jeans fall to his ankles, leaving him with his shirt fronts billowing and the front of his sports briefs bulging.

Cinder used her foot to push the coffee table out a little, giving Gian more room. He was imposing enough in clothes, but shrugging off his shirt and stepping out of the pool of denim at his feet, he seemed to expand until he filled her view. Her eyes traced the thick veins and cords standing out against his skin as he hooked his thumbs into the waist band of his briefs, the muscles of his arms and chest lengthened and bunched as he bent over to lower them. Shadows filled the hollows of his hip muscles when he stepped out of his briefs and lightly kicked them to one side.

He straightened, displaying the definition of his abdominal muscles, trying to read Cinder's expression. Was she pleased? Frightened? Standing before her, he could hide nothing, especially the fact that her gaze affected him as strongly as her touch might have. Only her eyes moved as they traveled over him. They lingered in certain areas, places that responded painfully to her interest. Just when he would have begged her to allow him to do so, she asked him to sit.

"You have so many scars," she murmured, touching the trio of pale, smooth slash marks striping his left pectoral muscle.

"I got into a fight with Wolverine," Gian joked. When Cinder didn't laugh or smile, Gian continued more soberly. "I got that in a skirmish with locals outside Kandahar. They were farmers armed with spades and hoes. One of them got in a good lick with a tiller before we drove them back."

She scooted closer to him, leaning in to stroke the raised, jagged line of scar tissue just under his navel. "And this?"

"Homemade machete," he said simply. "That was the last time I underestimated the power of handmade weaponry."

Cinder repositioned him to recline against the corner of the sofa, his legs up and outstretched. She sat facing him, her hip to his. Her right hand came to rest lightly on his thigh. "May I touch you?"

"I think I might die if you don't."

Cinder's slim hand whispered over his skin, her touch as stimulating as an electric current. Gian breathed deeply through his nose, closing his eyes when she cupped his face, her thumb lightly stroking over his lips once before she ventured to the solid column of his neck.

She took his shoulders and sat on his upper thighs, her knees flanking his hips. She took his wrists, guiding his arms up and above his head, his hands far out of reach of her.

She leisurely reacquainted herself with a man's body, with Gian's body. She paid careful attention, intent on learning his textures, how he tasted, smelled, and responded. She threaded her fingers through his hair and found it soft, but so unlike hers. His hair was very straight with a cowlick that would have been more noticeable had his hair been longer. She leaned forward, her bosom in his face, to study his scalp. His maple-gold hair was thick with little space between the follicles. She pressed her nose to his head and inhaled, approving of the fresh, clean scent that reminded her of the forest after a heavy rain.

She liked his ears, deeming them perfect—not too big, not too small. They were sensitive, given the way he tensed when she took the rim of his ear between her teeth, traced it with her tongue and suckled his earlobe before trailing her lips lower. The scent of his neck was very different from that of his hair. No less pleasant, it was warmer, stronger, more him, as distinct as the scent of fresh bread yet decidedly male.

At the hollow of his throat, his pulse drummed against her lips. With the tip of her tongue, she sampled the velvety texture of his skin. His chest was naturally bare, so she had a smooth path to his nipples. The tawny pips hardened, the darker skin around them puckering in response to the moist heat of her tongue. Cinder's own flesh reacted in kind, tightening when Gian let his head fall back. He took a deep breath that expanded his chest and rocked her back a bit.

Gian kept silent, although he wanted to tell her how much he liked the dance of her fingers over the ridged muscles of his rib cage and the defined squares of his abdomen. A thin trail of golden-brown hair originated at his navel and led downward. Cinder scooted down his legs to settle more comfortably upon him while following the trail of hair, which ended in a silky nest of darker fur from which reared the eager prominence of Gian's not-so-little soldier.

Cinder nuzzled its base with her nose, inhaling his earthy fragrance. He smelled delicious, his aroma inviting her to taste the hard instrument grazing her cheek. She raised her head enough to catch its tip between her lips. Pinching her lips into a snug ring, she lowered her head, drawing him farther into her mouth. Gian's arms tensed, his abdomen and buttocks flexing, his hips lifting reflexively to drive himself deeper. His hands clenched into hard fists eager to grab Cinder, but Gian knew that he couldn't, not until she invited him. If they were to proceed any further, he had to follow her lead and respond within her parameters.

Cinder's hands went beneath him, clasping his backside so hard her blunt fingernails creased his skin.

Helpless, Gian groaned low in his throat, the sound emanating from the depths of his pleasure. His hands opened and closed as he pushed his shoulders into the back of the sofa, his hips pumping in rhythm with Cinder's head. The softness of her inner cheeks, the thrilling rasp of her tongue and the wet heat of her mouth combined to render him ignorant of all but her exquisite attention.

Cinder measured her breathing, taking him deeper with each down stroke. She removed her hands from his shaft and stroked his legs, smoothing her hands over the hard muscles under his skin.

With a loud grunt, Gian reached the limit of his endurance. He surrendered with a shudder, his elbows and heels digging into the sofa. Cinder held onto the back of the sofa with one hand to keep him from throwing her off as his hips seemed to move on automatic, his noises of relief waning as his excitement subsided.

"Cinder," he gasped, his body relaxing, "when you said touch, I didn't think you meant like that."

She discreetly swiped a napkin across her mouth and tidied him before she lay atop him, resting her head on his shoulder and draping an arm over his chest. Gian considered that an invitation, and he fastened her tight in his arms.

"You aren't annoyed with me?"

He laughed. "Annoyed is so not the word to describe how I feel right now. Why would you think I'd be annoyed?"

"Because I did what I wanted to do, and you didn't get to do anything."

"I understand why you had to do what you just did."

She shifted, lacing her fingers on his chest and resting her chin on them to face him. "Good. Explain it to me."

He lovingly touched a fingertip to the end of her nose before tracing the line of her jaw. "I think you want me."

She giggled. "Really? Is it obvious?" He gave her a half grin that made her want to reach between his legs once more.

"When was the last time you were with a man?"

She dropped her eyes. "My ex-husband is the last man I was with."

"I think that you needed to establish control," he said. "You needed to see that you could trust me. That I wouldn't hurt you or try to force you into something you didn't want."

Her head went back to his shoulder and her left arm circled his head, her fingers moving through his hair. "There were a couple of men who were interested in me when I first moved here," she said. "The first one tried to kiss me after we'd gone to a gallery exhibit. I couldn't let him. Every time he touched me, it reminded me of Sumchai. It was worse with the second man. We never made it to the end of the first date. He took control of everything. He ordered for me at the restaurant, and chose my bowling ball for me. It made me so nauseous, I just ran out on him. I know how silly and stupid that is, but—"

"It's not stupid," Gian assured her. "And it's not your fault. Your ex is the one responsible for the fact that you link innocent gestures and words to pain."

"How do you know so much about things like this?"

Gian stroked her arm with his fingertips. He sighed and said, "My sister Lucia was a runner. She used to work out in a different park every month. There's so many of them in and around St. Louis because some society lady at the turn of the century decided that parks should be available to everyone, not just the rich folks who lived in the painted ladies downtown."

"What's a painted lady?"

"That's a nickname for the Victorian houses in the neighborhood surrounding Lafayette Park, down on

Mississippi, Missouri, and Park Avenues," Gian said. "In the past couple decades, the houses have been remodeled and painted. The area is real upscale now."

"Zae took me to Lafayette Park once," Cinder said. "It's really pretty. There's a bridge crossing over a little creek, and with the trees bowing low over it and all the water lilies and moss-covered stones in the water, it looks like something from an old-fashioned book of fairy tales."

"Lucia liked the bridge, too. It's the main reason she liked running down there. One Saturday afternoon, though, the park was crowded, and she had to park her car about three blocks away. The neighborhood wasn't very good, but she hadn't expected anything to happen in the middle of a sunny Saturday with so many people out on the streets."

A weak shudder moved through Cinder, and Gian held her closer, sweeping his lips across the top of her head in a reassuring kiss.

"She was never able to tell us how many assailants were involved, but a group of young thugs grabbed her and dragged her between two dilapidated buildings. She's a real fierce kid, but those creeps outnumbered her. On a day when so many other people had gone to the park to enjoy the weather, these monsters thought it would be fun to spend the afternoon beating and raping my baby sister."

Gian's chest heaved. He struggled to hold back emotions Cinder could only guess at—fury, sorrow, pain, and frustration top among them. She comforted him with soft kisses to his temple and the backs of his fingers.

"It's been four years," he went on. "I don't expect her to bounce back and be the same person she was before the attack. I know it doesn't work that way. But I want her to get through it. To come out on the other side knowing that she survived it. She's still here and she's stronger and tougher and better than the bastards who hurt her because she survived it. I haven't been able to hug her or kiss her, or even touch her unexpectedly, since it happened. She can't bear to be touched by a man, not even by her own brothers. When I first met you, I saw the same apprehension in your eyes that I see in Lucia's. The difference between the two of you is that you've got the courage to arm yourself against the monsters."

"Was anyone ever charged with your sister's assault?" Cinder asked.

"No. DNA was collected and Lucia gave the best descriptions she could, but the offenders apparently weren't in the system. Pio and I stay on top of the cops, getting them to run the samples once a year, just in case they get a hit. I can't imagine that Lucia was the last person those bastards hurt. They'll get a hit one of these days. I just hope it happens before the statute of limitations runs out."

"Maybe that's the problem," Cinder suggested. "Lucia hasn't had the chance to confront her monsters. When Sumchai went on trial, I had to force myself to walk into that courtroom and sit down. The next day, I had to force myself to look at him. By the end of the trial, I stared him straight in the eye as he was led back to prison. I didn't realize it at the time, but that was the moment I started rebuilding my life. I moved to Webster Groves a few months later, and a year after that, I walked into Sheng Li." She caressed his cheek with the backs of her fingers. "I met you. And now I want so much of what I've missed out on. True love. A family. A dog."

"What kind of dog?"

"A big one. Something loyal and protective."

"A German Shepard in bulletproof armor would blend right into your little fortress here." Gian chuckled.

"This is one of only two places I feel completely safe," Cinder said.

"Where's the other one?"

"Right here." She kissed his neck. "Right here in your arms."

"I was just thinking the same thing."

"I don't need you to protect me, I told you that," she said.

"You're misunderstanding me. I was just thinking about how safe *I* feel in *your* arms. You got me in your arms and my heart in your hands. I can go into a skirmish outnumbered and underarmed without blinking an eye, but when it comes to women, I never put up a fight because I never wanted to lose. I love you, Cinder. I'll fight for you, die for you—"

She kissed him, stopping his declarations. Gian's arms circled her, pressing her into his body as he returned her kiss.

"Would you get the ice cream for me?" she asked once they broke for air.

Gian laughed lightly. "Can I put my clothes back on now?"

"I'd rather you didn't."

Cinder watched his leisured movement to and from the kitchen. He handed Cinder a spoon and opened the flaps of the waxed ice cream carton. "Ladies first." He offered her the first taste of the milky-gold dessert.

"What flavor is this?"

Gian watched her savor the confection, his smile broadening. Cinder's eyes widened, her eyebrows arched higher, and she licked her upper lip.

"Bacon!" She laughed, plunging her spoon into the carton once more and digging out a hearty bite.

CHAPTER 7

"Is there meat in all the side dishes, too?" Cinder muttered under her breath. Zae's Labor Day spread was impressive in quantity, quality, and the sheer overabundance of meat. Just about every animal in the barnyard had been on the grill, and Zae's guests sat around her backyard chomping on ribs, chicken breast, lamb chops, sirloin steak, hamburgers, hot dogs and Johnsonville brats.

Grasping a heavy-duty paper plate, Cinder slowly moved down the buffet table Zae had set up along one end of her deck. Though she had asked guests not to bring anything, many had, and Zae had quarantined their dishes to a rusty old card table bereft of even a tablecloth. Before Zae could see her and stop her, Cinder helped herself to a ladleful of Chip's fruit salad, a vivid, fragrant combination of watermelon, cantaloupe, blueberries, seedless green and red grapes, and sliced starfruit sprinkled with fresh mint leaves. She also took a few of the homemade taro chips Sionne had brought, eager for her first taste of Samoan food.

Gian had enlisted his mother to make lasagna, and she'd clearly thought Gian had intended to feed five hundred rather than fifty. The lasagna pan was so wide and deep, it looked like a toddler tub. Absently licking her lips, Cinder cut herself a huge square of lasagna. Seven tiers of curly-edged noodles, herbed ricotta cheese, sauce, and mozzarella started her stomach rumbling as she wrangled stretchy strands of melted cheese and clumps of fragrant sauce free from her portion before setting it on her plate.

Cinder turned to leave the potluck table and nearly collided with Zae. Arms folded stiffly, the right side of her mouth pinched in a derisive smirk, Zae glared at Cinder's plate.

"What?" Cinder asked innocently.

Zae stood close to her and spoke in a low voice. "Every year these people come to my Labor Day barbeque, and every year I tell them not to bring anything. And every year, they all bring some watery casserole or some tasteless, mayonnaise-based salad, or some gruesome bakery product from the day-old shelf. Meanwhile, they eat up everything I cook and leave me with their nasty potluck contributions."

"Zae, your friends are just trying to be polite," Cinder said. "I think they made a pretty good showing. I've never seen taro chips at a barbeque before, and Chip's fruit salad is beautiful." She held her plate up to Zae's nose. "Doesn't the basil and garlic in the lasagna smell so—"

"I know, I know." Zae impatiently pushed Cinder's plate back at her. "It smells like Italy!"

Cinder choked back a laugh. "You don't have to worry, you know."

"Worry about what?"

"About someone bringing a dish that steals the attention from your cooking."

Zae grunted. "Honey, I'm not worried about that. My barbeque is the best this side of Gates in Kansas City."

"Then what's the problem?"

"The only time I bring food to a barbeque is when I know the host is a terrible cook. What does it say when my best friends bring food to a party where food is the main reason for the gathering?"

Cinder silently stared at Zae for a moment. "You're really weird."

"But I'm right, aren't I?"

"Are you for real?"

"Look," Zae demanded, "all I'm saying is that if a perfectly good feast is waiting someplace for you, why on God's great green Earth would you bring something else to eat?"

Though Zae was speaking to her, Cinder noticed Zae's line of sight led beyond her, somewhere over her left shoulder. She turned to see a few of Zae's colleagues from the university and three of her daughters' friends from Webster Groves High School. And through them, she spotted Chip smiling at the perky blonde he'd brought to the barbeque.

"You didn't tell the guys that they couldn't bring dates," Cinder said.

Zae took her arm and pulled Cinder toward the deck stairs, almost making Cinder lose her food. Cinder offered the "excuse me's" and apologies as Zae shuttled her through the guests milling on the deck.

"Cory didn't bring a date," Zae pointed out once she and Cinder were deep in the tree-shaded backyard, far out of earshot of the other guests. "Sionne didn't bring a date. Gian didn't bring a date."

"I'm Gian's date," Cinder said.

"That isn't the point!" Zae snapped. "If Chip was going to bring someone, he should have at least asked me first."

"You didn't seem to mind when Cory brought a date to your July fourth barbeque," Cinder said. "Why do you care that Chip brought a girlfriend?"

Cinder had always envied Zae's practiced calm. Her face never revealed her emotions or mood unless she wanted it to. But right now, stealing glances at Chip and his laughing date, Zae's face was as easy to read as a cloudy Missouri sky. The heavens were about to open.

"You really like him, don't you?" Cinder asked.

"That child is young enough to be . . . my younger brother," Zae scoffed.

"He's a grown man. And you're a beautiful, healthy woman who's been single for a long time. It's okay to be attracted to him, Zae."

"I'm not." She folded her arms resolutely.

"Then why does it bother you so much to see him with a date?"

"I'm not used to it, that's all."

"He probably hasn't had much time for dating, between training you for the tournament—"

"We don't spend any more time training than you and Gian do," Zae argued.

"—and going to the gym with you—" Cinder continued.

"If you must know, I need to build my upper body strength," Zae informed her. "Chip knows which machines and exercises are best for me, and he keeps me motivated."

"—and to the physical therapist with you—"

"I'm forty-two years old, soon to be forty-three," Zae said testily. "These old joints and muscles need some attention from time to time."

"And you two have gone out for dinner a couple of times, too," Cinder said. "Gian and I saw you going into Isis a few nights ago when we were leaving Sheng Li. We saw you at the Kirkwood Farmer's Market, too, sharing one of those big apples."

"People gotta eat," Zae whispered loudly. "And those Honeycrisp apples are the size of softballs. I can't eat one by myself!"

"It's all right to spend time with him," Cinder said. "If he makes you happy, you should—"

"Have you and Gian had sex yet?"

Cinder's cheeks burst into flame.

Zae stepped closer to her and lowered her voice. "I'm sorry. I wanted to change the subject, and that's the first thing that popped into my head."

With Zae following her, Cinder moved a few yards to the black wrought-iron bench beneath Zae's biggest willow. The long, lazy fronds seemed to enclose them in their own little world as they sat, Cinder's plate between them. Zae picked pieces of deliciously browned cheese from the lasagna as Cinder spoke.

"We fool around a lot." Cinder peered through the willow fronds and the guests on the deck to see Gian, whose animated hand gestures made him seem bigger and taller as he talked with Zae's twins, Cory, and a few other people. "Every time I see him, I want to kiss him. I'm going to get my ass kicked at the tournament because every one of our training sessions ends with us groping and rolling over each other in the private studio."

"Gian told Chip that you're getting really good," Zae said through a mouthful of lasagna.

"Gian's just being nice." Cinder kicked her feet, staining the toes of her canvas sandals in the freshly cut grass. "He's so nice to me, Zae. And so patient."

"He's not stupid," Zae remarked. "He knows that some things are worth the wait. But why are you making him wait?"

"I don't mean to. Every time we're tangled up in each other, I go so far with him before it's not just us anymore. Chai creeps in."

"Oh, baby . . ." Zae cooed.

"Gian came over to watch a movie last week, and we ended up falling asleep on the sofa. I had the dream again."

"That bastard is in your head and you have to get him out," Zae said forcefully. "You can't let him keep controlling your life."

"He was really good at it, you know. He did it for so long without me even noticing it. He would tell me that he was just looking out for me, or wanted what was best for *us*. Remember when I accepted the promotion at MetaGraphica?"

Zae crunched into a taro chip. "Vaguely."

"My first big assignment was for Calvert Caldwell Incorporated. They're based in Baltimore, and their network is enormous."

Zae nodded. "Three of my literature grads are at Missouri U. on scholarships awarded by Calvert Caldwell. It's amazing how much the company does to help low-income and impoverished women advance themselves."

"I did the graphics for a national campaign they planned to launch for their new Women's Technology Services division. The focus was on how the WTS would provide no- or low-cost training in computer education for women re-entering the job market, or women who speak English as a second language—for whatever reason a woman needed to have computer skills. Men can go out and get well-paying jobs in construction or something if they don't have computer skills, but a woman without a degree usually has to trade on her looks if she wants to earn a good living. The whole concept behind WTS was that of empowering women, so that they could compete in today's job market using their brains and ambition."

"Sounds good," Zae said. Having finished off the lasagna, she used her finger to mop up the last of the sauce on Cinder's plate.

"On the day of our big presentation, everything was going great. The client loved the treatments we came up with, both in terms of the copy and the art. They really liked one of the logos I designed. Just when they were about to leave to go see the treatments the other company up for the job had done, in comes a singing telegram. From Chai."

Zae looked up, her black eyes wide.

"My birthday was a week off, but he sent a singing telegram to the office as a surprise. He'd chosen strippers, and not just any strippers. The women were twins, identical right down—or up—to their enormous breasts. He hired Bitty and Kitty McTittie to dance and sing an absolutely horrible song for me. The lyrics of the song were worse than their dancing. When they stripped off their sequined 54DDD brassieres and tossed them in the air, that was it. The Caldwell Calvert reps had all they could take. They stormed out, I got called before the vice president of personnel. I was demoted to the Lenny Orsatti Used Car account, and Caldwell Calvert ended up going with the campaign treatment our rival created."

"That wasn't your fault."

"Yes, it was. I shouldn't have talked about my promotion so much. I should never have let Chai know how much the Caldwall Calvert account meant to me. That's why he took it away. He didn't want anything in my life to compete with him for my attention."

"Is that why you went two years without calling or writing or visiting me after you got married?"

"It was just easier to keep the peace than to argue or deal with his silent treatments if he found out that I'd been talking to you," Cinder said.

"He never could stand me. I always stood up to him, and he hated that."

"How could I not have seen it at the time? What was wrong with me?"

"The problem was never with you," Zae insisted. "It was him. When you introduced me to Sumchai Wyatt for the first time, I fell half in love with him myself! He was smart, funny, he seemed to worship the ground you walked on with those big ol' size nines of yours, and the man was beautiful."

"I don't want my past interfering with my future," Cinder said firmly. "Gian deserves that."

"So do you, honey," Zae assured her. "Just keep doing what you've been doing. Everything will work out the way it's supposed to. Say your prayers, and God will manage your mess into a glorious outcome." She patted Cinder's bare knee. "Now let's go see if Chip's little friend has any food allergies."

"I'm too old for this," Cinder grunted as she pulled herself onto a higher branch of the oak tree at the far end of Zae's backyard.

"If you're too old at thirty-one, then I'm definitely too old." Gian, his hands on her hips, gave her a boost onto the cargo netting moored between two branches of the tree. The rough synthetic cable formed a triangular web nearly thirty feet above the ground. Zae had installed the web for her twins' tenth birthday as a compromise to getting a tree house, something Zae knew the twins would quickly outgrow.

Hesitant, Cinder crawled over the web, fearful that it might not support her weight. Gian braced his feet on a lower branch and grabbed the netting. He gave it a good shake, scaring a shriek out of Cinder, who bounced onto her back and stiffly splayed her arms and legs. She gripped the wide squares of the netting as tightly as she could.

"I'm sorry." Gian chuckled. "I didn't mean to scare you. I wanted to assure you that the web would hold."

"You're lucky I didn't kick you in the windpipe," Cinder replied. "I know what to do with my startle reflex these days, you know."

Gian hummed a noise of acknowledgement. "Guess what?"

"What?" Cinder asked. Framed by the leafy canopy in the early darkness, he looked like a mythical forest denizen, or perhaps a mischievous demi-god.

"You're not wearing any panties."

Convinced that the wide web would indeed support her, Cinder relaxed, pillowing her head on her laced fingers. "Yes, I am."

Gian made a production of peering under her short black skirt. "No, you're not. I've got a great angle and I can see your—"

"It's my Chocolate Silk." She laughed, clapping her knees together and crossing her legs at the ankles.

"That's a fancy name for it." Gian grabbed her ankles to drag her closer to him. "I call mine Soldier."

Cinder laughed harder, succumbing to a full attack of the sillies. "I'm wearing my Chocolate Silk *panties*," she clarified. "I've got Va-Va-Voom Vanilla, Strawberry Sweetness, Naked Nectarine. Those are see-through orange silk."

Gian licked his lips with a noisy slurp. "You know," he started, peeking through the branches to get a look at the house a few hundred yards away, "everyone's on the deck having dessert. We're the only ones out here."

"I want a slice of Zae's coconut cream pie." Cinder sat up.

"I want what's right here."

It might have been a trick of the moonlight, but the playful gleam in Gian's eyes turned into something else as he stood there, his upper body framed between her feet. The specifics of his desire went unspoken, but Cinder perfectly understood what he meant. What he wanted.

Beckoning him with an index finger, she lay on the web. Gian heeded her silent invitation. He climbed onto the web, crawling over her until his face aligned with hers.

"Now about these panties of yours," he said, his voice low. "Are they edible?"

"No." She giggled. "They're from an online company called Cashmere & Charisma. It's owned by two African-American women, Cashmere Connolly and Charisma O'Meara. They started the business as an intimate party planning service, to pay for college. It was so successful, they branched into merchandising their brand. They sell lingerie, gourmet food, bath and beauty products—"

"If you'd stop talking, I could kiss you."

"Well, if you'd kiss me, I'd stop talking."

Gian's mouth came down on Cinder's; she raised her head to meet him. He supported his weight on his knees, his heavier body lowering that end of the web to bring her more upright. His hands gently closed around her forearms, then slid up to her wrists before he threaded his fingers through hers. Kissing had become one of their favorite pastimes. It came very easily, so much so that it was merely another way of using their lips to speak to one another.

Gian's kisses held nothing back. They revealed everything about his feelings for Cinder. The flick of his tongue and pinch of his lips at her earlobe, the nip of his teeth at her lower lip, the gentle vacuum of his mouth at her neck; in so many ways he told her how much he cared for her and wanted to please her.

Cinder responded in kind, tonight more than ever. She found herself someplace she had never expected to be. She had shared a bed with Gian, but only to sleep in his arms. They had made out like teenagers, Gian never moving faster or further than she desired. She desired him now, suspended between Heaven and Earth, far from every reminder of her painful past and uncertain future. Joyfully, she reveled in the present, a blissful place shared with a man whose kindness, patience, and tolerance heightened his beauty.

He cupped her face to set the most tender of kisses on the tip of her nose and eyelids. Arms outstretched, she gripped the web. Gian's gaze held her face in place while his hands moved under the soft cotton pleats of her skirt. Goose bumps rose in the path taken by his fingers as they glided over her thighs and hips to the waistband of her Chocolate Silk panties.

"Do you want me to stop?"

She responded with a shake of her head.

"Tell me."

"I don't want you to stop," she whispered, her words as soft and raspy as the language of the wind-stirred leaves.

The give of the web made an awkward task of removing her panties, but Gian managed, draping them carefully over the nearest branch. He kissed her then, his hands roaming freely beneath her skirt.

His long, strong fingers pressed into her lower back, his thumbs stroked her hips. He kissed her deeply, clasping her left buttock in one hand while cupping his right hand between her legs. The warmth of her liquid silk wet his fingers as he parted the slippery seam hidden in her moist curls. His tongue slipped between her lips to suckle the tip of her tongue. His thumb and forefinger found the firm tip protruding from its fleshy hood, and he mimicked the action of his lips and tongue.

The joints of the cable creaking, Cinder gripped the net even tighter, her arm muscles hard. Running his hands along her thighs, Gian felt the tension in her legs. He broke the kiss to whisper, "Imagine that your muscles are like honey."

Soft kisses and even softer caresses helped her do just that, until she released the web and put her hands on

Gian. He took them, kissing them, before granting her leave to touch him as she wished. She cradled his head to her body as he nipped and gnawed at her breasts through her knit top. Her back arched, thrusting her hard nipples at him. He raised her top, exposing her Chocolate Silk bra to the night. Leisurely, Gian suckled her through the shiny satin, darkening it. Cinder closed her eyes and surrendered to sensation. Her hips bucked toward Gian, the empty heat within her aching for fulfillment.

Gian read her signals and obliged her, lowering himself until his mouth covered her dark opening. He drew on her long and with enough firmness to leave her arched in pure pleasure, her mouth open, her eyes shut.

Her doctor was the last man to have touched her in the places Gian touched, only Gian's touch thrilled her. No fright laced the luscious, thickly sensual waves of warmth and desire he generated as he learned her body and its responses. His muscular frame was pleasantly hard, but his strength and size were not used to intimidate or dominate her. He used his body in ways meant only to please.

His arms cradled her thighs, positioning her bottom against his chest. The former Marine became an explorer and he expertly used his tools to discover every detail of her. His tongue delved and excavated, his teeth tested textures and firmness. Cinder writhed beneath him, gritting her teeth. Gian's left arm slid up her body so his fingertips could graze the cool, smooth skin of her jaw.

"Relax," he told her, the word an erotic murmur against her most sensitive flesh. "Just let it come."

Cinder concentrated, her attention turned inward, rather than out. She told her big muscles to slacken, her little ones to soften. Her eyes drowsed shut, her lips slightly parted as she made herself stop gritting her teeth. She let the breeze inflate her lungs and fill her nose with the scent of eucalyptus and lavender from a neighbor's aroma garden. She ignored the scratch of the web cable under her arms and focused only on Gian and the magic he performed between her thighs.

Her abdomen jumped when he splayed his hand over it to stoke her with his thumb while his tongue plunged into her with a spongy firmness that both scandalized and delighted. Whatever apprehension she had left was freed by the hungry pellet under Gian's thumb. Much more blissful sensations radiated from it as her body danced to the silent music of sexual pleasure. Arms outstretched above her head, she stifled her moans in her left bicep. One word ran on a loop in her mind, the word she managed to gasp when Gian replaced his thumb with his tongue and his tongue with two fingers.

"Gian."

Her breathy utterance stoked Gian's own fires beyond bearing. Every part of him hurt, from his tightly curled toes and the hot knot behind his fly on up to his biceps and the tips of his ears. He made love to her with his entire face, parting her with his nose and running its length along her pliant heat before lapping at her as though she were his favorite dessert and he was determined to collect every drop.

Clutching handfuls of his T-shirt at his shoulders, Cinder trembled. Gian stood on his knees, grabbed his shirt between his shoulders and tugged it over his head, carefully wiping his face before flinging it behind him, where it landed on a branch. Cinder took off her top and skirt, and with Gian's help, eased out of her bra.

As much as it pained him not to touch her, he couldn't stop looking at her. He'd seen naked women before, lots of them, from his first sexual encounter at fifteen up to his last interlude with Kuriko. Cinder was the first woman he'd seen who looked prettier dressed in dappled moonlight and the shadows of oak leaves than in clothing. She was so lovely, he couldn't think of her as naked. He thought of her only as his.

His eyes roamed the places his hands and mouth wanted to search. The hollows behind her collarbones and in her throat. The angle of her jaw and the warm place where it met her earlobe. The unlined space between her finely arched eyebrows and the apples of her cheeks. Her lower lip, still plumped from earlier kisses.

The action of her hands at his fly broke his contemplation of her. Quickly, he finished what she'd started, slipping his jeans and briefs down and scrambling out of them, careful not to fall backwards out of the tree. He had to turn and sit with his back to Cinder to kick off his athletic shoes, one of which popped out of his grasp. By the time the shoe hit the ground, Gian's jeans were slung over a branch with the rest of their clothes, giving the tree a lived-in look.

Gian scooted back and positioned Cinder on top of him. He preferred having the coarse plastic cable biting into his skin rather than hers, not that he noticed the spiky scratch of the web once he had the view of Cinder astride his hips. It was too dark to make out more detail than the outer curve of her breasts, the sensuous lines of her arms, the inward arcs of her waist and the swell of her hips. Her silhouette had weight and warmth, and when her thighs hardened under his hands to raise herself on her knees, Gian shivered in anticipation of what else it offered.

Bracing her hands on his chest, Cinder lowered herself on him, swallowing his thickness all at once. A burst of sudden pain stole her breath, and she stilled, taking deep breaths until her body acclimated to the sudden invasion.

"It's been so long," she said breathily. "It's like . . ." She struggled to find the right words. "Retroactive virginity. Like the first time all over again."

Gian wanted to respond, to comfort her in some way. But he couldn't, not with the heat of her tight center robbing his will to let her take the lead. It took all of his self-control to stop himself from grabbing her hips and taking the satisfaction he had wanted for so long. He was no stranger to battles. He knew that patience and control were the only weapons needed to win this one, which would have no losers if he kept it together and followed her lead.

Slowly, with rhythmic pulses of her strong leg muscles, Cinder rose and sank upon him. She leaned back and grabbed the highest branches within reach so she could smoothly rock forward and back. Her sighs and quiet moans harmonized with the rustle of the wind through the leaves and the call of crickets, forming a primitive song of carnal bliss with lyrics of one word.

"Gian," she gasped, his hands coming to her breasts to knead and pinch them in ways that left her smiling into the night.

"Gian," she sang once more when he contracted his abdomen to sit upright, to guide her breast to his mouth.

Her breasts were small; their shape, firmness, and sensitivity more than compensated for their size. Her nipple reacted to the brush of his thumb, the dot of flesh growing even harder and more pert. Gian took it gently between his teeth, then closed his lips around it, taunting it with the rapid flick of his tongue.

Cinder cradled his head to her shoulder, her chest heaving. Her abdomen bunched and relaxed in a cycle that left Gian burying his sweaty face in her neck.

"Sweet heaven," he murmured. "Take me with you, baby."

Arms around her middle, he held her as close as he could. Her gaze locked with his, she smoothed errant locks of sweat-drenched hair from his face. There was so much more she wanted to give him but couldn't, not with the tide of passion cresting within her. Gian caught her mouth with his and she tasted her sweetness, inhaled her distinctive pungency. His kiss propelled her to the summit of sensation. Her thighs shaking, her hips drove harder and faster and her inner muscles fastened around him in strong, rhythmic pulses that forced Gian's head back and locked his jaw in a grimace of ecstasy. He shuddered within her and beneath her, his arms like steel around her as he joined her in passion's ultimate embrace.

Tears seeped from Cinder's closed eyes. She reveled in her discovery of true rapture, of how thoroughly love could be expressed without words. Sumchai's touch had elicited all the wrong colors and tension. Sex with her ex had been black and empty, electric in a way that shocked without pleasure.

Cinder felt no embarrassment or self-consciousness with Gian. In his eyes, she saw herself as he made her feel—perfect. She blinked, and the discomfort of the cold grays, blacks, and stark whites she'd always seen with Sumchai transformed into deep reds and purples, striking blues and passionate oranges, blinding yellows and explosive golds erupting with volcanic heat and force, stirring to life something within she'd thought dead.

She surrendered to the want of her body, the need of her soul, her union with Gian Piasanti satisfying in too many ways to name, all vital. Gian took no more than she could give him, and his understanding made it so easy to give him everything, heart and head, sex and soul.

This was passion without fear or worry, only mutual joy at fully sharing each other. His concern outweighed his desire for her, and in his eyes she'd found the one truth she most needed—that he would never hurt her. Causing her pain would never be a requirement for his pleasure. He had waited for her, sure that his patience would be rewarded.

"Are you okay?" Her breathing slowly returned to normal.

Still panting, he kissed her moist brow. "I was going to ask you the same thing." Without leaving her, he fell back on the web, bringing her to rest on top of him. Cinder's lithe body cloaked him, a sheen of perspiration adhering her torso to his. It also helped the breeze carry off their radiant heat, so he wrapped his arms around Cinder to keep her warm.

"I'm fine," he said, kissing her chin. "Thank you."

"Thank *you*," she whispered. Moonlight sparkled in the tears above her lower eyelashes. "I'm sorry you had to wait so long."

"Almost forty years, and worth every second." He wiped away her tears with the pads of his thumbs.

"That's not what I meant."

"I know. But I did mean what I said. I didn't realize it until now, but I've waited my whole life for you. I've never known a woman like you."

"There's nothing special about—"

"What would you say if I asked you to marry me?"

She stopped breathing, resuming only after her lungs began to burn and her head went fuzzy. "That's not a fair question."

"I know, I know," he groaned in frustration. "I shouldn't have phrased it that way."

"You shouldn't have asked at all."

Gian looked stricken.

"If you asked, I'd want to say yes." She smiled somberly. "But I'd have to say no."

"Because of him."

She nodded.

"I'm not scared of Sumchai Wyatt."

"Neither am I. Not anymore."

"He can't control your life anymore. He's in jail. He can't hurt you. I won't let him."

"He won't be in jail forever. When he gets out, he will look for me. Chances are, he'll find me. That's when it'll end, one way or the other."

"Why can't it end my way? With you and I getting married. I'm not getting any younger, you know, and my biological clock is starting to sound like a hammer striking a steel drum. I don't want to die an old maid."

Cinder laughed. Gian widened his legs to maintain balance, to stop her from rolling off him.

"We could have the ceremony at my house," he went on. But then he paused, his expression a bit more serious. "Why don't you ever want to come to my house?"

"You know why." She laid her head on his chest. "I feel safer in my apartment."

"You've never been to my place, so you don't know if you'd feel safe there or not. What could happen to you there?"

"The same thing that could happen to me anyplace else, only it might happen to you, too. I won't put you in harm's way."

"I think you're being too . . ." He finished with a sigh.

"Paranoid?" Cinder scooted off him and lay on her right side, close to him.

Gian rolled onto his left side to face her. "If there's a word less offensive than paranoid that means the same thing, that's what I should have said."

"I'm cautious," she said. "Not paranoid. I know Sumchai. He won't just let me have a life. He'll want payback."

"You didn't do anything to him."

"He doesn't see it that way. He blamed me for everything that went wrong in his life. If he was late for work, it was my fault for not having the coffee ready on time. If his softball team lost a game, it was my fault because I didn't wash his lucky socks. Never mind that he had a weak throwing arm and no coordination."

"Cinder," Gian began carefully, "couldn't you tell that he wasn't quite right before you married him?"

"He had quirks, like everyone else, but when we were dating, they seemed charming. It wasn't until a few months after we were married that he started packaging insults and pinches and little slaps with his quirks. Once I was his, his charm disappeared."

She pillowed her head on the crook of her right arm. Her left hand moved over Gian, her fingers lightly dancing over his skin. Gian inhaled deeply when her gentle touch stirred the flesh between his legs. It rose to meet her belly, prodding her with the impatience of a greedy child.

Gian caught Cinder's hand. "I want to finish talking."

"Okay. Why aren't you married?"

Gian's soldier retreated an inch.

"You're the one who wanted to talk," Cinder reminded him.

"I never met the right girl." He leaned in for a kiss, which Cinder avoided by turning onto her back.

"That's what old unmarried people always say. There had to have been a lot of women in your life. You're a handsome guy, you're straight, you're employed, and you're a hero. Women must have been falling from trees to be with you."

"Speaking of trees . . ." Gian started to sit up, reaching for his jeans.

Cinder pressed him back down and half covered him with her body. Speaking directly into his face, she said, "Have you ever proposed to anyone before?"

"No."

"Why not?"

He opened his mouth, but no words came. He tried again, and still nothing. Just when Cinder was about to shake the words from him, he said, "I know the difference now between love and what I thought was love. There were a couple of women I really liked, but I never imagined what they would look like wearing my bathrobe on a Sunday morning, or if they smiled in their sleep. I never had dreams about a golden-brown little girl with your nose and my ears calling me Daddy. I never drove by Memorial Field and wondered what it would be like to coach a little boy with my throwing arm and your strength in Little League. It's easy to have sex with someone and enjoy going to a movie or out to dinner with them. It's a lot harder to imagine building a life with someone. But it's so easy with you. Those are the things

I want . . . with *you*. I think that's what real love is. And that's the way I feel about you."

"Let's just stay up here."

Cinder's reply was casual, but the quiver in her voice showed Gian how much his declaration affected her.

"It's a little windy, don't you think?"

"I like it." She took a deep, refreshing breath. "It reminds me of New England."

"I'm confused now. You won't come to my house because you don't think you'll feel safe, but you're willing to live in this web? It's totally exposed."

"No one would think to look for me here," Cinder said. "People never see what's right in front of them."

"Hey, Tarzan!"

Gian and Cinder jumped, startled by the shrill call of Zae's voice from the ground.

"How 'bout you and Jane getting dressed and getting your asses outta my tree? I need some help cleaning up the deck."

"We're coming!" Cinder and Gian responded together.

"In that case," Zae said more quietly with a knowing side-eye at the tree, "take your time."

CHAPTER 8

"This is a lot more comfortable than that web," Gian laughed as he came up for air. He'd thrown Cinder's light flannel bed sheet off his head before crawling up her torso. Cinder draped her arms around his neck and kissed him, shifting to align her hips with his. She opened her legs and tilted her pelvis upward, massaging Gian's hardness with her tidy V of curls.

"That feels so good," he murmured, sinking into her. "That's even better."

Cinder stifled his compliments with kisses and wrapped her legs around his hips. Gian's hands were everywhere at once—stroking her thigh, cradling her head, clasping her bottom, and kneading her breast. She'd had him twice and was having him again, and already thinking about the next time she would wrap herself around him to take him within her. Rain had come to her drought-stricken nation, and she craved every drop Gian gave her.

Two hours earlier at Zae's, they'd dressed and climbed out of the tree. After making quick work of Zae's clean-up, they had left her and Chip arguing about whether or not plastic bakery packs could be recycled. Gian had walked Cinder home, stealing kisses in every shadow. Once Cinder had secured her apartment, she had invited

Gian into her bedroom simply by stripping off her skirt, top, and Chocolate Silk.

Like locusts on new corn, Gian had landed on her, struggling to undress as he kissed her. With Cinder's help, he had gotten rid of his shirt and freed himself from his jeans and briefs. There had been no preliminaries this time, not when their hunger was so fierce. With his jeans and underpants bunched at his ankles and Cinder's calves braced on his shoulders, he thrust into her with primitive force, earning a loud, lengthy gasp of relief from Cinder. She'd had nothing stronger than sun-brewed herbal tea at Zae's, yet her body hummed with the pleasant buzz of intoxication.

Gian was responsible for that. She felt needed, wanted, in his company. Even when he wasn't touching her, a mere glance from him was all it took to let her know that he craved her. He'd taught her so many things, not the least of which was the carnal magic of love-making. Even as her body responded once more to him, the rhythmic pulses of her body stacking and intensifying, enough reason remained for her to appreciate what had truly happened between them.

They knew each other completely. Not in details, but in the way two hearts and souls had of finding each other and knowing they were part of the same whole. Gian stiffened on top and inside her, his muscular arms compressing her shoulder blades in an unyielding embrace. She locked her ankles at the small of his back, her hips bucking in a dance of rapturous surrender over which she had no control.

Their acts strengthened her as they weakened Gian, empowering her with the vulnerability he shared with her. She took his head in her hands and raised his face to catch his gaze. The sweaty ends of his hair fringed his face, and Cinder stroked them off his forehead only to have them flip back.

"Forget the tree web," Gian said, a tremble in his voice. "I want to live right here."

"My apartment is so small." Cinder smiled. "There's barely enough room just for me."

"I want to live *here*." He nodded toward her hips, giving his own a slight wiggle. "I could stay right there forever."

"You're nuts." Cinder giggled. "How would you teach your classes?"

"I could get a *gi* big enough to cover you up. We'd look like conjoined twins."

Cinder laughed as Gian rolled onto his back, one hand on her bottom to keep them from separating. "I wouldn't be able to work like this. It would be really hard to reach my drafting table with you wedged between my legs."

He chuckled. "It doesn't sound as romantic when you say it like that." He pressed his chin to his chest to get a better view down the length of his body. His thumbs went to the base of his soldier, which was attempting to retreat. "You're gonna have to do something about this."

"About what?" Cinder glanced down. "Your soldier?"

Gian nodded.

"It's takes longer for men to recover as they get older, doesn't it?"

" 'Older?' " His eyes widened. "I got your older . . ." Gian braced his fingers at the crease of her hips and thighs and brought his thumbs to the dark silk veiling the tiny heart of her pleasure. He found the candy-pink tip hidden under its delicate hood, and, mindful of its over-sensitivity, he worked his thumbs on either side of it with the softness of a whisper. Cinder abruptly sat back, gripping his thighs to support herself. Her thighs hardened, securely flanking Gian's. The taut muscles of her abdomen flexed and relaxed as her lower body moved to meet Gian's thumbs.

"You are impossibly beautiful," Gian said, his breathing rate increasing along with his length and girth.

Cinder moaned, taking one corner of her lower lip between her teeth as Gian filled her anew. The pressure and friction inside and out brought her quickly to another climax, one so strong her legs threatened to cramp. Her breathy cry of release combined with the sight of her supple brown body sent Gian over the top, his groans joining hers.

He pulled Cinder down to lay beside him, his arms too weak to do more than pillow her head with his arm.

"That . . . was awesome," he sighed. "I can't get enough of you. You know, I think your flexibility has improved. Your stamina has always been good, but—"

"You're not my trainer now," Cinder told him. "Don't critique my performance the way you do at Sheng Li."

"That wasn't a critique. I just wanted you to know that I think you're in great physical shape. I could teach you a couple of things, though."

"Oh, really?"

"You forget to breathe," he said.

Cinder sat up on her knees, her hands primly folded in her lap. Unlike Gian, she was energized by their acts rather than depleted. "I can hold my breath for three minutes. Easy."

"Okay. If you say so."

She crossed her arms prettily over her chest. "You don't believe me?"

"Sure, I do." Gian yawned. He dragged one of her pillows to the center of the bed and gave it a punch before resting his head on it.

"I can prove it."

Gian smiled. "Oh, yeah?"

"Yeah."

"How?"

⁂

Gian watched the clock, but he was only scarcely aware of the movement of the seconds hand. It swept past the stylized six, seven, eight and nine on the broad face of the black and white newsroom clock mounted high on the bathroom wall. Each second dragged on yet raced past at the same time as Gian's concern for Cinder battled with the sensations mounting below his waist.

He sat wedged at the back of Cinder's bathtub. His elbows braced on the pale yellow tile at the back of the deep tub, his biceps tensed. Beneath the billowy bubbles floating on the surface of the deep water like whipped dessert topping, Gian's legs and toes tensed in a rictus of pleasure. The water softly buffeted Gian's torso as Cinder, her water-slicked backside exposed like a chocolate heart, showed Gian exactly what she could do to him in the three minutes she could hold her breath.

The first minute had been amusing, fun even. But fifteen seconds into the second minute, Gian had begun wrestling with the urge to bring her up for air and his growing need to take the sides of her head and steer her head faster and himself deeper.

At two minutes and forty-five seconds, Cinder's left arm went around his waist and her right shoulder pressed farther into his crotch. Gian's head fell back, clunking against the tiled wall, when Cinder did something that he could only describe as . . . swallowing.

The warm, soft walls of her cheeks pulled in around him, which gave him a tantalizing thrill of its own, but then that unique snugness grew even tighter when he felt himself drawn so deep that Cinder's nose pressed into his lower abdomen. Gian sounded the three-minute warning with a shudder and a loud groan as Cinder's throat generated a vacuum effect that left him pounding his fists on the tile.

At three minutes, ten seconds, Cinder rose from the water, standing on her knees before Gian. Her chest heaved as she took deep breaths and asked, "How long?"

"It's a new record," Gian grumbled before taking her by the waist with one arm and reversing their positions. "Three minutes, ten seconds. Wanna see how long I can hold my breath?"

"Sure." Cinder smiled.

Gian went under, his bigger body only partially obscured by the water and bubbles. His hair danced in the water, caressing her skin with feathery strokes. Cinder's back arched when she felt his nose open her, followed by greedy laps of his tongue that covered more and more territory with each lick. His fingers dug into the meat of her buttocks as he spread her wider and tilted her upward to fully enjoy her. The scrape of his lower teeth and the rasp of his tongue against the puckered ring between her buttocks gave her a dizzying erotic charge. Gian nibbled her hard, hot pearl while using two fingers to taunt the sensitive bed of nerves inside her.

She almost screamed in frustration when Gian burst through the surface, flinging water from his hair as he looked at the clock. "Two minutes, eleven seconds," he gasped.

Cinder sat up straight and might have put him in a chokehold if he hadn't said, "I can't hold my breath for long, but there's other things I can do for hours."

He stood on his knees and took Cinder's ankles. He pressed them to her buttocks and drove the rigid, heavy weight between his legs into her. Cinder held onto his shoulders, allowing him to control the speed and depth of their union. Their position was perfect, giving Gian's mouth access to her breasts. He licked droplets of bathwater from her nipples, then he suckled them, drawing just hard enough to put a curl in her toes. Cinder held his head to her bosom, her upper back and shoulders butting into the back of the tub as Gian increased his speed, burrowing deeply. Cinder tried to hold on, to outlast him as she had under the water, but the nip of Gian's teeth at her right nipple forced a blissful surrender. She clamped around him, her fingernails marking crescents in the meat of his shoulders. She closed her eyes and happily, eagerly, lost her mind to the universe of warm, bright color turning over itself with each thrust of Gian's hips.

～⁓～

Gian kept still.

His heart drummed faster from the effort of trying to remember every detail of the moment he awakened in Cinder's bed. She lay with her back to his chest, her hands under the left side of her head, folded as if in prayer. Her bedroom was a study in muted shades of green, gold, and umber, her furniture sturdy and well crafted in distressed hardwoods. Books neatly packed her shelving units. Gian was a little surprised to see her comic book collections. Matt Groening's *Life is Hell, Calvin & Hobbes, Bloom County, The Boondocks, The Far Side,* and *Peanuts* were well represented alongside romance novels by Kitty Kincaid, Khela Halliday, and Victoria Ronaldinho. He knew that she had to have had a sense of humor at some point to handle being friends with Zae, and he'd seen traces of it. Her taste in comics proved that she had a sardonic streak that needed to be resurrected.

Paperback classics—*To Kill a Mockingbird, Being Plumville, The Color Purple, A Separate Peace*—their bindings creased from multiple readings, sat prominently at eye level along with slim, glossy graphic design trade manuals.

She had no photos of friends of family in her bedroom, or anywhere else in her apartment. All of her clothes and shoes fit in her bedroom closet and one five-drawer bureau with room to spare from what he'd seen when she'd selected a pair of white cotton briefs and a matching slip gown to sleep in.

The only area of her apartment that seemed lived in was her drafting table, which occupied the corner of the bedroom that best received the northern light. Her work area exploded with color. Her drawings and designs were tacked to giant corkboards mounted on adjacent walls, and they represented everything from cartoonish grocery store and austere pharmaceutical company logos to an ornate, Asian-style painting of a serpent dragon. That image captivated Gian, reminding him of the silkscreens he'd seen in dojos in Japan.

Gian stroked Cinder's upper arm with the backs of his fingers, marveling anew at the wonder of the woman tucked into the hollow of his body.

"It's early," came Cinder's quiet, sleep-raspy voice.

Gian kissed her exposed shoulder. "I didn't realize you were awake."

"I'm a light sleeper."

Gian lay on his back, his hands laced over his torso. Cinder turned onto her other side to look at him. "Something's wrong," she said and sighed.

"I don't like the way you live," he stated bluntly.

"Why not? I'm happy here."

"No, you aren't. You're in a holding pattern. You're waiting. The tragic part of it is that you're waiting for something that probably won't ever happen."

Cinder slipped out of bed. She opened her pale, heavy curtains, allowing a blast of early morning sunlight to strike Gian's face like a laser beam. Squinting, he sharply turned away.

"I think I know my ex-husband a great deal better than you do," she began evenly, leaning against the wall between the window and her workspace. "This can go two ways. If it's gonna be our first fight, let's get on with it so we can get to the make-up sex before you have to open Sheng Li. Or, you could apologize and change the subject. We might be able to squeeze in a nasty little breakfast entrée between the sheets before you have to go to work if you calm my fur enough. Pick your pleasure, Gian."

He saw that there was no point in further pursuing the matter with her. She refused to see reason, at least for the moment. A veteran of all sorts of conflict, Gian surrendered with his pride intact. "Cinder, I'm sorry. Tell me about that serpent dragon on your wall."

Her pleasant, relaxed demeanor restored, she unstuck the clear push-pin holding the art in place. She returned to Gian's side, sitting cross-legged with the eleven-by-seventeen-inch poster propped on her knees.

"The arena is going to be so big, and Zae wanted to make sure that her family and friends would be able to see her when she competed in the tournament," Cinder started, her excitement waking her fully. "She asked me to design some kind of symbol that she could embroider on her *gi*, something to represent Sheng Li. I did some research, and I came up with this."

Leaning against Gian, Cinder pointed out the details she had so carefully incorporated into the design. "Green represents health, vigor—"

"Wealth," Gian put in.

"That, too." Cinder smiled. "But that's why I shadowed some of the scales in gold. To represent longevity, value, and wealth."

Gian peered closer at the work. "That looks like real gold."

"It is. It's only 10K, but it's real. I ordered the paint from a distributor in Japan. The gold detail came from a story about the discovery of the gold Kannon."

"I don't know what that is."

"According to myth, two brothers discovered a gold statue of Kannon, the goddess of mercy, when they were fishing the Sumida River. Gold dragons flew out of the river when the discovery was made."

"So I guess the brothers got stinkin' rich."

"One could suppose." Cinder chuckled.

"This is really beautiful, Cinder. It looks like an authentic *tatsu*."

"I'm a good artist and a good researcher," she stated with pride. "One of the first things I read about dragons is they don't have the same stigma in the Far East that they have in Western culture. They don't breathe fire and watchdog captive princesses. They're benevolent, but powerful. They symbolize power, strength, and the balance between might and wisdom. Buddhist traditions view the dragon as a mythical representation of the hardships we have to face and overcome before we can obtain enlightenment. I wanted to honor Sheng Li and the man who created it. The dragon was the perfect emblem."

"I would be so honored, so pleased, to wear this into combat," Gian said. He put an arm around her and drew her in close. "I want all my fighters to wear it, too. It's perfect."

Cinder fastened her arms tight around his middle and stared at the dragon. Everything it stood for was something she believed in. Gian personified the ideals behind the emblem, and Cinder wanted to represent them, too. After a moment of introspection, she said, "I'm sorry I struck out at you about what you said. You're right, and I know it. It's just hard to hear someone say it out loud."

Gian leaned back against the high, slatted headboard and brought Cinder to rest on his chest. "Last night was the first time you fell asleep before I did."

"I was tired. I could hardly keep my eyes open once we got out of the tub."

"You're so beautiful when you're awake, but when you're asleep, you look like an angel. I've never seen you so relaxed."

"I'm comfortable with you. You know that."

"Is that all?"

Beneath her cheek, Cinder was certain that his heartbeat pounded harder. "No," she said. "I trust you. I sleep easy with you because I trust you."

"And?"

"And what?"

"Is there anything else you want to tell me?"

"I'm hungry," she said matter-of-factly.

"Woman, I've had just about—"

"I love you."

Gian's heart slammed against her cheek, and she turned her face up to his. "Is that what you wanted me to say?"

"Only if you mean it."

"I do."

"Yeah?"

She felt his smile in his whole body. "Yeah. That was practice, by the way."

"For what?"

"When we get married."

"Yeah?"

"Yeah."

Gian pulled her over his lap, cradling her in his arms. "Are you sure?" His joyful gaze bored into hers.

"I want to get on with living my life," she said. Gian began layering kisses on her face. "I want to live it with you. I don't want to waste another second worrying about something that might never happen."

But if it does, she thought before giving herself over to Gian's kisses, *I'll be ready . . .*

CHAPTER 9

With an enigmatic grin aimed at her feet, Cinder walked through the leaves that had been raked into the curb along Taylor Avenue. "Don't you just love that sound?" she asked Zae, who kept pace with her on the wide, tree-lined sidewalk. "It sounds like potato chips!"

"It won't smell like potato chips if you happen to kick up some of the dog poop mixed in with those leaves," Zae warned. "I smell a hot one now."

Cinder threw up her arms and gave the leaves one last kick, sending them on their second flight of fall before she hopped back onto the sidewalk.

"What's gotten into you?" Zae asked, casting Cinder a suspicious glance. "You and Gian must have kept the party going after you left last night. Want to tell me why you were so late meeting me?"

"I had to finish up a nasty little breakfast entrée." Cinder hid a sly smile behind her crooked index finger.

"You went to Muttermann's Diner again?"

"No, I had breakfast in bed this morning."

Zae's eyes widened in understanding. "Did you now," she remarked. "What was on the menu?"

"Italian sausage and a couple of boiled eggs." Cinder chuckled.

"Hard or soft?"

"Soft, by the time I was done with them."

"That man is bringing out the worst in you," Zae teased. "And I'm so glad to see it."

"We had a good night. And we made some plans for later."

"Are you going to the International Festival in Tower Grove Park on Friday?" Zae adjusted the wicker grocery basket hanging from her right arm so it wouldn't snag the sleeve of her orange cashmere cardigan. "Chip said he and Gian wanted to catch the capoeira demonstration at the Brazilian section."

"Our plans are for later than that," Cinder said.

Zae stopped and drew Cinder up short at the entrance to the Kirkwood Farmer's market. "I haven't seen you this happy since we were kickin' it back in college. What exactly do you and Gian have planned?"

Fall was Cinder's favorite season in St. Louis. The bright heat of the sun was friendly, rather than oppressive as it was in the summer, and the absence of humidity assured that her hair looked great every day with little effort or product. The leaves were not as bountiful in color in a St. Louis fall as in New England, but the milder temperatures allowed her to wear adorable khaki short shorts instead of heavier Bermuda shorts. And Kirkwood Market, the place where she and Zae got all their best produce in summer, was a riot of fall festiveness.

The sweet cinnamon-laced scent of freshly pressed apple cider flavored the air, competing with the drool-inducing aroma of kettle corn popped as it was ordered. Bales of fresh hay added their own distinct odor and ambience. Cinder led Zae to one of those bales and sat her down. "Gian asked me to marry him, and I said yes. He didn't want me to tell anyone, but I had to tell you."

Cinder knew that Zae would have a strong reaction to the news, but she was completely stunned when Zae burst into tears.

"Zae, don't," Cinder softly pleaded, placing her hand on the knee of Zae's dark brown slacks. "Gian and I aren't rushing into a wedding. But I love him, and I can't imagine not being with him. He's not like Sumchai, and—"

Full-out bawling, Zae threw her arms around Cinder and wept. Loudly. Her shoulders shaking, Zae wet the collar of Cinder's white button-down shirt. "Baby, I'm happy," she exclaimed through slobbery tears. "I have been so worried about you." She fished a wad of crumpled tissues from her Coach bag and mopped her face. "I wanted you to meet a good man and settle down and have a nice, long, boring life."

Cinder chuckled. "I hope by 'boring' you mean a life with a big home office and a big friendly dog."

"Don't forget about a man who loves you."

Pensive, Cinder picked at the nail of her left thumb. "Are you disappointed that he isn't a black man?"

Zae took Cinder's hand and gave it a firm squeeze. "The only criteria your man has to meet is that he loves you. Really, truly, all the way through with his whole head, heart, and ass. I don't care if he's black, white, tall, short, fine, ugly, rich or poor. He better love you and take care of you the best he can. And I know Gian can."

"So can Chip," Cinder murmured.

Zae sat up straight. The tear tracks striping her foundation evaporated. "What's Chip got to do with anything?"

"Chip is a good man, too. And I think he likes you."

Zae dismissed her with a lazy wave of her hand and picked up her shopping basket. "Chip is fun to mess with, that's all."

"Okay."

"We're talking about you now, not me," Zae said defensively.

"Fine." Cinder smiled.

"There's no law that says just because we spend time together here and there, we're in love."

"I know." Cinder laughed.

Zae suddenly stood. "I'm going to get my apples." She gave her cheeks one last swipe and resumed her usual regal posture. "You can come, if you want to." With a sassy sway of her hips and an exaggerated swing of her free arm, Zae strutted toward the Summit Farms booth.

Still laughing, Cinder caught up to her, overjoyed at the big step she had taken to move on with her life.

Zae grabbed Cinder's arm and tugged her close, snatching her away from the tiny paper cups holding free samples of Summit Farms freshly pressed apple cider.

"What is it?" Cinder whined low, her cider splashing over the rim of the cup.

"Look," Zae whispered loudly, turning her right shoulder into Cinder and pointing over it with her left index finger. "Look who's crating Jonagold apples over there."

Cinder peeped over Zae's shoulder to see Karl Lange in a sweaty T-shirt. He used a stubby knife to pry open wooden crates of apples, and then dumped them onto a big, padded produce scale. He steadied the scale with two fingers, his sweat-shiny arm muscles glistening. Once it reached the desired number, he tipped the bed of the scale into a half-bushel basket adorned with a Summit Farms sticker.

"He looks like Tom Joad," Cinder said.

Zae hid a laugh behind her hand.

"I wasn't trying to be funny," Cinder told her. "How could he go from autoworker to karate teacher to apple guy?"

"It's his temper," Zae said. "Karl is smart, and he's handsome. He has more blessings than most people, but he throws them away with both hands. He'd better get a hold of himself before he ends up in jail or the morgue, because one day he's going to pick a fight with someone bigger, meaner, and crazier than he is, at the rate he's going, and that person is going to whoop his ass for him." Zae looked at her watch. "We'd better get a move on. I've got people coming for dinner tonight, and I haven't even started marinating my meat yet."

"Who's coming?" She glanced back at Karl as she and Zae headed back the way they had come, past angled stands of vibrant fresh produce and homemade candies wrapped in shiny cellophane.

"Just a prospective M.U. student who wants to know more about the school," Zae said matter-of-factly.

"Who?"

Zae mumbled a name but Cinder couldn't understand her.

"Chiclets? Is that what you said?" Cinder laughed lightly. "Come on, tell me who you've got coming over."

"Chip Kish." Zae stopped in front of a tiny, dark wood booth where Thai street food was being served, and she dug for her car keys in her purse. "Chip is coming over tonight."

Cinder peered at the contents of Zae's basket. "Just a casual business dinner to talk about school, huh?"

"Yeah, that's about it." Wallet in hand, Zae stepped into a long line at the checkout, where a woman with flat blonde hair used a stubby pencil and the back of a paper bag to calculate totals due.

"Fresh fiddleheads," Cinder persisted. "Asparagus, fresh feta cheese, and imported black olives . . . sounds like the ingredients for your asparagus salad, the one you only make at Christmas and Easter. You know, maybe I'll stay for dinner at your house, since it's just a casual get-togeth—"

"I'll shoot you on sight if I see you within ten yards of my house tonight," Zae warned. "The kids have an overnight with their grandparents, so Chip and I have the house to ourselves."

"I don't understand why you need a whole house to yourselves for business talk about Missouri University," Cinder said.

Zae glared at her before pursing her lips and punching Cinder in her arm.

"I guess that means you don't want to talk about this anymore?" Cinder chuckled.

Pointedly ignoring her, Zae stepped up to the cashier's table and unpacked her basket. Cinder stood close to Zae, her mind turning toward her own plans for that evening. Gian had invited her to dinner and planned to take her to a Brazilian restaurant he knew in the Central West End. He had told her twice to dress comfortably in something sporty, so Cinder had her suspicions that dinner wasn't all Gian had planned.

She watched Zae pluck a few bills from her wallet to pay for her produce, all the while wondering why Zae was so determined to hide her growing attraction to Chip. Cinder wanted to climb onto a roof and shout her engagement to Gian, perhaps even send a telegram to the Massachusetts prison Sumchai Wyatt currently called home.

Cinder couldn't understand why Zae would be ashamed or self-conscious about falling in love with Chip. They certainly made an interesting pair, one that made sense specifically because of their differences.

Zae was a proud Republican with centrist views more in line with older Southern Democrats than the typical modern Republican. Chip, a registered Democrat, often argued with Zae about his liberal beliefs.

Chip taught at Sheng Li while he figured out what course of study he wanted to pursue at Missouri University with his G.I. Bill. Zae, who had earned a doctorate in English Literature from Princeton, was a tenured professor at Missouri University with seven highly-regarded publications to her credit.

Tennessee born and reared, Chip had that unassuming charm unique to Southern gentlemen. That charm combined with his golden good looks to make him irresistible to most women, and Chip was something of a libertine. Zae had married young, at twenty-two, to the man of her dreams, but she'd lost him to illness after fifteen years. Chip never dated a woman for more than six months. Eight years after her husband's death, Zae had yet to loosen her hold on his memory enough to give another man a fair chance at winning her heart.

Chip was thirty-four and Zae was almost eleven years older, and Cinder could understand a little hesitancy on Zae's part. They were as different as two people could be, yet those differences were what gave their partnership its excitement.

Cinder almost told Zae so, but she thought better of it as they returned to Zae's car. She had faith that all would work out as it was supposed to, in spite of Zae's efforts to control the one thing no man or woman could—the course of true love.

~~~

Fresh mums in hearty reds and eye-popping yellows and oranges adorned the rear patio of Brasileria. Sparkling gold lights hung from the rough-hewn rafters overheard, giving the appearance of dining under a second canopy of stars to the few patrons sitting at the outdoor tables. As Gian led her across the patio, Cinder thought they would have dessert or wine outside following their meal. But, holding her hand, Gian pulled her to a short flight of stairs, across a small plot of neatly cut grass, through a box hedge wall and to an empty lot where tall tiki torches burned into the dark.

"Wh-What is—" was all she got out before a chorus of male voices loudly greeted Gian in English and Portuguese.

"Cinder," Gian started, "I'd like you meet some friends of mine."

The darkness hid their true number, but it seemed to Cinder that at least thirty half-dressed men stepped forward to greet her.

"Hello," she said with a slight laugh, and she tried to catch the eye of as many of them as she could.

"This is another place where I like to train," Gian told her.

Cinder raised an eyebrow. Through the trees edging the wide, open expanse of matted grass, she could just make out the distant silhouettes of playground equipment. Tiki torches of varying heights gave the immediate area an unearthly aura heightened by the drum and bass-heavy beats emanating from a boombox the size of a small sofa. The boombox rested atop a scuffed Coleman cooler with little heaps of discarded clothing and shoes piled around it.

Training? Cinder thought, easing closer to Gian. *It looks more like they're preparing for a human sacrifice.*

"You didn't tell me that your 'someone' was so pretty," said a dark-skinned man, heavy with chiseled muscles, who stepped up to Gian and Cinder. The man's face and chest dripped with sweat, which caught the firelight. He wiped his hand on his loose-fitting dun trousers before he offered it to Cinder. "Luiz Weickart," he said, his hand swallowing Cinder's. "I understand you'll be working out with us tonight?"

Cinder was the only woman among dozens of men. She knew Gian wouldn't bring harm to her, but she couldn't say that with any certainty about Luiz Weickart or the others. Studying the nearest men more closely, Cinder noticed their calloused knuckles, and the grass and dirt stains on their skin and clothing. One of the men set the boombox on the ground so he could open the cooler and grab a handful of ice. He wrapped it in a white T-shirt that quickly began to turn red when he tilted back his head and pressed the bundle of ice to his bloody nose.

"Gian," Cinder began hesitantly, "is this some kind of fight club?"

He smiled at her before catching Luiz's eye. "Didn't I tell you she was smart, too?" he said to Luiz before turning to Cinder. "Yes. That's exactly what it.is. I think you'll learn a lot of things here that'll help you in the tournament."

Gian started toward the boombox, Cinder close at his back. "Gian, you can't be serious," she said anxiously, keeping her voice low. "The only thing I could learn here is how to get my ass beat!"

The man with the bloody nose smiled in greeting and stepped aside, giving Gian room to return the boombox to the cooler.

"I want to go home now," Cinder said firmly.

Gian grabbed the tail of his T-shirt and drew it over his head. Bare-chested, he spread his arms wide and then reached back, stretching his pecs and biceps before dropping his shirt to the ground.

"I'm not fighting with these men, and I won't watch you do it, either!" Cinder snapped through gritted teeth. She turned to leave when Gian raised the volume on the boombox.

The fast, lively music stopped her as cleanly as the sight of the men arranging themselves in a loose circle. Some of them clapped to the rhythm of the drums while others faced off, performing something that looked like a hybrid of a traditional fight stance and a breakdancing move.

"We do capoeira here," Gian explained, stepping up behind Cinder and lightly resting his hands on her shoulders. "It's a Brazilian form of fighting that relies on rhythm and timing. Come on and watch for a little while. If you want to give it a try, Luiz and the others can show you a few basic moves."

Gian ushered her to the perimeter of the fight circle, and two men scooted aside to make room. Gian began to clap, but Cinder stood rapt, watching.

The two combatants lacked the grace of proper dancers, but there was a certain elegance to their moves. Long muscled arms swinging in time to the music, backs hunched and knees unlocked, they began sparring, striking at each other in sweeping, roundhouse punches.

They kept their centers of gravity low, which helped them stay on their feet when their opponents attacked. One of the men, grabbed around the waist by an opponent who tried to take him down, spun out of the man's grasp. In the next second, he was on his hands in a cartwheel maneuver that caught the aggressor in the jaw with a heel.

Cinder cheered and clapped, impressed by the move. "That was incredible!" Cinder turned to tell Gian, only to find him gone.

She searched the faces of the men on either side and behind her, but she didn't find Gian until she again faced the fight circle. Gian stood on the opposite side, swinging his arms in wide circles in the proximity of the other fighters waiting for a turn in the circle. Cinder had seen him do that before, to stretch his muscles and move blood through them prior to sparring.

Oh, God, she thought in horror. *Please, keep him safe.*

Cinder clapped, but the anxious pounding of her heart was louder in her ears than that of the tribal rhythms echoing into the dark sky. Gian's style of fighting was so different from that of the swarthy, acrobatic men before her. Cinder's mind's eye tormented her with images of Gian's beautiful face covered in heel-shaped bruises.

But the second he entered the circle, her fears ebbed. Gian lacked the musicality of the other fighters, but he had rhythm and strength. Added to his power and precision timing, Gian's skills made him an effective capoiera fighter. The wind whistled when he sliced an arm through it for a near miss of his opponent's jaw. Cinder cheered out loud when he went into a handstand to deliver two glancing kicks to his sparring partner's head and chest.

Cinder swelled with pride and desire watching the easy, languid movement Gian brought to the circle. Power, physical and emotional, were truly aphrodisiacs.

The fights were short, and almost as soon as he entered the circle, Gian and his partner were backing out of it. Everyone waited for two more to enter, and that was when Gian raised his hand and beckoned to Cinder.

"Hell, no," she murmured, shaking her head.

"Come on!" Gian moved a step toward her.

Knowing he would pull her in if she didn't get in there on her own, Cinder slowly approached him. The clapping of the spectators grew more raucous.

"Are you wearing anything under this?" Gian asked, giving her short cotton skirt a little tug.

"Yes, bike shorts," she answered.

Squatting before her, Gian took her skirt by its hem and eased it down to her ankles. His eyes gleamed with the smile his pursed lips held at bay while Cinder braced herself with a hand on his shoulder. Hoots and whistles temporarily drowned out the pounding music as Cinder stepped out of the pool of white fabric and faced the crowd wearing skin-tight black bike shorts and a matching sports tank.

Gian dragged his fingertips along her calf and thigh as he stood, her skin tingling along their path.

"This is your basic move." Gian demonstrated the stooped, sweeping arm motion that prefaced a match. Luiz stepped up on Cinder's other side and fell into rhythm with Gian. Cinder quickly picked up the routine, and she instantly understood the point of it. It was easier to change positions if you were already moving, and the hunched posture protected the torso. The arm movements could be defensive blocks or offensive strikes.

"You got it," Gian praised her. "Good girl. You want to try some kicks?"

"Do I really have a choice?"

"Nope."

Luiz stepped forward and showed her a basic kick, one where she raised her knee hip-high, then kicked out straight, hard and fast. Cinder envisioned the effective emasculation of an attacker she used the kick on, and it gave her a little tickle of glee. Her joyous confidence escalated with each new block, strike, and kick. To the casual observer, Cinder might have looked like she was learning the individual steps of a complicated dance, but Cinder reveled in the knowledge that if she sped up the moves and put power behind them, she could defend herself against almost anyone, or at least hurt an assailant badly enough to make him regret his decision to target her.

"Did you have fun tonight?" Gian asked as he caressed her upper arms.

193

"I can't remember the last time I laughed so much." Cinder smiled. "Thank you." She cupped his face with a gentle hand. "I wish I could give you as much as you've given me."

Gian's grin faded. He took her hands and curled her fingers around his, holding her hands close to his heart. "Kid, you don't owe me anything. I—"

"You taught me karate," she spoke over him.

"You paid for those lessons," he pointed out.

"And Webster Groves is starting to feel like home because of you," she added.

"I think Zae and Chip and the guys at Sheng Li had something to do with that, too."

"And you make me love being in love with you."

Gian had no response, at least not in words. He bowed his head and kissed her, nestling their clasped hands under his chin. His lips, warm, pliant yet firm, sampled hers politely, then with more eagerness accompanied by a tightening of his hands around hers. Right there on her shadowed doorstep, he would have peeled off her sweaty bike shorts and hoisted her to his waist, sheathing himself within her. But Cinder pulled a hand from his and, after a bit of fumbling, blindly unlocked the front door, leading him inside with their kiss.

Cinder made it up all three flights of stairs with Gian tugging at the back of her skirt and slipping his hand under it. She never got the chance to lock the door to her apartment.

Gian, his chest to her back, pressed her to the door, pinning her there with one knee between hers. Breathless from the jaunt up the stairs, he panted in her right ear as he lowered his trousers and threw up the back of her skirt. Cinder poked out her backside to help him wrestle her bike shorts to her knees. Hot and heavy, rigid and seeking, he found his entry and boldly shoved into her.

Gritting his teeth, Gian forced himself to move slowly, to give her the same pleasure her slippery sheath gave him.

Cinder had no desire for generosity, nor patience. She reached back and grabbed his bum, urging him deeper, faster. His thighs hard, Gian supported her weight in an incredible show of strength when he pulled her to his chest, allowing their snuggest fit possible. His left hand went to her breast while his right middle finger targeted the sweating kernel hidden within her damp folds.

A few quick, light strokes of his finger was all it took to send bullets of carnal rapture shooting through her. Her fingers clenched, her nails digging into the meat of his buttocks. She threw her head back, nearly butting him in the mouth. Her warmth constricted around him over and over, wringing everything he had from him.

"You leave me weak," he gasped, his thigh muscles burning and shaking.

Cinder released him and turned in his arms to face him. With the pads of her thumbs, she swiped perspiration from his temples. "That's odd," she said. "Because you give me such strength."

"It doesn't come from me," he said softly. "It was always right in here." He laid his fingers over her heart.

They righted their clothing and went into Cinder's apartment. Gian, stroking her back, followed her into the bathroom. Cinder started the taps in the bathtub, sprinkling a handful of Epsom salts into the running water. Gian sat on the edge of the tub as it filled. He took Cinder by her waist and tugged her between his widespread knees. For the second time that night, he took Cinder's skirt off her.

"Gian," Cinder started as Gian helped her out of her bike shorts and sports tank, "why do you like fighting so much?"

"I don't," he said, his tone and expression solemn. "I hate fighting."

"Then . . . why Sheng Li and the capoeira—"

"I've experienced enough combat to last three lifetimes. I hate it. Unfortunately, it's something I'm really good at. When I was in the service, I needed to know how to defend myself. I do what I do with the hope that by teaching people to fight, they won't ever have to."

"That doesn't make any sense."

"Sure, it does. If you have the same or better weapons than an opponent, they're less likely to attack you."

"That just means that everyone will be walking around with the ability to kill anyone they want."

"I hope that people use what they have up here," Gian said, touching his temple, "to avoid using what they have here." He held up his fist, which opened to cup her face. "Some people need the weapons I can provide."

She nodded in full agreement.

He smiled, breaking the tension. "Your tub is so small compared to mine."

"This is an antique. I love the lion's paw feet."

Gian hugged her close, pushing his face between her breasts. He inhaled her scent, enjoying the sweet organic aroma of her sweaty skin. Tempted to flick out his tongue to taste her, he stood to remove his clothing. Gian settled into the tub first, then welcomed Cinder. She slipped into the cradle of his legs, resting her back on his chest with her knees poking out of the water, which sloshed over the edge of the tub every time Gian moved.

"You could seat seven in the tub in my master bath," Gian told her. He lathered his hands with a bar of apricot-scented soap. "Your whole bathroom could fit in it."

"Gian," Cinder began, "are you rich?"

"Why do you ask?"

She almost forgot as he moved his soapy hands over her shoulders and chest, paying special attention to her breasts and their tips, which hardened under his touch.

"The guys at Sheng Li talk about your house as though it were a palace," she said. "And if you have a tub big enough to seat seven, I'm thinking your house must be pretty fancy."

"It's a green house and it cost me next to nothing," Gian said softly, his lips so near her ear, his words caressed its sensitive lobe. "My brother Pio is the family moneybags. He builds ecologically friendly homes called green houses. I bought one of his displays. He sold it to me for an eighth of the market price."

"What's the market price for one of his green homes?" Cinder asked, her eyes slowly drowsing shut. Gian pinched her nipples just hard enough to trigger urgent pulses between her legs.

"In Webster Groves? A little over three-quarters of a million."

Cinder gasped. Gian wasn't sure if was because of the price he'd named or the busy work of his fingers.

"He recently sold one in Santa Monica for six million," Gian said.

"I suppose it all comes down to location." Cinder tilted her head back and turned her face to Gian, catching his mouth with hers. They shared a deep, penetrating kiss that harmonized with the action of Gian's right hand, which had found the heat between Cinder's legs. Two of his long fingers filled her while his thumb mined her hard, extended jewel. She reached back to thread her fingers through the hair at his nape, her backside grinding against his stiffened length.

Still kissing him, Cinder braced her toes against the front of the tub. Her shoulders bore her weight as she slid her wet, soapy body upward until the rigid tool at her back popped out between her opened legs.

Cinder maneuvered herself into position to receive the instrument Gian now guided lightly with his fingertips. He aimed it toward Cinder's yearning darkness and she did the rest, lowering herself until she was filled.

Gian's head fell back, his body trembling. Thoughts of Heaven and eternity swirling through his mind, Cinder's thighs began working once more, allowing her to rise and fall in long, deep strokes countering the rapid, feathery flicks of Gian's fingers at her eager pink pearl.

Cinder took her neglected right breast in hand and raised the firm round of flesh as high as she could. Awkwardly, desperately, Gian craned his head over her shoulder to take the straining nipple into his mouth. Cinder kissed him as he suckled her, her own tongue laving her flesh along with his.

Sensation overloaded her, and her orgasm ripped through her with enough force to make her cry out. She clamped around Gian so tight that he came suddenly, his jaw locking. His teeth fastened around Cinder's nipple, adding another dimension of pleasure to her carnal response. Breathing hard, her jaw clenched and she rode out each rapturous pulse, her hips moving on their own in an ancient rhythm meant to draw everything Gian had.

Her abdominal muscles ached by the time Gian's soft kisses to her head and tender caresses to her torso and legs brought her back to her tub and the man withdrawing from her.

"I'd like you to come to my place for dinner tomorrow night," Gian told her.

Cinder sat up, her hips still wedged between his legs. Methodically, she lathered a washcloth and stroked it across her shoulders and chest.

"You don't want to?" Gian asked.

She ran the washcloth over his left knee, making soapy patterns in the whorls of dark hair covering his skin.

Gian took the towel to wash her back. "Why won't you come to my house? You don't have a problem having me over here, so I know it's not me."

"It's me."

"I don't understand."

"I'm safe here." She relaxed into the weight and warmth of Gian's hands on her shoulders.

"You don't feel safe with me?"

She bowed her head. "None of this is about you."

"I understand."

Her head popped up. Had there been room to do so, she would have turned to face him. "Do you?"

"Your apartment is a controlled environment. You know your security, you know your neighbors, you know the building and when the mailman comes, when the meter reader drops by. There aren't that many unknowns. My place is a whole new world. You're not ready for it yet. I get it."

"How is it that you can explain it so well when I can't?"

"Experience, I guess. I know a few things about fear and what it can do to you."

"Lucia?"

"She hardly ever leaves my mother's house. We don't know what to do. You can't reason with fear, you know?"

"Yes," she sighed. "I know."

CHAPTER 10

"This is the last time we draw cards to pick costumes, and the very last time we have a theme." Gian's testy declaration echoed through the empty dojo. The soft plastic soles of his stretchy red boots stuck to the bamboo floor with each step he took around the big vinyl mat. He surveyed his instructors, his shame growing. "Look at yourselves. Sionne, you look like a parade float."

Sionne spread his arms wide. The top to his Spiderman costume was stretched so tight over his belly, it rolled itself up like a window shade every time he moved. Pulled so far out of shape, the spider emblem on his chest looked like an overfed waterbug. The skin-tight pants worked themselves up to Sionne's knees. The back seam appeared to be on a suicide mission as it struggled to contain the considerable dimensions of Sionne's butt.

Gian swung his gaze to Cory, who kneeled beside Sionne at the edge of the mat. Like a sail, Cory's tattered white shirt flapped in the breeze from the open lobby door. His ripped brown breeches, which were supposed to go to his knees, instead reached his skinny green ankles. The brilliant idea of going to a tanning salon had been too effective. Instead of having his own brown skin coated an unnatural shade of gold or orange, Cory had paid the technician to spray him with green vegetable dye. Cory's natural nut-brown complexion was now as green as the Busch Stadium infield.

"This is the perfect example of why drawing cards is dangerous," Gian complained. "Why are you Spiderman?" He indicated Sionne with one hand, while gesturing toward Cory with the other. "And why is he The Incredible Hulk?"

"We traded cards," Cory explained simply.

"He wanted to be the Hulk," Sionne stated indifferently.

"Hulk *SMASH*," Cory grunted, hunching over and flexing his biceps. Which were the approximate size and shape of baseballs.

"Honest to God, you guys need your heads examined." Gian turned to Chip. "Speaking of heads . . ."

Chip looked down at himself. "What's wrong with my costume?"

"Red underpants." Gian plucked the leg band of part of his own costume. "I never wore red underpants even when I was a kid. Last year I had to be Optimus Prime, this year it's Superman. Why do I leave it up to you knuckleheads to pick the costumes?"

Chip snickered.

"Laugh it up, Blondie," Gian growled. "You're not even wearing underpants."

Chip looked down again. "You can tell?"

"Can we tell?" Cory laughed. "Man, we can tell that your mom and pop didn't believe in circumcision. You can't hand out candy with that thing starin' the kids in the eyes."

"I'm gonna go change," Chip decided. He got to his feet and started for the locker room. Before he disappeared around the corner, he turned back to the dojo, the tall black ears of his headgear standing like daggers. "Gian, you want these briefs? Batman doesn't wear red, but I don't think the kids will mind."

"Hell no!"

"You don't wear gray underpants, either?"

Gian rolled his eyes and stared at the ceiling. "Do I really have to explain myself on this one?"

"I don't see what the problem is," Chip said.

"I don't wear underpants that have been rubbing against another guy's junk," Gian clarified. "Go put on a cup."

Chip and his ears vanished. Gian flipped his red satin cape over his shoulder, convinced that he would trip over the thing at least ten more times before the night was over. "Where's Aja? Isn't she supposed to be here?"

"She's handing out treats to the kids at the Children's Home of St. Louis," Cory said. "She told you she wouldn't be here tonight."

"I wish Zae and the twins would get here already," Gian fussed.

"Me, too!" Cory's eyebrows bounced in enthusiasm. "I can't wait to see their costumes."

"There you go," Sionne said, tipping his chin toward the lobby.

Cinder, closely followed by Zae and her twins Dawn and Eve, entered Sheng Li carrying bulging plastic grocery bags, trays covered in foil and a big brown box.

"Hi, all," Zae called, hurrying ahead of Cinder.

Gian's eyes and mouth opened wide at Zae's entrance. "What the heck are you supposed to be?" He eyed her super-short leather skirt and huge longbow. Her long hair was slicked back and held off her face with a thick leather band similar to the one around her right upper arm. A quiver of arrows peeked from her left shoulder. But it was the lopsided contents of her revealing leather halter that held Gian's eye. "Did you leave something at home?"

"I'm Hippolyta, Queen of the Amazons," Zae stated regally. "Amazons burned off their right breast so it wouldn't interfere with their archery."

"So . . ." Cory started, staring at the less pronounced right side of her halter. "How did you . . . ?"

"I taped it down," Zae grinned. "And I have padding on the left side, to make it look bigger so the right side seems flatter."

"Cool," Cory chuckled. He went to Dawn and took the big box from her.

"Those are candy apples and popcorn balls, so be careful," Dawn warned.

In spite of his mood, Gian smiled at the sight of Dawn in her sweetly sexy devil costume.

"Your costume suits you," Cinder said, approaching Gian.

His bad mood and collection of complaints disintegrated in his contemplation of her. She had refused to tell him her costume, but he immediately knew who she was. Sheer white silk wrapped around Cinder's body, leaving one shoulder exposed and covering everything that needed covering while still starting Gian's mouth watering. Accents in gold—a corset that looked as if it had been fashioned of gold wire, an arm bracelet in the shape of a snake, flat sandals with gold ties that criss-crossed to the middle of her calves, and a fine gold thread draped across her forehead—gave her a divine sparkle.

"You're either Aphrodite or Helen of Troy," Gian murmured through a kiss. "Either one, and you're still the most beautiful woman I've ever seen."

"Zae talked me into it." Cinder smiled. "I wanted to be Charlie Chaplin."

"I'm glad you went with Zae's choice." He wound a dark tendril of her new long hair around his index finger. "I like this. Your short hair is gorgeous, but long hair suits you."

"I like your tights." Cinder grinned. "Blue is your color."

"Don't remind me," Gian groaned. "Superman has the silliest superhero costume. I can't wait to get out of this getup."

Cinder stood on her toes to whisper in his ear. "Do we really have to wait?"

They began backing out of the dojo, but before they could get too far, a parade of princesses, witches, clowns, pumpkins, cartoon and gaming characters and their parents raced into Sheng Li.

"We're on," Gian said. "Happy Halloween."

Cinder squeezed his hand. "Same to you. We'd better give them treats before they unleash their tricks."

"Slow down, slow down!" Dawn, Zae's oldest by three minutes, yelled at the gang of Pokemon-costumed children charging the table where bowls of miniature treats sat.

"Quit yelling at them," Sionne told her. "They're excited. They're kids."

"They're hobgoblins dressed up as kids dressed up for Halloween," Dawn said, a moue of disgust wrinkling her nose. She adjusted the tinsel halo circling her head and carelessly tossed a handful of candy into a trick or treater's bag.

"It's so funny that Eve is dressed as a devil and Dawn is dressed as an angel." Gian snickered.

"I guess the twins switched personalities for the night," Cinder supposed. She smiled at the sight of Eve, who laughed at the antics of the little ghost in her arms, who put handful after handful of gumballs into his pumpkin bucket.

"I didn't think there would be so many kids," Gian sighed. "I hope the candy lasts. Hey, where's C.J.?" he asked, referring to Zae's eleven-year-old son.

"He's at a party. He wanted to hang out with his friends tonight. Don't worry about the candy supply. Natasha has tons," Cinder said, referring to Natasha Usher, the owner of the bookstore next door. "She said we can get some from her if we run out."

"Great," Gian said. "Time for Superman to get to work."

"Have fun." Cinder gave him a kiss, then watched him march off with his own very special treat: coupons for free introductory karate lessons.

CRYSTAL HUBBARD

Cinder took her place at the temporary tattoo table in a corner of the dojo. Children, and even a few teenagers, lined up to choose a martial arts-themed tattoo, which Cinder applied to a hand, arm, cheek, or forehead with a damp sponge.

During her first lull in business, Cinder tidied her supplies. She looked up to see a six-foot Batman staring down at her. "Shift's up," he said. "My turn to stick paint on these little candy grubbers."

"Where should I go now?" Cinder asked. "Gian didn't give me anything else to do."

"Two kids lost their mom, so Gian took 'em into the office to call the police," Chip said. "So there's no one manning the door and handing out Gian's coupons."

"I can do that." Cinder left Chip with a long line of tattoo seekers and went to the front door. She found a stack of Gian's coupons on top of a wire newsstand piled high with *Webster-Kirkwood Times, Riverfront Times,* and *Auto Sales Daily* magazines. Coupons in hand, she stepped out onto the sidewalk as a half-dozen children pushed past her to get into Sheng Li.

"Hi, Natasha," she said and smiled, greeting Gian's neighbor.

"Hey, Cinder," Natasha called from the center of the children gathered around her. "This is some turnout tonight."

Offering smiles and coupons as she went, Cinder worked her way closer to the bookstore. Natasha, the only African-American business owner on Lockwood, met her halfway. "Is it like this every Halloween?" Cinder asked.

"I can't remember the last time it was this warm for Halloween," Natasha said. "The heat seems to have brought everyone out tonight."

Lockwood Avenue, Webster Groves's main street, teemed with ordinary citizens and otherworldly creatures. Across the street in the public parking lot, an inflatable Haunted House entertained dozens of children who shrieked with laughter as they bounced inside. Next door to the lot, employees of Grogan's Superette, dressed as crash test dummies, offered apples and oranges wrapped in tissue stamped with GROGAN'S SUPERETTE *We're the Best!* Every restaurant was decorated and full of customers, with Pelligroso's Pizza and MacDuff's Sub Shop enjoying the most business.

Business was slowest at The Sweet Shoppe, the only candy store on Lockwood. Proprietress Maggie O'Brien didn't seem to mind. Dressed as Glinda the Good Witch, she handed out puzzle and activity books, super bounce balls, paper doll kits, and kazoos instead of candy.

Cinder had been outside for a little over an hour when finally, the initial trick-or-treating rush dissipated. Natasha took off her tall, pointy black hat and swiped the back of her wrist across her forehead. "I should have worn a toga, too," she grinned, her twinkling brown eyes taking in Cinder's costume. "It's too hot for all this black satin."

"I think you look fantastic," Cinder said, and she meant it.

"I wonder who that is?" With a subtle tip of her head, Natasha led Cinder's gaze to a lone figure in black standing under one of the remodeled street lights in front of Grogan's Superette. "He's been standing there for the past hour or so."

"That long?" Cinder hadn't noticed him, not with what seemed like a thousand candy-crazed kids demanding treats, forcing jokes and riddles on her, and pulling at her bracelets and corset. She looked at the figure now. The longer she did so, the more sure she was that he was staring back at her. Her throat, suddenly very dry, she had difficulty swallowing.

"It's probably Karl Lange, considering the ninja costume." Natasha lowered her voice, even though it was unlikely the man in the nimbus of light could hear her from so far away. "He's been talking mess about Sheng Li and Gian ever since he got fired. I don't even go to Grogan's for lunch anymore because I'm sick to death of hearing him crab and moan about getting fired."

Cinder took a slow sidestep toward the entrance to Sheng Li.

The ninja's head followed her.

"Cinder?"

Startled, she jumped a foot to the left when Cory appeared on her right, calling her name. "Get Gian," she croaked, her throat too dry to provide amplitude.

"I'm on my way out," Cory explained happily. "The little kiddies are going in and now it's time for us college kiddies to come out. Mrs. Usher, Gian wants you and your daughters to come over for some Halloween cake. You better hurry. Sionne's already had four pieces."

"The girls will like that," Natasha said. "I'll be right there after I close the store."

"Please, Cory, tell Gian to come out here," Cinder quietly begged him.

"Sure," Cory replied, his smile fading. "Are you okay?"

She stared him straight in the eye and said, "Get him. *Now.*"

Cory stuck his head back in the door. "Gian! C'mere!"

Cory's voice hadn't finished echoing through the dojo before Gian appeared, his red satin cape swirling at his ankles. "What's the ma—"

"That man across the street," Cinder blurted, pressing close to him. "He's been staring over here for a long time."

Gian had to wait for a rowdy group of young adults, likely students from nearby Webster University, to pass before he could see anyone past the traffic. Once the street cleared, Gian looked about. "I don't see anybody."

"He was right there!" Cinder moved closer to the curb and scoured the street in each direction. "He was dressed as a ninja. Natasha saw him, too."

"I believe you." Gian joined her, stepping into the street to better see. "He's gone now, whoever he was." Pulling her close, he wrapped her in his cape. "You had yourself a real Halloween spook, didn't you?"

"He was watching me. I know he was."

Rubbing her back, Gian gave the street one more look. Halloween was a night for fun and sweets, a time for pretend monsters to roam the night. Someone had scared Cinder, and that was enough to make that monster real. "Whoever it was—"

"Natasha thought he might have been Karl."

"That wouldn't surprise me," Gian said. "Let's close up the dojo and I'll take you home. There's probably some gut-slashing, blood-splattering movie on cable we can watch."

"I thought you wanted to get out of that costume," Cinder reminded him. Within the safety of Gian's cape, her adoration and affection for her super man overrode the creepy feeling the ninja had given her.

"I do. The sooner the better." His hands roamed down to her buttocks, and for an instant, he wondered how far he could go with his voluminous cape concealing his actions.

"Cory invited Natasha and her girls over for cake. You still have a little bit of entertaining to do before we can leave."

"I'll make them a to-go platter," Gian said. "I can't wait to climb into bed with the most beautiful woman in history."

"In your history, at any rate." Cinder winked.

～～)

Gian moved through the darkness.

So familiar with Cinder's apartment, he disturbed nothing and made no sound as he looked for her. The bathroom was empty, but for the blue-grey moonlight flooding through the skylight. She wasn't in the kitchen as Gian had first suspected. The spacious living and dining room area initially appeared empty, and Gian quickened his step to return to the bedroom to put clothes on and see if she had gone outside for some reason.

But then he caught sight of a pretty brown foot poking from behind Cinder's sectional sofa. Rounding it, he found her lying on the plush bench positioned behind the sofa to face her wide, slanted living room windows.

Aware of his presence, she sat up, curling a small piece of paper in her hand. Gian sank beside her.

"Did I wake you?" Her voice was raspy.

"Not at all. How long have you been out here?"

Staring at her hands in her lap, she shrugged a shoulder.

Gian raised an arm to embrace her. Before he could, she swung her legs back onto the bench and laid her head in his lap, her hands tucked under her chin.

"Are you still creeped out by the ninja?"

"No."

He stroked her hip through her thin cotton shift. She wore nothing under it, Gian discovered, his hand roaming freely over her abdomen and backside. "Did you have fun tonight?"

She nodded.

Gian forced himself to ignore the effect the movement had on the sleeping creature at the back of her head. "Are you going to tell me what pulled you out of bed, or are we going to keep playing twenty questions?"

"I keep thinking about Danielle."

Gian chuckled. "About the frosting she got all over her cheeks when Sionne challenged her to a cake eating contest, or how she laughed her head off when she flattened Chip?"

Danielle, Natasha's youngest, had been little more than a baby when Gian founded Sheng Li. The little girl had taken her first steps in the cushioned safety of the dojo, and she seemed to believe that the entire world was safe for her explorations, with cushions to soften her landings and a handful of strapping surrogate uncles who would protect her. Danielle had everyone at Sheng Li wrapped around her pinky so tightly, Chip hadn't hesitated—and no one had stopped her—when she decided to demonstrate the GEFS defense technique Gian had created specifically for his youngest students.

"She's nine years old, and she can already defend herself better than I ever could," Cinder said quietly.

"Is that what's bothering you?"

"No."

"This is frustrating." Gian took her by her shoulders and sat her up. The paper scroll in her hand jostled to the floor. Cinder made a dash for it, but Gian got to it first. Without thinking, he unfurled it. "What is this?" The murky black and white image made no sense to him. "Is it a constellation?"

Her face drawn, her eyes wide and melancholy, Cinder shook her head.

"Damn it, Cinder, tell me what's wrong," Gian insisted. Sitting naked in the moonlight, he had never felt more helpless. He could fight almost anything with a better than good chance of coming out the victor, but he was powerless against the haunts in her head.

"I always wanted a daughter."

Her voice, quiet as a sigh, combined with her words and the photo to hit Gian hard in a place a punch would never reach. He took the photo from her and studied it more closely. "This is a sonogram."

"I should have told you when you proposed to me," she nearly whispered. "But I can't be a mother."

Her eyes searched his. The tension in her neck and hands, the tremble in her lower lip, and the sadness emanating from her served as warning. He had to choose his next words with great care.

"Sure you can."

She chuckled sadly, wiping away the tears that had escaped the trap of her lower lashes. "Two very good OB/GYNs would disagree with you."

"You don't have to get pregnant to be a mother. There are a million kids who need parents like us."

Cinder covered her face with her hands and wept, her shoulders shaking with the release.

"I can't promise that we'll take the whole million, but I'm good for two or three. Five, tops."

Cinder climbed into his lap, tightly hugging his neck to smear his face with tears and kisses.

"Sometimes the family you pick is even better than the family born to you," he went on, fastening her in his embrace. "I'm a lucky man, Cinder. I got to pick you. Our kids will be the luckiest kids in the world because they're going to have you for a mom."

Gian entered Grogan's Superette with the sole intention of picking up lunch. Or so he kept telling himself as he walked the convoluted path to the salad buffet in the middle of the store.

Founded in 1952 as a tiny neighborhood grocery store, Grogan's had since tripled its floor space and evolved into a landmark specializing in whole and organic foods. Though it had kept the unassuming label of "superette" in its name, Grogan's was the only place for miles where one could find canned snails imported from France, pancetta flown in from Italy twice a month, and fresh panko straight from Japan shelved alongside Missouri staples such as Vess soda, C&H sugar, and Mama Toscana's toasted ravioli. The current owner, Sean Grogan III, had brought the store into the twenty-first Century by giving it an online presence with a website from which patrons could order home deliveries.

The long line at the salad buffet, the best in St. Louis County, gave Gian a chance to look around. Not for a beverage to accompany his meal, but for a Grogan's employee. Specifically, former karate instructor Karl Lange.

Gian's stomach rumbled. The scents of the day's hot entrees—lasagna, chicken parmesan, fried eggplant, and grilled chicken breast—tickled Gian's nose. Hunger could wait. Gian wanted immediate satisfaction of a different kind once he spotted Karl in the soda aisle chatting with Jalesa Usher, Natasha's oldest daughter.

Jalesa, a freshman at Webster University, was exactly the sort of target Karl preferred. She was young, and with her sparkling brown eyes and pretty smile, she was too attractive for Karl to ignore. Gian had trained Jalesa for eight years and he knew that she was no fool. But he left his place in line at the buffet to let Karl know that Jalesa was off limits.

Or so he told himself.

"I loved your costume last night," Karl was saying as Gian approached. "I saw a lot of diva princesses last night, but you were definitely the cutest one."

"Thank you, Mr. Lange," Jalesa said without looking at Karl, who had rolled the sleeves of his T-shirt to display his big deltoids.

"You're eighteen now, right?" Karl folded his arms over his chest and stepped closer to her.

Studying the label of a grapefruit soda from Italy, Jalesa offered no more than a disinterested grunt of affirmation.

"Hey, kid," Gian greeted.

Jalesa looked up and smiled. "Mr. Piasanti, hi," she said brightly.

Karl scowled.

"Danielle and I had such a good time at Sheng Li last night," Jalesa went on. "My mother told me to thank you for inviting us over."

"No problem, kiddo," Gian told her, although he was staring at Karl. "I'm hosting a mini-tournament on Thanksgiving Day. You and your sister should come by and watch the fights. It's in the morning."

"Good," Jalesa said and laughed. "Because my dad won't want to miss any of his football games."

"Then I'll count on seeing you."

"Great. See you, Mr. Piasanti."

Grapefruit soda in hand, Jalesa started away. Karl leaned to his right to peer past Gian, watching the young woman go. "Natasha sure makes beautiful girls," he said, leering at her. "Where does the time go? I remember when she was in braids, bouncing around Sheng Li in the Beginners class. She was a long way from braids in that leather skirt and tiara last night."

"You saw her last night?" Gian asked.

Karl straightened and fixed his stare on Gian. "So what if I did?"

"Who else did you see?"

"What's it to you?"

"Just answer the question."

"I don't answer to you. Not anymore."

"Stay away from Cinder."

A deep laugh stuttered from Karl. "What?"

"If I ever catch you trying to scare or intimidate her again, I'll—"

"You'll what?" Karl sneered.

"If you have a beef with me, take it up with *me*. Don't take your petty grudges out on Cinder."

"Kiss my ass," Karl spat. "I got better things to do than fool around with Cinder White." He cracked his knuckles and played with the tiny knot fastening his long white stockboy's apron around his hips. "Although I hear you don't. I hear that little fox has you so whipped, you can't walk straight unless she's leading you by the nose."

Gian grinned. "Still jealous that I got the girl, huh?"

"It's not like anyone else had a chance. We all thought you were teaching her karate in the private studio, when all along you were getting paid gigolo-style to dip your stick in her—"

Gian cut the insult off with a quick jab to Karl's mouth, sending the big stock boy reeling into a display of sugar-free two-liter sodas. He charged forward, clashing with Karl, who had lost none of his agility in his weeks away from the dojo. Shoppers stood frozen in shock, watching a very real battle between former sparring partners. Grunts and sweat flew in every direction, plastic bottles of soda bounced onto the gray and white floor tiles, six-packs of canned beverages clattered from shelves. A few cans landed on their rims, popping their tops to send fruity, carbonated sprays of purple, orange, and brown into the air.

Gian and Karl battled on, slipping and sliding on the remains of hissing cans bleeding their contents. In a white button-down, jeans, and athletic shoes, Gian had a little less of the mobility his *gi* allowed, but he moved well enough to counter Karl's ferocious strikes.

In their sparring matches, Karl had always let frustration and temper get the better of him, and this contest was no different. He picked himself up from the collapsed pyramid of ginger ale cases Gian had thrown him into and took a running start to launch himself into a whirling crescent kick. Underestimating the width of the aisle, he cleared a dozen eight-packs of flavored water from their home on an eye-level shelf before he crashed to the floor.

Gian straddled him, using his legs to render Karl's useless. His right fist poised to strike, he clenched his teeth and drew his right elbow back farther, to get as much power as possible behind the impending blow.

"That's enough!"

Chip's bellowing voice couldn't stop the descent of Gian's fist, but Chip's hand did. He caught Gian's wrist and, with a neat twist, deflected the shattering blow meant for Karl's face.

"What the hell is the matter with you two?" Chip positioned himself to back Gian away from Karl. "If you want to brawl, do it in the dojo or in the alley. You don't bring it out in the open. You're scaring folks."

"And embarrassing others." Zae spoke low between her teeth, glaring from Gian to Karl. "Idiots."

"Oh, my God," moaned the day manager, who had emerged from the safety of an endcap loaded with the week's special, 3 for $11 cases of generic diet cola. He clutched his balding head as he entered the soda aisle, the soles of his leather uppers giving him no purchase on the wet and sticky floor. "Who's going to pay for this? Lange, what the hell happened? Mr. Grogan isn't going to like this, not at all!"

"Just a disagreement between old friends," Chip said and smiled. "Gian and Karl had some things to work out, and, well . . ." Chip tightened his grip on Gian, who continued to glower at Karl. "They're all out now. Right, boss?"

"This isn't over by a long shot!" Karl swore. Like the biggest bull in Pamplona, Karl got to his feet and snorted, squaring his shoulders. His head down, he sneered and charged toward Gian.

"Yes, it is, Karl." The manager, hands raised, stepped into Karl's path.

Karl clipped the manager's shoulder as he lunged at Gian, spinning the man in a complete circle. His feet twisted, and he hit the floor. A rainbow of soda instantly tie-dyed his white shirt. He landed on his big belly, instantly flipping onto his back like a beetle. His skinny arms and legs flailed until he rocked himself onto his side and struggled to his feet in a puddle of soda.

"It's time to cool it, Karl." Zae caught him, easily stopping him with an arm hold. "You can't take on all three of us."

Despite her high-heeled T-straps, tight tweed skirt, pale silk blouse, and heavy tortoiseshell-framed glasses, Zae looked perfectly capable of throwing down if Karl forced her. Gian enjoyed a fleeting second of pride knowing that the sexy schoolmarm had his back.

One last angry snort, and Karl jerked out of Zae's grip. "This ain't the last, Gian. Not by a stretch."

"Get your things and go home, Karl," the manager panted. "You'll be lucky if Mr. Grogan doesn't fire you." He shook soda from his hands. "Dear God, this mess is gonna cost a fortune to clean up, never mind what this will do to my waste account for the day . . ."

"Mr. Piasanti will pay for the damages and your losses," Zae assured the manager. "He's a business owner right across the street. Sean Grogan knows where to find him."

The manager, his saturated polyester trousers hanging off him, worked his mouth, capable of no sound other than a soft whimper. Chip helpfully used the toe of his sneaker to push a spinning, spraying two-liter to one side of the aisle.

"We're gonna get Mr. Piasanti back across the street," Chip said, offering an awkward smile.

"And back on his meds," Zae snapped. Her voice cleared a path through the stunned gawkers. "Don't you people have jobs to get back to? The matinee is over. Get on with your business. Folks act like they've never seen a throw down in a grocery store before." She turned back to the manager, who had been following them. "This is what happens when you overprice your boneless chicken breast. It's a dollar and a half cheaper everywhere else in town."

Chip grabbed Zae by her arm and pulled her out of the store. "I've got my hands full with Gian," he chided her. "Can you save your comparison shoppin' for later?"

~~~

"If I'd heard it from anyone other than Jalesa, I never would have believed it," Natasha said. She met Gian and his entourage outside Sheng Li and followed them into the office. Gian kicked out his chair and dropped into it, giving his desk an extra kick out of frustration.

"Look at your hands," Natasha admonished. "You tore the skin right off your knuckles."

"More like scraped it off against Karl's face," Chip noted. He offered Karl's old swivel chair to Zae, who refused it.

More prepared than any Boy Scout, Natasha whipped her keys from the pocket of her full peasant skirt. She rounded the desk and took Gian's right hand. She sorted through the policeman's whistle, store cards, and mini Swiss Army knife attached to her keychain and selected a tiny yellow and green canister of antibacterial spray. Each of Gian's knuckles got a blast while Chip retrieved the first aid kit from the top of a tall filing cabinet.

"Jesus!" Gian exclaimed. "That stuff stings."

Natasha pursed her lips with an impatient sigh. "You just finished tearing up a man's head with your bare hands, and you're going to bellyache about a squirt of antiseptic?" She gave his knuckles another spray and grinned when he winced.

"You should be ashamed of yourself, Gian," Natasha said. She ripped open a half dozen bandages. "What will Cinder think when she finds out that you went over there to beat up Karl?"

"I did it for her. I don't want Karl thinking he can scare her and get away with it."

"Women don't need to be saved," Natasha insisted. "Men just want to be heroes."

"That sounds familiar," Gian said, remembering something Cinder had once told him.

"That's a good way of putting it," Zae told her.

"It's not mine," Natasha said. "I read it in a book. But the lesson applies here."

"Amen, sister," Chip agreed.

Gian narrowed his eyes at him. "Whose side are you on?"

"I don't know what the hell is going on," Chip admitted. "One minute I'm scoopin' the best lasagna in town into my paper hot box for our lunch, the next I'm in the middle of Mortal Kombat. I don't know what to think, boss."

"You said my mother's lasagna was the best," Gian reminded him.

"Your mom's is the best *ever*," Chip clarified. "Grogan's is the best in the Groves."

"Are we seriously having a debate about lasagna right now?" Zae snapped.

"Karl dressed up as a ninja on Halloween and stood outside Grogan's, staring at Cinder while she and Natasha treated the kids," Gian explained. "He had the black mask, the sword, the whole nine yards."

"If he was in a mask, how'd you know it was Karl?" Zae asked.

"I told you that it *could have* been Karl," Natasha argued. "It could have been anybody."

"Who else would be out there deliberately trying to scare Cinder? She's been through so much. This is the last thing she needs, another crazy bastard torturing her."

Zae's gaze flickered toward Natasha before she said, "Cinder told you? About . . . ?"

Gian spread the fingers of his right hand wide, allowing Natasha to wrap bandages around each of his knuckles. "I got a lot of it from the internet, but she told me the rest."

"Have I missed something?" Chip asked. "I thought we were talking about Karl."

Natasha shared a look with Chip. Zae broke the silence. "Remember when I left town for a few days? It's been almost two years now."

"You were gone ten days," Chip recalled. "You upped and left without telling anybody."

Zae's elegant eyebrows arched in surprise.

"Those were the most peaceful ten days we ever had at Sheng Li," Chip remarked, a sardonic grin aimed at Zae. "How could I forget them?"

"I went up north, to Massachusetts. For Cinder. She was recovering from a serious . . . accident."

"Accident?" Gian blurted. "Her ex-husband deliberately tried to kill her."

Chip was taken aback. "Hold on . . . What?"

Gian started to explain, but Zae stopped him with a raised hand. "Cinder married a man who knew how to charm. He was beautiful—"

"So was Lucifer," Gian interjected.

"—and smart. But he was a fraud. After she married him, his true colors came out. He picked her clothes, picked her friends. Picked 'em off, is more like it. Every time I talked to her, more and more of her conversation centered around her life with Sumchai Wyatt. Work and Sumchai. She never talked about her parents or her friends. It got to the point where I didn't hear from her unless I called her. She even stopped sending me Christmas cards. When she called me and told me that she left him, I was so happy, I did cartwheels. But when she told me why she'd left, I wanted to shoot Sumchai Wyatt in the head."

"I thought Cinder looked familiar when I met her," Natasha said, pensive. "I think I saw her on a television news show a couple of years ago. That story broke my heart."

"Well, I didn't see it, so I'm the only one in the dark here," Chip broke in. "What did he do to her?"

Gian answered. "He raped her, for starters."

Zae continued the tale. "That's what finally forced her to see what that man really was. She left him after that, but it still took her about a year to decide to divorce him. She was moving out of their farmhouse when he came in. Cinder said she never even saw him, that one minute she was sealing a box, and the next, she was waking up in the hospital two weeks later."

"Jesus Harold," Chip gasped.

Gian closed his eyes and flexed his sore knuckles against the images conjured by Zae's account.

"He beat her. He stabbed her two dozen times. He cut off her hair. He would have killed her if one of the moving men hadn't stopped him."

"What happened to her ex?"

"He was arrested and got a domestic abuse assault charge instead of attempted murder or manslaughter because he and Cinder were still married when it happened. His attorney argued some horsecrap about extreme emotional distress contributing to his state of mind at the time of the attack. The prosecutor tacked on as many charges as he could—assault, battery, conspiracy to commit premeditated murder—"

"How did they argue that last charge?" Natasha asked.

"There was a policeman outside the house the day Cinder was moving," Zae said. "According to the officer's statement, Sumchai asked the officer's permission to enter the house. The cop, who was there to protect her from him, told him he could go in as long as he made it quick. The prosecution tried to work that into conspiracy."

Natasha shook her head. "I don't understand why he let the man go into the house."

"He said Sumchai looked like 'a nice guy,'" Zae told her.

"Don't they all, until they break their wives in half or shoot them to death," Chip speculated.

"The defense convinced the judge that there was no premeditation, and so Sumchai pleaded out to the lesser charge," Zae said. "He was convicted and sentenced to three years in prison."

"You gotta be kidding," Chip said.

"His attorney pulled some strings and got him a parole hearing six months into his sentence." Zae moved to stand at the back of Chip's chair. "Cinder spoke at it and he was denied. She knew she had to get out of Massachusetts before he was released. She called me and I went up there to help her settle things. A few months later, she moved down here. She's finally starting her life over."

"I won't have Karl giving her a second of fear or unhappiness," Gian vowed.

"Do you think she'll be happy when she finds out you went over there and nearly caved in his face?" Natasha asked.

Gian attempted to defend his actions. "The man needed a warning. He got it. It's over, as far as I'm concerned."

"It better be, or we'll have to form a line to whoop Karl's ass," Chip promised.

"You can't fight a phantom, Gian," Zae pointed out. "You can't triumph over a phantom."

Gian gathered the bandage wrappers and balled them up. "I don't understand."

"Any man who scares or hurts Cinder will make you think of Sumchai Wyatt," Zae started. "When you went after Karl, you were really going after Sumchai."

"I thought your degrees were in English and Literature," Gian said. "Don't assign amateur psychology to—"

"Zae's right, and no one needs a psych degree to know that you are in stupid love with Cinder," Natasha put in. "You'd do anything to keep her safe. What wouldn't you do to undo what happened to her?"

"Nothing," Gian exhaled.

Zae went to Gian. She warmly clasped his shoulder, then sat on the edge of his desk, facing him. "You can't fight the monsters of her past, Gian. You know that."

"You're right. I can't. But for now and the future, I can do my best to keep the rest of the monsters away from her."

CHAPTER 11

His elbows resting on his desk, Gian laced his fingers at the crown of his head and closed his eyes. He relaxed his face—no easy task, considering he had been smiling for five straight hours.

After Natasha had gone back to her store, Gian had tried to direct conversation in the office to Chip and Zae, and why they had been at Grogan's together at lunch. Without answering, they had fled the dojo, each escaping in different directions. Hunger had begun to override his anger, and Gian had been deciding where to go for a late lunch when a man in a sharp business suit trotted across the street from Grogan's.

Great, Gian had thought, both dismayed and amazed at how quickly Sean Grogan had gotten his attorney involved following the melée at his store.

The well-dressed man with his severe side part was an attorney, but he hadn't come to Sheng Li on behalf of Grogan's, which Gian discovered when, hand outstretched, the man greeted him in the lobby. "Hi, my name is Michael Steele and I'd like to sign up for lessons. Are you taking new students?"

Michael Steele looked like he'd be more comfortable on the back nine, brokering a deal between major corporations rather than punching and kicking barefoot in the dojo. But then Gian remembered all the coupons he'd given out the night before. He always had an influx of new students in the days after Halloween.

"The coupon is only good for one free lesson," Gian emphasized as he led Mr. Steele into the dojo. "But if you sign up for a full package, I'm sure we can work out a discount of some kind."

"I don't have a coupon," Mr. Steele said. Following Gian's example, he removed his shoes and bowed before stepping onto the mat. "I was picking up lunch at Grogan's a couple of hours ago, and, well, I got quite an eyeful."

Gian stopped halfway to his office. "I'm sorry, who did you say you were representing?"

"I'm not here on business." Mr. Steele laughed. "I want to learn to fight like you did. I just came from Grogan's. I asked about you and they sent me here." He boomed with laughter. "You should see the soda section. They've got it cordoned off like a hazmat site!"

"That really wasn't my proudest moment," Gian said and grimaced. "What I did over there this afternoon goes completely against the philosophy of self-discipline I teach at Sheng Li. If you came here because you want me to teach you how to behave like a complete dumbass, then you've got the wrong dojo."

"I was told that you were fighting over a woman," Mr. Steele mentioned.

"For. Not over."

"I'm not here to learn to be a bully. I travel overseas quite a lot for business," Mr. Steele said. "I want to be able to handle myself, should something untoward occur. And of course, I want to know that I can protect my loved ones if the need should arise. Proud moment or not, you couldn't ask for better exposure than your fight in Grogran's." Mr. Steele tipped his head toward the lobby. "See for yourself."

Gian looked back. Several men and women, one of whom he recognized as a Grogan's cashier, stood reading his glossy, tri-fold brochures. A few more people were entering. Stunned, Gian took his cell phone from his back pocket. He ushered Mr. Steele into his office, then stepped into the corridor to call Chip.

"Hey," Gian said once Chip answered. "Do you think you could come down to the dojo?" He peered into the studio. The small lobby was quickly filling. "No, I haven't beaten anyone else up . . . I'm the one who'll take a beating if you don't get here as soon as possible . . ."

Having skipped lunch, Gian was starved by the time he climbed up to Cinder's apartment, taking the steep pine stairs two at a time. He knocked on her door, announcing himself as well to hasten the time-con-suming process of dislodging her police bar, unfastening security chains at the sides and top of the door, and turning each of the deadbolts.

As always, Cinder left the chains for last, peeking through the door gap before opening it. She greeted him in silence, but that wasn't the thing that tipped him off.

Cooking was perhaps her favorite pastime, and she went at it with a concentration and determination that baffled him. There had been times when he had arrived to see a half dozen pots and skillets bubbling, sizzling or steaming. Whenever he visited, he stuck his nose in the air to figure out what she had prepared. The heady perfume of oregano, basil, and garlic mixed with the succulent scent of ground veal, pork, and sirloin let him know that one of her Italian specialties was in the works. Cardamom, nutmeg, cumin, and cinnamon reminded him of the few good things about his military deployments to the Middle East. Her skill with Asian ingredients wasn't limited to her expertise at balancing aromatics like five-spice, aniseed, and chili peppers. It also encompassed her fearlessness at working with atypical fare—live eels, octopus, squid, and even sea cucumber.

Usually, the aromas from her kitchen started him drooling before he even knew what she was preparing. But instead of a gourmet meal, Gian smelled the faint citrus of furniture polish and the exotic floral spice of the scented candles she favored. She hadn't cooked, and right then he knew that she had learned of his run-in with Karl.

Small town living, he thought with a sigh, entering and securing the door.

"I'm sorry I'm so late," he told her. He kissed her temple. "I had a rush of new students sign up tonight."

She said nothing, only padded into the living room. Sitting in her favorite spot on her sofa, she tucked her legs beneath her.

"So I guess you heard what happened today." He paused at the kitchen, peeping in to make certain that no dinner awaited.

"I heard."

Her eyes seemed darker, shinier. They followed him as he approached. He sat opposite her in an overstuffed library chair. "Did Zae tell you?"

"It doesn't matter who told me."

"No, I guess it doesn't. If I'd known a public brawl would be so good for business, I'd have kicked Karl's ass a long time ago."

"Do you think what you did this afternoon is funny?"

"I'm not laughing."

"I've lived here in peace and quiet for over a year, and in one day, you've turned me into the subject of town gossip. That's the one thing I've assiduously tried to avoid—having people talk about me!"

"They don't know your name."

"Don't they?"

"Do you really think this will get back to him? Come on . . ."

"Everybody knows somebody who knows somebody who knows you! The world is a lot smaller than you think it is! It's only a matter of time before he finds me, and comes here." Her voice cracked.

"And gets his ass kicked or killed," Gian assured Cinder, moving to sit beside her.

"You can't protect me. I know you want to, and that means so much to me, but you're not like him. You don't fight to kill."

"No? I think my body count is higher than his."

"You never used deadly force against anyone because you *wanted* to. That's the difference between you and Sumchai Wyatt."

"I'm not a five-and-a-half-foot-tall woman who tops the scale at 140. Your ex will have to go through me and all of Sheng Li to get to you."

"What are you going to do? Take him out back and beat him up?" She gave him an exasperated shake of her head.

"No. You will. That's why you came to me, isn't it? So that your ex could never hurt you again?"

"There are ways to hurt people other than hitting or stabbing them." She articulated each word. "When he canceled our plans to go to a wedding at the last minute, when he accidentally—or so he claimed—erased the presentation I was going to give at work when I was in the running for a major account, each time he neglected to tell me that my mother had called . . ." She paused to catch her breath. "There are thousands of ways to wound someone without laying a hand on them, and Sumchai is a master at it."

"You have your own life now, sweetheart. What can he take from you?

"You," she answered quickly. "Or Zae, or Chip. He might go after my parents in Massachusetts, or—"

Gian pulled her into his arms and held her close. "My God, you're tense." He rubbed her arms, hoping to soften her muscles and still the fluttering of her heart. "I'm sorry, doll. I'm so, so sorry. If I'd known—"

She touched her fingertip to his lower lip. "Don't be too sorry. A part of me is glad that you went after Karl."

"Well, which is it? Are you pissed or proud that I got into it with Karl?"

"Both." She rested her head on his chest, right under his chin. "I was so scared when I saw him staring at me from Grogan's. I froze. Sumchai used to do that. He would just stare at me, and I'd go nuts trying to figure out what was out of place, what was dirty, what I'd bought that I shouldn't have. It was torture.

"Even though Natasha was with me that night, I started to feel that old anxiety and nausea that would make my stomach and head hurt while I waited for Sumchai to finally say something insulting that would point out my 'mistake'. The worst was when he'd grab me by the back of my neck and point me toward what I'd done wrong, as if I were a poorly trained dog. You did to Karl what I wanted to do to Sumchai. That sounds so awful."

"It sounds human. There's only so much a person can take before they snap."

"Did you ever snap when you were in the service?"

"No. The pressure was there, for sure, and sometimes it was hard to separate the business of a mission from the personal feelings it might evoke. But I never lost control."

"Karl brought out the beast in you?"

"I guess so." He pressed a kiss to the top of her head.

Gian's stomach growled. The rumbling resonated through his torso and into Cinder's ear. She laughed, finally relaxing in his embrace.

"I haven't eaten since breakfast," he said.

"I could rustle up something." Cinder rolled off the sofa and went into the kitchen.

Tired, Gian was slow to follow. By the time he pulled himself to his feet and went after her, she was returning, a foil-covered hump on a plate in one hand and a sweating bottle of beer in the other.

"Leftovers?" Gian's salivary glands reacted immediately to the promise of food, at long last.

Cinder set the plate on the low table before the sofa. She removed the foil as she sat.

Gian moaned. "That is the most beautiful thing I've seen all day." He sat down and cracked open the beer. "Present company excepted, of course," he added with a beer-bottle salute.

Cinder curled up on the sofa. With her right knee pulled to her chest, she laced her fingers together over her right foot, propping her chin on her knee. She smiled, watching Gian dive into his meal.

Hungry as he was, Gian spent a short moment marveling at the sandwich—which was no mere sandwich— she had prepared. It was a classic Dagwood elevated to culinary art. He identified five different meats, including mortadella— his favorite— and at least three varieties of cheese layered between the halves of an eight-inch ciabatta roll. Romaine lettuce, red onion, tomato, and green bell pepper slices complemented the cold cuts. Gian devoured three hearty bites. "What else is on here?"

"I made a sandwich spread. Minced black, green, and kalamata olives, capers, sautéed shallots, Dijon mustard, and a few spices mixed into a little basil oil. I also splashed a bit of white balsamic vinegar on top of the vegetables. Do you like it?"

Smiling around bulging cheeks full of the sandwich, he leaned over and kissed her, smearing a corner of her mouth with oil.

"That good, huh?" She laughed lightly.

"Better," he answered, chomping off another bite.

Cinder got up for napkins.

Gian licked his fingers. He was wiping his hand on his jeans when Cinder returned. "I'm starting you on something new this month. Make sure you bring your mouth guard to class tomorrow night."

Cinder gave him a few paper napkins. "That sounds interesting. What are we doing?"

He grinned. "Weaponry. Every two weeks between now and the tournament, you're going to learn a new weapon, and you'll learn how to improvise them in the field."

"What field?"

"Home. The street. The middle of a department store." He licked his fingers. "The field is anyplace you find yourself having to defend yourself."

"Why would I have to defend myself in the middle of a department store?"

"It was just an example. Hopefully, nothing ever happens at Macy's that would lead to you busting skulls. But if you ever have to, you'll know how."

"Sounds fun." She giggled.

Gian finished the sandwich and followed it with two cups of coffee and a slice of gooey butter cake. In her darkened living room, he and Cinder cuddled on the cushioned bench behind the sofa to watch a meteor shower. She kissed him every time they saw a shooting star. With the shooting stars coming more frequently and the kisses lasting longer, Gian decided to bid her good-night while he thought he still could.

"I can't stay, sweetie. I've got fifty new students to process." He gave her a final nip to her lower lip and started for the door. "They want to start immediately, and I've got to get them on file for insurance purposes before they can work out in the dojo."

"Are you sure you can't stay?" Pressing her chest to his back, she slipped her right hand into his pants. He stopped abruptly at the door. "I think one of you might want to stay awhile longer." She nuzzled his back with her nose. "He's at full attention now. He definitely wants to stay."

Her fingertip traced delicate circles over the sensitive bed of nerves at the back of his little soldier's head. Not so little anymore, it seemed to buck and rear to battle its way out of his jeans. "I suppose we could stay for a few more minutes."

"Minutes?" She flicked her tongue over his earlobe, then suckled it.

Gian moaned, his response incoherent.

"What was that?"

"I'm not going anywhere." In one rough motion, he turned and kissed her, taking her by her backside to lift her. Her arms and legs locked around his neck and waist. Pressing her into the wall, his hands went into her hair, clutching her head. He spoke to her in the language of desire. Through the fluency of his kisses, he showed her that there was nothing he wouldn't do for her, this woman whose kisses blessed him, whose body gave him new life every time she shared it with him. Her strength was total, and elastic in the way it stretched over him, giving him the invincibility that weapons and fighting skill never could.

"I love you." He stroked her hair from her face, caressing her cheek, her lips.

The earnest intensity of his declaration seemed to startle her out of their kiss. She cupped his face, holding his gaze. He wondered . . . hoped . . . she saw the weight and truth of his love.

Her lower lip trembled. Tears glistened, but failed to fall, from her lower lashes. "I know," she said.

Gian touched his forehead to hers. There was no arrogance in her response, only humble gratitude and acceptance. He carried her into the living room and fell into the comfortable depths of the sofa with her, determined to show her, in every way he knew, how very much he loved her.

"Did you get a cat?"

Gian looked up from the applications and insurance forms spread over his desk to see Chip enter his office. Chip's fresh white *gi* temporarily blinded Gian. "No, I don't like cats," Gian answered, returning to his paperwork. "Why do you ask?"

"Your face. Looks like you got into a fight against something with sharper claws than Karl."

Absently touching his face, Gian remembered the nicks he'd given his jaw and neck during his hasty morning shave. "I really wish people would stop mentioning that."

"They will," Chip assured him. He took the chair facing Gian's desk. "Just as soon as something more interesting happens around here. You're the talk of the town. I was at the university last night, and a lot of people asked me about it there."

"What were you doing at Webster?"

"Lecture." Chip scratched his chin, his gaze toward the ceiling. "Nothin' big."

Gian set down his ballpoint pen and leaned back in his chair, his fingers laced over the knot of his *obi*. "Since when are you interested in lectures?"

"Since recently. It ain't no thing, Gian." Chip forced a cough. "I'm gonna grab a bottle of water before my first class, boss."

"Hold up." Gian grinned. "What was the lecture on?"

Chip's gaze seemed unable to find Gian. "Just some talk on woman warriors . . ." His voice dropped off, his words running together unintelligibly.

"What's that again?" Gian tried not to laugh as Chip squirmed.

Chip sighed. "Waking the Warrior in Every Woman," he drawled.

"Is there a woman warrior in particular who interested you in the subject?"

"Don't go there, man."

"I'm not trying to pry. I just didn't know you had an interest in that sort of thing."

"Neither did I," Chip replied, "until the speaker started talkin'. It was . . . enlightening."

Enlightening? That was a Professor Zae Richard word if Gian had ever heard one. "Did you go alone?"

Chip hopped out of the chair and went to the desk that had once been Karl's. "Hey, I got my applications processed." He took up a sheaf of forms and gave them to Gian. "I finished 'em before I left last night. What time did you finally get outta here?"

"Around eight. I got involved with something and didn't get home until early this morning. I wanted to come in early to process the applications I took yesterday." Gian glanced at the wall clock. "I've been here since six."

"You've been at this for three hours?"

Gian nodded. "I had to get them done. Our first group of new students came in at seven-thirty for the first Dangerous Housewives class of the day." He reached back and tapped the schedule with the tip of his pen. "Aja's got two new Brees, two Gabbys, one Susan, and one Edie."

"No new Lynettes?"

Gian bent over his work. "The Lynettes don't tend to need self-defense classes."

"Have you talked to Cinder yet?"

"Yeah. We're good."

"Are *you*?"

Gian raised his eyes to Chip. "I don't follow."

Chip sat back down. Resting his elbows on his knees, he leaned in toward Gian. "Don't take this the wrong way, but I don't think you're using your brain when it comes to Cinder."

Gian's face hardened. If anyone else had said that, chances were good that he'd be brawling again. He waited until the muscles in his jaw relaxed before he said, "Cinder and I have more than a physical relationship. We couldn't be more different, but in the ways that matter, we understand each other. I find balance with her, and I think I give that to her, too. If you think I went after Karl yesterday because I'm being led by my dick, then—"

"That's not what I meant," Chip cut in. "I think your heart leads you when it comes to Cinder. Your brain takes a backseat. When we were on tour, you were the best commander because you were so logical. So reasonable. You didn't let emotion figure into the choices you had to make, and I know how hard some of them were for you. I think . . ." Chip chose his words very carefully. "I think you should balance the heart with the brain when you run into situations like what happened on Halloween."

"When did you get so wise?"

Chip smiled. "Not wisdom. Just good horse sense."

"Maybe it's the company you're keeping," Gian suggested.

Chip stood and turned, unsuccessfully hiding a grin and a blush.

"Who did you say you went to that lecture with?" Gian persisted, enjoying Chip's discomfort.

"I didn't." Chip looked at the place on his wrist where a watch would have been, had he been wearing one. "Look at the time, boss. I think I'll go help Aja set up for her next class since she's got so many new students."

"Good idea." Gian chuckled. Right before Chip cleared the door, he called, "Hey . . ."

Chip turned in the doorway.

"Thanks."

"Anytime, boss."

CHAPTER 12

Cinder shouldered her way through the crowded lobby and hurried past the students lining one wall of the dojo. Gian had told her that he had new students, but he hadn't mentioned numbers. Chip's beginning taekwondo class appeared to have doubled in size while at least ten more new students in the lobby waited for the start of the five-thirty Strength & Conditioning class.

Cinder was turning into Gian's office as Gian rushed out, and he had to catch her by her shoulders to keep from stampeding over her.

"You weren't kidding," Cinder said. "There are so many new faces here today."

"Every class has been packed," Gian told her. "I have to split up Aja's five o'clock because I don't think she can adequately manage all the new students. I had to call one of my former students in to help me teach since Aja's working with you tonight."

"Why?" Cinder clutched the braided strap of her gym bag a little tighter.

"You're starting weapons tonight, remember?"

"Aren't you teaching me?"

"Gian!" Chip stuck his head around the archway. "Could you come out here? I've got someone who wants to sign up for classes, but he wants to talk to you about a payment plan for his tuition."

"I'll be right there," Gian told Chip. He cupped Cinder's face. "Aja's better at weaponry than I am. You're ready, honey."

"I know, it's just . . ." She stared at her feet, but then looked up at him with a slight smile of confidence. "I'm so used to you."

He gave her a quick kiss. "You'll like Aja." He backed toward the dojo. "Everyone does. Stay focused and you won't get hurt."

"Thanks," she muttered at his back as he disappeared.

Her step less eager, Cinder went to the private studio.

Aja had remained an enigma in the course of Cinder's association with Sheng Li. Like "Maris" from *Frazier*, Aja existed for Cinder only through hearsay. Curious and wary, she entered the private studio.

According to Zae, Aja was Sheng Li's most experienced instructor. She was the most decorated, with seventy fighting titles and belts. Tough and resourceful, Aja had emigrated alone to the United States from Japan at seventeen years old. Cinder admired her for that even as she feared Aja's prowess with weapons she had only seen in Ninja Turtle movies.

I have the wrong movies in mind, Cinder told herself after stepping into the studio. *She's Yoda.* Shock obliterated Cinder's nervous jitters. No Asian version of Zae awaited her at the tall cabinet in the far corner. Not unless Zae had been hacked off at the knees and aged thirty years.

The small woman turned around. "Miss White?"

"Yes," she nodded. "Yes, sensai." Cinder bowed.

The little woman approached. Though she appeared to have no difficulty walking, she carried a staff a foot taller than she was. Cinder doubted Aja topped five feet. Her *gi*, if it could be called that, consisted of a tunic that appeared to be two rectangles of coarse, drab fabric hand-sewn at the shoulders and sides. The unfinished edges of the armholes were frayed, and Cinder was tempted to reach out and pluck the loose threads fluttering at the hard muscles of Aja's shoulders.

Aja's gnarled toes poked from crude rope sandals. Her formless trousers swam around her hips and legs. When she smiled up at Cinder, her craggy face splintered into a thousand wrinkles that radiated from the corners of her black eyes and her mouth. Wispy silver and black strands of her hair had freed themselves from the loose bun at her nape to elegantly frame her broad face. Cinder found her oddly beautiful, like a perfect piece of driftwood, or desert dunes after a windstorm.

The hand gripping the staff was all knuckles, its deeply cracked, heavily lined skin revealing a long life of hard work. The old woman moved with the strength and agility of a gymnast, and the muscles bunched in her arms and shoulders looked hard and strong as she flipped the stick horizontally, shoving it at Cinder. She issued a rapid-fire command in heavily-accented English.

"I'm sorry," Cinder started, struggling to steady the staff, which was heavier than it looked. "I didn't quite understand you."

"Find the balance," Aja repeated more slowly, and a bit more loudly.

"I don't underst—"

Aja grabbed the staff back, gripping it firmly at its midpoint, her hands a few inches apart. She gave it a little shake. "Find the balance. Find the center of the bo to find its strength."

Cinder took the staff. She adjusted her grip, copying Aja. The bo seemed much lighter once she had it centered.

Aja marched back to the cabinet. She took two sticks the approximate length of her arms from a lower shelf. Smiling, she started back to Cinder. Ten feet away, Aja began swinging the sticks, screaming shrill fight cries that brought the fine hairs on Cinder's arms to attention.

Instinctively, she warded off Aja with the bo, holding it horizontally to block slashing strikes, vertically to avoid side-to-side swings that whistled through the air. The staccato notes of the bo clacking against the shorter sticks echoed in the studio. Aja didn't stop her charge until she'd backed Cinder into the wall.

"Good, good," she praised, holding her sticks under one arm to give Cinder a proud clap on the shoulder. "Gian taught you well."

"We've never used weapons before," Cinder admitted, panting. "This is my first time."

Aja's second proud slap to Cinder's arm nearly rocked her off her feet. "You got good instincts," Aja said. "You want to survive a fight. Your head trusts your body to know what to do to protect itself."

"Does my grip make a difference?"

"You're a smart girl, very smart. That is a very good question."

Again, Aja snatched the bo. Holding it in an overhand grip, she said, "This is wrong. This is how you hold oars to row a canoe. Do you think you will fight a canoe?"

"No, sensai," Cinder answered.

Aja switched her hold, one hand over, the other under. "You hold it like this, the right way. You get more control. You can switch direction faster without losing your grip or the strength in your block or swing." She demonstrated, her movements powerful and precise as the bo slashed gracefully in every direction.

After nearly an hour of practice and sparring, Aja led Cinder to the cabinet. She opened the doors. Cinder expected to see more weapons, and she did. But she also saw a box of spaghetti, a canister of air freshener, and a few long wooden dowels. Aja selected a dowel.

"See this?" She held it, hands wide apart. "It's the same size as the stick of your broom or mop. What will you do if an intruder comes into your home? Do you have your own cabinet with the bo, the club or the bolo? No!"

Cinder jumped, startled by the sharpness of Aja's last syllable.

"But you have a broom." Aja grinned, her eyes gleaming with animal cunning. "And you have a mop." She raised the dowel and snapped it over her knee. "And now, you have your own pair of eskrima sticks." The jagged ends of each half aimed at Cinder, she worked them in slow circles as she had her other pair of sticks.

"Your home will protect you," Aja continued, placing the dowel halves in the cabinet alongside her genuine eskrima sticks. "A package of spaghetti, a can of air freshener, your rolled up newspaper—all are weapons."

"I don't see how you can hurt someone with spaghetti," Cinder said.

Aja pulled one strand of uncooked spaghetti from its box. Cinder almost giggled when Aja hit her forearm with it. "One is good for nothing." She took the entire box of spaghetti. "But together . . ." She whapped the side of the cabinet with it.

Cinder winced at the resultant *BAM!*, imagining the package crashing into human flesh.

Aja jabbed at her with it, showing her another defensive maneuver. Impressed, Cinder studied Aja's every move, especially her use of a newspaper as a weapon.

Aja held up a flat-folded issue of the *St. Louis Post-Dispatch*. "Like this, what happens when I hit someone?" She swatted at Cinder with the newspaper. The sections slid apart harmlessly, the sales circular floating to the mat. "Paper flies all over," Aja answered herself. She rolled the paper into a tube, her forearm muscles working as she gave it a savage twist. She lunged at Cinder, driving her back in a move the Three Musketeers would envy. "What's black and white and red all over?"

"I have no idea," Cinder nearly whimpered.

"Your opponent, after you beat his ass with this." With a loud clap, Aja brought the end of the newspaper down into the palm of her left hand. "You can easily break the cartilage of the nose or the larynx with this. You can jab an eye or his tenders."

Cinder's eyebrows drew closer, relaying her confusion. *Tenders?*

Aja jabbed at Cinder's crotch, pulling the blow an inch from her target.

"That would be really bad news for someone dumb enough to attack you," Aja chuckled, handing the newspaper to Cinder.

Cinder tested it herself, lightly tapping it against her palm and her thigh. The twist in the tube made all the difference. The newspaper was hard, almost like wood.

"A roll of aluminum foil is just as good," Aja instructed. "In or out of its box."

Cinder sparred with Aja a little longer, taking a turn with the eskrima sticks and snapping a dowel in half, which hurt her knee a little more than she thought it would. At the end of the class, she thanked Aja, who told her that she'd see her in two days for their next lesson. Her future decided for her, Cinder took a quick shower and dressed in her jeans and cable-knit sweater. She looked for Gian, but his office was empty and his new instructor was finishing the class in the dojo.

I'll call him later, she thought. Her gym bag slung over one shoulder, she left to walk home.

Pedestrian and road traffic was light. The glow of brightly lit storefronts warmed the November night, taking any chill Cinder might have felt. Fall in Webster Groves was very different from that in New England. The few people Cinder encountered had bundled themselves in heavy pea coats, parkas, scarves, gloves, mittens, and knit hats. Compared to the twenty-degree nights she'd known in Manchester-by-the-Sea, Webster Groves's current thirty-nine degrees was positively balmy.

Her left thumb hooked through her belt loop, Cinder was comfortable in nothing more than jeans, a thick sweater, and her cross trainers, even with her hair still slightly damp from her shower. She took a deep breath as she walked past Kenary Florist, A-1 Printing, and the other shops lining Lockwood Avenue. Webster Groves smelled like . . . Webster Groves. Fresh and pleasant with the smell of snow, the air was bereft of the scents Cinder most loved: burning leaves, pine trees, crushed crabapples, and wood fires.

She sighed, not unhappy, but not entirely happy, either.

New England was home and always would be. Webster Groves had yet to engender that level of comfort and contentment within her. She turned right at the corner of Lockwood and Elm, proceeding south on Elm. Dense canopies of tall sweet gum trees still partially dressed in their fall colors obscured the light from the street lamps. She made a game of her last block home, deliberately stepping into the puddles of light dappling the sidewalk.

Webster Groves might not yet feel like home, but Cinder was closer to that feeling than she'd ever been. Zae, certainly, had done her best to welcome Cinder into her world, to help her start living her own life again. Sheng Li had been Zae's greatest gift toward that. Gian and his team were like family. Chip, the older brother she'd never had, was protective almost to a fault. Cory alternated between annoying younger brother and amusing cousin. Aja, now that Cinder had finally met her, was the wise matriarch, someone who existed outside the day to day relationships yet remained an integral part of everyone's life. Sionne defied explanation, but Cinder knew that he would kill or maim to protect her, just as he would for any other member of the Sheng Li family.

Cinder paused on her front porch. That was it, really. With Gian at its helm, Sheng Li had become her family.

She didn't rush right into the house and up to her apartment. Instead, she set her gym bag on the narrow planks of the wood floor. She swept dead leaves from the porch swing, then sat to wait for Gian.

The porch swing gave her a great view up and down Elm and of the house across the wide street. The family inside had their dining room drapes tied back, so Cinder had a front-row seat to their dinner hour. A modern-day Norman Rockwell scenario played out before her, with an attractive, smiling mother using oven mitts to set a steaming casserole dish in the center of the dining table. Three children, two boys and one girl, sat around the table. The older boy, surely a high-schooler, talked to his father, who sat at the head of the table. The other two children seemed to be bickering.

Cinder imagined that the scene before her was occurring in dining rooms throughout the world. What made this one special to Cinder was its proximity. Right before her, she saw everything she had ever wanted, everything she could have for herself. It was near enough to touch.

Perfect might be too much to ask, Cinder reasoned. *I could be happy with good enough.*

God, Fate or some other divine force must have been listening in on her peaceful musing, because at that moment, snow began to fall. Cinder went to the porch rail. She stuck her hand into the night and let the dry, sparkly flakes collect on her palm. More like flecks of ice, the snow glittered in the yellow-gold glimmer of street lights transforming the quaint, tree-lined street. It looked like a scene in a snow globe, until she heard quick footsteps pounding the sidewalk. Gian came into view in his faded jeans and beat-up leather car coat, and right then Cinder realized that she had better than good enough. She had perfect after all.

She met him with a kiss on the walkway to the front door. She smiled into it, the cold tip of his nose giving her a tickle as it brushed hers.

"Hey," he greeted her, his hands at her waist. "Why didn't you wait for me?"

"I didn't know how long you'd be." Holding his hand, she led him to the front door of the Victorian. "It's a nice night. I had a good walk home."

"Are you just getting here?" Gian blew on his hands while Cinder unlocked the door.

"No, I sat out here for a while." She opened the door, allowing Gian to enter the brightly lit foyer first. "I was watching the family across the street."

"Gettin' the hang of small town life, huh," Gian said and laughed.

Cinder closed the door. "I guess." She bolted the deadlock. "They—" She stopped short, hooding her eyes with her hand to better see into the night. She thought she'd spotted a thread of reddish-orange light zig-zagging within the tall yew bushes lining the front lawn of the house she'd been spying on.

"What is it, honey?" Gian stood atop the first stair-well leading to the attic.

Cinder spent another silent moment watching the yew bushes shudder as something within them moved from one end of the house to the other and around the corner. The hairs on her back of her neck and arms stood, and not because of an autonomic response to the cold air. She strained her eyes, trying to make out the creature moving in her neighbor's front yard.

Was it a cat in the neighbor's tall hedgerow? A possum? A person . . . ?

Her mouth went dry. Her hand trembled on the doorknob.

"Cinder?" Gian walked down a few stairs. "Are you okay?"

She might have shared her sudden apprehension with Gian if she hadn't seen a big gray body with a long, bushy striped tail weave out of the hedgerow and back into it.

"I'm fine," she finally answered, relaxing. Joining Gian on the stairs, she wanted to kick herself. No one had seen Karl Lange in days, not since he'd been fired from Grogan's. She realized how absurd it was for her to think that Karl would sneak onto her neighbor's property to spy on her.

Wasn't it . . . ?

CHAPTER 13

"Aja was wonderful." Cinder took off her sweater and slung it over the back of a dining room chair. "I learned so much from her. The hour just flew by. I think I might sign up for her class. " She ran her fingers through her hair to discharge the static electricity the removal of her wool sweater had put there.

"I think that would be a good idea," Gian said. "But you'd better do it soon. I'm going to have to set a limit on class sizes, because we were swamped tonight. Although at least a quarter of my new students will quit within three weeks and another quarter will stop showing up within two months."

Cinder took his jacket and hung it in the foyer closet. "Don't be so pessimistic."

Gian wearily sank onto the sofa. "I'm just stating a fact. That's why I give the free trial classes, so that potential students can see what they're getting themselves into before they make the investment."

Cinder sat beside him and let him fold her into his side. "I think you're going to be surprised. You won't lose many students. You run a really good shop."

"I try."

"You're going to have even more students after the International Martial Arts tournament."

"Speaking of that," Gian started, "you have to think up a name to use in the exhibition match. Zae chose Hippolyta."

"She's getting a lot of mileage out of her fascination with Amazons."

"I'm trying to get her to change it to something a little more crowd-friendly." Gian ran his hand over Cinder's hip.

"Why do we have to use pseudonyms anyway?"

"It's part of the fun of the exhibition matches."

"Why didn't you put me in the fight round?" Her head on his shoulder, she tipped her face to look at him.

"Because most of the competitors in your weight class won't have been taught one-on-one by a seventh-degree shodokan for six months," he explained. "You're better trained than ninety percent of the people who'll enter the tournament."

"What about the other ten percent?"

Gian's abdomen jumped as he chuckled, lightly jostling her. "They'd probably play with you for a while before wiping the mats with you."

"What's Aja's skill level?"

"She's probably forgotten more fighting techniques than I'll ever learn. As good as her physical skills are, her mental skills are even better. Her greatest weapon is her ability to focus. Aja is the perfect example of lethal calm when she fights."

"She says that the home is an arsenal," Cinder told him. "There are at least a hundred weapons in my kitchen right now."

"When it comes to combat, most people are ignorant. Not defenseless," Gian said.

"She showed me how to use a broom handle to defend myself." Cinder sat up and faced Gian. "If an attacker came in here, I could throw salt, sugar, even vinegar or coffee in his eyes to buy myself a few crucial seconds to escape. I could hit him with a frozen jug of milk, or club him with a ketchup or salad dressing bottle. The bathroom has even more potential weapons. Will she teach me how to use throwing stars or samurai swords?"

"I don't allow my instructors to teach the use of any weapon that could easily be turned against them. If you own a gun, you'd better be prepared to shoot to kill if an intruder gets into your home. Because if you're not, and he gets the gun from you, you're the one who'll end up dead."

"I don't want to own a gun, Gian. I would like to know how to use one, though."

He mulled over her request. "There's a place in Maplewood that could help you out. It's run by good people, and the instructors are excellent."

"Why can't you teach me?"

"Cinder, if I never pick up a gun again in my life, it'll still be too soon."

"I'm sorry." She remembered that Gian knew better than most how lethal guns were. Cinder had no problem with ordinary citizens owning guns. Her problem was that so many of those ordinary gun-owning citizens were also dumbasses.

Cinder hugged him. "I've learned so much from you. Thank you." She settled into his lap and kissed him.

"Now these are lethal weapons." He stroked her lower lip with the pad of his thumb. "My heart stops every time you kiss me."

Gian was impressed by the change in her confidence level. Five months ago, she'd looked like a frightened kitten when she first came to Sheng Li to learn how to fight. Though she had never asked him to, she had been overly grateful when he offered to walk her home after class. He'd made certain that if he couldn't do it, that someone else did. Tonight, she'd gone home alone. Not only that, she'd enjoyed it. Convinced he was seeing the Cinder he would have known had she never been temporarily diminished by Sumchai Wyatt, Gian asked her the one question he'd most wanted to ask her since Labor Day.

"Will you marry me?"

"You already asked me that once."

"No, I asked you what you'd say *if* I asked you to marry me. I never officially proposed."

She brought her fingertips to her mouth in surprise, her eyes wide. "I'm so embarrassed. I told Zae a long time ago that you'd proposed. And that I'd said yes."

"You told Zae that you'd say yes, but you left me hangin' all this time?"

"I'll say yes." She laughed. "Ask me again, and I promise, I'll say yes."

"I'm offended," Gian teased. "I'll ask some other time. Unless I forget . . ."

"Gian!"

Grinning, he cleared his throat. "I want to do this right." He got on one knee and pulled a ring from his breast pocket. He looked up at her, his bright, beautiful eyes shining with every hope and dream two people in love could ever hope to share. He took her left hand. "I never imagined that I would fall in love, until I saw you. I never thought about getting married and building a family, until you. Nowadays, that's all I think about. I love you. I want to share the rest of my life with you. Cinder, will you marry me?"

Tears blurred her vision, and emotion clogged her throat. Smiling so wide it hurt, she nodded. Her hand shook as Gian slipped the blinding twinkle of a square-cut, two-carat diamond on her ring finger. Cinder blinked away tears to see that Gian's eyes were misty, too. She framed his face in her hands, moving in to kiss him. Her lips took his to trigger a response that transformed her mute acceptance into something hotter, more insistent.

She wanted to marry him. She wanted him.

Their clothes were cast away and his flesh met hers, generating invisible sparks that sent a current running through them, one that heightened every sensation, deepened every kiss. Every part of them moved in harmony—lungs and hips pumped, backs and necks arched, thigh and jaw muscles hardened and relaxed.

Cinder now knew what it truly meant to belong to someone. Not in a possessive, degrading way as practiced by Sumchai Wyatt, but to belong to someone as the sun belonged to the sky.

Cinder slipped a hand between them to feel Gian's movement in and out of her. That part of him was so distinct from her own body, yet closing her eyes, she couldn't tell the difference between her flesh and his. He ended where she began, and that was where she wanted to spend the rest of her life.

～～～♪

Kneeling at the edge of the mat, Gian leaned over and whispered to Cinder. "Sionne is one and seven against this guy. This should be a very interesting match."

Cinder wondered which of the huge men kneeling on the opposite edge of the mat was Sionne's opponent. Each one of them had a chest like the side of a cliff, arms and legs built for crushing, and fists like small canned hams. Cinder knew that Sionne would be fighting someone named Clarence Clark, but when the referee called that name, none of the big men rose. Instead, every head turned toward the archway leading to the locker rooms, where a fighter in a black *gi* stood with his fists propped on his hips and his chest thrust forward. Cinder gasped. "*That's* who Sionne's fighting?"

"Clarence Clark's only loss to Sionne came when they fought the day after Clarence's pet gecko died," Gian whispered. "Clarence's head just wasn't in the match."

"I can't believe you're going to let this happen," Cinder muttered.

"Sionne can beat him. He's been training harder than ever. This is his last preparation match before the Internationals tomorrow."

Cinder turned to face Gian. "This kid is the size of the sub Sionne ate for lunch."

Chuckling, Gian shushed her, and the match started.

Clarence and Sionne circled each other. Slight and sinewy, Clarence couldn't have been more than twelve or thirteen. A beautiful kid with a nut-brown complexion and a sharp fade, Clarence put Cinder in the mind of a Jack Russell terrier circling a buffalo. Agile and quick, Sionne dropped his weight and lunged at Clarence, who skirted free of Sionne's grasp to deliver three quick punches to Sionne's ribs. Whirling in a blur, Sionne got in one blow toward Clarence, who again dodged it, suffering no more than a brush of Sionne's knuckles at the side of his *gi*. Sionne gave the contest his best, showing off some of his strongest moves, yet nothing fazed Clarence, who toyed with his much bigger opponent. With no points scored and two minutes remaining in the match, Clarence darted behind Sionne. He used Sionne's right calf as a step to climb onto the bigger fighter's back. The boy's skinny arms captured Sionne's head in a tight hold.

Sionne pulled at Clarence's arms, he turned and shook, but nothing weakened Clarence's grip. His face reddened, Sionne struggled to breathe, spittle shooting from his lips.

Gian rushed onto the mat. "Clarence, that's enough! We don't choke opponents to unconsciousness in tournaments!"

His dark eyes innocent, Clarence released Sionne and backed off. "Well, when *can* we choke somebody out?"

"When that somebody is trying to shove you into the back of a van." With a little push to his back, Gian sent Clarence to his coach. "What are you teaching your students? You know the rules of tournament competition."

Cinder went to Sionne while the two sensais argued. She roused him with light pats to his cheeks. "Are you all right?"

"That kid," Sionne panted. He sat up, shaking his head to jostle his wits back into place. "I hate that kid so hard."

Cinder helped Sionne stand, nearly collapsing under his bulk.

"Would you feel better if you came to Mama's for dinner with us?"

Sionne straightened, almost good as new, at Gian's invitation. "Thought you'd never ask, boss."

Sionne's match was the final for the day. He quickly showered and dressed while Gian emptied Sheng Li. Sionne rode with Gian and Cinder for the short drive to the Piasanti house in South St. Louis. The battle didn't affect his appetite any. After everyone sat for dinner and Gian said grace, Sionne stacked his plate high at the Piasanti's Thanksgiving table. Sionne recounted his fight between bites. "This kid is fast. He climbs like a lemur."

"How long has he been training?" Pio Piasanti, Gian's younger brother, asked from the opposite end of the table. Or tables. Josefina "Mama" Piasanti lived in the upper west apartment of a classic four-family flat. The rooms were lined up and connected by a long corridor stretching from the living room to the bigger of two bedrooms. The small dining room shrank further with two tables set end to end, accommodating Josefina, her sister, her two sons, her daughter, a daughter-in-law, two grandsons, a granddaughter, Cinder, and Sionne.

Gian sat at the head of the table for the meal, his traditional seat since the death of his father when he was fifteen. Pio sat at the opposite end, his pretty, dark-haired wife Isabel to his right, Josefina to his left. Cinder, and Gian's sister Lucia occupied the place settings at Gian's elbows.

From the middle of the table, Sionne reached left and right, helping himself to food from every platter, dish, and tureen on the loaded table. "Clarence Clark must have started training in his mama's belly," Sionne said. He picked up a sautéed green bean that slipped off its serving spoon, and he popped it into his mouth. "I first saw him in competition when he was seven. He's good."

"He's got solid skills but he needs discipline," Gian put in. "His sensai is creating monsters."

"We're signing the boys up after New Year's," Pio said. "They seem genuinely interested in it now, and who better to teach them than their Uncle Gian?"

Cinder looked from Pio to Gian and back again, noting the similarities and differences between them. They both had distinctively beautiful blue-green eyes that sparkled when they smiled and darkened when they didn't. Pio's raven black hair was several shades darker than Gian's chestnut scruff, and perfectly salon-styled. Not a hair was out of place, his line razor precise. Where Pio's casual holiday dress consisted of a starched collared shirt under a wool blazer with leather elbow patches, Gian wore an old white T-shirt under a formless crewneck sweater with what looked like paint stains on one cuff.

The Piasanti brothers were a genetic odd couple on the surface, but underneath, they were exactly alike in their humor, quickness to smile, and affection for their mother and sister.

Cinder tried not to stare at Lucia, whose remarkable beauty made it difficult. Her shoulder-length black hair complemented her alabaster skin. All three Piasanti children had full, overly sensuous mouths, with Lucia's naturally ruby lips forming a Cupid's pout. She sat between her mother and one of her nephews, overshadowed by her mother's talkativeness and her nephew's rambunctiousness. If her posture was any indication, Lucia wanted to be anywhere but at the dining table.

"Your lady friend is so dark," Gian's elderly Aunt Veronica said, drawing out her last word. She peered over her glasses. The lenses were thicker than the crystal butter dish. "She's from the north, isn't she?"

Gian hid his mouth with a loosely curled hand and leaned toward Cinder. "She thinks you're from northern Italy," he explained.

"The northerners are so dark-skinned," Veronica went on. "She's a beautiful girl, Gianni. You done good."

"Thanks, Aunt Vee," Gian said. "But Cinder is from Massachusetts. She's not Italian."

"Are you sure?" Veronica squinted at Cinder, her wrinkled face resembling a dried apple. "She looks just like a northerner."

"Yeah, I'm sure, Aunt Vee."

Aunt Veronica directed a fresh round of queries toward Sionne, who happily shared his Samoan origins.

Gian clasped Cinder's knee under the table. He stroked her inner knee and thigh, enjoying the feel of her silky black hose. "Do you know why I wanted you to see Sionne's match today?"

Cinder swallowed the bite of winter squash she had been chewing. "Of course. You wanted me to see that a fighter's size doesn't matter as long as he has proper skills. When Danielle brought down Chip on Halloween, I saw the effectiveness of proper training. She punched him in the groin, which brought his head down so she could gouge his eyes. She stomped on his foot and kicked him in the shin, which would have hindered him chasing her. G-E-F-S. It's perfect for a kid or a short adult, especially if an attacker isn't expecting it." She dabbed at the corners of her mouth with a napkin, then helped herself to a few stalks of marinated asparagus.

"You're smart." Gian smiled.

"Sometimes . . ."

Josefina's loud voice drew Cinder's attention to Lucia, who had sunk another two inches in her chair. Lucia's large, somber eyes glanced at Cinder before returning to her untouched plate heaped high with turkey and a few of the eleven side dishes. Lucia was present, but she wasn't there. She seemed to withdraw further under her mother's scrutiny.

"I seen on one of those afternoon talk shows, how sometimes women who have been attacked grow to become lesbians," Josefina said loudly. Isabel cringed and glanced at her sons. "I want Lucia to get herself out there and start dating and meet a nice man, get married, have a family, before it's too late." She set down her fork as a judge would a gavel, then stared at the table over the top of the glasses perched on the end of her nose.

"You shouldn't watch that garbage, Ma," Pio said. "Hey, Gian, did you call someone to flush out your sprinkler system? It's supposed to get cold later this week."

"The boys are really looking forward to the International Martial Arts tournament tomorrow," Isabel offered brightly. "They're looking forward to seeing Sheng Li compete."

Josefina ignored the efforts of Mr. and Mrs. Pio Piasanti to change the subject. As squat and chubby as a down-stuffed pillow come to life, Josefina hunkered in her chair and said, "Gianni, isn't there someone you can fix Lu up with? And Pio, that fella you brought to Christmas dinner last year . . . is he still single?"

"I try not to mix business with family," Gian said, although his choice of dinner guests belied that statement.

"Jason is engaged," Pio answered. "The wedding is set for June, I think."

"May," Isabel corrected.

"Another good one gets away," Josefina cried. She leaned around her grandson to talk at Lucia, her pale blue eyes flashing. "I love all my children equally, God knows I do, and I'll love them no matter what, but I want more grandkids. You're in this house all day, every day,

Lu. You look like a vampire with that pale skin. You need to get out, start livin' your life again. Look at your brother! He's got a beautiful wife, beautiful kids, a house, and a life. And Gianni's almost there, I guess." Her sharp gaze zeroed in on Cinder. "Goodness knows, he's never brought any of his other girlfriends home to meet me and Auntie Vee. This one might be the one."

"She is," Gian said. "I've asked Cinder to marry me."

Cinder's face reddened. Josefina finally shut up.

All at once, congratulations came from Sionne, Pio, and Isabel. Pio stood, dropping the napkin from his lap onto his chair. He squeezed past his wife, between Sionne and an antique floor radio, and gave Cinder kisses on each cheek. Aunt Veronica took off her thick glasses to wipe away her tears.

Josefina clapped her hands and aimed a silent prayer heavenward. But then she turned to Lucia. "You're the only one left, Lucia," she nagged. "Let me fix you up with one of the nice boys from church. Once you get back out there, you'll—"

"She'll date when she's ready," Cinder said. All eyes swung toward her. "She'll leave the house when she's ready. She'll take a walk around the block, or go running again, when *she's* ready. You can't rush someone's recovery. You can't make them live on your timeline. Unless you know what she's been through, you shouldn't be trying to force her into anything."

Isabel pinched back a smile. Cinder's future nephews, wide-eyed, stared uncertainly from their grandmother to Cinder and back again.

"What'd she say?" Aunt Veronica asked. "I didn't catch all that, what'd she say?"

Just when Cinder was about to apologize, Lucia spoke up. "She said Mama should leave me alone. And I agree with her."

Lucia left the table. Her footsteps sounded in the long corridor, ending with the soft slam of the back door.

"She's so sensitive about everything," Josefina muttered, dismissing Lucia's exit with a wave of a wrinkled hand. "I'm just trying to help."

"I'll go get her," Gian volunteered.

Cinder took his forearm. "Let me."

Gian nodded. Cinder excused herself.

The family ate in silence for a minute . "I have an uncle-in-law from northern Italy," Sionne finally said.

Josefina and Veronica jumped on the subject, peppering him with questions that allowed everyone else to eat in peace.

The meal didn't last much longer. Gian and Pio helped Isabel clear the table while Josefina and Veronica retired to the living room with Sionne and the two boys. Josefina tried to sneak into her bedroom at the other end of the house, but Gian followed her.

Josefina led him to the window. They saw Cinder and Lucia in the backyard. "What're they doing?" Josefina asked, wrinkling her nose.

Gian smiled, his heart filling his chest. "She's teaching Lu how to fight." Specifically, Cinder was teaching Lucia the GEFS technique, which was very effective and very easy. Cinder demonstrated blows and kicks, striking the groin, eyes, foot, and shin of an invisible attacker. Lucia copied the moves perfectly, although with far less power than Cinder.

"What will the neighbors think?" Josefina fretted. "I'm bringing them inside, right now."

"Leave 'em alone, Ma. We've spent thousands on therapy for Lu, and none of it did for her what Cinder's doing."

"Dr. Hardy is a professional," Josefina argued. "He has experience with cases like Lucia's."

"So does Cinder," Gian said quietly, his gaze never leaving the two women in the yard.

CHAPTER 14

The heavy bass of a Papa Roach song reverberated throughout the near-empty arena. Cinder stood with the rest of the contingent from Sheng Li, staring at the banners hanging from the rafters. Though veterans of International Martial Arts tournaments, Gian, Chip, and Sionne seemed as awed as Cinder, who had never even seen the event on television before.

"They're beautiful," Cinder muttered.

Hanging banners represented each competing dojo. The size of bed sheets, they were as colorful and ornate as museum tapestries. Cinder's mouth audibly popped open when she saw the banner for Sheng Li.

"That's my dragon," she gasped. "Gian . . . ?"

"I hope you don't mind." He draped an arm over her shoulders, drawing her in for a hug. "I've tried to find a symbol for Sheng Li since I opened the place, but nothing felt right." He tipped his head toward the banner. "This is perfect."

"It's great, Cinder," Chip drawled. "I want to get it tattooed on my back."

"No, you don't," Zae snapped.

"It's my back, I can do what I want to it," Chip argued.

"What do you think a dragon tattoo will look like on your shriveled, droopy ol' back when you're eighty years old? It'll look like the dragon melted." Zae patted her hair, making sure none of it had escaped her ponytail.

"What do you care? You won't have to look at it," Chip told her.

Grumbling under her breath, Zae threw a nasty look at Chip. "Where are the locker rooms? I want to change into my *gi* and mingle before the crowd starts coming in."

An event volunteer directed Zae, and Cinder accompanied her. The venue was enormous, and Cinder found it daunting at first. But as she passed the fighting mats lining the floor where the St. Louis Blues ordinarily played, she realized that with so many matches going on at once, it was unlikely that many people would be paying specific attention to any one fight. Taking comfort in the anonymity offered by a crowd, she settled her nerves and looked forward to enjoying the meet.

Since they were competing in the Exhibition half of the event, Zae and Cinder didn't have to adhere to the rules for the Combat half. Instead of traditional white *gis*, they could wear any color they wanted. Zae exited the women's locker room in a traditional blood-red *gi* that warmed the brick undertones in her dark complexion. Cinder wore black, her *gi* the rough-sewn, beltless peasant style Aja favored.

"Baby, you look like you're about to go work in a rice paddy," Zae said. "I wish you'd gotten the silver traditional one."

"I like my new *gi*." Cinder spotted the Sheng Li table. Gian was already there, speaking with a silver-haired Asian man in a very nice suit, and a tall, willowy woman in a skirt so short, she risked revealing all of her secrets if she were to bend over. "It's comfortable, and—"

Zae grabbed the tail of Cinder's tunic to pull her along faster. "Who the hell is that tall drink of trouble at our table?"

"I don't know," Cinder responded. She didn't care, either. The beautiful, long-haired woman stood close to Gian, speaking in his ear, but Gian's gaze was fixed on Cinder. He tracked her journey from the opposite side of the arena to his side.

"Pritchard, Kuriko, I'd like to introduce you to Cinder White," Gian said.

Kuriko narrowed her eyes, propping a hand on her right hip.

"She's his fiancé," Zae volunteered, clearly enjoying Kuriko's displeasure.

They shook hands all around, Kuriko refusing to meet Cinder's gaze as she did so.

"Are you competing for Sheng Li this afternoon?" Pritchard asked Cinder.

"Yes, on the Exhibition side," Cinder said. "I haven't studied the art long."

"She's one of my best students," Gian stated proudly. "Taught her everything I know."

"Everything?" Kuriko echoed, one of her eyebrows arched higher.

"Could I ask your ancestry?" Cinder asked Kuriko.

"My father is Ethiopian and Russian," she said dismissively. "My mother is Japanese."

"You're remarkably beautiful," Cinder replied.

"She's a'ight," Zae grumbled under her breath.

"Gian, I'd like you to meet some of my executives," Pritchard said. "Could I steal you for a moment?"

Gian nodded. "Zae, would you mind rounding up our guys? I want everyone assembled before the introductions."

Reluctantly, Zae disappeared into the growing crowd of fighters and spectators to do as Gian asked, leaving Cinder and Kuriko alone at Sheng Li's station. Kuriko, in her immaculately fitted suit, studied Cinder from head to toe. "Are you a fighter, too?" Cinder asked to break the silence between them.

"Only when I have a chance of winning," Kuriko sighed.

"I've never done anything like this before," Cinder admitted. "It's exciting." She eyed the floor, where sixteen smaller mats had been arranged around a large one raised on a dais. High above, big spotlights beamed down, most of them directed toward the center mat. Television cameras from local stations, ESPN, HDNet Sports, and several Asian sports stations were positioned throughout the arena. Advertisements for the sponsors of the tournament, Pritchard Hok Industries, Nike, Gatorade, Trojan, and numerous martial arts suppliers foremost among them, lined the outer rim of the competition floor.

"This is more than just a competition for Gian," Kuriko said. "If Sheng Li does well, Pritchard Hok

Enterprises will partner with him to open Sheng Li dojos across North America. This tournament will determine the course of Gian's future."

"Gian's fighters won't let him down," Cinder said. "They've been training for months. They're really good."

"What about you, little one?" Kuriko smiled, but there wasn't a note of friendliness in it. "How good are you?"

"I'm not in the medal rounds. My performance doesn't matter much."

Kuriko bared her teeth in a grin. "Yours matters most of all. You are Gian's prized pupil. You came to him with no experience, yes?"

Cinder nodded.

"You are the embodiment of the Sheng Li technique. Everything he has worked for, everything he represents rests on your little shoulders. If you fail, so does Sheng Li. So does Gian." Kuriko snickered as though she looked forward to it.

Cinder again turned toward the mats. Kuriko made sense, in a way, but Cinder thought it ridiculous to hinge the quality of an entire discipline on one rookie's performance. She looked back at Kuriko and came to two conclusions, both of which she shared with her. "I won't let my sensai down," she said evenly. "And you're a bitch."

~~~

The arena quickly filled with spectators in the stands, competitors on the floor, and media in the broadcast booth. The mingled conversations sounded like the hum of electricity, and excitement rippled throughout the building. Sitting on a three-tiered portable bleacher behind the Sheng Li table, Cinder's heart lurched when the lights went down, plunging the venue into semi-darkness. The lights came back on with the loud blare of a Cheap Trick song and thunderous applause, over which came the voice of the announcer, a local sportscaster named Duff Brownley.

"Welcome to the fifteenth annual International Martial Arts tournament broadcast live from the heart of the Midwest, St. Louis, Missouri," Duff announced.

" 'Missourah?' " Cinder whispered to Zae, repeating Duff's pronunciation.

"He's from Springfield," Zae said. "A lot of the folks down there say Missou*ruh* instead of Missou*ree*."

Duff introduced the dojos, their representatives standing to applause. Cameramen from each local network affiliate, as well as those from ESPN and a few other cable networks, moved between the dojo stations, panning over the fighters. Cinder bowed her face when the cameras shot Sheng Li. She resisted the urge to jump off the bleachers and hide beneath them.

Once the matches started, she forgot about the cameras.

Sixteen fights took place at once, one on each mat. Cinder tried to follow more than one at a time until a Sheng Li fighter took to the mat, and then she gave her full attention to her dojo-mate.

Sionne fought in the heaviest weight class. He made quick work of his opponent, collecting his three-point win in nine minutes. Cinder was sure that the match would have ended in five minutes if Sionne had been less generous. When Sionne took to the center mat for the final, he didn't hold back. The mighty Samoan displayed incomparable agility and flexibility. He scored his third point six minutes into the match with a slicing strike to his opponent's midsection to collect Sheng Li's first gold medal of the tournament.

Gian gave Sionne a standing ovation. "Let's keep it going," he shouted above the noise of the crowd as Chip took to the floor in his weight class.

Cinder watched Gian cheer his fighters. He defended them when their competitor fought dirty and praised them even if they lost a point in a valiant effort. He looked so handsome in his white *gi* with the new Sheng Li emblem embroidered on the back. High on pride, Cinder began to look forward to her match.

Zae's running commentary, which rivaled that of Duff Brownley, ended when Chip squared off against a fighter from a rival dojo, the one to which Clarence Blake belonged. Cinder smiled, watching Zae more than Chip. Zae's hands were clasped tightly under her chin. She cheered each time Chip scored, winced when he was flipped onto the mat. When Chip scored his third and winning point, Zae flew to her feet, clapping and cheering for him.

One by one, Gian's fighters earned gold medals, which were awarded on the center mat. The excitement level went up after the medalists returned to their respective stations.

"This is the moment we've all been waiting for," Duff began from the control booth. "The Exhibition round!"

Gian walked Cinder to the eighth mat, where she would meet her first opponent. "Are you nervous?"

"Yes," she whispered.

"Are you scared?"

She nodded.

"Don't be."

She laughed, the sound brittle and hard with nerves.

Gian took her by her upper arms and gazed into her eyes. "You're ready for this. I wouldn't have you here if you weren't."

"I know."

"I really want to kiss you now."

"Don't," she said. "Sionne and Chip might get jealous since you didn't kiss them before their matches."

Gian chuckled. "Go get your three, baby." And just as he had to Chip and Sionne, Gian sent her to the mat with a swat on the butt.

Cinder bowed to the mat, and then she stepped onto it. It seemed to have more give than the firmer mats at Sheng Li. She reminded herself to account for that once her match started.

In a traditional *gi* the same shade of yellow as her hair, Cinder's opponent took to mat eight. "Hi," the young woman said, offering a hand to Cinder. "I'm Bunny Dearborne. I fight out of American Krav Maga in Fenton. This is my third IMA tournament. I had a baby three months ago, so I thought I'd get back into tournament action by competing in exhibitions first. How long have you been fighting?"

"Not long." Cinder swallowed hard, unsure which intimidated her more—Bunny's experience level, or the fact that she seemed to be hopped up on amphetamines.

"I'll go easy on you," Bunny said with a wink. "We'll give 'em a good show."

Bunny's continued jibber-jabber kept Cinder from hearing the names and dojos of the fighters paired on the other mats. The woman shut up mid-word when Duff said, "Fighters ready?"

A chorus of battle barks answered. Everyone on the mats struck their fighting poses.

The fight buzzer sounded.

Cinder's heart leaped into her chest. With the shriek of a banshee, Bunny's pleasant smile morphed into a homicidal sneer. She charged, fists flying. On automatic, Cinder went into defense mode. She dodged right, avoiding Bunny's left fist. She ducked left, allowing Bunny's right foot to sail past her rather than make contact with its target, her right hip. In the quick second it took Bunny to reset her balance, Cinder threw out her right arm, spun to punch with her left hand, and finished with a low kick that left Bunny on her butt.

Three bells sounded from Judging Table Eight.

One of the two judges raised a placard with the word VIXEN printed on it in neat block letters.

"In thirty-nine seconds, Vixen wins on mat eight! Vixen makes it to round two!" Duff announced.

"I'm so sorry," Cinder said, genuinely concerned as she helped Bunny off the mat. "I didn't mean to do that. You came at me so suddenly, and I just reacted without thinking."

"What are you?" Bunny asked as they left the mat, her eyes wide in shock. "A ninja?"

Bunny never got her answer. Gian, Chip and Zae swept Cinder into a huddle. "That was awesome, girl!" Chip said enthusiastically.

"Damn," Zae whispered emphatically. "You took your fighter down faster than I took mine!"

Gian, his arm around her waist, walked her back to Sheng Li's station. "I think you caught their attention," he said quietly. "Look."

Cinder followed Gian's gaze. Spectators cheered her and clapped, some shouting, "Vixen!" as she passed their section of seats.

"I'm Vixen?"

"I had to think of a name for you on the fly," Gian explained. "I was at the registration desk, and you and Zae were going into the locker rooms. You looked so good. I couldn't call you Sexy, so I decided on Vixen."

"Because I'm a fox," Cinder groaned.

"I should have named you Champ."

"Don't bet on it," Cinder scoffed. "Bunny scared me into the fight. I didn't have any kind of battle plan other than to keep her from beating my butt."

Back at their station, Gian sat Cinder on the lowest bench of their bleachers. Massaging her calf muscles, he said, "I don't know who you'll meet in Round two." He looked over his shoulder. "Weight and experience don't factor into the exhibitions, so you might get someone a lot bigger than you are."

"Bunny had to outweigh her by twenty pounds," Zae offered from the middle bench. "She took care of her with no problem."

"From what I've seen so far, I'd put Cinder up against any—"

"Congratulations, Gian."

Gian turned at the familiar voice.

Karl Lange stepped up to him. He wore a black *gi* tied with a gold *obi*. Around his neck hung official IMA volunteer credentials.

"You gotta be kidding," Gian grumbled.

"I wouldn't miss this tourney for the world." Karl's black eyes glittered at Cinder. "Ever since I got fired from Grogan's, I've been taking whatever work I can get. IMA was glad to have me. They don't often get volunteers with my level of experience and knowledge of the sport."

"Is there something I can help you with?" Gian asked impatiently.

"Yeah, actually. I'm here on official IMA business. One of your fighters has a wardrobe problem."

Gian rolled his eyes. "What? Who?"

"Aja Oshiro didn't remove her sandals before she took to mat one for her exhibition match." Karl snickered. "She was disqualified."

"We got an exemption for Aja," Gian nearly shouted. He reached around Karl and took a piece of paper from the table. He shoved it in Karl's face.

Still smiling, Karl took it and glanced at it. "I guess you did. Too bad the judges didn't know that before they gave her the DQ. Better luck next time, G." He dropped the exemption on the table and moved on, a slight bounce in his step.

"What a dick," said Cory, who had won his exhibition match and arrived as Karl delivered his news. "He knows Aja *always* fights in her sandals."

Gian gathered his fighters. "You guys have to be careful out there," he said. "Karl's working this thing, and, obviously, he's working against us. Zae, Cory, Cinder, you guys are fighting in round two. Make sure you observe all the protocols and rules before, during, and after you step on the mat. I need to find Aja and see if I can't get her DQ reversed."

Cinder watched Gian go. He had never looked more magnificent. His posture and demeanor set him apart from the other fighters, elevating him in such a way that heads turned to follow his progress.

I love you, Cinder thought. She swelled with pride, adoration, and respect for the man who had taught her how to drop a fighter in thirty-nine seconds. *I love you, and I'm going to make you proud today . . .*

~~~

Zae toyed with her first- and second-round opponents before beating them. While the crowd loved her showy antics, her third-round opponent wasn't so easily amused.

CRYSTAL HUBBARD

"Poor thing," Cinder murmured to Gian, commiser-ating with the fighter facing off against Zae. "I'd hate to have to fight someone so much bigger than I am."

"Cory can handle her," Gian said. "He's a goofball in the dojo, but he knows how to settle down and turn it on once he hits the mat."

Cinder was impressed with Cory's performance. Zae had four inches and thirty pounds on him, but his youth and experience gave him the match. At the end of it, Zae and Cory were the only duo to hug after leaving the mat, much to the crowd's enjoyment.

Gian pulled Cory aside when he returned to their sta-tion to rest before his round three match. "We have a problem."

Zae's smile melted. "What's the matter?"

"Cory's next opponent scratched," Gian said.

"What does that mean?" Cinder asked.

"The kid pulled out with an injury," Chip said. "Although he looked fine when Karl was talking to him after his second round fight."

"So my fight is cancelled?" Cory fretted.

"The meet organizers found an alternate," Gian told him.

"Who?" Cory asked.

Duff Brownley answered. "Viper is out of the tourney with a back injury. He will be replaced in round three by last year's IMA middle-weight champion, Karl 'The Caveman' Lange!"

"Crap," Cory muttered.

"It gets worse," Gian went on. "Since Cinder won her match, she's in the final. She'll have to fight whoever wins your match, Cory."

"No pressure then, huh?" Cory laughed uncomfortably.

"I could go in for Cory," Chip offered. "I'll get the three off Karl."

"These are friendlies," Cory reminded them. "He's not gonna try anything in front of twenty-five thousand witnesses. If I can beat Zae, I can beat Karl. He's not as strong as she is. Besides, I've never scratched or forfeited in a tournament. I'm not about to start now."

Gian spent a moment thinking. "Keep it super clean, Cory. Karl is a man without a dojo out there. The audience will automatically be on his side because he's solo and a past champion. I don't want the energy of the crowd giving him an advantage."

"Sure," Cory agreed.

Cinder remained on the bleachers while Gian paced near mat six, where Karl "The Caveman" Lange stood toe-to-toe with Cory "Widowmaker" Blair. Darkly impressive in his *gi*, Karl stood several inches taller than Cory, whose sinewy forearms seemed to dangle from his wide sleeves. Cory's *gi* was printed with characters from *The Simpsons* and tied with an *obi* the bright blue of Marge Simpson's hair.

Cinder's spine stiffened at the sound of the fight buzzer. With each punch and kick, she expected Karl to do something cruel. He fought clean and hard, and emerged the victor twenty-six minutes later. Cinder was convinced that had Cory been fresh, like Karl, he would have taken him.

As apprehensive as she'd been for Cory's fight, Cinder was doubly so for her own. She had fought one man and two women to earn her way into the Exhibition final, and none of her opponents had been terribly challenging. Her longest match had lasted seven minutes; she spent more time waiting between matches than she had in combat.

Walking to the center mat when her fight name was called, she understood that fighting Karl would be different. Everyone else she had fought had taken the mat for fun. She wasn't sure what Karl's motives were.

"I don't like this," Gian said quietly, accompanying her on her last few steps to the mat.

"I'll be fine," Cinder assured him. "Cory was right. What's he going to do in front of all these people?"

Gian fiddled with her collar to buy another moment with her. "I can call this off. I'll scratch you."

"Don't you dare. I'm the best example of the Sheng Li technique and style. I can't walk away from this match. Every rookie watching me is a potential Sheng Li student if Pritchard Hok likes what he sees today. Kuriko told me—"

"Too much, evidently," Gian interrupted.

"I won't let you down, sensai." Cinder executed a neat bow toward Gian and another toward the mat. She didn't look back at Gian before climbing onto the dais.

The glare of the bright spotlights obscured the crowd. The pounding of a Kid Rock song drowned out all noise but for Duff Brownley's voice as he told the audience that the championship exhibition round would last until one fighter scored three points on his or her opponent.

While Duff introduced the judges and thanked the event sponsors, Cinder tried to acclimate. She saw only Karl, standing tall and impassive before her like a live oak. A barefooted referee wearing a whistle stood at one edge of the mat.

She took a few deep breaths, exaggerating the movement of her diaphragm. Pulling back her shoulders to breathe in, she flexed her abdominal muscles to force the air back out. She replayed in her mind everything Gian taught her. Envisioning Chip, Sionne, Cory, and Zae in their matches, she recalled what worked for them and what hadn't.

Breathe, she told herself. *Concentrate. Focus.*

The buzzer sounded.

Roaring, Karl came at her hard. His big feet flying, his spinning kicks drove her to the out-of-bounds line at the far edge of the mat. The referee's quick reflexes stopped her from hitting the floor two feet below the fighting area.

"You okay?" the ref asked, ushering her back into the fighting circle. "You want to go on with this?"

"I'm fine," she insisted a bit too strenuously. She straightened her tunic and returned to the center of the mat, urged on by light applause.

One side of his mouth hooked in a sinister grin, Karl struck his fighting stance, flexing his arms so that his veins stood out against his muscles. "Having fun yet?"

Cinder answered with the twitch of an eyebrow. She silently vowed to wipe the smirk off his face.

A short blast from the referee's whistle restarted the match. Again, Karl threw himself at her in full attack. She stood her ground against a string of quick, hard punches, blocking them or dodging them entirely. Karl dropped and swept out his leg, tripping her to the mat. She rolled clear of a stomping kick that would have won Karl his first point and possibly broken one of her ribs.

Only vaguely aware of Gian protesting at the judges' table, Cinder shoved a foot between Karl's legs, sending him crashing to the mat. In a showy move she'd seen only on dance floors, he flipped back onto his feet as she regained her own footing. Dropping into a crouch, she awaited his next volley, more comfortable on defense rather than offense.

Sneering, Karl signaled his next combination with a loud cry. A series of kicks flew at Cinder, all of which she deflected. He surprised her with a vicious strike to her midsection, earning his first point. Duff Brownley was still announcing the point to the polite applause of the crowd when instead of stopping the fight to reset in the center of the mat as Cinder had, Karl delivered one more punishing kick.

She caught his huge foot right in the face.

Horrified gasps rose from the stands. Cinder clumsily fell to the mat on her elbows and knees, her hands cupped over her bleeding nose. Writhing in pain, she heard Gian shouting at the judges to stop the match. The referee leaped between her and Karl, backing him away from her. First aid personnel reached her as she rolled off the dais, but Gian was there first with a white towel to press to her nose.

During the two-minute injury timeout, the crowd quieted. Pumped up on adrenaline, Karl traveled over the mat as if he owned it, bouncing on the balls of his feet while Duff Brownley announced the loss of Karl's point, the penalty for a dirty blow.

"That son of a bitch," Gian growled in hushed tones. "He can't beat me so he goes after you? I'm stopping this right now."

"No," Cinder said. "I'm ready to fight him."

Gian gave his head a little shake, grimacing in confusion.

"I never really fought him before," she quietly explained. "I've got a feel for the way he moves now."

His jaw firm, Gian said, "Baby, he's a third-degree black belt. You can't—"

She grabbed his wrist and pulled down the towel. "Watch me."

"Do you think you can go on?" asked the paramedic who'd come to her aid.

"Absolutely."

Gian's heart pounded painfully hard. Cinder climbed onto the dais, and while the crowd cheered, it took every bit of willpower Gian possessed to stop himself from grabbing her and pulling her into the shelter of his embrace.

He moved back a few steps at the referee's bidding, but he had no intention of straying too far from the mat. He didn't care if he got kicked out of the venue or risked everything with Pritchard Hok. If Karl drew one more drop of her blood, Gian would hop onto the mat and finish what he'd started at Grogan's Superette.

On the mat, Cinder faced off with Karl, who stared at her while the referee sternly warned him to keep the fight clean. The ref's whistle sounded, and the fight resumed.

"How's your nose, little girl?" Karl taunted, circling her.

Cinder stood her ground, her weight low but centered, her fists at the ready.

"Gian's crazy to let you back on the mat," Karl chuckled. "He's so whipped."

"So are you," Cinder said. "You just don't know it."

She didn't give Karl a chance to digest her reply. She spun, turning her back to him as she raised her leg. As her body rotated, she took a quick jump on her second step, propelling herself into a flying roundhouse kick. The tornado kick was one of her favorites for its beauty and power, and it hit its target—Karl's thick neck.

Both hands clutching his throat, he fell to the mat, noisily gasping for air. On his elbows and knees, he scuttled away from Cinder. The audience roared and cheered as Duff Brownley announced, "Point, Vixen!"

"Ten seconds, Caveman," the referee told him. "Get on your feet or forfeit the match."

Karl used every one of his ten seconds to recover before regaining his footing. His upper lip curled into a snarl. He breathed in short, hard snorts, like an angry bull. He seemed to shudder with anger in the center of the mat, and when the referee restarted the match, he lunged at Cinder.

She calmly ducked under his right arm. His momentum carried him forward, but she helped him along with a jab to his back from her right elbow.

"Point, Vixen!"

Duff Brownley's excited cry riled the audience. Cheers and applause shook the venue.

Gian, one hand cupping his elbow, the other covering his mouth, allowed himself a very brief moment of relief. "One more point, baby," he whispered. "One more point and you're outta there."

On the mat, the fighters reset. Karl's arm muscles hardened, his knees seemed to bounce in his eagerness to resume the fight. At the ref's whistle, he bellowed and charged. He threw his punches faster, mixing in kicks that Cinder barely avoided. His longer arms and legs gave him an advantage, but she negated it with her calm focus.

Karl's blows crashed into her forearms, his vicious kicks glanced hard off the outside of her knees and hips. The angrier he got, the sloppier he fought. He was taller, heavier, more determined to hurt her. Cinder fought back with speed, agility, and unerring focus. She prowled, taking advantage of every opening Karl gave her. The complicated dance of battle lasted for six full minutes before Karl ratcheted up his intent. Arms upraised, he brought both hands down in a strike meant to hit both of Cinder's shoulders at the same time. Such a strike would have brought her to the mat, where she would have been within range of a dozen debilitating strikes from Karl's feet.

Before his hands could make contact with her shoulders, Cinder initiated a front low kick. It landed in his midsection, driving him back. She took two quick steps and let her right leg fly in a high kick to Karl's face.

Performed correctly, such a kick could deliver six hundred and fifty pounds of force. Cinder had no idea if her kick was that powerful, but it was strong enough to send Karl's head snapping back, his huge body following. He hit the mat like a bag of wet sand.

"Point three and match, Vixen!" whooped Duff Brownley.

The arena shook with cheers, applause, and rock music. The Sheng Li contingent rushed the center mat. Cinder leaped off the dais and into Gian's arms. He hugged her, kissing her as he whirled her in a circle.

"Finally, the warrior in you woke up!" Zae hollered joyfully over the noise.

The same paramedic who had seen to Cinder's nose tended to the unconscious Karl while she and Gian led the procession back to Sheng Li's station. She looked into the stands and saw so many familiar faces—Natasha, her husband Kurt, and her daughters Jalesa and Danielle; Zae's children, Eve and Dawn and her son C.J.; Mama Piasanti, Aunt Veronica, Pio and his family, and Lucia; and Sheng Li students both old and new. They celebrated her success, and Cinder had never been more proud of herself.

She took to the awards podium and graciously accepted her gold medal. Next to her, on the second place step, Karl still looked slightly dazed as the silver medal was slipped over his head. Cory took the bronze to give Sheng Li five of the top six awards in the tournament.

"We should go to Isis or someplace to celebrate," Zae said afterward.

"Sounds good to me," Chip said.

"I'm a little tired." Cinder smiled. "I'm gonna pass."

Gian looked at Cinder, who sat a few feet away on the bleachers. Her gym bag stood open between her feet. Her elbows on her knees, she looked at her gold medal before dropping it into the bag. As if she'd just finished another ordinary lesson with Gian, she spent a moment mopping perspiration from her face and chest.

"What about you, Gian? You comin'?" Chip asked.

"No," Gian answered. "I've got some business to tie up with Pritchard Hok. You guys go and have fun. If you end up at Isis, tell the manager to charge everything to my tab."

"Thanks, boss," Chip said.

"You should go with them," Cinder told Gian as Chip and Zae led everyone else out of the arena. "This was a really big day for Sheng Li."

Gian squatted in front of her. He zipped up her gym bag and hung it over his shoulder as he stood. He took her hand, drawing her to her feet. She moved slowly, a little awkwardly. "The only thing I want to do right now is get you home," he said.

~⁂~

Gian took her home. To his home.

Too tired and in too much pain to protest, Cinder let him open the car door and help her from the front seat of his SUV. Gian's house, a multi-level contemporary, was spacious and airy. The foyer led to an open floor plan with the chef's kitchen on one side and the living and dining rooms on the other. Gian guided her into the kitchen. He opened a door to set their gym bags in the laundry room, then got her a bottled water. "You need to hydrate, baby," he told her. "Drink up."

Cinder sipped a bit directly from the bottle.

"Have I told you how proud I am of you?" Gian asked.

"About ten times. Do you think Pritchard Hok was impressed?"

"I don't care. I couldn't have asked for better from you guys. Whether Pritchard Hok sees it or not, I know I have the best dojo in the world."

Cinder smiled and nodded.

"In ancient times, when a warrior returned from battle, he had attendants to see to his aftercare. Only his most trusted, most loyal devotees were granted that honor."

"Makes sense," Cinder said softly. She sat heavily on one of the blond wooden stools at the center cooking isle. "The warrior would have been most vulnerable after a tough battle. It wouldn't do to have enemies creeping around to take advantage of his weakness."

"I want to take care of you." He took her hand and kissed the back of it. "Will you let me?"

Gian moved between her knees. She wrapped her arms around his neck. Her legs went around his waist and Gian held her tight. She closed her eyes and rested her head on his shoulder as he carried her upstairs. "I can walk, you know," she murmured.

"I know." He didn't put her down until he reached the master bedroom. Gian set her on his bed, then kneeled at her feet. He slipped off her sneakers and socks. Cinder raised her arms to help him pull her tunic over her head. She leaned back on the bed, lifting her hips, to make it easier for him to tug off her pants.

He exited through a pocket door on the other side of the room, and Cinder curled up on the big bed. The fluffy comforter, cool and soft against her skin, cradled her as she imagined a cloud would. Through his deep, wide windows, Cinder sleepily gazed at the rich purples and pinks of the setting sun. *I could sleep for a thousand years,* she thought.

Gian had other plans.

"Baby, come on," he gently urged. He took her hand and walked her into the master bathroom.

Cinder paused, stunned. The room was huge, the muted champagne, ivory, and hunter green color scheme echoing that of the master bedroom. The centerpiece of the room was a deep, wide tub recessed in the floor. A built-in bench seat draped with thick, fluffy white towels dominated the shallower end. The tub filled from the opposite end, the water flowing from set-in fixtures that lay flat against the tub wall. The tub was filling, but the arrangement of the fixtures allowed it to do so silently. Centered above the tub, three big, square skylights provided a full view of the gorgeous twilight sky.

"Gian, your home is so beautiful," she remarked as he peeled her sports bra and panties from her.

"It's missing something," Gian said. He helped her into the tub and sat her on the bench seat.

"What's that?" She leaned back, letting the water take the weight from her joints.

"You."

Smiling, she closed her eyes. On his knees at the edge of the tub, Gian lathered his hands with a citrus-scented soap and worked them over her shoulders. His strong hands kneaded out the tightness before moving to her upper right arm. By the time he lifted her right leg to massage the weary muscles of her thighs, Cinder was half-asleep and half-drugged on the pure pleasure of being cared for so thoroughly.

She let Gian wash her hair, her scalp receiving the same attention he had given the rest of her body. He rinsed her from head to toe, then bundled her in a big white towel. Back in his room, he laid her on her belly close to one edge of the bed.

Gian wasn't sure if she was asleep or not, but her eyes were closed with no movement behind her eyelids. Her head pillowed on her forearms, she didn't stir when he eased onto the bed, straddling her upper thighs. He took a small bottle of oil from the pocket of his jeans, where he'd kept it throughout her bath to warm it. He poured a small quantity of the oil into his palm, then set the bottle on his nightstand.

Gian dribbled the oil along her spine, then began working it into the muscles of her back. The faint scent of ginger and camphor rose with each stroke of his hands as the warmth of her skin activated the oil meant to replenish and heal her skin. He was careful with her hips and shoulders, where bruises were blooming.

Her legs received special attention. He massaged them long and hard, getting rid of the lactic acid that would otherwise lead to soreness and cramping later on. Leisurely, Gian saw to every part of her, even her fingers and toes. When he was finished, he lay beside her, his right elbow propping up his head.

The waning light of the sunset left soft strokes of color on her bare body. She was as lovely as a Rodin sculpture. Gian found that if he squinted, he could blur out all of her scars, leaving her body absolutely perfect.

He ran his fingers over a long, smooth line of scar tissue curving from under her right breast to her back. He'd seen enough war wounds to know that something very sharp had made the cut. He counted seven more similar scars of varying lengths, even one across her left buttock, and he marveled that she'd managed to survive the blood loss that would have resulted from such wounds.

"My warrior," he murmured, pressing a kiss to her head. "My queen." He smiled, a hard surge of love for her moving through his heart. "My wife."

Cinder stirred. She rolled onto her left side to face Gian. "Was I asleep long?"

Gian shook his head. "About an hour. You needed it. You had a big afternoon."

"Gian . . . thank you."

He hooked a finger under her chin and stroked her lower lip with the pad of his thumb. "For what?"

It took her a moment to figure out how to articulate the reason for her gratitude. He had given her so much more than knowledge. Respect, confidence, friendship, passion—by giving her those things, he'd given her a new foundation for her life. She couldn't string together the proper combination of words, so she cupped the back of his head and drew him in for a kiss.

His right arm went around her; she rolled onto her back, drawing him half atop her. Gian's mouth came down on hers. Delicately, and with patience sorely tired by the massage he'd given her, he kissed her, the ache deep within him flaring. He rubbed her lips with his, nipping and sucking at the lower one, determined to make her ache as he did.

Cinder's tongue met his and he groaned, sampling the succulence of her mouth. His tongue craved the warm, wet heat of her mouth just as another part of him craved the warm, wet heat between her legs, and he positioned that solid weight on top of her. She widened her legs, thrusting upward with her hips to feel him there, at the entrance to the emptiness yearning to be filled.

Gian's lips moved over her as his hands had, covering her with kisses that stoked the fire deep within her. She pressed her head into a pillow, bringing Gian's head to her left breast. He framed the soft globe in his hand, holding it in place to sup at her nipple. It hardened, lengthening with each pull of his lips. She kneaded and pinched her other nipple, multiplying her pleasure until Gian saw to it.

Her right nipple peeked between the fingers of her right hand, and Gian needed no further invitation. He turned his attention to it, lapping at it between her busy fingers while slipping a hand between her thighs. His longest finger parted her lips, circling the sensitive flesh there without nearing the hooded treasure straining for contact. Cinder moaned and arched against him, mutely pleading for more.

Gian didn't give it to her, instead taking her breasts and bringing them together, to suckle both nipples at once. Cinder cried out and pounded the bed with her fists, her hips still seeking the creature coiled behind the fly of Gian's jeans.

He wanted to take his time, to love her with the same patience and thoroughness with which he'd cared for her body after her bath. With Cinder tugging at his shirt and kissing him with the abandon of a succubus, he couldn't make himself wait another moment longer. With her help, his shirt and jeans came off quickly. His sports briefs and socks soon joined them on the floor.

Skin to skin, they wrapped themselves in each other. Cinder sat astride him, holding his gaze. She took him gently with her fingertips and guided him toward her center. Gian stroked her thighs, working his hands over her hips and back to her buttocks. He spread her wide as she lowered herself on him, stopping halfway.

Reaching back, she gripped his shins to steady herself as she pumped her hips in hard, short strokes, allowing his swollen cap to massage the internal bed of nerves previous lovers had never found. She moaned in blissful agony, keen waves of pleasure radiating to her limbs.

Gian raised his hips and her along with them, eager to plunge himself completely within her. Cinder, her head lolling back on her shoulders, closed her eyes and concentrated on squeezing him with each upward stroke.

Gian gritted his teeth so hard it hurt, every part of him aching for more. Without dislodging himself from her, he sat up, forcing her weight onto him. Impaled, Cinder cried out and fastened her arms tight around his neck, her legs firmly around his waist. Gian gripped her hips, aiding the movement of her strong thighs as she raised and lowered herself, faster and faster until the solid bed began to creak.

He buried his face in her neck, reveling in the utter pleasure of their union. Her breasts flattened against his chest, her breath came hard and heavy in his left ear. Her tongue snaked out and traced the shell of his ear before she suckled his earlobe. The sensual simplicity of it triggered a reaction that zoomed straight to his loins, and he erupted with a ragged groan. His body stiffened, his thighs and buttocks hardening, his arms tightening around her. He pumped himself into her until he felt himself shrinking. Not quite ready to exit her slick temple, he eased a hand between them and found the slippery hood at the apex of their union. He drew it back, just enough to expose the treasure beneath it to the friction provided by his coarse nest of hair.

A rolling, guttural moan issued from Cinder's throat. She shifted her hips, working them in tiny circles with each forward movement. Gian brought her left breast to his lips and clamped the nipple between his teeth. Quick flicks across it with the tip of his tongue jolted Cinder to a climax that left her frozen but for the pulsing of the muscles imprisoning Gian.

With a ragged cry, she pressed her face to his neck, kissing beads of sweat from his skin. Behind her closed eyelids, she saw every color, each shattering into a kaleidoscope of blissful sensation. As the colors faded, so did the intensity of her orgasm. She held onto Gian, pumping her hips into his to achieve it once more.

Gian spent a second cursing the failings of the male anatomy and its inability to recover as quickly as women did. But what his soldier couldn't give her, another part of him could. He laid her on her back, earning a short noise of protest from Cinder when he pulled out. He quickly settled between her thighs, hooking them over his shoulders.

Long, firm strokes of his tongue sent her fingers burrowing in his hair. Her fingernails dug into his scalp; her strangled groans answered each lick and nip at her overly sensitive flesh. His tongue found the hard seed from which her rapture would bloom, and he sucked it, starting her hips bucking. Gian curled his arms around her thighs to keep her from breaking contact with his mouth.

Panting, she tugged at his hair, the muscles of her abdomen bunching as she tried to sit up. Relentless, Gian continued, gently scraping his upper teeth against her most sensitive place while his tongue thrust into her.

"Gian," she gasped sharply. "Please! It's too much! I . . . I . . ."

He took her hardened pellet between his teeth. Not hard, but with enough pressure to force broken grunts of mindless bliss from her. As if an electric charge had been administered to her, her body went rigid, then twitched. Over and over, her backside clenched, her hips rose and her abdominal muscles contracted.

Cinder melted. Her arms and legs turned to pudding, she lay on the bed, completely helpless in the aftermath of perfect pleasure. Tears trickled toward her ears.

"Sweetie, what's the matter? Did I hurt you?

She shook her head and mustered a smile for him. "I always suspected something better or stronger, or whatever you want to call it, was there. I've had orgasms before, you know that. But I've never felt *that* before."

Gian grinned. "I kinda wanted to see what would happen if I took you past the twitch. Now I know."

" 'The twitch?' "

He stroked light fingertips over her belly. Her skin jumped, still highly sensitive. "That point past orgasm," Gian explained. "Orgasms stop, eventually. But once you go past the twitch, you find whole new secrets to taste. It can go on and on . . ."

"Until your heart stops." Cinder laughed. "Or dehydration sets in."

Gian cupped her between her thighs, his thumb lightly caressing her bare mound. "This is different," he remarked.

"Zae and I went for pedicures and manicures yesterday." She grinned. "The salon offered a package deal."

"They'll shave your kitty with every mani-pedi," he teased.

"They waxed." Cinder laughed lightly. "I'd never done it before. It felt like the technician was using a flamethrower, but after it was over, it was okay. I was surprised at how sensitive the area is once the fur coat came off. Do you like it?"

"I do now. You're just as smooth and juicy as a fresh nectarine."

"You're making me hungry." She dragged a fingertip along the trail of fine, dark hair arrowing toward his groin. She kept it moving past his pelvis until her fingertip was tracing the instrument between his legs, which grew with the movement of her finger.

"I was just thinking about seconds, myself."

Cinder sat up. She pushed Gian onto his back. She stifled a giggle at the sight of his "little" soldier at full attention.

"What's so funny?" Gian asked.

"Talk about perpendicular." She emphasized the third syllable of her last word. She threw a leg over Gian's chest and sat on him.

"Nice." He gave Cinder's bum a little slap, since it was now in his face.

"Behave," she directed over her shoulder. She hunched forward and took him in her mouth. Gian groaned, a slight bend appearing in his knees as his feet flexed and his toes spread. He caressed Cinder's buttocks, lightly stroking a finger between them as she tormented him with the soft, wet walls of her warm cheeks. Gian inhaled deeply, the ginger musk of her scent heightening the action of her tongue and lips. The lines of her shoulders, back and bum, exquisitely beautiful in the semi-darkness, changed as she switched position.

Lifting her backside, she supported her weight on her knees to add both hands to the work of her mouth. Gian's girth overfilled one hand, so she laced her fingers together to fully circle him, twisting her hands up and down his shaft while she sucked his smooth, taut cap.

"God Almighty," he grunted. He clasped her thighs right at her hips and dragged her back until he could reach her with his mouth. He braced his elbows on the insides of her knees, forcing them as far apart as possible. With a satisfied moan, he devoured her, lapping and nibbling her, mimicking everything she did to him.

One of her hands fondled the fleshy package trying to crowd his base. He responded by dragging his tongue along the full length of her seam, finishing with kisses to the dimples just above her buttocks. Cinder squealed, her hips taking on a life of their own to exuberantly delight in the skill of Gian's tongue, teeth, and lips.

Cinder took him deeper, the rhythm of her mouth matching that of her hips. On each downstroke, she took him all the way to the back of her throat, dragging her lips in a tight "o" along his length on the upstrokes.

When he grabbed her thighs and held her to his mouth, kissing her nether lips as deeply as he would the lips on her face, she gored her throat with him, taking him deeper than ever before. Frozen in a rictus of pleasure, Cinder kept him entombed. She pressed her tongue against him, the only movement she had room to do, and slowly pulled off of him. The rasp of her tongue over the nerve endings gathered at the base of his cap sent that part of him coddled in her hand crowding upward. He twitched between her lips and she shoved her head down on him once more. His length pulsated between her cheeks, his liquid heat bypassing her tongue.

Gian's arms locked around her thighs, holding her in place as he once again took her past the twitch. Lying flat atop him, her face pressed into his right thigh, she held onto his legs and let the intensely strong orgasms carry her to that place where her state of being dissolved into pure sensation.

CHAPTER 15

"So what do you think of the place?"

Gian ended her tour of his home in the same room it had started, the kitchen. Cinder leaned on her elbows on the center cooking isle and watched Gian take covered plastic containers out of the stainless steel refrigerator.

"It's wonderful," Cinder answered. "It's so airy. When you said it was environmentally friendly, I imagined an adobe cottage with a goat instead of a lawnmower, and oil lamps instead of electric lights."

"Just think of all the good times you could have had here, if you'd been willing to leave your tower." He set a wooden bowl of red grapes before her.

"I hope you'll give me the chance to make them up." She plucked a few grapes, then caught his gaze. "I like it here. I feel . . ."

"Comfortable," he suggested.

"Safe."

Gian rounded the cooking isle and put his arms around her, lacing his fingers loosely at her back. "Where is that timid little woman who came into my dojo so long ago?"

"She's gone. You turned her into a warrior. You gave her the skills to take care of herself."

"My beautiful warrior." He cupped her face and kissed her forehead. "The day you walked into my dojo was the best day of my life. I can't imagine my life without you."

"You say the most wonderful things." She hugged him, fitting her head under his chin.

He laughed. "Your hair is tickling me." He scrubbed his fingers through it. "It's so curly."

"I didn't blow dry it after we showered," Cinder explained. "This is what it does naturally."

"I like it." He gently tugged one of her spiraling curls and watched it spring back into place just as a bell chimed. "Whoa, that was cool. It has sound effects."

"That was your phone." She chuckled.

It rang once more before Gian trotted into the foyer to answer his cell. Cinder hung back in the kitchen to give him privacy. She went to the sliding glass doors that led to his deck. Since it was so dark outside and light inside, the doors acted as a mirror. Cinder wore the change of clothes she'd brought to the arena, a pair of black pull-on pants and a short-sleeved shirt. Both garments were made of cotton jersey and were as soft and comfortable as an old T-shirt.

The glass doors reflected Gian's return to the kitchen, and Cinder turned to get a proper view of him. In a pair of black sports briefs, he looked like an Olympic athlete, and she couldn't wait to get him out of his shorts again. She looked at his face and her wanton thoughts vanished. Gian didn't speak. His phone pressed to his ear, he listened, his expression growing more grave.

Cinder went to him and rested a hand lightly on his arm.

"Someone attacked the kids," Gian said after disconnecting the call. "That was Zae. She's at the Crestwood police station."

"What?" Cinder asked, horrified.

"Jalesa, Eve, and Dawn went to a movie with Cory after the tournament," Gian explained. He started for the stairs. "After the show, they were at their car and a guy in a balaclava grabbed Eve." Gian took the stairs two at time, Cinder right behind him. He went into the bedroom and headed straight for the walk-in closet. Dressing quickly in jeans and a crewneck sweater he yanked from an upper shelf, he said, "The kids turned the tables on him. All four of them attacked him."

"Are they all right?" Cinder sat on the edge of Gian's bed and put her sneakers on. "Was Eve hurt?"

"They're rattled, but they're okay. Zae says Cory got a good kick in. The guy will be walking around with a bruise on his face for a while."

"Where are we going?" Cinder followed Gian back downstairs.

He cracked a brittle grin. "Zae didn't think the cops were taking the assault seriously enough. She made a bit of a scene."

Cinder cringed. She could only imagine what kind of scene Zae might have made in the interest of protecting her children.

At the front door, Gian took Cinder's fleece jacket from the coat tree and helped her into it. He grabbed his car keys from the pocket of his car coat and opened the door for her. "The police are holding Zae until 'a responsible adult' comes for her," Gian said. "She called me because I've conducted a lot of training seminars with the Crestwood Police Department. They know me. Hopefully, they won't have arrested her before we get there."

"Were the kids able to describe the guy?"

"No," Gian said. He locked his front door behind them. "It's Black Friday. There were a ton of people at the mall, shopping and going to the movies. This is the start of the parking lot mugging season."

Gian led Cinder to his SUV and unlocked the passenger door. "I'm just glad everybody is all right," she said as Gian opened her door.

"Me, too. But that'll teach the bastard not to mess with Sheng Li students."

"Ma'am, I assure you, we're working with mall security to do everything we can to find this guy," an officer stated for what must have been the tenth time, because he sounded thoroughly annoyed. "Officers are canvassing the area and an alert has gone out to all the stores and the cinema. There's not much we can do without an accurate description."

"Officer, Mrs. Richardson has understandably been under duress," Gian started. "Her daughter was attacked at eight o'clock in a crowded parking lot. It takes balls to do something like that. You're looking for someone who is potentially very dangerous."

"Gian, you think I don't know that?" the officer said. "From what I heard from these kids, our perp got the worst of it." He lowered his voice. "I don't think we'll ever get this guy. Looked like a classic grab and go. He went for the girl's purse, couldn't get it—"

"Got his ass kicked," Cory chimed in.

"He's in the wind now," the officer finished. "We see a lot of this type of crime on Black Friday. There are so many shoppers out, the perps get bold and greedy."

"Can we get Zae and go home?" Cinder asked. No fan of the police to begin with, Cinder was irked by the officer's cavalier acceptance of defeat.

"Can we?" Gian directed his question to the officer.

"Absolutely," he said. "I'll go get her. I had to put her in a holding cell. She got real belligerent."

"I'm sure she was just upset about her daughter being attacked," Gian said.

"Upset or not, there was no reason for her to call me a 'monosyllabic morphodite.' I don't know what that is, but it didn't sound like anything good."

Leaving Gian, Cinder and the kids in the tiny lobby, the officer disappeared behind a door to retrieve Zae. They heard her before they saw her upon her release.

"It's irresponsible to ignore a perfectly good lead, that's all I'm trying to explain to you," came Zae's voice. She kicked open the door, making no move to stop it from slamming back into the officer on her heels. "Karl Lange is a troublemaker. He's got an ax to grind against

Gian Piasanti, and what better way to hurt him than to strike out at his students?" Zae saw Gian. "Tell him, Gian."

"Tell him what? The kids don't know who the guy was. It could have been a random crime of opportunity."

"Cory's the one who assumed it was Karl," Zae argued.

At the nearby vending machine, Cory shrugged his shoulders and put up his hands. "He was the first person to pop into my head. He lives near here, right over on Sappington Road. He's pissed at Gian and all things Sheng Li."

"How would he know that you would be at the mall tonight?" Cinder asked.

"He could have heard us talking about it at the tournament," Eve said, her stern expression a younger version of her mother's.

"He was all over the place, fake volunteering," Dawn added.

"I couldn't see the mugger's face," Cory said, "so I can't say for sure who it was. I just think Karl is the most likely suspect."

"Likely isn't good enough, ma'am," the officer directed at Zae. "I can't go around arresting people without evidence."

"You'll get your evidence," Zae said. "But by then, he might have killed someone."

"I'd consider it a personal favor if you could look into this a little deeper," Gian told the officer. "Zae and these kids are like family to me, and I need to know that everything possible is being done to catch this guy."

"Sure thing, Gian," the officer said.

With a hand at their backs, Gian guided Zae and Cinder to the vending machines, where Eve sat in a plastic chair, surrounded by her sister, Jalesa and Cory. "Eve, are you okay?" Gian asked.

She nodded, though the hand holding a can of Sprite shook. "He came right at us. It was so weird."

"He must not have known that we were karate students," Dawn said.

"Then that would rule out Karl," Jalesa said.

"Karl is nuts," Zae replied. "He probably figured he could take on all of you. Losing to Cinder this afternoon probably made him snap."

"I think it's time we get out of here," Gian suggested. "Hopefully, the police will catch—"

Gian's cell phone rang. He pulled it from his back pocket, glanced at the call number in the text window and answered it. The call lasted seconds, and Gian's end of the exchange consisted only of four words. "I'm on my way."

He turned to Cinder. "That was the Webster Groves police. The silent alarm was triggered at Sheng Li. I've gotta go check it out."

"What the hell is going on tonight?" Zae muttered.

"Let the police handle it," Cinder insisted. It suddenly didn't seem so unlikely that Karl was on some sort of rampage of revenge for his tournament loss.

"The cops are meeting me there," Gian told her. "Could you get a ride home with Zae? I don't know what's going on at Sheng Li, so I don't know how long I'll be."

"Sure," she said and nodded. "Please, be careful."

"I can handle Karl Lange." Gian gave her a reassuring smile, although his comment convinced everyone that he'd reached the same conclusion Zae had. "Leave a light burning for me, baby. I'll be looking for thirds later tonight." He kissed her, and it lasted so long, everyone around them grew impatient.

"For heaven's sake," Zae groaned. "You act like you're never going to see her again."

Gian reluctantly pulled out of Cinder's embrace. "Wait up for me, baby."

"I will," Cinder said, sending him off with a smile.

Gian squatted at the broken glass scattered over one end of the studio. "Can I pick this up?"

"Sure," answered one of Webster Groves's finest. "It's evidence, but we can't dust it for prints."

Gian carefully leaned over and picked up the brick that had been thrown with such force, it broke the plate glass window in Sheng Li's lobby and traveled another ten feet to shatter the observation glass between the lobby and the studio.

"The guy's got an arm, I can tell you that much," the officer said. "The Cards could use him."

Gian grunted a noncommittal sound of acknowledgement. Someone had caused him a small fortune in damage. The last thing he wanted for the culprit was a spot in the Cardinals bullpen. Clutching the brick, he stood and faced the officer, who leaned against the frame of the doorway between the lobby and the studio.

"It's pretty obvious that burglary wasn't the intention here," Gian said. "Or else the guy would have used the brick to break the glass of my front door so he could unlock it. Someone just wanted to cause me some grief."

"Can you think of anyone who'd want to damage your property, Mr. Piasanti?" the officer asked.

"What?"

"Who'd you piss off," the officer stated more plainly. "A student, a neighbor . . . ?"

Karl. That was the only name that came to mind. Gian hesitated before saying, "My club competed in a martial arts tournament today. My fighters took most of the medals. There might have been a sore loser with an axe to grind."

"I'll canvas the area tomorrow morning when the stores open, to see if your neighbors saw anything," the officer said. He used the edge of his notepad to shove up the brim of his cap. "I gotta tell you, whoever did it was pretty fearless. All the shops on the street are open late tonight, what with this being the busiest shopping day of the year, supposedly. There must have been witnesses."

"What about Natasha?" Gian asked. "She said she heard the crash and called 911."

"Mrs. Usher?" The officer had to consult his notes. "Yeah, the bookstore owner next door. She placed the call to emergency, but by the time she got outside, the guy was gone. I'll re-interview her. Sometimes witnesses remember details once their nerves have settled."

"She locked up early tonight," Gian said. "You'll have to catch her at home. Her daughter was involved in a mugging or something tonight over at Crestwood Mall."

"All the head cases are out tonight, huh?"

"Seems like it." Gian dropped the brick, his shoulders falling. "I need to get someone here to board up my storefront. I don't want the rest of the glass to fall out and slice some poor passerby into lunchmeat."

"I'll file this report as soon as I get back to the station. If you could come by in the next couple of days to sign it, I'd appreciate it. I have to tell you, though, Mr. Piasanti, chances are we're not gonna find the person who did this. You got insurance, right?"

"I'm covered. I'm glad I got the full package, even though I didn't think I'd ever need it."

"Unless you need me to stay, I'm going to get started on my report."

"I'm good." Gian shook the officer's hand. "Thank you."

With a tip of his cap, the officer left. Gian scrubbed his hands over his face, through his hair. The day had started out so well only to end with perhaps thousands of dollars of damage to Sheng Li. If, in fact, Karl was responsible for the attack on Eve and the broken windows, Gian hoped that he had gotten it all out of his system before someone was genuinely hurt.

On his way to his office to get a phone directory, Gian debated whether or not to call the officer and tell him specifically about Karl. But with no concrete evidence, anything he said would be pure speculation. As angry as he was at Karl, he had no desire to malign the man any more than necessary.

That wouldn't stop him from kicking Karl's ass again, given the chance. *Or maybe I'll let Cinder do it.* Gian amused himself with that thought as he opened a bottom drawer of his desk and pulled out the AT&T Business Directory. He sat on the edge of his desk, the phone book propped against his belly, and leafed through the WINDOWS section.

"Custom, Supplies, Repair . . ." He read the various categories. "Here we go. Board-up services." To his surprise, there were dozens, most of them offering twenty-four hour service. Gian choose the one in Maplewood for its proximity to Webster Groves.

A very friendly woman answered when he called. Her friendliness intensified after Gian offered to pay in cash with a bonus for the repairman if he arrived within the hour. Gian wanted to finish up and get back to Cinder as soon as possible.

After his call, he replaced the phone book and started back into the studio, dialing Cinder's phone number on his cell as he went.

"Hello, Mr. Piasanti."

Gian froze.

In the archway between the studio and the back corridor, he looked up to see a man standing near the broken glass at the far end of the mat.

"Sorry, I'm closed . . ." Gian started. The stranger looked familiar. He was tall and broad through the chest and shoulders. He wore a denim jacket with a black

T-shirt underneath it. His black trousers were a size too big and threadbare at the knees. Straight black hair fell to his shoulders, and deep-set black eyes glittered above his long, thin nose. His eyes were distinctly Asian in shape. Most revealing was the ugly bruise on his left cheekbone, and Gian recalled where he'd seen the stranger's face.

"Cinder has a standing order of protection against you," Gian said. "You aren't to be within—"

"Five hundred feet, I know," Sumchai Wyatt said. "But Cinder's not here. She lives a quarter of a mile away, so I'm in no danger of violating the court order. Yet."

That one detail was more than Sumchai should have known about Cinder. Gian worried that he'd already been to her place. "If you've hurt her . . ." he warned.

Sumchai laughed lightly. "I'm saving the best for last. My wife and I have a lot of catching up to do."

"You're gonna have to go through me to get to her."

"I've heard a lot about you around town, Mr. Piasanti." Sumchai slowly moved farther into the studio. "You're an ex-Marine—"

"There's no such thing as an ex-Marine."

Exaggerating a bow, Sumchai placed his right hand over his heart. "Forgive me," he said, overly gracious. "Once a Marine, always a Marine?"

"Something like that." Cautious, Gian approached Sumchai.

Stepping onto the mat, Sumchai circled around the broken glass. "And now you're a respected business owner. A regular pillar of the community, give or take a public brawl here and there."

"What do you want?" Gian demanded.

"To see the great Giancarlo Piasanti. To meet the man who's trying to steal my wife."

"She's not your wife."

The upper left side of Sumchai's mouth twitched. "She took a vow. What God has joined, no man, not even you, can put asunder."

"She divorced you, or didn't you get the memo?"

Sumchai kept moving, maintaining his distance from Gian. "One of the women at the market across the street told me a lot about you. It's amazing what these back-water bottle-blondes will give up, once you get them yapping. She said you were smart." He shot a look at Gian. "She doesn't know you very well, does she? You see, a smart man would know when to back off and let another man repair his relationship with his wife."

"You'd need tweezers and airplane glue to piece your relationship with Cinder back together."

Sumchai responded with a sarcastic smile. "Again, I'm just not seeing this smart side of you."

"Quit backing away from me and I'll show it to you."

Sumchai stopped well out of Gian's reach. "Have you laid her yet?"

Gian pushed up his sleeves.

"No answer is an answer, jarhead." Sumchai grinned. "I can tell you have just by looking at you. You look like you want to kill me, because you know I had her, too. I had her *first*. You're good looking. Resourceful." He looked around, nodding in approval at the studio. "I suppose you're successful." Sumchai shoved his hands into the pockets of his jacket. "But I know one thing you're not."

"What's that?" Gian challenged.

"Bulletproof."

The blast of the gun concealed in Sumchai's jacket pocket threw him back a step, revealing his inexperience with such a weapon. *But he knows enough,* Gian thought, clumsily falling to his knees. His right hand went to the bright, hot pain just above the crest of his right hip. Without looking, he knew the wetness quickly filling his hand was blood. He struggled to his feet, staggering toward Sumchai. *If I can reach him, I can disarm him.*

Gian's effort was met by a second shot, this one striking his right shoulder to spin him before dropping him to his knees. Gritting his teeth against the pain, he panted, curses flying from his lips. His legs worked but his feet could gain no purchase on the bloody mat. He fell forward, his entire right side ignoring the desperate orders issued from his brain. Forcing his forehead into the mat, Gian tried to roll himself over.

Sumchai's worn and dirty sneakers came into view, and with them, another shot that sent Gian's body into spasms of agony that nearly rendered him unconscious.

Jesus, he cried in his mind, refusing to give Sumchai the pleasure of seeing his pain. *Sweet Jesus, help me get him,* he pleaded. He threw out his left hand, hoping to snag Sumchai's ankle or the cuff of his trousers.

Sumchai neatly stepped out of reach.

Gian writhed, digging his elbows into the mat to drag his bleeding body after Sumchai. Pain, jagged and hot, rocketed through his body, and it was so intense, he couldn't tell where the third shot had hit him.

He was too familiar with the sound of gunfire, and he hoped that someone on the street had recognized it, too. With each passing second, Gian's limbs grew heavier, his clothing heavier with his blood. He had been through two wars, dozens of dangerous missions behind enemy lines, and had emerged with little more than a few minor injuries.

Gian refused to die in his own dojo.

Keeping out of Gian's reach, Sumchai backed toward the lobby. "Cinder won't mourn you for long," he taunted. "I'll make sure of it. But before I put her out of her misery, I'm going to make sure she pays for the hell she put me through. Two years in prison, another ten on probation . . . I'm a felon because of her."

Grunting, Gian took a swipe at Sumchai's ankle.

Sumchai stepped into the lobby.

"I never thought she would hook up with anyone else, not after what I did to her," Sumchai continued, stealing peeks over his shoulder to check the street. "I made her mine. I took her skin, her tears, her hair, her blood. I'm sure you can understand my dislike for you, Mr. Piasanti. You tried to take my wife. I deserve satisfaction, and I'll have it, the second I tell Cinder that you bled to death at my feet."

Gian coughed. Thick clots of blood sputtered from his mouth, the salty, metallic taste of it sickening him. His lungs, hard and heavy as concrete, fought to drag in one more breath, and another, then another.

"You should have seen her the last time I was with her," Sumchai said. "She was all bloody and twitchy, kind of like you are right now. She pissed herself once I started cutting. Smells like you pissed yourself, too, *sensai*."

Gian could pull himself no further. Shaking his head to clear the fog from it, he grabbed the brick lying on the floor.

"You bring a brick to a gunfight," Sumchai laughed. "Big dumb Marine."

Gian drew his arm back, and with the last of his strength, he sent it hurtling forward.

The brick whistled past Sumchai, missing him by more than a foot. Sumchai laughed, but the sound of it was abruptly drowned out by the violent crash of the front door breaking as the brick sailed through it.

Gian's thoughts grew filmy, and everything around him darkened.

He heard Sumchai utter a profanity, then flee. An eternity after, a man's voice called his name. But he couldn't answer, not when something within pulled him farther into darkness, the weight of it pressing on him from every direction. The sound of his heartbeat in his ears, he was aware of movement around him, but he couldn't feel it.

Is this dying, he wondered. *No, it can't be . . .*

Gian traveled the in between places, the corridor between warm and cold, life and death, love and emptiness, and he found Cinder. He thought life was supposed to flash before your eyes at a time like this, but all Gian saw was the woman he loved.

Cinder asleep in her pale white shift, the shadowy outline of her body a thing of beauty in the moonlight. Cinder, her skin glistening with perspiration, twirling a bo with the grace and power of a samurai. Cinder's lazy half smile of good morning on a pillow they shared. Cinder's lips parted in sensual surrender in that moment when their bodies and souls fused, that brief infinity when they were truly one.

He forced his eyelids open and fixed his gaze on the hazy silhouette of the man looming over him. "Cinder," he sputtered through blood. "W-Warn her . . . Wyatt is coming for her . . ."

CHAPTER 16

The call had come from Gian's cell phone, but the voice on the other line wasn't his. The words the caller spoke replayed in her head as she frantically dragged a small suitcase from the back of her bedroom closet.

Wyatt is coming for you. He has a gun.

The suitcase contained clothing, toiletries, cash, copies of her insurance, and medical records—everything she needed to make a quick getaway. The suitcase had been packed and ready from the day she moved into the apartment. She had hoped that she'd never have to use it.

She put on her fleece jacket, grabbed her purse and car keys, and began unbarring and unlocking her front door. Her breath caught in her chest, sweat ran down her spine, her vision blurred. Dizzy with panic, she fumbled with the locks, her fear growing with each passing second.

Her skull seemed too tight for her brain, forcing her thoughts to jumble into a senseless knot. She threw open her front door to hear the crash of glass from three stories below. Her throat closed, stopping the scream building in her lungs, and her bladder threatened to empty. Forcing herself to keep her cool even as she heard slow footsteps climbing the stairs, she closed her door and locked it.

The fire escape.

She dragged the suitcase into her bedroom and unlocked her window. Cinder threw the suitcase out first. In less than thirty seconds, she would be in her car and on her way to the police department. After that, she would head to a new town to make a new start. One foot on the fire escape and the other dangling in her bedroom, she straddled the window sill.

A new start.

How many of those had she already gone through? How many were in her future? How many times would she have to escape from Sumchai Wyatt?

She had tried to escape Sumchai once, and he'd nearly killed her to stop her. Here he was again, forcing her to run. From him. From Zae. From Gian. She hadn't spent six months learning to fight only to run. Not when she had so much to fight for.

Sumchai wasn't looking for a fight, she was certain of it. He had nothing to fight for. He wanted revenge, plain and simple.

She hadn't asked for this war, but Sumchai had brought it to her door. He wouldn't have the advantage of a blitz attack, not this time. This time, she would see the enemy coming. If nothing else, Gian had taught her the most important thing about war.

"Stand or surrender," she murmured.

She pulled her leg back inside.

Cinder's dark leather library chair faced her front door, and it was there she sat, her legs crossed, her arms on the wide armrests, when Sumchai stepped into view. The door stood wide open. Cinder wanted him to know with absolute certainty that he was welcome to enter.

He entered slowly, his steps deliberate, perhaps even cautious, as he stepped into the foyer. Without taking his eyes off Cinder, he closed the door behind him. He locked it, securing the chains as well.

Her lips pursed, Cinder watched her ex-husband approach. He was still tall and handsome, although prison had eliminated the softer aspects of his features. The planes of his face were hard, his skin appeared to be stretched too tightly over his high cheekbones, one of which sported a purple-black bruise. New lines curved around his eyes and wide mouth. A scant crop of gray hairs glinted at his temple. Accustomed to seeing him in well-tailored clothing purchased with her income, it took her a moment to get used to him in his off-the-rack denim jacket, no-name work pants, and scuffed sneakers.

"What?" His tone was casual as he walked toward Cinder with open arms. "No hug?"

"If you touch me, I'll kill you."

Despite the gun loosely held in his right hand, his steps faltered. Cinder gave him a grim smile.

His eyes raked over her ribbed tank top. "You look good, kitten," he said, using the nickname she most hated. "The past couple of years have been real good to you." He sat a few feet away on the arm of the sofa, his gun hand resting on his right knee. "I love your place. It's a lot bigger than it looks from the outside. The high ceilings are really special. I figured I'd have to hunch over like Quasimodo up here."

"You came here to talk architectural details?"

A deep cackle rose from his chest. Cinder squinted and locked her jaw to stop herself from screaming. Sumchai had the laugh of a cartoon witch. It was completely incongruous with his physical appearance, and there had been a time when the mere sound of it had made Cinder laugh, too. But now she cringed at the high-pitched, wheezy sound with its broken, staccato notes. It was the laugh she heard in her nightmares.

"No, I didn't come here to talk about your new digs. I want to talk about us."

It was Cinder's turn to laugh. "You really are insane, aren't you?"

"I was here for two weeks before I finally saw you, on Halloween. It was like love at first sight all over again. I saw you there on the street, and you were more beautiful than the day I met you. I was surprised at how fast your hair grew back. But then I saw you at that karate school the next day, and I realized you'd been wearing a wig. I loved your hair long, but I like that you're still wearing my mark."

"What you like isn't really my concern anymore. I don't have a choice when it comes to your marks. They're all over my body. Plastic surgeons did what they could, but I'll have my scars for the rest of my life."

"I meant your hair." He drew a fine gold chain from his collar. "I had this made while I was in lockup. See that?" Pulling it taught over the tip of his thumb, he leaned forward to show it to her. "You probably can't see it from over there, but I've got one strand of your hair woven in it. Just one strand. That's all I've had of you for the past couple of years. It's the only thing that's kept me connected to you. That, and the internet. You'd be surprised at how well-equipped the prison library is. My cellmate runs an online dating service for cons and the women who love them. He posted profits of more than fifty grand last year."

"That's fascinating," Cinder said dismissively. "You didn't find me on the internet. I don't use your surname or my maiden name, and my clients don't list me on their websites. Nothing significant comes up if you search the name I use now."

"Yes, I realized that a few months into my search. And your parents . . . they were no help at all. I searched their house from top to bottom, and they didn't have so much as a holiday card from you."

Cinder's skin broke out in gooseflesh. "If you hurt my mother and father . . ."

"They were at the Cape when I broke in," he said blithely. "But I didn't leave entirely empty-handed. Did you know that they use your birthday for the combination to the safe behind the bookcase in their den? They really should change it. Birthdays are so obvious. Very easy to guess."

"What did you take?"

"Just a few pieces of jewelry. Your mama is like a raccoon. She likes anything that sparkles. She probably never even noticed anything missing. It was like Blackbeard's treasure in there."

She stood, slowly, so as not to startle him into firing the gun. She moved toward the kitchen. "Why did you rob them?"

Sumchai followed her, keeping close. "I needed fun money for this little vacation to Webster Groves. My parents have me on an allowance, can you believe it? It's barely enough to cover my bar tab, let alone to travel halfway across the country and woo back my wife."

"How did you find me?" Cinder made a point to stay clear of the cordless phone mounted on the wall just inside the kitchen. She went to the freezer and took out a half-gallon of milk.

"Zae."

With a loud thunk, the frozen milk landed on the butcher block counter. Shocked, Cinder's tongue seemed too thick as she said, "She wouldn't . . . liar."

"Oh, she didn't tell me where you were. But Professor Azalea Richardson was an easy search online. I knew that if I found her, you would be close by. I almost came to you on Halloween. I dressed as a ninja, in keeping with your current interest in martial arts."

"Why did you attack Zae's daughter?" Cinder asked abruptly.

"Zae screwed around in our life for too long. I figured it was time to screw her right back."

"By going after one of her children? Why didn't you go after *her*?" She smiled bitterly. "Oh, right. Zae would have ripped your nuts off and force-fed them to you. Is that why you always hated her so much? I used to think it was because she's a tenured, published professor, while you couldn't even get a job teaching primary school. Then I thought maybe it was because she's the only one of my friends you couldn't intimidate and drive away. It's pretty obvious to me now that it's because she's ten times the man you'll ever be."

He didn't rise to the bait. "That mouth of yours is always what got you into so much trouble. Got you out of it, too, especially when you did that thing where you circle your tongue—"

"I don't do that with Gian."

Sumchai flinched.

"Gian's a lot bigger than you are." She opened a cabinet above the counter and took out a drinking glass. "I don't have the room to maneuver the way I did with you. Of course, I could have shoved a whole Twinkie in my mouth alongside you . . ."

Snarling, Sumchai charged her, only to be caught in the face with a quick, hard whack with the frozen milk. A comical squawk of pain and surprise flew out of Sumchai's mouth, along with a bloody tooth and a pink rope of saliva. With a dull tink, the tooth landed on the vinyl tile floor. Cinder's second blow, which connected with his chin, knocked him off his feet.

On his hands and knees and drooling blood, Sumchai glared up at her. "I'm going to kill you slow this time, kitten."

He lunged at her, only to introduce his chin to her heel. It came at him fast and hard enough to drive his head backward, his body flopping after it. He scrambled out of the kitchen, grabbing the gun he'd tucked into his waistband. Relentless, she didn't stop to gauge the effect of her first kick. She pursued him, a series of powerful ax kicks driving Sumchai toward the living room wall.

Her final kick, a sweeping roundhouse aimed at his head, missed its target. Sumchai clumsily ducked under it and vaulted over her sofa, positioning himself on the far side of it to give himself a chance to regroup and catch his breath.

Fists clenched, Cinder stood ready for her second big battle of the day, a deadly smile cloaking any fear or reservations she might have had about resorting to lethal force. "Threaten all you want, Chai," she stated evenly. "I'll have an answer for you. Gian's a really good teacher. But I guess you know that, since one of his former students kicked your face in at the mall earlier tonight."

He cocked the gun, almost playfully aiming it at her. "His students might show a bit of talent, but your big boyfriend was off his own game tonight. He couldn't dodge a single bullet. Are your reflexes any better?"

Cinder's heart seemed to stop. Her lungs ceased function. Her brain couldn't digest Sumchai's implication. The warning call. It had come from Gian's phone, but Gian hadn't made it . . .

Sumchai spat out a gooey clot of blood. "Only three bullets left."

"Y-You—"

"He took the first two on his knees," Sumchai sneered through a sinister laugh. "He was flat on his back for the last one. Some hero. He's a lot tougher on paper than in real life."

Cinder withstood his taunts, battling with her stomach to keep its meager contents inside her. She swallowed hard, over and over, fat beads of sweat tickling down her face. "Did you kill him?"

"No. The bullets did."

Cinder's eyes closed. She fell to one knee, bitter fluid lurching from her stomach in a hot rush that ran through her fingers. On her hands and knees, she couldn't stop the convulsions of her belly, even after it had emptied.

"Holy cow, that stinks!" Sumchai laughed. "I think I might get sick, too." Walking sideways to keep from turning his back on her, he went to one of her living room windows and opened it wide, the action awkward because of the gun in his hand.

A gust of chill night air, faintly scented with burning leaves and damp earth, helped cool Cinder's brow and settle her stomach. Most important, the fresh air helped her think clearly.

"Remember the time we went to my brother's rugby game, and he got hit in the nuts?" Sumchai stood in the window. The darkened windowpane his mirror, he used the tail of his shirt to wipe blood from his chin. "He vomited on the field, and it made two of his teammates vomit. It started a chain reaction that had guys on both teams vomiting everywhere." He cackled again, the sinewy muscles of his exposed abdomen jumping. "God, that was funny!"

There was nothing funny to Cinder about his stop on Memory Lane. The thing she best recalled about that rugby game was his insistence that she wear a thin, tight-fitting sweater to the field, one that showed off her body but did nothing to protect her from the frigid day. She had been flattered at the time, pleased that he wanted to show her off. Now, she wanted to slap herself for her stupidity in confusing his pride in her appearance with pride in a possession.

But I'm not stupid anymore. She had learned his lessons well, gaining an understanding he hadn't counted on. She stood and slowly walked into the bathroom.

Close behind her wielding the gun, Sumchai watched her wash her hands, rinse her mouth, and splash cold water on her face. Sparkling droplets of water dripped from her eyebrows, nose, and chin as she stared at her eyes in the mirror.

He's not dead. He's not. If he was, I'd know it. I'd feel it . . .

She gripped the clean white porcelain of the basin, the sleek muscles of her arms and shoulders assuring her that she had the power to pay Sumchai Wyatt what she owed him for every bruise, scar, nightmare, and tear he had ever caused her.

She slowly turned to face her ex-husband. "Put the gun away, Chai."

He giggled. "Why?"

"You aren't going to shoot me."

"The jury's still out on that, kitten. I haven't decided what I'm going to do to you." His black eyes zeroed in on the front of her white tank top. The ribbed cotton was wet and translucent in places, molding itself to her flesh. Sumchai licked his lips, perhaps recalling the days when he'd been permitted access to that flesh.

"You're not going to shoot me because you won't have your gun."

He raised it, bringing it close to her head. "Is that righ—"

Cinder moved forward, meeting the nozzle of the weapon. In seemingly one motion, she spun into Sumchai's body, her back to his chest. Before he could complete a howl of pain, she had taken his gun arm, bent it backwards over her own, and twisted the revolver from his grip. She used the butt of it to strike him across the face before she helped him out of the bathroom with a very well-placed flat-footed kick to his solar plexus.

Sputtering for breath, Sumchai landed on the living room floor, paralyzed and in pain long enough for Cinder to grab the mesh lingerie bag on top of her laundry hamper. She dropped the gun into the bag, pulled it closed, and wrapped the drawstring around her fist a few times.

Standing over Sumchai, she clenched her teeth and swung the bag as though it were a bolo. But instead of throwing it to somehow ensnare Sumchai, she battered him with it, landing a hard blow to his torso. He grunted and struggled onto his elbows and knees. Cinder delivered another vicious blow, this one hitting Sumchai's ribs with a sickening crack. She bit back a smile, hoping that she'd broken at least one of his ribs. She deposited her third shot in the same place.

His paralysis worn off, he shrieked, throwing himself at her with one hand hooked into a claw while he clutched his injured ribs with the other.

Cinder deftly dodged him, letting him crash into her sofa. She ran for the front door, Sumchai close behind her. She had the door open when he grabbed the back of her tank, yanking her off her feet. Swinging her homemade bolo, she landed hard on her tailbone, crying out more from anger than pain over having missed her target.

Sumchai's fingers burrowed into her hair, using it as a handle to drag her back into the living room. Kicking and screaming, Cinder dropped the bag containing the gun to claw at his fingers.

"I loved you more than anything, you bitch, and you threw it away," he roared at her. He heaved her ahead of him.

"You never loved me! You wouldn't know love if it sat on your face! You gave me obsession, jealousy, distrust, rage, selfishness, and your damn insecurity! You possessed me. You never loved me."

"I tried to give you everything."

"You tried to kill me." He blocked her path to the front door, and there was every chance he would reach the gun before she could if she tried to race him for it. She drew her final weapon. "That night you tried to kill me? That wasn't all you did to me, was it?"

Sumchai smiled. A filmy coat of blood covered his upper teeth. "A husband has the right to enjoy sexual congress with his wife."

Striking away sudden tears, Cinder pressed on. "Tell me, was it good for you? Did you like it better with your partner unconscious? Bleeding. Dying! As horrible as that day was, you actually managed to give me the one thing I'd ever wanted from you."

Sumchai stared at her, perplexed. Then, understanding broke over his face. For the merest second, his expression relaxed, and he looked like the man she'd once loved. "A baby?" His head whipped left and right as he scanned her bookshelves, walls, and tabletops. "Why don't you have any photos? Where is—"

"He's dead."

"He? You aborted him," Sumchai shouted. "You killed my son?"

Cinder closed her eyes and took a few quick, deep breaths. She had spent most of her marriage and the months following Sumchai's attack in a state of constant anxiety. Sumchai's absurd, cruel accusation was the catalyst she needed to allow that sickening, tense feeling to evolve into the one emotion she had kept corralled deep inside for too long. It seeped from its hiding place, permeating her cells, flooding her brain, hardening her heart.

Anger. That was the one thing Sumchai had never tolerated, the thing that earned his wrath fastest.

From the first time he had hurt her for being cross with him, she had kept her anger caged as one would any wild, unpredictable thing. With her hair around his neck, her skin under his nails, and her future beyond this night in peril, the anger within her began to smolder. The heat of it reached Cinder's skin, searing her from the inside out.

She began to burn.

"*YOU KILLED HIM!*" Her arms stiff at her sides, her fingers rigidly splayed, Cinder screamed so loud, she tasted blood at the back of her throat. "I didn't know I was pregnant until almost three months after you attacked me. I was still in the hospital, and I started to bleed. He couldn't survive." She hooked her fingers into her abdomen. "How could he, not after the way you cut me! *You* killed him, Chai. You killed your own son."

"My son . . ." The words quivered from his lips as he stared at Cinder, tears shining in his black eyes.

"When he died, so did any shred of forgiveness or pity I might have had for you."

Sumchai wavered on his feet, and Cinder hoped he might actually pass out. He ground his fists into his eyes, his shoulders quaking. "My son," he moaned, staggering toward the front door. He picked up the bag containing the gun and returned to the living room, taking the gun from the lingerie bag. "He would have been my legacy. He would have had my name."

"He would never have known you existed," Cinder declared, her teeth clenched.

His misery turned to fury, Sumchai roared and flung forward his gun hand.

Cinder dropped to the floor, sweeping her right leg in a circle as hard as she could. Her inner right ankle struck Sumchai's shins, bringing him crashing to the floor. The shot meant for her went wild, shattering one of her living room windows instead of her chest.

Still on the floor, Cinder raised her right foot and brought it crashing down on Sumchai's right hand. The bones cracked around the gun and he shrieked, calling her the worst names hateful men had for women. Faintly from outside, Cinder heard activity, then a man's voice, loud and clear through a bullhorn. "Sumchai Wyatt, this is the Webster Groves Police Department."

On her hands and feet, her butt in the air, Cinder crawled clear of Sumchai's reach while he used his left hand to uncurl the fingers of his right from his gun. "The residents of the building have been evacuated and armed officers with authorization to fire are located throughout and around the residence. Exit the building and surrender yourself and your hostage."

Cinder found her feet and ran for the door. The gun now in his left hand, Sumchai fired at her once more, the sound of the shot startling her. Clipping the doorframe with her left hip, she spun into the stairwell and into three policemen crowding the landing outside her door.

The officers passed Cinder down the stairs as though she weighed no more than a doll, her feet scarcely touching the floor. On the lower landing, in full combat gear, they surrounded her, shielding her.

Eleven steps above on the landing outside her door, Sumchai emerged, his gun drawn, to find three automatic rifles pointed at his head and chest. Through the officers in their heavy black gear, he searched for Cinder. Spotting her, he smiled, cracking the blood drying on his face.

"Lower the gun, mister," one of the officers said, his voice slightly muffled by his helmet. "You've still got a chance to walk out of here."

Cinder wanted to look away, but she couldn't, not with Sumchai so intensely holding her gaze. "He won't," Cinder murmured. "He won't stop until he does what he came here to do."

The officer nearest her pressed closer to Cinder. "What's that?"

"Kill me."

Sumchai gritted his teeth and fired at Cinder. She drew in her shoulders, closed her eyes. The officers around her huddled tighter, leaving her too little room to expand her chest to breathe. Gunfire erupted in the close stairwell, temporarily deafening Cinder. When the officers eased off her, she opened her eyes. Two of them started to hustle her down the stairs, but she looked back over her shoulder. Before she lost sight of her doorway, she saw an officer on one knee tucking Sumchai's gun into a chest pocket of his flak jacket. The soles of Sumchai's feet faced the narrow balusters of the railing. He lay flat on his back, unmoving, his blood spilling over the landing in a ruby trickle.

Zae and Chip stood together near the nurses' station in the Critical Care Unit of Missouri Medical Center. Cinder was tempted to call out to them, but decided against it. Not that she could move words past the hot lump of emotion plugging her throat as she passed the glassed-in rooms of the hospital's most imperiled patients.

This is my fault, she thought dismally. *Eve and Gian . . . they were targeted because of me.*

No amount of guilt would force her from the ward, not until she saw Gian with her own eyes. If Zae and Chip ostracized her for bringing Sumchai into their lives, they would just have to do it after—

"Baby girl," Zae sobbed, rushing to Cinder with her arms wide. Chip greeted her, too, throwing his arms around her and Zae. "I had no idea what was going on until I got here and talked to Karl. I would have gone over to your place if—"

Cinder drew away from her. "Karl?"

Chip squeezed her shoulder. "He saved Gian's life."

"Honey, are you okay?" Zae cupped her face, stooping a little so she could look into Cinder's eyes. "Sumchai didn't get to you, did he?"

"Yes, he did," Cinder answered absently. She peeled Zae's hands from her face, and looked beyond her to the big man in blue scrubs sitting on a padded bench in the wide hallway. "Excuse me, please."

She went to the bench and sat down.

Karl, who had been staring at his hands, looked up at her.

"That was you who called me," she said softly.

"Gian's phone was the closest one," Karl replied. "You're number one on his speed dial. Before he passed out, he told me to warn you."

They sat in silence, the pariahs. She for bringing Sumchai into Gian's well-ordered life, he for being the distraction that had thrown them off the scent of real danger.

Karl broke the silence by clearing his throat. "I was at Grogan's, asking for my old job back. I saw the front window of Sheng Li had been busted, then a brick came flying through the door. Some guy ran out, and I went over there." He took a long, shuddering breath and ran his hands over his thighs. Cinder took his left hand and held it in hers. Blood darkened the crescents of his fingernails and filled the cracks of his knuckles. *Gian's blood* . . .

At Karl's feet sat a clear plastic bag filled with blood-stained clothing. Cinder stroked the back of Karl's hand, then closed it in hers, resting it on her lap.

"I called Gian's mom and Chip and Zae once Gian was in surgery. I owe you such a big apology, Cinder," Karl said softly. "Gian, too. I've been so angry and unhappy since the auto plant closed, and I took it out on everyone around me. I'm so sorry, Cinder. I—"

She cupped his face, turning it to hers, and she pressed a tender kiss to his cheek. She gave him one more kiss, and said, "I think we're even. No more apologies."

They sat hip to hip, awaiting news of Gian. Zae and Chip joined them, Chip leaning against the wall with no room on the bench. The minutes dragged by, their vigil broken only when Zae stopped a nurse to ask for an update on Gian's surgery.

Gian's mother, brother, and sister arrived, and a nurse moved their larger group to a private waiting area. Mama

Piasanti stoically counted off her rosaries while Pio paced before the window overlooking the parking lot. Lucia wiggled in beside Cinder and put a comforting arm around her shoulders.

Four hours after Gian went under the knife, the gray-haired surgeon who took care of him walked into the waiting area. "He's being wheeled into recovery," he said. "Mr. Piasanti suffered three gunshot wounds. We recovered bullets from his upper arm and liver. The third was a through-and-through. That bullet entered at the right crest of Mr. Piasanti's ilium and passed straight through, exiting near his kidney without penetrating it. Thank God for small blessings."

"Will he be okay?" Pio asked.

"As long as he remains free of infection, I see no reason he shouldn't make a full recovery."

Mama Piasanti slumped against Lucia in relief, murmuring a prayer of thanks.

The surgeon turned to Karl. "Mr. Lange?"

"Yes," Karl said.

"One of the bullets nicked Mr. Piasanti's brachial artery. I was told that you were the one who placed the tourniquet on his arm."

"Yeah, that was me."

The surgeon offered his hand. Karl shook it. "You saved his life. He would have bled out in a matter of minutes if you hadn't been there."

"Miss White?"

"Miss White, wake up."

Cinder opened her eyes and sat up, careful not to disturb Karl. She hoped the nurse didn't notice the wet spot on his shirt, where she'd drooled.

The nurse crouched in front of her. "Mr. Piasanti is awake," the nurse whispered. She grabbed Cinder's knees, keeping her seated a moment longer. "He's asked for you. You should go in before everyone else wakes up."

Cinder followed the nurse to Gian's room. She impatiently allowed her to tie a disposable gown on her before she slid open the glass door and approached Gian.

A thin sheet covered him to his waist. His chest was bare, the wounds in his upper arm and torso bandaged around drainage tubes. Electrode pads stuck to his chest and rib cage monitored his heart, and an oxygen reader was clipped to his right forefinger. A pale green tube snaked around his head and fed him oxygen through his nose.

The stiff curtains had been opened, and the sunrise washed him in bright, clean light. His pale body gleamed, his chest rising and falling evenly.

Cinder slipped in among the machines monitoring his vital signs and medication to take his left hand, careful not to move it since his IV line ran into the crook of that arm.

"My head feels like it's made of cement," Gian said in a raspy whisper, his throat raw from the removal of his intubation tube. "I can't see you."

Cinder leaned farther over him.

"Baby," he whispered. "I was so worried about you."

"I was worried about you, too." She kissed his temple, his cheek, his ear. The tears she fought to hold back seeped out to wet his pillow.

"I couldn't stop him," Gian said. "I couldn't protect you."

Cinder gazed into his eyes. His humble admission seemed to cause him more pain than his injuries.

"I pissed my pants." A tear pushed its way from the corner of his eye.

"So did I," Cinder admitted.

They chuckled sadly over the peculiar bond.

"I want two minutes with him," Gian said. "Just two."

Cinder held his hand a little tighter. "He won't bother us again. He won't ever bother anyone again."

Gian instantly understood her meaning. "You?"

"The Webster Groves police. It's over, Gian. All of it. I don't ever want to look back. When you leave this hospital, I'm leaving with you. When I came to Webster Groves, I told myself it was because I wanted a new start. What I wanted was a place to hide. You gave me the one thing I needed to face my worst nightmare. You gave me knowledge. You taught me how to defend myself and you pushed me to stand, not surrender. You're my hero, Gian. The fact that you're here right now proves that Sumchai Wyatt was wrong about every damn thing he ever said." She laughed. "Even that you're not bulletproof, 'cause you're still here."

"I want to go home with you." His eyes drowsed shut.

"Then you're already there," she whispered, bringing her lips to his. "My home is wherever you are."

The End

ABOUT THE AUTHOR

Burn is Crystal Hubbard's eighth romance novel for Genesis Press. She is also an award-winning children's book author. The mother of four, Crystal resides in St. Louis, Mo. She spends her free time promoting cancer awareness and conducting writing workshops for grade school children.

BURN

2011 Mass Market Titles

January

From This Moment
Sean Young
ISBN: 978-1-58571-383-7
$6.99

Nihon Nights
Trisha Haddad and Monica
   Haddad
ISBN: 978-1-58571-382-0
$6.99

February

The Davis Years
Nicole Green
ISBN: 978-1-58571-390-5
$6.99

Allegro
Patricia Knight
ISBN: 978-158571-391-2
$6.99

March

Lies in Disguise
Bernice Layton
ISBN: 978-1-58571-392-9
$6.99

Steady
Ruthie Robinson
ISBN: 978-1-58571-393-6
$6.99

April

The Right Maneuver
LaShell Stratton-Childers
ISBN: 978-1-58571-394-3
$6.99

Riding the Corporate Ladder
Keith Walker
ISBN: 978-1-58571-395-0
$6.99

May

Separate Dreams
Joan Early
ISBN: 978-1-58571-434-6
$6.99

I Take This Woman
Chamein Canton
ISBN: 978-1-58571-435-3
$6.99

June

Doesn't Really Matter
Keisha Mennefee
ISBN: 978-1-58571-434-0
$6.99

Inside Out
Grayson Cole
ISBN: 978-1-58571-437-7
$6.99

2011 Mass Market Titles (continued)

July

Rehoboth Road
Anita Ballard-Jones
ISBN: 978-1-58571-438-4
$6.99

Holding Her Breath
Nicole Green
ISBN: 978-1-58571-439-1
$6.99

August

The Sea of Aaron
Kymberly Hunt
ISBN: 978-1-58571-440-7
$6.99d

The Finley Sisters' Oath of
Romance
Keith Thomas Walker
ISBN: 978-1-58571-441-4
$6.99

September

October

November

December

Other Genesis Press, Inc. Titles

2 Good	Celya Bowers	$6.99
A Dangerous Deception	J.M. Jeffries	$8.95
A Dangerous Love	J.M. Jeffries	$8.95
A Dangerous Obsession	J.M. Jeffries	$8.95
A Drummer's Beat to Mend	Kei Swanson	$9.95
A Good Dude	Keith Walker	$6.99
A Happy Life	Charlotte Harris	$9.95
A Heart's Awakening	Veronica Parker	$9.95
A Lark on the Wing	Phyliss Hamilton	$9.95
A Love of Her Own	Cheris F. Hodges	$9.95
A Love to Cherish	Beverly Clark	$8.95
A Place Like Home	Alicia Wiggins	$6.99
A Risk of Rain	Dar Tomlinson	$8.95
A Taste of Temptation	Reneé Alexis	$9.95
A Twist of Fate	Beverly Clark	$8.95
A Voice Behind Thunder	Carrie Elizabeth Greene	$6.99
A Will to Love	Angie Daniels	$9.95
Acquisitions	Kimberley White	$8.95
Across	Carol Payne	$12.95
After the Vows	Leslie Esdaile	$10.95
(Summer Anthology)	T.T. Henderson	
	Jacqueline Thomas	
Again, My Love	Kayla Perrin	$10.95
Against the Wind	Gwynne Forster	$8.95
All I Ask	Barbara Keaton	$8.95
All I'll Ever Need	Mildred Riley	$6.99
Always You	Crystal Hubbard	$6.99
Ambrosia	T.T. Henderson	$8.95
An Unfinished Love Affair	Barbara Keaton	$8.95
And Then Came You	Dorothy Elizabeth Love	$8.95
Angel's Paradise	Janice Angelique	$9.95
Another Memory	Pamela Ridley	$6.99
Anything But Love	Celya Bowers	$6.99
At Last	Lisa G. Riley	$8.95
Best Foot Forward	Michele Sudler	$6.99
Best of Friends	Natalie Dunbar	$8.95
Best of Luck Elsewhere	Trisha Haddad	$6.99
Beyond the Rapture	Beverly Clark	$9.95
Blame It on Paradise	Crystal Hubbard	$6.99
Blaze	Barbara Keaton	$9.95

Other Genesis Press, Inc. Titles (continued)

Blindsided	Tammy Williams	$6.99
Bliss, Inc.	Chamein Canton	$6.99
Blood Lust	J.M. Jeffries	$9.95
Blood Seduction	J.M. Jeffries	$9.95
Blue Interlude	Keisha Mennefee	$6.99
Bodyguard	Andrea Jackson	$9.95
Boss of Me	Diana Nyad	$8.95
Bound by Love	Beverly Clark	$8.95
Breeze	Robin Hampton Allen	$10.95
Broken	Dar Tomlinson	$24.95
Burn	Crystal Hubbard	$6.99
By Design	Barbara Keaton	$8.95
Cajun Heat	Charlene Berry	$8.95
Careless Whispers	Rochelle Alers	$8.95
Cats & Other Tales	Marilyn Wagner	$8.95
Caught in a Trap	Andre Michelle	$8.95
Caught Up in the Rapture	Lisa G. Riley	$9.95
Cautious Heart	Cheris F. Hodges	$8.95
Chances	Pamela Leigh Starr	$8.95
Checks and Balances	Elaine Sims	$6.99
Cherish the Flame	Beverly Clark	$8.95
Choices	Tammy Williams	$6.99
Class Reunion	Irma Jenkins/ John Brown	$12.95
Code Name: Diva	J.M. Jeffries	$9.95
Conquering Dr. Wexler's Heart	Kimberley White	$9.95
Corporate Seduction	A.C. Arthur	$9.95
Crossing Paths, Tempting Memories	Dorothy Elizabeth Love	$9.95
Crossing the Line	Bernice Layton	$6.99
Crush	Crystal Hubbard	$9.95
Cypress Whisperings	Phyllis Hamilton	$8.95
Dark Embrace	Crystal Wilson Harris	$8.95
Dark Storm Rising	Chinelu Moore	$10.95
Daughter of the Wind	Joan Xian	$8.95
Dawn's Harbor	Kymberly Hunt	$6.99
Deadly Sacrifice	Jack Kean	$22.95
Designer Passion	Dar Tomlinson Diana Richeaux	$8.95

Other Genesis Press, Inc. Titles (continued)

Do Over	Celya Bowers	$9.95
Dream Keeper	Gail McFarland	$6.99
Dream Runner	Gail McFarland	$6.99
Dreamtective	Liz Swados	$5.95
Ebony Angel	Deatri King-Bey	$9.95
Ebony Butterfly II	Delilah Dawson	$14.95
Echoes of Yesterday	Beverly Clark	$9.95
Eden's Garden	Elizabeth Rose	$8.95
Eve's Prescription	Edwina Martin Arnold	$8.95
Everlastin' Love	Gay G. Gunn	$8.95
Everlasting Moments	Dorothy Elizabeth Love	$8.95
Everything and More	Sinclair Lebeau	$8.95
Everything but Love	Natalie Dunbar	$8.95
Falling	Natalie Dunbar	$9.95
Fate	Pamela Leigh Starr	$8.95
Finding Isabella	A.J. Garrotto	$8.95
Fireflies	Joan Early	$6.99
Fixin' Tyrone	Keith Walker	$6.99
Forbidden Quest	Dar Tomlinson	$10.95
Forever Love	Wanda Y. Thomas	$8.95
Friends in Need	Joan Early	$6.99
From the Ashes	Kathleen Suzanne	$8.95
	Jeanne Sumerix	
Frost on My Window	Angela Weaver	$6.99
Gentle Yearning	Rochelle Alers	$10.95
Glory of Love	Sinclair LeBeau	$10.95
Go Gentle Into That Good Night	Malcom Boyd	$12.95
Goldengroove	Mary Beth Craft	$16.95
Groove, Bang, and Jive	Steve Cannon	$8.99
Hand in Glove	Andrea Jackson	$9.95
Hard to Love	Kimberley White	$9.95
Hart & Soul	Angie Daniels	$8.95
Heart of the Phoenix	A.C. Arthur	$9.95
Heartbeat	Stephanie Bedwell-Grime	$8.95
Hearts Remember	M. Loui Quezada	$8.95
Hidden Memories	Robin Allen	$10.95
Higher Ground	Leah Latimer	$19.95
Hitler, the War, and the Pope	Ronald Rychiak	$26.95
How to Kill Your Husband	Keith Walker	$6.99

Other Genesis Press, Inc. Titles (continued)

Other Genesis Press, Inc. Titles (continued)

Mae's Promise	Melody Walcott	$8.95
Magnolia Sunset	Giselle Carmichael	$8.95
Many Shades of Gray	Dyanne Davis	$6.99
Matters of Life and Death	Lesego Malepe, Ph.D.	$15.95
Meant to Be	Jeanne Sumerix	$8.95
Midnight Clear	Leslie Esdaile	$10.95
(Anthology)	Gwynne Forster	
	Carmen Green	
	Monica Jackson	
Midnight Magic	Gwynne Forster	$8.95
Midnight Peril	Vicki Andrews	$10.95
Misconceptions	Pamela Leigh Starr	$9.95
Mixed Reality	Chamein Canton	$6.99
Moments of Clarity	Michele Cameron	$6.99
Montgomery's Children	Richard Perry	$14.95
Mr. Fix-It	Crystal Hubbard	$6.99
My Buffalo Soldier	Barbara B.K. Reeves	$8.95
Naked Soul	Gwynne Forster	$8.95
Never Say Never	Michele Cameron	$6.99
Next to Last Chance	Louisa Dixon	$24.95
No Apologies	Seressia Glass	$8.95
No Commitment Required	Seressia Glass	$8.95
No Regrets	Mildred E. Riley	$8.95
Not His Type	Chamein Canton	$6.99
Not Quite Right	Tammy Williams	$6.99
Nowhere to Run	Gay G. Gunn	$10.95
O Bed! O Breakfast!	Rob Kuehnle	$14.95
Oak Bluffs	Joan Early	$6.99
Object of His Desire	A.C. Arthur	$8.95
Office Policy	A.C. Arthur	$9.95
Once in a Blue Moon	Dorianne Cole	$9.95
One Day at a Time	Bella McFarland	$8.95
One of These Days	Michele Sudler	$9.95
Outside Chance	Louisa Dixon	$24.95
Passion	T.T. Henderson	$10.95
Passion's Blood	Cherif Fortin	$22.95
Passion's Furies	AlTonya Washington	$6.99
Passion's Journey	Wanda Y. Thomas	$8.95
Past Promises	Jahmel West	$8.95
Path of Fire	T.T. Henderson	$8.95

Other Genesis Press, Inc. Titles (continued)

Path of Thorns	Annetta P. Lee	$9.95
Peace Be Still	Colette Haywood	$12.95
Picture Perfect	Reon Carter	$8.95
Playing for Keeps	Stephanie Salinas	$8.95
Pride & Joi	Gay G. Gunn	$8.95
Promises Made	Bernice Layton	$6.99
Promises of Forever	Celya Bowers	$6.99
Promises to Keep	Alicia Wiggins	$8.95
Quiet Storm	Donna Hill	$10.95
Reckless Surrender	Rochelle Alers	$6.95
Red Polka Dot in a World Full of Plaid	Varian Johnson	$12.95
Red Sky	Renee Alexis	$6.99
Reluctant Captive	Joyce Jackson	$8.95
Rendezvous With Fate	Jeanne Sumerix	$8.95
Revelations	Cheris F. Hodges	$8.95
Reye's Gold	Ruthie Robinson	$6.99
Rivers of the Soul	Leslie Esdaile	$8.95
Rocky Mountain Romance	Kathleen Suzanne	$8.95
Rooms of the Heart	Donna Hill	$8.95
Rough on Rats and Tough on Cats	Chris Parker	$12.95
Save Me	Africa Fine	$6.99
Secret Library Vol. 1	Nina Sheridan	$18.95
Secret Library Vol. 2	Cassandra Colt	$8.95
Secret Thunder	Annetta P. Lee	$9.95
Shades of Brown	Denise Becker	$8.95
Shades of Desire	Monica White	$8.95
Shadows in the Moonlight	Jeanne Sumerix	$8.95
Show Me the Sun	Miriam Shumba	$6.99
Sin	Crystal Rhodes	$8.95
Singing a Song...	Crystal Rhodes	$6.99
Six O'Clock	Katrina Spencer	$6.99
Small Sensations	Crystal V. Rhodes	$6.99
Small Whispers	Annetta P. Lee	$6.99
So Amazing	Sinclair LeBeau	$8.95
Somebody's Someone	Sinclair LeBeau	$8.95
Someone to Love	Alicia Wiggins	$8.95
Song in the Park	Martin Brant	$15.95
Soul Eyes	Wayne L. Wilson	$12.95

Other Genesis Press, Inc. Titles (continued)

Soul to Soul	Donna Hill	$8.95
Southern Comfort	J.M. Jeffries	$8.95
Southern Fried Standards	S.R. Maddox	$6.99
Still the Storm	Sharon Robinson	$8.95
Still Waters Run Deep	Leslie Esdaile	$8.95
Still Waters...	Crystal V. Rhodes	$6.99
Stolen Jewels	Michele Sudler	$6.99
Stolen Memories	Michele Sudler	$6.99
Stories to Excite You	Anna Forrest/Divine	$14.95
Storm	Pamela Leigh Starr	$6.99
Subtle Secrets	Wanda Y. Thomas	$8.95
Suddenly You	Crystal Hubbard	$9.95
Swan	Africa Fine	$6.99
Sweet Repercussions	Kimberley White	$9.95
Sweet Sensations	Gwyneth Bolton	$9.95
Sweet Tomorrows	Kimberly White	$8.95
Taken by You	Dorothy Elizabeth Love	$9.95
Tattooed Tears	T. T. Henderson	$8.95
Tempting Faith	Crystal Hubbard	$6.99
That Which Has Horns	Miriam Shumba	$6.99
The Business of Love	Cheris F. Hodges	$6.99
The Color Line	Lizzette Grayson Carter	$9.95
The Color of Trouble	Dyanne Davis	$8.95
The Disappearance of Allison Jones	Kayla Perrin	$5.95
The Doctor's Wife	Mildred Riley	$6.99
The Fires Within	Beverly Clark	$9.95
The Foursome	Celya Bowers	$6.99
The Honey Dipper's Legacy	Myra Pannell-Allen	$14.95
The Joker's Love Tune	Sidney Rickman	$15.95
The Little Pretender	Barbara Cartland	$10.95
The Love We Had	Natalie Dunbar	$8.95
The Man Who Could Fly	Bob & Milana Beamon	$18.95
The Missing Link	Charlyne Dickerson	$8.95
The Mission	Pamela Leigh Starr	$6.99
The More Things Change	Chamein Canton	$6.99
The Perfect Frame	Beverly Clark	$9.95
The Price of Love	Sinclair LeBeau	$8.95
The Smoking Life	Ilene Barth	$29.95
The Words of the Pitcher	Kei Swanson	$8.95

Other Genesis Press, Inc. Titles (continued)

Order Form

Mail to: Genesis Press, Inc.
P.O. Box 101
Columbus, MS 39703

Name _____
Address _____
City/State _____ Zip _____
Telephone _____

Ship to (if different from above)
Name _____
Address _____
City/State _____ Zip _____
Telephone _____

Credit Card Information
Credit Card # _____ ☐ Visa   ☐ Mastercard
Expiration Date (mm/yy) _____ ☐ AmEx   ☐ Discover

Qty.	Author	Title	Price	Total

Use this order form, or call 1-888-INDIGO-1

Total for books	_____
Shipping and handling:	
$5 first two books,	
$1 each additional book	_____
Total S & H	_____
Total amount enclosed	_____

Mississippi residents add 7% sales tax